SCARLET

BY STEPHEN R. LAWHEAD

King Raven Trilogy
Hood
Scarlet
Tuck

STEPHEN R. LAWHEAD

SCARLET

King Raven: Book Two

www.atombooks.co.uk

ATOM

First published in the United States in 2007 by Westbow Press,
a division of Thomas Nelson, Inc.
First published in Great Britain in 2007 by Atom
This edition published in 2008 by Atom
Reprinted 2009, 2010 (twice), 2013

A CIP catalogue record for this book
is available from the British Library.

ISBN 978-1-904233-73-2

Typeset in Centaur by M Rules
Printed and bound in Great Britain by
Clays Ltd, St Ives plc

Papers used by Atom are from well-managed forests
and other responsible sources.

MIX
Paper from
responsible sources
FSC
www.fsc.org FSC® C104740

Atom
An imprint of
Little, Brown Book Group
100 Victoria Embankment
London EC4Y 0DY

An Hachette UK Company
www.hachette.co.uk

www.atombooks.net

To the dedicated
men and women at
UWMC and SCCA,
without whom . . .

KING RAVEN

England and The March

1080 - 1100 A/D

RHI BRAN'S WORLD

to Lundein

King's Road

to Lundein

Wintan Caestir
(Caer Winton)

CHAPTER I

S o, now. One day soon they hang me for a rogue. Fair enough. I have earned it a hundred times over, I reckon, and that's leaving a lot of acreage unexplored. The jest of it is, the crime for which I swing is the one offence I never did do. The sheriff will have it that I raised rebellion against the king.

I didn't.

Oh, there's much I've done that some would as soon count treason. For a fact, I et more of the king's venison than the king has et bread, and good men have lost their heads to royal pikes for far less; but in all my frolics I never breathed a disloyal word against the crown, nor tried to convince any man, boy, horse, or dog to match his deeds to mine. Ah, but dainties such as these are of no concern when princes have their tender feelings ruffled. It is a traitor they want to punish, not a thief. The eatin' o' Red William's game is a matter too trifling – more insult than crime – and it's a red-handed rebel they need. Too much has happened in the forests of the March and too much princely pride hangs in the balance to be mincing fair about a rascal poaching a few soft-eyed deer.

Until that ill-fated night, Will Scarlet ran with King Raven and his band of merry thieves. Ran fast and far, I did, let me tell you. Faster and farther than all the rest, and that's saying something. Here's the gist: it's the Raven Hood they want and cannot get. So, ol' Will is for the jump.

Poor luck, that. No less, no more.

They caught me crest and colours. My own bloody fault. There's none to blame but the hunter when he's caught in his own snare. I ask no pardon. A willing soul, I flew field and forest with King Raven and his flock. Fine fun it was, too, until they nabbed me in the pinch. Even so, if it hadn't a' been for a spear through my leg bone they would not a' got me either.

So, here we sit, my leg and me, in a dank pit beneath Count de Braose's keep. I have a cell – four walls of stone and a damp dirt floor covered with rotting straw and rancid rushes. I have a warden named Guibert, or Gulbert or some such, who brings me food and water when he can be bothered to remember, and unchains me from time to time so I can stretch the cramps a bit and wash my wound. I also have my very own priest, a young laggard of a scribe who comes to catch my wild tales and pin them to the pages of a book to doom us all.

We talk and talk. God knows we've got time to kill before the killing time. It pleases me now to think on the dizzy chase we led. I was taken in the most daring and outrageous scheme to come out of the forest yet. It was a plan as desperate as death, but light and larksome as a maiden's flirting glance. At a blow, we aimed to douse the sheriff's ardour and kindle a little righteous wrath in lorn Britannia. We aimed to cock a snook at the crown, sure, and mayhap draw the king's attention to our sore plight, embarrass his sheriff, and show him and his mutton-headed soldiers for fools on parade – all in one fell swoop. Sweet it was and, save for my piddling difficulties, flawless as a flower until the walls of the world came crashing down around our ears.

Truth is, I can't help thinking that if we only knew what it was that had fallen plump into our fists, none of this would have happened and I would not be here now with a leg on fire and fit to kill me if the sheriff don't. Oh, but that is ranging too far afield, and there is ground closer to home needs ploughing first.

A h, but see the monk here! Asleep with his nose in his inkhorn.

'Odo, you dunce! Wake up! You're dozing again. It ill becomes you to catch a wink on a dying man's last words. Prick up your ears, priest. Pare your quill, and tell me the last you remember.'

'Sorry, Will,' he says. He's always ever so sorry, rubbing sleep from his dreamy brown eyes. And it is sorry he should be — sorry for himself and all his dreary ilk, but not for Will.

'Never feel sorry for Will, lad,' I tell him. 'Will en't sorry for nothing.'

Brother Odo is my scribe, decent enough for a Norman in his simpering, damp-handed way. He does not wish me harm. I think he does not even know why he has been sent down here amongst the gallows birds to listen to the ramblings of a dangerous scofflaw like myself. Why should he?

Abbot Hugo is behind this wheeze to scribble down all my doings. To what purpose? Plain as daylight in Dunholme, he means to scry out a way to catch King Raven. Hugo imagines languishing in the shadow of the noose for a spell will sober me enough to grow a tongue of truth in my head and sing like a bird for freedom.

So, I sing and sing, if only to keep Jack o'Ladder at arm's length

3

a little longer. Our larcenous abbot will learn summat to his profit, as may be, but more to his regret. He'll learn much of that mysterious phantom of the greenwood, to be sure. But for all his listening he'll hear naught from me to catch so much as a mayfly. He'll not get the bolt he desires to bring King Raven down.

'So, now,' I say, 'pick up your pen, Brother Odo. We'll begin again. What was the last you remember?'

Odo scans his chicken tracks a moment, scratches his shaved pate and says, 'When Thane Aelred's lands were confiscated for his part in the Uprising, I was thrown onto my own resources . . .'

Odo speaks his English with the strange flat tongue of the Frank outlanders. That he speaks English at all is a wonder, I suppose, and the reason why Hugo chose him. Poor Odo is a pudgy pudding of a man, young enough, and earnest in faith and practice, but pale and only too ready to retire, claiming cramp or cold or fatigue. He is always fatigued, and for no good reason it seems to me. He makes as if chasing a leaking nib across fresh-scraped vellum is as mighty a labour as toting the carcass of a fat hind through the greenwood on your back with the sheriff's men on your tail.

All saints bear witness! If pushing a pen across parchment taxes a man as much as Odo claims, we should honour as heroes all who ply the quill, amen.

I am of the opinion that unless he grows a backbone, and right soon, Brother Odo will be nothing more in this life than another weak-eyed scribbler squinting down his long French nose at the undiluted drivel his hand has perpetrated. By Blessed Cuthbert's thumb, I swear I would rather end my days in Baron de Braose's pit than face eternity with a blot like that on my soul.

Perhaps, in God's dark plan, friend Will is here to instruct this

4

indolent youth in a better lesson, thinks I. Well, we will do what can be done to save him.

When Thane Aelred's lands were confiscated for his part in the Uprising, I was thrown onto my own resources, and like to have died they were that thin.'

This I tell him, repeating the words to buy a little time while I cast my net into streams gone by to catch another gleaming memory for our proud abbot's feast. May he choke on the bones! With this blessing between my teeth, I rumble on . . .

CHAPTER 2

Thane Aelred was as fair-minded as the Tyne is wide, and solid as the three-hundred-year-old oak that grew beside his barn. A bull-necked man with the shaggy brown mane of a lion and a roar to match as may be, but he treated his people right and well. Never one to come all high and mighty with his minions, he was always ready enough to put hand to plough or scythe. Bless the man, he never shirked the shearing or slaughtering, and all the grunt and sweat that work requires. For though we have lived a thousand years and more since Our Sweet Jesus came and went, it is a sad, sad truth that sheep will still not shear themselves, nor hogs make hams.

There's the pity. Toss a coin and decide which of the two is the filthier chore.

Under Aelred, God rest him, there was always a jar or three to ease our aching bones when the day's work was done. All of us tenants and vassals who owed him service — a day or two here, a week there — were treated like blood kin whenever we set foot on the steading to honour our pledge of work. In return, he gave neither man nor maid worse

6

than he'd accept for himself or his house, and that's a right rare thane, that is. Show me another as decent and honest, and I'll drink a health to him here and now.

Not like these Norman vermin – call them what you like: Franks, Ffreinc, or Normans, they're all the same. Lords of the Earth, they trow. Lords of Perdition, more like. Hold themselves precious as stardust and fine as diamonds. Dressed in their gold-crusted rags, they flounce about the land, their bloody minds scheming mischief all the while. From the moment a Norman noble opens his eye on the day until that same eye closes at night, the highborn Frankish man is, in Aelred's words, 'a walking *scittesturm*' for anyone unlucky enough to cross his path.

A Norman knight lives only for hunting and whoring, preening and warring. And their toad-licking priests are just as bad. Even the best of their clerics are no better than they should be. I wouldn't spare the contents of my nose on a rainy day to save the lot of them . . .

Sorry, Odo, but that is God's own truth, groan as you will to hear it. Write it down all the same.

'If it please you, what is scittesturm?' Odo wants to know.

'Ask a Saxon,' I tell him. 'If bloody Baron de Braose hasn't killed them all yet, you'll learn quick enough.'

But there we are. Aelred is gone now. He had the great misfortune to believe the land his father had given him – land owned and worked by his father's father, and the father's father before that – belonged to him and his forever. A dangerous delusion, as it turns out.

For when William the Conqueror snatched the throne of England

7

and made himself the Law of the Land, he set to work uprooting the deep-grown offices and traditions that time and the stump-solid Saxons had planted and maintained since their arrival on these fair shores – offices and traditions which bound lord and vassal in a lock-step dance of loyalty and service, sure, but also kept the high and mighty above from devouring the weak and poorly below. This was the bedrock of Saxon law, just and good, enforcing fairness for all who sheltered under it. Like the strong timber roof of Great Alfred's hall, we all found shelter under it however hard the gales of power and privilege might blow.

The thanes – freeholders mostly, men who were neither entirely noble nor completely common . . . Willy Conqueror did not understand them at all. Never did, nor bothered to. See now, a Norman knows only two kinds of men: nobles and serfs. To a Norman, a man is either a king or a peasant, nothing else. There is black and there is white, and there is the end of it. Consequently, there is no one to stand between the two to keep them from each other's throats.

The Welshmen laugh at both camps, I know. The British have their nobility, too, but British kings and princes share the same life as the people they rule. A lord might be more esteemed by virtue of his deeds or other merits, real or imagined, but a true British prince is not too lofty to feel the pinch when drought makes a harvest thin, or a hard winter gnaws through all the provisions double-quick.

The British king will gladly drink from the same clay cup as the least of his folk, and can recite the names of each and every one of his tribesmen to the third or fourth generation. In this, King Raven was no less than the best example of his kind, and I'll wager Baron de Braose has never laid eyes on most of the wretches whose sweat and blood keep him in hunting hawks and satin breeches.

Like all Norman barons, de Braose surveys his lands from the back of a great destrier – a giant with four hooves that eats more in a day than any ten of his serfs can scrape together for the week. His knights and *vavasors* – hateful word – spill more in a night's roister than any hovel-dweller on his estate will see from Christmas Eve to Easter morn, and that's if they're lucky to see a drop o' anything cheerful at all.

Well, de Braose may never have shaken hands with one of his serfs, but he knows how much the man owes in taxes to the nearest ha'penny. That's a kind of talent, I suppose, give him that.

I give him also his shrewd, calculating mind and a farsighted sense of self-preservation. He could see, or maybe smell, the right way to jump a long way off. The old goat rarely put a foot wrong where his own vital interests were concerned. The king liked him, too, though I can't think why. Still and all, royal favour never hurts a'body while it lasts. Making it last: aye, there's the grit in the loaf.

So, when William the Conquering Bastard got himself killed in a little foray in France – took an arrow, they say, just like poor King Harold – *that* upset the apple cart, no mistake. And Thane Aelred was one of those ruddy English pippins as got bounced from the box.

Aye, heads rolled everywhere before the dust settled on that one. Stout Aelred's lands were confiscated, and the good man himself banished from the realm. All of us vassals were turned out, thrown off the land by the king's stinking sheriff and his bailiffs; our village was burned to the last house and pigsty. Aelred's holding was returned to forest and placed under Forest Law, devil's work.

Most of us, myself included, lingered in the area awhile. We had nowhere else to go, and no provision made for us. For, like the others in Aelred's keep, I was born on his lands, and my father served his father as I served him. The Scatlockes have been vassals ever and always, never lords . . .

Yes, Odo, that is my real name – William Scatlocke,' I pause to explain. 'Y'see, it's just some folk have it hard with such a ragged scrap between their teeth, and *Scarlet* has a finer sound.'

'I agree,' says he.

'Splendid,' I tell him. 'I will sleep so much better for knowing that. Now, where was I?'

Odo scans what he has written, and says, '. . . you were telling about Forest Law. You called it the devil's work.'

Aye, and so it is. Forest Law – two perfectly honest and upright words as ever was, but placed together they make a mad raving monster. See now, under Forest Law the crown takes a piece of land useful and needful for all folk in common and at a stroke turns it into a private hunting park forever closed to common folk for any purpose whatsoever. Forest Law turns any land into king's land, to be used by royals only, them and their fortune-favoured friends. The keep of these so-called parks is given to agents of the crown known as sheriffs, who rule with a noose in one hand and a flamin' hot castration iron in the other for anyone who might happen to trespass however lightly on the royal preserve.

Truly, merely setting foot in a royal forest can get you maimed or blinded. Taking a single deer or pig to feed your starving children can get you hung at the crossroads alongside evil outlaws who have burned entire villages and slaughtered whole families in their sleep. A petty thing, hardly worth a morning's sweat, as it may be. Yes, that dark-eyed deer with the fine brown pelt and tasty haunches is worth more than any fifty or a hundred vassals, be they serfs or freemen, and there's a fact.

Forest Law is what happened to Thane Aelred's lands – hall, barn, sty, granary, milkhouse, and mill all burned to the last stick and stake, and the ashes ploughed under. The age-old boundary stones were pulled up, and the hides taken off the registry books, and the whole great lot joined up to the lands of other English estates to be declared king's forest. Aelred himself was hauled away in chains, leaving his poor lady wife to make her way as best she could. I heard later he and his were dumped aboard a ship bound for Daneland with other miserable exiles, but I never really knew for sure. The rest of his folk were turned out that same day and herded off the property at the point of long Norman spears.

Those of us without friends or relations we might flee to for aid and comfort took to the greenwood. We aimed to live off the land in spite of the threat of death hanging over us if we were caught. As one of Aelred's foresters this was no great hardship for me, but others who were not used to such stark conditions suffered mightily. Cold and fever took a heavy toll, and the sheriff's men took more. They killed us whenever they could, and chased us always.

I t was no kind of life, Odo lad, let me tell you.' He glances up with his big dreamy eyes, his soft mouth caught in a half smile. 'You would not last above three days.'

'I might be stronger than I look,' says he.

'And looks are ever deceiving,' I reply, and we go on . . .

E ventually, with winter coming on and the sheriff and his men growing wise to our ways, the few of us that had survived those many months broke company and drifted off to other parts. Some went north where the Harrowing had desolated the land; in those empty parts it was said honest folk might begin again. Trouble there was that too many dishonest folk had gathered up there, too, and it was fast becoming a killing ground of another kind.

Me, I decided to go west, to Wales – to Wallia, land of my mother's birth.

I'd always wanted to see it, mind, but there was more to it than whim. For I had heard a tale that stirred my blood. A man, they said, had risen in defiance of the Norman overlords, a man who flew in the face of certain death to challenge King William himself, a man they called King Raven.

CHAPTER 3

Lundein

Cardinal Ranulf de Bayeux stepped from the small, flat-bottomed boat onto the landing stone set into the soft shore of the River Thames. The rank brown water was awash in dung and garbage, awaiting the estuary tide to rise and bear it away. Pressing the cloth of his wide sleeve against his nose, he motioned impatiently to his companions as they clambered from the boat.

Two men-at-arms had travelled down to Lundein with the cardinal and they followed his lead, remaining a few paces behind, the red pennants atop their spears fluttering in the breeze. Clutching the skirts of his scarlet satin robe to avoid the mud, Ranulf tiptoed up the embankment to the wooden walkway that led to the city street and passed the walls of the White Tower. The new stone of that magnificent fortress glowed in the full light of a warm sun, a blazing milky brilliance against the yellow leaves and dazzling blue autumn sky.

King William had returned from Normandie two days previous and had summoned his chief advisor straightaway – no doubt to review the accounts which Ranulf carried in a velvet pouch beneath his arm. It had been a good year, all things considered. The treasury was showing a small surplus, for a change, so Ranulf was to be congratulated. Thanks to his tirelessly inventive mind, the king would have money to pay his bribes and his troops, with a little more besides.

Oh, but it was becoming ever more difficult. The people were taxed to the teeth, the nobles likewise, and the chorus of grumbling was becoming a deafening din from some quarters, which is why Ranulf — a man of the cloth, after all — could no longer travel about the land alone, but went with an armed escort to protect him from any who felt themselves particularly aggrieved by his efforts on the king's behalf.

William, of course, was ultimately to blame for the resentment festering throughout his realm. It was not that the king was a spendthrift. Common opinion to the contrary, William the Red was no more wastrel than his father — a man who lived well, to be sure, although far less so than many of his barons — but war was a costly business: much expenditure for piddling little gain. Even when William won the conflict, which he usually did, he almost always came away the poorer for it. And the warring was incessant. If it wasn't the Scots, it was the Bretons; and if not foreign troublemakers it was his own brothers, Prince Henry and Duke Robert, fomenting rebellion.

Yet today, if only for today, the news from the treasury would please the king, and Ranulf was eager to share this good news and advance another step towards reaping a substantial reward for himself — the lucrative bishopric of Duresme, perhaps, which was empty now owing to the death of the previous incumbent.

Cardinal de Bayeux and his escort passed through the wide and handsome gate with but a nod to the porter. They quickly crossed the yard where the king's baggage train still waited to be unloaded. Ranulf dismissed his soldiers and commanded them to remain ready outside, then entered the tower and climbed the stairs to the antechamber above, where he was admitted by the steward and informed that the king was at table and awaiting his arrival.

Entering silently, Ranulf took one look at his royal patron and read the king's disposition instantly. 'His Majesty is displeased,' declared Cardinal Ranulf from the doorway. He made a small bow and smoothed the front of his satin robe.

'Displeased?' wondered William, beckoning him in with a wave of his hand. 'Why would you say displeased? Hmm?' Rising from his chair, the king began to pace along the length of the table where he had lately enjoyed a repast with his vavasours. The king's companions had gone, or been sent away, and William was alone.

'Why, indeed?' said the king, without waiting for Ranulf's reply. 'My dear brother, Robert, threatens war if I do not capitulate to his ridiculous whims . . . my barons find ever more brazen excuses to reduce their tributes and taxes . . . my subjects are increasingly rebellious to my rule and rude to my person!'

The king turned on his chief counsellor and waved a parchment like a flag. 'And now this!'

'Ill tidings, *mon roi*?'

'By the holy face of Lucca!' William shouted. 'Is there no end to this man's demands?'

'Which man, Sire, if you please?' Ranulf moved a few paces into the room.

'This jackanapes of a pope!' roared the king. 'This Urban – he says Canterbury has been vacant too long and insists we invest an archbishop at once.'

'Ignore him, Sire,' suggested Ranulf.

'Oh, but that is not the end of his impudence,' continued the king without pausing to draw breath. 'Far from it! He demands not only my seal on a letter of endorsement, but a public demonstration of my support as well.'

'Which, as we have often discussed, you are understandably loath to give,' sympathised the cardinal, stifling a yawn.

'Blast his eyes! I am loath to give him so much as the contents of my bowels.' William, his ruddy cheeks blushing hot with anger, threw a finger in his counsellor's face. 'God help me if I ever suffer one of his lick-spit legates to set foot in my kingdom. I'll boil the beggar in his own blood, and if Urban persists in these demands, I will throw my support to Clement – I swear I will.'

'Tell him so,' suggested Ranulf simply. 'That is what the Conqueror would have done – and did, often enough.'

'There! There you say it, by Judas!' crowed William. 'My father had no illusions about who should rule the church in his kingdom. He would not suffer any priest to stick his nose into royal affairs.'

It was true. William's father, the Conqueror, had ruled the church like he ruled everything else on his adopted island. Not content to allow such a wealthy and powerful institution to look to its own affairs, he continually meddled in everything from appointing clerics to the collection of tithes – ever and always to his own advantage. Ranulf knew that the son, William the Red, was peeved because, try as he might, he could not command the same respect and obedience from the church that his father had taken as his due.

'Mark me, Bayeux, I'll not swear out my throne to Urban no matter how many legates and emissaries he sends to bedevil me.'

'Tell His Eminence that his continued attempts to leech authority from the throne make this most sacred display of loyalty a mockery.' Cardinal Ranulf of Bayeux moved to a place across the table from his pacing king. 'Tell him to stuff the Fisherman's Ring up his sanctimonious—'

'Ha!' cried William. 'If I told him that, he would excommunicate me without a second thought.'

'Do you care?' countered Ranulf smoothly. 'Your Majesty holds Rome in contempt in any of a hundred ways already.'

'You go too far! My faith, or lack of it, is my own affair. I'll not be chastised by the likes of you, Bayeux.'

Ranulf bowed his head as if to accept the reprimand and said, 'Methinks you misunderstand me, Sire. I meant that the king of England need spare no thought for Pope Urban's tender feelings. As you suggest, it is a simple enough matter to offer support to his rival, Clement.'

William allowed himself to be calmed by the gentle and shrewd assertions of his justiciar. 'It is that,' sneered William. The king of England surveyed the remains of his midday meal as if the table were a battlefield and he was searching for survivors. 'I much prefer Clement anyway.'

'You see?' Ranulf smiled, pleased with the way he had steered the king to his point of view. 'God continues to grace your reign, Sire. In his wisdom, he has provided a timely alternative. Let it be known and voiced abroad that you support Clement, and we'll soon see how the worm writhes.'

'If Urban suspected I was inclined to pledge loyalty to Clement, he might cease badgering me.' William spied a nearby goblet on the table; there was still some wine in it, so he gulped it down. 'He might even try to woo me back into his camp instead. Is that what you mean?'

'He might,' confirmed Ranulf in a way that suggested this was the very least William might expect.

'He might do more,' William ventured. 'How much more?'

'The king's goodwill has a certain value to the church just now. It is the pope who needs the king, not the other way around. Perhaps this goodwill might be bartered for something of more substantial and lasting value.'

William stopped pacing and drew his hand through his thinning red hair. 'The pope has nothing I want,' he decided at last. He turned and stumped back to his chair. 'He is a prisoner in his own palace. Why, he cannot even show his face in Rome.' William looked into another cup, but it was empty so he resumed his search. 'The man can do little enough for himself; he can do nothing for me.'

'Nothing?' asked the cardinal pointedly. 'Nothing at all?'

'Nothing I can think of,' maintained William stubbornly. 'If you know something, Bayeux, tell me now or leave me alone. I grow weary of your insinuations.'

'Given Urban's precarious position – a position made all the more uncertain by the king's brother . . .'

'Robert?' said William. 'My brother may be an ass, but he has no love for Rome.'

'I was thinking of Henry, Sire,' said the cardinal. 'Seeing that Henry is courting Clement, it seems to me that Urban, with the proper inducement, might be willing to recognize the English crown's right to appoint clergy in exchange for your support,' suggested the cardinal. 'What is that worth, do you think?'

William stared at his chief justiciar. 'The wheels of government grind slowly, as you well and truly know,' he said, his pale blue eyes narrowing as he considered the implications of his counsellor's suggestion. 'You are paid to see that they do.'

'Yes, and every day a pulpit stands empty, the crown collects the tithe, as *you* well and truly know.'

'A tithe which would otherwise go to the church,' said William. 'Ultimately to Rome.'

'Indirectly, perhaps,' agreed Ranulf. He buffed his fingernails against the sleek satin of his robe. 'Urban contests this right, of course. But if the pope were to formally relinquish all such claims in favour of the crown . . .'

'I would become head of the church in England,' said William, following the argument to its conclusion.

'I would not go so far, Sire,' allowed Ranulf. 'Rome would never allow secular authority to stand above the church. Urban's power ebbs by the day, to be sure, but you will never pry that from his miser's grasp.'

'Well,' grumped the king, 'it would amount to the same thing. England would be a realm unto itself, and its church an island in the papal sea.'

'Even so,' granted Ranulf gallantly. 'Your Majesty would effectively free the throne of England from the interference of Rome for good and forever. That would be worth something.'

'How much?' said William. He leaned across the table on his fists. 'How much would it be worth?'

'Who can say? Tithes, lands – the sale of benefices alone could run to—'

William might not understand the finer points of the papal dispute that had inadvertently thrown up two rival claimants to Saint Peter's golden chair, but he knew men and money. And clerics were the same as most men in wanting to ease the way for their offspring in the world. A payment to the church to secure a position for an heir was money well spent. 'Thousands of marks a year,' mused William.

'Pounds, Sire. Thousands, yes – thousands of pounds straight into your treasury. It would only take a letter.'

William looked at the empty goblet in his hand, and then threw it the length of the room. It struck the far wall and tumbled down the tapestry. 'By the Blesséd Virgin, Flambard, you are a rascal! I like it!'

Returning to his chair, William resumed his place at the table. 'Wine!' he shouted to an unseen servant lurking behind the door. 'Sit,' he said to Ranulf. 'Tell me more about this letter.'

The cardinal tossed the black velvet bag onto the bench and sat down; he cleared a place among the crumbs and bones with the side of his hand. Choosing a goblet from those on the table before him, he emptied it and waited for the servant to appear with a jar. When the cups were filled once more, the king and his chief advisor drank and discussed how to make best use of the pope and his predicament.

CHAPTER 4

Brother Odo is dozing over his quill again. Much as I like to see him jump, I won't wake him just yet. It gives me time. The longer I stretch this tale, the more time I have before the tale stretches me, so to speak. Besides, I need a little space to think.

What I think on now is the day I first set eyes on King Raven. A pleasant day it was, too, in all its parts. Crisp, bright autumn was descending over the March. I had been months a-wandering, poking here and there as fancy took me, moving ever and always in the direction of the setting sun. I had no plan other than to learn more of this King Raven, and find him if I could. A fellow of the forest, such as myself, might make himself useful to a man like that. If I did, I reckoned, he might be persuaded to take me under his wing.

I kept my ears sharp for any word of King Raven, and asked after him whenever I happened on a settlement or holding. I worked for food and a bed of straw in barn or byre, and talked to those who were bold enough to speak about the abuses of the crown and events in the land. Many of those I spoke to had heard the name — as well they might, for Baron de Braose, Lord of Bramber, had set aside a right hand-some reward for his capture. Some of the folk had a tale or two of how this Raven fella had outwitted the baron or abbot, or some such; but none knew more than I did of this elusive blackbird or his whereabouts.

The further west I wended, however, the pickings got better in one respect, but worse in another. More had heard of King Raven, to be sure, and some were happy enough to talk. But those who knew of him held that this Raven was not a real man at all. Rather, they had it that he was a phantom sent up from the lowest infernal realm to bedevil the Normans. They said the creature took the form of a giant, high-crested bird, with wings to span a ten-foot pike, and a wicked long beak. Deadly as plague to the Normans, they said, and black as Satan's pit whence he sprung, he was a creature bred and born of deviltry — although one alewife told me that he had given some kinfolk of hers aid in food and good money when they were that desperate for it, so he couldn't be all that bad.

As green spring gave way to summer, I settled for a spell with a swineherd and his gap-toothed wife on their small farm hard by Hereford, where Baron Neufmarché keeps his great stone heap of a castle. Although Wales is only a few days' saunter up the road, I was in no hurry just then. I wanted to learn more, if more was to be learned, and so I lay low, biding my time and listening to the locals when they had cause to speak of matters that interested me.

When the day's work was finished, I'd hie up to town to spend a fair summer evening at the Cross Keys, an inn of questionable repute. The innkeeper was a rascal, no mistake — it's him they should be hang-ing, not Will — but he served a worthy jar and thick chops so tender and juicy your teeth could have a rest. I came to know many of the local folk who called at the Keys, and they came to trust me with their more private thoughts.

Always, I tried to steer the talk towards happenings in the March, hoping for a word or two of King Raven. Thus, it fell out one night that I met a freeman farmer who traded at Hereford on market days. He had come up to sell a bit of bacon and summer sausage and, seeing me cooling my heels, came to sit down beside me on the low wall that fronted the inn. 'Well,' said I, raising my jar, 'here's hail to the king.'

'Hail to the king, devil take him when he will.'

'Oh? Red William gone out of favour with you?' I ask.

'Aye,' says the farmer, 'and I don't care who knows it.' All the same, he glanced around guiltily to see who might be overhearing. No one was paying any mind to a couple of tongue-wags like ourselves, so he took a deep draught of his ale and reclined on his elbow against the wall. 'I pray for his downfall every day.'

'What has the king done to you to earn such ire?'

'What hasn't he done? Before Rufus I had a wife and a strapping big son to help me with the chores.'

'And now?'

'Wife got croup and died, and son was caught in the greenwood setting rabbit snares. Lost his good right hand to the sheriff's blade. Now he can't do more'n herd the stock.'

'You blame the king for that?'

'I do. If I had my way King Raven would pluck out his eyes and eat his right royal liver.'

'That would be a sight,' I told him. 'If that feathered fella was more than a story to tell on a summer night.'

'Oh! He is,' the farmer insisted. 'He is, right enough.'

My vengeful friend went on then to relate how the dread bird had swooped down on a passel of Norman knights as they passed through the March on the King's Road one fine night.

'King Raven fell out of the sky like a venging angel and slew a whole army o' the baron's rogues before they could turn and run,' the farmer said. 'He left only one terrified sot alive to warn the baron to leave off killin' Brits.'

'This creature – how did he kill the knights?' I wondered.

The farmer looked me in the eye and said, 'With fire and arrows.'

'Fair enough,' says I. 'But if it was with fire and arrows, how do they know it was the phantom bird who did it, and not just some peevish Welshman? You know how contrary they can be when riled.'

'Oh, aye,' agreed the farmer. 'I know that right enough. But it was the King Raven, no mistake.' He shook his head with unwavering assurance. 'That I know.'

'Because?' I prodded lightly.

'Because,' says he with a slow smile, 'the arrows was black. Stone tip to feather, they was black as Beelzebub's tongue.'

This bit of news thrilled me more than anything I'd heard yet. Black arrows, mind! Just the kind of thing ol' Will Scarlet might think up if he was about such business as spreading fear and havoc among the rascal brigade. In this tetchy farmer's tale, I saw the shape of a man, and not a phantom. A man that much like myself it gave me the first solid hope to be getting on with.

I lingered on the holding through harvesttime to help out, and then, as the leaves began to fall and the wind freshened from the north, I took my leave and, one bright day, took to the road once more. I walked from settlement to settlement, pausing wherever I could to seek word of King Raven.

Autumn had come to the land, as I say, and I eventually arrived at the edge of the March and entered the forest. Easy in my own company, I remained alert to all around me. I travelled slow and with purpose, camping by the road each night. On those clean, clear mornings

I rose early and made for a high place, the better to watch and listen and learn what I could of the woodland 'round about.

See now, the Forest of the March is an ancient wood, old when Adam was a lad. A wild place not like any forest I'd known in England. Denser, darker, more tangled and woolly, it clutched tight to its secrets and held them close. Mind you, I am a man used to forest ways and byways, and as the bright days chased one another off toward winter, I began to get the measure of it.

One morning, just as the weather turned, I woke to a chill mist and the sound of voices on the King's Road. I had seen wolf scat on the trail before sunset and decided a prudent man might do well to sleep out of reach of those rangy, long-toothed hunters. So, having spent the night in the rough crook of a stout oak within sight of the King's Road – a stiff cradling, to be sure – I stirred as the daylight broke soft on a grey and gusty day, and heard the sound of men talking on the trail below. Their voices were quiet and low, the easy rhythmic tones familiar, even as the words were strange. It took me a moment to shake the sleep out of my ears and realise they were speaking Welsh. My mother's tongue it was, and I had enough of it from my barefoot days to make myself understood.

I heard the words *Rhi Bran y Hud* and knew I was close to finding what I was looking for, so . . .

'Yes, Odo, what is it?' My scribe rouses himself from his snooze and rubs his dream-dulled eyes.

'These words *Riban Hood*,' he asks, yawning wide. 'What do they mean?'

'If you would let a fella get on wi' the tellin', God knows you'd find out soon enough,' I say. 'But, see here now, it en't *Riban Hood*, as you will have it. It is *Rhi Bran* – that part means 'King Raven.' And *Hud* means . . . well, it means 'Enchanter.' It is what the British folk call the phantom lord of the Marchlands.'

'Ree Bran a Hood,' he says, dutifully writing it down. 'A good name.'

'Aye, a good name, that,' I agree, and we rumble on.

W ell, I shinnied down to join those fellas on the road and see what they could tell me of this mysterious bird.

'Here now,' I called, dropping lightly from the last branch onto the bank above the road. 'Can you fellas spare a traveller a word or two?'

You would have thought I'd dropped down from the moon to see the look on those two faces. Two men, one big as a house and the other slighter, but muscled and tough as a hickory root. They were dressed in odd hooded cloaks with greenery and rags sewn on, and both carried sturdy longbows with a quiver of arrows at their belts. 'What!' cried the big one, spinning around quicker than you'd have thought possible for so large a lump of humanity.

This one has spent a fair bit of time in the greenwood, thinks I, his knife is in his hand that quick. 'I mean no harm, friend,' I said. 'And full sorry I am if I startled you. I heard you talkin' and was hopin' for a little chin music, is all.'

'You lurking devil,' growled the slight one, thrusting forward, 'we'll not be singing for you.' He looked to the big one, who nodded slowly. 'Not until we know more about you.'

'Well, I've got time enow if you do,' said I. 'Where would you like me to begin?'

'A name if you have one,' said he. 'That will do for a beginning.'

'My name's William Scatlocke,' I told them. 'Think what you like, but there's some as tug a forelock when they hear that name.' I give him a smile and a wink. 'But a doff o' the hat will do nicely just now.'

'I am Iwan,' replied the big one, warming up a little. 'This here is Siarles.'

'Scatlocke's a Saxon name,' observed the slight one with a frown. 'But William, now that's Ffreinc.' He seemed ready to spit to show me what he thought of Normans.

'Saxon and Ffreinc, aye,' I agreed politely. 'My mother, bless her dear, sweet, well-meaning soul, thought a Frankish William would make my life that little mite easier seeing as our land was overrun by the vermin. With a William to go before me, they might mistake me for one of their own, see, and give me an easier ride.'

'Do they?' he asked, suspicion making his voice a threat.

'Not as I've noticed,' I said. 'Then again, it en't as if I'd been named Siarles. Now, there's a name just begging for trouble, if ever I heard one.'

The slight one bristled and bunched up his face, but the big one chuckled aloud, his voice like thunder over green hills. 'You are a bold one, give you that,' said he. 'But you're in the March now, friend. What causes you to be dropping from our good Welsh trees, Bold William?'

'Friendly folk call me Will Scarlet,' I answered. 'Forester by trade, I am – just like my father before me. I see you two know your way around leafland yourselves.'

'That we do, Will,' Iwan said. 'Are you running from someone, then?'

'Running to, more like.'

Well, they wanted to hear more, so I went on to explain about Thane Aelred getting banished and his lands taken in Forest Law and all that ruck. I told about taking to the greenwood, and all my travels since then. They listened, and I could feel them relaxing their distrust as I described hiding from the sheriff and his men on land that used to belong to my good thane, and poaching the king's precious deer to survive. Pretty soon, they began nodding and agreeing, siding with me in my plight. 'Thing is, since then I've been on the move all summer looking for this fella they call King Raven. Naturally, when I heard you mention Rhi Bran, my ears pricked right up.'

'You speak Cymru?' asked Siarles then.

'Learned it on my dear mum's knee,' I told him. 'Same mum, in fact, that named me William. I also bothered myself to learn a little Frank so I'd know what those buggers were up to.'

'Why do you want to see King Raven?' asked Iwan. 'If you don't mind my asking.'

'To offer my services,' I replied, 'and I'd be much obliged for any help you could give me in that direction.'

'Might we know the nature of these services?' asked Siarles, looking me up and down. He was softening a bit, but still a little brittle for my taste.

'Seems to me that if he is even half the man I think he is, he'll be needing a strong and fearless hand like Will Scarlet here.'

'What do you know of him?'

'I know he en't a phantom, as some would have it. I know Baron de Braose is offering fifty pounds of pure English silver for his fine feathered head on a pike.'

'Truly?' Siarles asked, much impressed.

'Aye,' I assured him, 'did you not know that?'

'We maybe heard something about it,' he muttered. Then a new thought occurred to him. 'And just how do we know you don't want to claim all that money for yourself?'

'Good question,' I allowed. 'And it deserves a good answer.'

'Well?' he said, suspicion leaping up lively as ever. Siarles, bless him; his grey eyes are quick and they are keen, but he distrusts most of what he sees. Half of it is living in the wildwood, I reckon, where your eyes and wits are your best and truest friends; but the other half is just his own leery nature.

'As soon as I think up an answer good enough, I'll tell you,' I said. This brought a growl from young Siarles, who wanted to run me off then and there.

Iwan only laughed. He had already made up his mind about me. 'Peace, Siarles,' he said. 'He doesn't want the money.'

'How can you be so sure?'

'Any man after the reward money would have thought of a better answer than that. Why, he'd have a whole story worked out and like as not say too much and get himself all tangled in the telling. Will, here, didn't do that.'

'Maybe he's just that stupid.'

'Nay, he isn't stupid,' replied Iwan. I liked him better and better by the moment. 'I'll wager my good word against anything in your purse that claiming the reward money never crossed his mind.'

'You would win that bet, friend,' I replied. 'In truth, it never did.' Seeing as how Iwan had made such a fine argument for me, I asked, 'Am I to be thinking that you know this Rhi Bran?'

Siarles, still suspicious, frowned as Iwan said, 'Know him, aye, we do.'

'Would you kindly tell me where he can be found?' I asked, nice as please and thank you.

'Better than that,' said Iwan, 'we'll take you to meet him.'

'Iwan!' snapped Siarles. He was tenacious as a rat dog, give him that. 'What are you saying? We don't know this Saxon, or anything about him. We can't be taking him to Bran. Why, he might be any-body – maybe even a spy for the abbot!'

'If he's Hugo's spy we can't be leaving him here,' countered Iwan. 'I say we take him with us and leave it to Bran to decide who and what he is — aye, and what is to be done with him.' Turning to me, he said, 'If we take you with us, do you swear on your life's blood to abide by our lord's decision whatsoever it may be?'

Ordinarily, I do not like swearing my life away on the whims of persons unknown, but seeing as he was only granting me the chance I'd been seeking all summer, I readily agreed. 'On my life's blood, I swear to abide by your lord's decision.'

'Good enough for me,' said Iwan. 'Follow us.'

'And see you keep quiet,' added Siarles for good measure.

'I'll be as quiet as you were when you woke me from my treetop perch just now,' I told him.

Iwan gave out a laugh and, in two quick strides, disappeared up over the bank and into the brushwood beside the road. 'After you,' said Siarles, prodding me with the tip of his bow. 'I'll come last, and don't you put a foot wrong, 'cause I'll be watching you.'

'There's relief, to be sure,' I replied. Stepping into the forest, I was led a merry chase to meet the man I'd crossed half the country to see. God save me, but I never imagined him the way he first appeared.

CHAPTER 5

The trail went on and on. My guides maintained a curious wolf-trot pace: three steps quick walk alternating with four steps slow running. It took a bit of getting used to, but, once I got the knack, I soon understood that it allowed a body to move quickly over long distances and still have breath enough and strength to do what you came to do when you reached your destination. I had never seen this neat trick before, and was glad to add it to my own tidy store of forest craft . . .

'You should try it, Odo,' I tell my bleary-eyed scribe. He raises his pudding face to see if I jest. 'It would do you good.'

'I will take you at your word,' he says, stifling a yawn. He dips his quill in the horn, and the wet nib hovers over the parchment. 'Where did they take you, these hooded strangers?'

'Where did they take me? Pay attention, and you'll learn soon enough. Now then, where was I?'

'Running through the greenwood to meet the Raven King.'

'Not the Raven King,' I tell him. 'It is King Raven – there is a difference, monk. Get it right.'

Odo gives an indifferent shrug, and I resume my tale . . .

Well, we ran miles that morning, and I am firmly persuaded most of it was just to confuse me so as to prevent me leading anyone else to their forest hideaway.

For the most part, it worked well enough. On a fella less firmly rooted in woodland lore, it would have been well-nigh confounding. As for myself, it produced only mild befuddlement, as Iwan probably guessed after a while. For we came to a place where a little clear water stream issued from beneath a natural rock wall, and after we'd got a few good mouthfuls, the big man produced a scrap of cloth from his quiver. 'Sorry, William,' he said, handing me the cloth. 'You must bind your eyes now.'

'If it makes you and yours feel better, I'm happy to do it,' I said. 'I'll even let Siarles here tie the knot.'

'Right, you will,' said Siarles, stepping behind me as I wound the cloth around my head. He tied the loose ends, gave them a sharp tug, and then we were away again, more slowly – this time Iwan leading, and me stumbling along with my hand on his shoulder, tripping over roots and stones and trying to keep up with his long-legged strides. It was more difficult than I would have thought – try it yourself in rough wood and see how you go. After a time I sensed the ground beginning to rise. The slope was gradual at first, but grew steeper as we went along. I heard birdsong high up, scattered and far off – the trees were getting bigger and farther apart.

Gaining the top of the ridge, we came to a stony ledge and

stopped again. 'Here now,' said Iwan, taking me by the shoulders and turning me around a few times, 'not far to go. A few more steps is all.'

He spun me around some more, and then Siarles spun me the other way for good measure. 'Mind your step,' said Siarles, his mouth close to my ear. 'Keep your head low, or you'll get a knock.' He pressed my head down until I was bent double, and then led me through a gap between two trees and, almost immediately, down a steep incline.

'Cél Craidd,' said Iwan. 'I pray it goes well with you here.'

'You better pray so, too,' added Siarles in tone far less friendly. He had taken against me, I don't know why – maybe it was that jibe about his name. Or maybe it was the cut of my cloth, but whatever it was, he gave me to know that he held me of small regard. 'Play us false, and it will be the last place you ever see.'

'Now, now,' I replied, 'no need to be nasty. I've sworn to abide, and abide I will, come what may.'

Siarles untied the binding cloth, and I opened my eyes on the strangest place I have ever seen: a village made of skins and bones, branches and stones. There were low hovels roofed with ferns and moss, and others properly thatched with rushes; some had wattle-and-daub walls, and some were made of woven willow withies so that the hut seemed to have been knitted whole out of twigs, and the chinks stuffed with dried grass, giving the place an odd, fuzzy appearance as if it wore a pelt in moulting. If a few of the hovels in the centre of the settlement were larger and constructed of more substantial stuff – split timber and the like – they also had roofs of grassy turf, and wore antlers or skull bones of deer or oxen at the corners and above their hide-covered doorways, which gave them the look of something grown up out of the forest floor.

If a tribe of Greenmen had bodged together a settlement out of bark and brake and cast-off woodland ruck, it would look exactly like this, I thought. Indeed, it was a fit roost for King Raven – just the sort of place the Lord of the Forest might choose.

Nested in a shallow bowl of a glade snugged about by the stout timbers of oak and lime and ash and elm, Cél Craidd was not only protected, but well hidden. The circling arm of the ridge formed a wall of sorts on three sides which rose above the low huts. A fella would have to be standing on the ridgetop and looking down into the bowl of the glade to see it. But this concealment came at a price, and the people there were paying the toll with their lives.

Our arrival was noticed by a few of the small fry, who ran to fetch a welcome party. They were – beneath the soot and dirt and ragged clothes – ordinary children, and not the offspring of a Greenwife. They skittered away with the swift grace of creatures birthed and brought up in the wildwood. Chirping and whooping, they flew to an antler-decked hut in the centre of the settlement, and pounded on the doorpost. In a few moments, there emerged what is possibly the ugliest old woman I ever set eyes to. Mother Mary, but she was a sight, with her skin wrinkled like a dried plum and blackened by years of sitting in the smoke of a cooking fire, and a wiry, wayward grizzled fringe of dark hair – dark where it should have been bleached white by age, she was that old. She hobbled up to look me over, and though her step might have been shambling there was nothing wrong with the eyes in her head. People talk of eyes that pierce flesh and bone for brightness, and I always thought it mere fancy. Not so! She looked me over, and I felt my skin flayed back and my soul laid bare before a gaze keen as a fresh-stropped razor.

'This is Angharad, Banfáith of Britain,' Iwan declared, pride swelling his voice.

At this the old woman bent her head. 'I give thee good greeting, friend. Peace and joy be thine this day,' she said in a voice that creaked like a dry bellows. 'May thy sojourn here well become thee.'

34

She spoke in an old-fashioned way that, oddly enough, suited her so well I soon forgot to remark on it at all.

'Peace, Banfáith,' I replied. I'd heard and seen my mother's folk greeting the old ones from time to time, using a gesture of respect. This I did for her, touching the back of my hand to my forehead and hoping the sight of an ungainly half-Saxon offering this honour would not offend overmuch.

I was rewarded with a broad and cheerful smile that creased her wrinkled face anew, albeit pleasantly enough. 'You have the learning, I ween,' she said. 'How came you by it?'

'My blesséd mother taught her son the manners of the Cymry,' I replied. 'Though it is seldom enough I've had the chance to employ them these last many years. I fear my plough has grown rusty from neglect.'

She chuckled at this. 'Then we will burnish it up bright as new soon enough,' she said. Turning to Iwan, she said, 'How came you to find him?'

'He dropped out of a tree not ten steps from us,' he answered. 'Fell onto the road like an overgrown apple.'

'Did he now?' she wondered. To me, she said, 'Pray, why would you be hiding in the branches?'

'I saw the sign of a wolf on the road the night before and thought better to sleep with the birds.'

'Prudent,' she allowed. 'Know you the wolves?'

'Enough to know it is best to stay out of reach of those long-legged rascals.'

'He says he is searching for our Bran,' put in Siarles. Impatient, he did not care to wait for the pleasant talk to come round to its destination as is the way with the Cymry. 'He says he wants to offer his services.'

'Does he now?' said Angharad. 'Well, then, summon our lord and let us see how this cast falls out.'

Siarles hurried away to one of the larger huts in the centre of the holding. By this time, the children had been spreading the word that a stranger had come, and folk were starting to gather. They were not, I observed, an altogether comely group: thin, frayed and worn, smudged around the edges as might be expected of people eking out a precarious life in deep forest. Few had shoes, and none had clothes that were not patched and patched again. At least two fellas in the crowd had lost a hand to Norman justice; one had lost his eyes.

A more hungry, haunted lot I never saw, nor hope to see – like the beggars that clot the doorways of the churches in the towns. But where beggars are hopeless in their desperation, these folk exuded the grim defiance of a people who exist on determination alone. And all of them had the look I'd already noticed on the young ones: an aspect of wary, almost skittish curiosity, as if, drawn to the sight of the stranger in their midst, they nevertheless were ready to flee at a word. One quick move on my part, and they'd bolt like deer, or take wing like a flock of sparrows.

'If your search be true,' the old woman told me, 'you have naught to fear.'

I thanked her for her reassurance and stood to my fate. Presently, Siarles returned from the house accompanied by a young man, tall and slender as a rod, but with a fair span of shoulders and good strong arms. He wore a simple tunic of dark cloth, trousers of the same stuff, and long black riding boots. His hair was so black the sun glinted blue in his wayward locks. A cruel scar puckered the skin on the left side of his face, lifting his lip in what first appeared to be a haughty sneer – an impression only, belied by the ready wit that darted from eyes black as the bottom of a well on a moonless night.

There was no doubt that he was their leader, Bran – the man I had come to find. If the right and ready homage of the ragged forest folk failed to make that clear, you had only to take in the regal ease with which he surveyed all around him to know that here was a man well used to command. His very presence demanded attention, and he claimed mine without effort to the extent that at first I failed to see the young woman trailing behind him: a fine, dark-haired lady of such elegance and grace that, though she was dressed in the same humble drab as the starvelings around her, she held herself with such an imperious bearing that I took her to be the queen.

'I present Rhi Bran, Lord of Elfael,' said Iwan, speaking loud enough for all gathered round to hear.

'Pax vobiscum,' said the tall young man, looking me up and down with a sweep of a quick, intelligent eye.

'God's peace, my lord,' I replied in Cymric, offering him the courtesy of a bow. 'I am William Scatlocke, former forester to Thane Aelred of Nottingham.'

'He's come to offer his services,' Siarles informed his lordship with a mocking tone to let his master know what he thought of the idea.

Bran looked me over once again and finding no fault, I think, replied, 'What kind of services do you propose, William Scatlocke?'

'Anything you require,' I said. 'From slaughtering hogs to thatching roofs, sawing timber to pollarding hazel, there's not much I haven't done.'

'You said you were a forester,' mused Bran, and I saw the glint of interest in his glance.

'Aye, I was – and a good one, if I say it myself.'

'Why did you quit?'

'Thane Aelred, God bless him, lost his lands in the succession dispute and was banished to Daneland. All his vassals were turned

37

out by Red William to fend for themselves, most like to starve, it was that grim.'

The dark-haired young woman, who had been peering from behind Bran's shoulder, spoke up just then. 'No wife, or children?'

'Nay, my lady,' I replied. 'As you see, I'm a young man yet, and hope burns bright. Still, young or old, a man needs a bit of where-withal to keep even one small wife.' I smiled and gave her a wink to let her know I meant it lightly. Unamused, she pressed her lips together primly. 'Ah, well, I was just scraping some of that wherewithal together when the troubles began. Most lost more than I did, to be sure, but I lost all the little I had.'

'I am sorry to hear it,' said Bran. 'But we are hard-pressed here, too, what with the care of ourselves and the folk of Elfael as well. Any man who would join us must earn his way and then some if he wants to stay.' Then, as if he'd just thought of it, he said, 'A good forester would know how to use a longbow. Do you draw, William?'

'I know which end of the arrow goes where,' I replied.

'Splendid! We will draw against one another,' he declared. 'Win and you stay.'

'If I should lose?'

His grin was sly and dark and full of mischief. 'If you would stay, then I advise you not to lose,' he said. 'Well? What is it to be? Will you draw against me?'

There seemed to be no way around it, so I agreed. 'That I will,' I said, and found myself carried along in the sudden rush – the people to the contest, and myself to my fate.

CHAPTER 6

'Obviously, you won the contest,' says Odo, raising his sleepy head from his close-nipped pen.

'You think so, do you?' I reply.

'Of course,' he assures me smugly. 'Otherwise, you would not be here in Count De Braose's pit waiting to be hung for a traitor and an outlaw.'

Brother Odo is feisty. He must have got up on the wrong side of his Hail Marys this morning. 'Now, monk,' I tell him, 'just you try to keep your eyes open a little while longer, and we'll get to the end of this and then see how good you are at guessing.' I settle myself on my mat of mildewed rushes and push the candle a little closer to my scribe. 'Read back the last thing I said. Quick now before I forget.'

'Siarles? Iwan? Your bows,' says Odo, in rough imitation of my voice.

'Oh, right.' And I resume . . .

The two foresters, Iwan and Siarles, handed Rhi Bran their long-bows and, taking one in either hand, he held them out to me. 'Choose the one you will use.'

'My thanks,' I said, trying first one and then the other, bending them with my weight. There was not a spit of difference between them, but I fancied winning with Siarles's bow and chose that one.

'This way, everyone!' called Bran, already striding off towards the far side of the settlement. We came to the head of a miserable patch of barley. They were about growing a few pecks of grain for themselves, but it was a poor, sad field, shadowed and soggy as it was. The people ranged themselves in a wide double rank behind us, and by now there were upwards of sixty folk — most all of the forest dwellers, I reckoned, saving a few of the women and smaller children. The grain had been harvested and only stubble remained, along with the straw man set up at the far edge of the clearing to keep the birds away. The figure was fixed to a pole some eighty or a hundred paces from where we stood — far enough to make the contest interesting.

'Three arrows. The scarecrow will be our mark,' Bran explained as Iwan passed arrows to us both. 'Hit it if you can.'

'It's been that long since I last drew—' I began.

'No excuses,' said Siarles quickly. 'Just do your best. No shame in that.'

'I was not about making excuses,' I replied, nocking the arrow to the string. 'I was going to say it's been that long since I last drew, I almost forgot how good a yew bow feels in my hand.' This brought a chuckle or two from those gathered around. Turning to Rhi Bran, I said, 'Where would you like this first arrow to go, my lord?'

'Head or heart, either will do,' Bran replied.

The arrow was on its way the instant the words left his mouth. My first shaft struck the bunched tuft of straw that formed the scarecrow's head, with a satisfying *swish!* as it passed through on its way to the far end of the field.

A murmur of polite approval rippled through the crowd.

'I can see you've drawn a longbow before,' said Bran.

'Once or twice.'

Lord Bran drew and loosed, sending his first shaft after mine, and close enough to the same place that it made no matter. The people cheered their lord with loud and lusty cries.

'My lord,' I said, 'I think you have drawn a bow once or twice yourself.'

'The heart this time?' he suggested, as we accepted our second arrows from Iwan.

'If straw men have hearts,' I said, drawing and taking good aim, 'his has thumped its last.' This time I sent the shaft up at a slight arc so that it dropped neatly through the centre of the scarecrow and stuck in the dirt behind it.

'Your luck is with you today,' sniffed Siarles as polite applause spattered among the onlookers.

'Not a bit of it,' I told him, grinning. 'That was so the lads wouldn't have to run so far to retrieve my arrow.'

'Then I shall do likewise,' said Bran, and again, drew and aimed and loosed so quickly that each separate motion flowed into the next and became one. His arrow struck the scarecrow in the upper middle and stuck in the ground right beside mine. Again, the people cheered heartily for their young king.

'Head and heart,' I said. 'We've done for your man out there. What else is left?'

'The pole on which he hangs,' said Iwan, handing over the last arrow.

'The pole then?' asked Bran, raising an eyebrow.

'The pole,' I confirmed.

Well, now. The day was misty and grey, as I say, and the little light we had was swiftly failing now. I had to squint a bit to even see the blasted pole, jutting up like a wee nubbin just over the peak of the scarecrow's straw head. It showed maybe the size of a lady's fist, and that gave me an idea. Turning to Bran's dark-haired lady, I said, 'My queen, will you bless this arrow with a kiss?'

'Queen?' she said, recoiling. 'I am not his queen, thank you very much.'

This was said with considerable vehemence . . .

Yes, vehemence, Odo.' My scribe has wrinkled his nose like he's smelled a rotten egg, as he does whenever I say a word he doesn't understand. 'It means, well, it means fire, you know — passion, grit, and brimstone.'

'I thought you said she was the queen?' objects Odo.

'That is because I thought she was the queen.'

'Well, was she or wasn't she?' he complains, lifting his pen as if threatening to quit unless all is explained to his satisfaction forthwith. 'And who is she anyway?'

'Hold your water, monk, I'm coming to that,' I tell him. And we go on . . .

This time we draw together,' said Bran. 'On my count.'

'Ready.' I press the bow forward and bring the string to my cheek, my eyes straining to the mark.

'One . . . two . . . three . . .'

I loosed the shaft on his 'three' and felt the string lash my wrist with the sting of a wasp. The arrow sliced through the air and struck the pole a little to one side. My aim was off, and the point did nothing more than graze the side of the pole. The arrow glanced off to the left and careered into the brush beyond the tiny field.

Bran, however, continued the count. 'Four!' he said, and loosed just a beat after me – enough, I think, so that he saw where my shaft would strike. And then, believe it or not, he matched it. Just as my arrow had grazed the left side of the scarecrow's pole, so Bran's sheared the right. He saw me miss, and then missed himself by the same margin, mind. Proud bowman that I was, I could but stand humbled in the presence of an archer of unequalled skill.

Turning to me with a cheery grin, he said, 'Sorry, William, I should have told you it was four, not three.' He put a friendly hand on my shoulder. 'Do you want to try again?'

'Three or four, it makes no matter,' I told him. Indicating the straw man, I said, 'It seems our weedy friend has survived the ordeal.'

'Arrows, Gwion Bach!' called Bran, and an eager young fella leapt to his command; two other lads followed on his heels, and the three raced off to retrieve the shafts.

Iwan walked out to examine the scarecrow pole. He pulled it up and brought it back to where we were waiting, and he and Angharad the banfáith scrutinized the top of the pole, with Siarles, not to be left out, pressing in between them.

'Judging by the notches made by the passing arrows,' announced the old woman after her inspection, 'Iwan and I say the one on the right has trimmed the most from the pole. Therefore, we declare Rhi Bran the winner.'

The people cheered and clapped their hands for their king. And, suddenly disheartened as the meaning of their words broke upon me,

I choked down my disappointment, fastened a smile to my face, and prepared to take my leave.

'You know what this means,' said Bran, solemn as the grave.

I nodded. 'The contest was fair – all it wanted was a better day.' I lifted my eyes to his, hoping to see some compassion there. But where the moment before they had been alive with light and mirth, his eyes were flat and cold. Could he change his demeanour so quickly?

'You deserved better,' said the dark-haired lady.

'I make no complaint,' I said.

'It is a hard thing,' Bran observed, glancing at the young woman beside him, 'but we do not always get what we want or deserve in this life.'

'Sadly true, my lord,' I agreed. 'Who should know that better than Will Scarlet?'

I lowered my head and prepared to accept my defeat, and as I did so I saw that he was not looking at me, but at the young woman. She was glaring at him – why, I cannot say – seeming to take strenuous exception to the drift of our little talk.

'But, sometimes, William,' the forest king announced, 'we get better than we deserve.' I looked up quickly, and I saw a little of the warmth ebbing back into him. 'I have decided you can stay.'

It was said so quick I did not credit what I had heard. 'My lord, did you say . . . I can *stay*?'

He nodded. 'Providing you swear allegiance to me to take me as your lord and share my fortunes to the aid of my *Grellon*, and the oppressed folk of Elfael.'

'That I will do gladly,' I told him. 'Let me kneel and I will swear my oath here and now.'

'Did you hear that, everyone?' His smile was suddenly broad and welcoming. To me, he said, 'I would I had a hundred hardy men as right ready as yourself — the Ffreinc would be fleeing back to their ships and reckoning themselves lucky to escape with their miserable hides.' With that Iwan—

B eg pardon?' says Odo, interrupting again.

'Are we never to get this told?' I say with a sigh of resignation, although I do not mind his questions as much as I let on, for it lengthens the time that much more.

'That word *Grellon* — what does it mean?'

'It is Britspeak, monk,' I tell him. 'It means *flock* — like birds, you know. It is what the people of Coed Cadw — and that means, well that's a little more difficult. It means something like *Guarding Wood*, as if the forest was a fortress, which in a way, it is.'

'Grellon,' murmurs Odo as he writes the word, sounding out the letters one by one. 'Coed Cadw.'

'As I was saying, Grellon is what Rhi Bran's people call themselves, right? Can we move on?' At Brother Odo's nod, I continue . . .

S o now, Iwan sent someone to fetch Bran's sword; and I was made to kneel in the barley stubble; and as the first drops of rain begin to fall upon my head, I plighted my troth to a new lord, the exiled king of Elfael. No matter that he was an outlaw hunted even then by every Norman in the territory, no matter that he had less in his purse than a wandering piper, no matter that a fella could pace the length and breadth of his entire realm while singing 'Hey-Nonny-Nonny,' and finish before the song was done. No matter any of it, nor that to follow him meant I took my life in my own two hands by joining an outlaw band. I knew in my heart that it was right to do, if only to annoy the rough and overbearing Normans and all their heavy-handed barbarian ways.

Oh, but it was more than that. It felt right in my soul. It seemed to me even as I repeated the words that would bind my life and fortunes to his that I had come home at last. And when he touched my shoulder with his sword and raised me to my feet, a tear came to my eye. Though I had never seen him or that forest settlement before, and knew nothing of the people gathered close around, it felt as if I was being welcomed into the fellowship of my own tribe and family. And nothing that has happened since then in all our scraps and scrapes has moved me from that stand.

The rain began coming harder then, and we all returned to the village. 'Your skill is laudable, William,' said Bran as we walked back together.

'Almost as good as your own,' said the lady, falling into step beside him. 'You may as well admit it, Bran, your man William is as good with a bow as you are yourself.'

'Just Will, if you please,' I told them. 'William Rufus has disgraced our common name in my eyes.'

'Rufus!' Bran laughed. 'I have never heard him called that before.'

'It is common enough in England,' I replied. Willy Conqueror's second son – the rakehell William, now king over us – was often called Rufus behind his back, on account of his flaming torch of red hair and scalding hot temper. His worthless brother, Duke Robert, is called Curthose owing to his penchant for wearing short tunics.

Thinking of those two ne'er-do-well nobles made me that sorry for Thane Aelred who, like all right-thinking men of his kind, had thrown in his lot with Robert, the lawful heir to the throne. Alas, Robby Shortshift turned out to be unreliable as a weathercock, forever turning this way and that at the slightest breath of a favourable wind from each and any quarter. That poor numbskull never could make up his mind, and would never fully commit himself to any course, nor stay one once decided. He was a flighty sparrow, but imagined himself a gilded eagle. The shame of it is that he led so many good men to ruination.

Aye, the only time he really ever led.

Of course, Red William held tight to the throne he'd stolen from his brother, and used the confusion over the succession – confusion he himself caused, mind – to further strengthen his grip. After he seized the royal money mintery, he had himself crowned king, sat himself on the throne, and decreed that what was in truth little more than a family disagreement had actually been a rebellious uprising, and all those who supported sad brother Robert were made out to be dangerous traitors. Lands were seized, lives lost. Good men were banished and estates forfeited to the crown. Only a small handful of fortune-kissed *aristos* came away scapegrace clean.

Turning to the lady, I said, 'Speaking of names, now that I've given mine . . .'

'This is Lady Mérian,' Bran said. 'She is our . . .' He hesitated.

'Hostage,' she put in quickly. The way she mouthed the word with such contempt, I could tell it was a sore point between them.

'Guest,' Bran corrected lightly. 'We are to endure the pleasure of her company for a little while longer, it seems.'

'Ransom me,' she said crisply, 'or release me and your trial will be over, my lord.'

He ignored the jibe. 'Lady Mérian is the daughter of King Cadwgan of Eiwas, the next cantref to the south.'

'Bran keeps me against my will,' she added, 'and refuses to set a price for my release even though he knows my father would pay good silver, and God knows the people here could use it.'

'We get by,' replied Bran amiably.

'Forgive my curiosity,' I said, plunging in, 'but if her father is only over in the next cantref, why does he not send a host to take her back by force?' I lifted a hand to the patched-together little village we were entering just then. 'I mean, it would not take much to overwhelm this stronghold, redoubtable as it is.'

'My father doesn't know where I am,' Mérian informed me. 'And anyway, it is all the baron's fault. I wouldn't be here if he had not tried to kill Bran.'

'Is that Baron de Braose?' I asked.

'No.' She shook her head, making her long curls bounce. 'Baron Neufmarché — he is my father's overlord. Bran took me captive when the baron turned traitor against him.'

'It is somewhat complicated,' offered Bran with a rueful smile.

'No,' contradicted Mérian, 'it is simplicity itself. All you need do is send a message to my father and the silver is yours.'

'When the time is right, Mérian, I will. Be sure of it. I will.'

'That's what you always say,' she snipped. To me she confided, 'He always says that — it's been a year and more, and he's still saying it.'

The way they talked a fella'd thought they were a married couple airing a grudge nursed through long seasons of living together. There was little hostility in it, and instead I sensed a certain restraint and even a sort of backwards respect. They'd had this discussion so often, I suppose, that the heat had gone out of it long ago and they were left with the familiar warmth of genuine affection.

'Forgive my asking, but why was the baron trying to kill you, my lord?'

'Because he wants Elfael,' said Iwan, coming up behind me. 'No Ffreinc usurper can ever sit secure on the throne while Bran is alive.'

'Elfael is a good place to stand if you're trying to conquer all

Cymru,' Bran explained. 'Elfael may be small, but it is a prize both de Braose and Neufmarché want to possess for their own. De Braose has it now, but that could change.'

'Aye,' said Iwan firmly, 'it will and one day soon.'

In this, I began to see the shape of the desperate necessity that had driven them into hiding. As in England, so in Wales. The Welsh now faced what Saxon England had suffered a generation ago. The difference was that now the Normans were far more numerous, far better supplied, and far more deeply entrenched in land and power than ever before. Restless, industrious, and determined as the day is long, the Norman overlords had stretched their long, greedy fingers into every nook and cranny of life in the Island of the Mighty. They are relentless, constantly searching out and seizing whatever they want and, often as not, destroying the rest. And now they had turned their attention to the hill-fast lands beyond the March.

I would not have given an empty egg for Wales' chances of surviving the onslaught. England in its strength, with its massed war host and bold King Harry leading the best warriors the land ever saw, could not resist the terrible Norman war machine. What hope in hell did proud little Wales ever have?

So now. Fool that I am, I had joined my fate to theirs, exchanging the freedom of the road and the life of a wandering odd-jobber for certain death in a fight we could never win.

Well, that's Will Scarlet for you — doomed beginning and end. Oh, but shed him no tears — he had himself a grand time between.

CHAPTER 7

Castle Truan

A little more than a year had passed since Baron William de Braose decreed that a market town would be built within the borders of his newly seized lands in Elfael. In that short time, the place had grown to respectable size. Already it was larger than Glascwm, the only other settlement worthy of a name in the region. True, the inhabitants had been moved in from the baron's other estates — some from Bramber and lands beyond the March and some from the baron's lands in France — for, unfortunately, the local Welsh shunned the place and refused to reside there. That, however, did not detract from the pride that Count Falkes felt in what he reckoned a considerable achievement by any measure: creating a town with a busy little market from a run-down, worthless monastery housing a few doughty old monks.

One day, thought Falkes as he surveyed the tidy market square, this town, his town, would rival Monmouth or perhaps even Hereford. One day, if he could just maintain order in the cantref and keep his uncle off his back. Baron de Braose might have many good qualities, but patience, like a lame hound, was lagging far to the rear of the pack.

Falkes was only too aware that his uncle chafed at what he considered his nephew's slow progress. In the baron's view, the conquest of Wales should have concluded long since. 'It has been almost two years,' he had said last time Falkes had visited him at Bramber.

It was at the first of summer that the baron had invited him, along with his cousin and closest friend, the baron's son, Philip, on a hunting foray in the south of England. The sunny, open countryside of his uncle's estate made a welcome change from grey, damp Wales. Falkes was enjoying the ride and basking in the warmth of a splendid summer day, if not in his uncle's good opinion.

'Two years!' said William de Braose as they paused beneath an elm tree to rest the horses. 'Two years and what have we to show for it?'

'We have a town, Uncle,' Falkes had pointed out. 'A very fine town. And, if I may be so bold to suggest, it has not been two years, but only a little more than one since work began.'

'A town.' William de Braose turned a cold eye on his nephew. 'A single town.'

'And an abbey,' added Falkes helpfully, casting Philip a sideways glance. 'The new church is almost finished. Indeed, Abbot Hugo is hoping you will attend the consecration ceremony.'

His uncle had allowed that while that was all well and good, he had far grander plans than this solitary town. Elfael was still the only cantref he had conquered in the new territories, and it was costing him more than he liked. 'Taxes are low,' he observed. 'The money collected hardly pays the supply of the abbey.'

'The British are poor, Sire.'

'They are lazy.'

'No, my lord, it may be true they work less than the English,' granted Falkes, who was beginning to suspect his uncle entertained a faulty understanding of the Britons, 'but their needs are less. They are a simple folk, after all.'

'You should be more stern with them. Teach them to fear the steel in your hand.'

'It would not help,' replied Falkes calmly. 'Killing them only makes them more stubborn.'

As Falkes had learned to his regret, the slaughter of the ruling Welsh king and his entire warband – while offering an immediate solution to the problem of conquering Elfael – had so thoroughly embittered the people against him that it made his position as ruler of the cantref exceedingly difficult and tenuous.

'Impose your will,' the baron insisted. 'Make them bend to your bidding. If they refuse, then do what I do – knock some heads, seize lands and property.'

'They own little enough as it is,' Falkes pointed out. 'Most of them hold land in common, and few of them recognise property rights of any kind. Money is little use to them; they barter for what they need. Whenever I tax a man, I am far more likely to be paid in eggs than silver.'

'Eggs!' sneered his uncle. 'I speak of taxes and you talk eggs.'

'It happens more often than you know,' declared Falkes, beginning to exhaust his own small store of patience.

'What about this creature of yours – this phantom of the forest? What do they call it?'

'*Rhi Bran y Hud*,' replied Falkes. 'It means King Raven the Enchanter.'

'The devil, you say! Have you caught the rascal yet?'

'Not yet,' confessed Falkes. 'Sheriff de Glanville is hopeful. It is only a matter of time.'

'Time!' roared the baron. 'It has been two years, man! How much more time do you need?'

'Father,' said Earl Philip, speaking up just then, 'may I suggest a visit to the commot? See it for yourself. You will quickly get the measure of Elfael. And you will see what Falkes is making of the place.'

'A worthy suggestion, Philip,' the baron had replied, curling the leather reins around his gloved fist as around the neck of an enemy, 'but you know that is impossible. I am away to Rouen within the month. If all goes well, I should return before Christmas.'

'I will speak to Abbot Hugo,' said Falkes, 'and we will hold the consecration at Christmas.'

'Rouen is where Duke Robert is encamped,' mused Philip, concern wrinkling his smooth brow. 'What takes you there, Father?'

Then, while the hounds and their handlers spread out across the field before them, Baron de Braose had confided his plans to meet in secret with a few like-minded noblemen who were anxious to do something about the incessant fighting between the king and his brothers. 'Their silly squabble is costing us money that would be better spent on the expansion of our estates and the conquest of Wales,' the baron fumed, wiping sweat from his plump round face. 'Whenever one of them thumbs his nose at the other, I have to raise an army and sail off to Normandie or Angevin to help the king slap down the knave. I've had a bellyful of their feuding and fighting. Something must be done.'

'Dangerous words, Father,' cautioned Philip. 'I would be careful about repeating any of that anywhere. You never know who is listening.'

'Phaw!' scoffed the baron. 'I would tell Rufus to his face if he were here. The king must know how his noblemen feel. No, the situation is intolerable, and something must be done. Something will be done, by heaven.'

Philip and Falkes exchanged a worried glance. Speech like this was dangerously close to treason. King William, who knew better than anyone else how little his nobles and subjects esteemed him, viewed even the slightest wavering of support as disloyalty; open disagreement was considered outright betrayal.

'If the king learns of this secret *société*, he will not be best pleased,' Philip pointed out. 'You will all be condemned as traitors.'

'The king will not learn of it,' the baron boasted. He drew off a glove and swatted at a fly buzzing before his face, then dragged his blue linen sleeve across his forehead. 'Special measures have been taken. We have appealed to the archbishop of Rouen, who has agreed to summon a council of noblemen concerning the papal succession.'

'The archbishop has recognised Urban as pope,' declared Philip, unimpressed with this revelation, 'as everyone knows.'

'Yes,' granted his father, 'but Urban's position is faltering just now. He is increasingly out of favour, and Clement occupies Rome. It would not take much to swing the balance his way.'

'Is this what you propose to do? Throw the weight of the nobles behind Clement?'

'For certain concessions,' the baron replied. 'A papal ban on this continual family warring would be a good beginning.'

'The king would ignore any declaration the pope might make – just as his father always did,' scoffed Philip. *'Comme le père, donc le fils.'*

The baron frowned and looked to Falkes. 'What say you, Count? Do you agree with my upstart son?'

'It is not my place to agree or disagree, Sire.'

'Hmph!' snorted the baron in derision. 'What good is that?'

'But if I might offer a suggestion,' continued Falkes, choosing his words carefully, 'it seems to me that while it is true the king is likely to ignore any censure by the church, were you to establish Clement firmly on the throne of Saint Peter, Clement would be in a position to offer William certain benefits in exchange for a signed treaty of peace between the king and his brothers.'

'Precisely,' agreed the baron. 'Is this not what I was saying?'

'To make good Clement's claim,' said Philip, 'you must first depose Urban for good. Blood would flow.'

'It may not come to that,' replied the baron.

'If it did?'

'*Qué será*,' answered his father. A drum began beating just then, and Baron de Braose gazed out across the field to a clump of beech trees where the handlers were waiting. 'If all goes well, you will receive a sign before Christmas. I will send it with the winter supplies.' With that, he put spurs to his mount and galloped away.

Earl Philip watched his father's broad back, his frown a scowl of displeasure. 'A word beyond this field and we are dead men,' he muttered.

'Count Falkes!' The baron called back to him. 'When you catch this phantom raven of yours, let me know. I think I'd like to see him hang.'

Well, thought Falkes de Braose as he rode into the town square, *we would all like to see King Raven hang.* And hang he would, there was no doubt about that. But there were other, more pressing matters on his mind than chasing down elusive thieves. And anyway, Elfael had been quiet lately — not an incident in many months. Most likely, the black bird and his band of thieves had been frightened away by the sheriff, and was now raiding elsewhere — someplace where the purses were fatter and the pickings easier.

Count Falkes paused outside Abbot Hugo's stone-built church. It was a handsome building. The abbot had spared no expense, commanding the finest materials available and gathering the best masons, and it showed.

The count had no great love for his abbot, a haughty, high-handed cleric who connived and conspired to get his way in everything — from the cloth of gold for the altar to the lead roof gleaming dully in the sun. That very roof Falkes paused to admire just now. Ordinary thatch was not good enough for Hugo; it had to be lead, cast in heavy sheets in Paris and shipped at great expense across the channel. And then there was the stonework – only the most skilled stonecutters were allowed to work on the archway carvings, producing the finest decoration money could buy. At the church entrance, Falkes stopped to examine a few of the finished sculptures – some of the last to be finished: a dragon with wings, chasing its tail for eternity; a centaur brandishing a sword; a lion and horse intertwined in mortal combat; Aquarius, the water man, with his bucket and ladle; an angel driving Adam and Eve from the Garden; a winged ox; a mermaid rising from the waves clutching an anchor; and more, all of them contained in dozens of small stone plaques around the arch and on the pillars.

Falkes traced the shapely outline of the mermaid with his finger. He had to admit that the work was extraordinary, but then, so was the cost – and increasingly difficult to bear. It meant, among other things, that he required constant support; he was still far too dependent for his survival on regular supplies from his uncle. True, the largest part of the problem was the baron himself, and his unquenchable zeal for conquest. If Baron de Braose was prepared to build slowly, to develop the land and settle the people, Count Falkes had no doubt that Elfael and the territories west could eventually be made to yield untold wealth. But the baron was not willing to wait, and Falkes had to bear the brunt of his uncle's impatience – just as he had to endure the umbrage of the abbot, whose spendthrift ways could well ruin them all.

Falkes entered the church. Cool and dim inside, it breathed an air of quiet serenity despite the steady chink of chisel on stone. He stood for a moment and watched the two masons on the wooden scaffold dressing the capitals of one of the pillars. One of them was carving what looked like a bear, and the other a bird.

'You there!' shouted Falkes, his voice loud in the quiet of the sanctuary. 'What is your name?'

The masons stopped their work and turned to look down at the count, striding down the centre of the nave. 'Me, Sire? I am Ethelric.'

'What is that you are carving, Ethelric?'

'A raven, Sire,' replied the sculptor, pointing to the leafy bough issuing from the face carved into the top of the pillar. 'You can tell by the beak, Sire.'

'Remove it.'

'Sire?' asked the mason, bewilderment wrinkling his brow.

'Remove it at once. I do not wish to see any such images in this church.'

The second stone-carver on the scaffold spoke up. 'Begging your pardon, Sire, but the abbot has approved of all the work we are doing here.'

'I do not care if the king himself has approved it. I am paying for it, and I do not want it. Remove the hideous thing at once.'

'There you are, Count Falkes!' exclaimed Abbot Hugo, moving up the nave to take his place beside the count. His white hair was neatly curled beneath a fine cloth cap, and his robe was glistening white satin. 'I saw your horse outside and wondered where you had gone.' Glancing at the two stone-carvers on the scaffold, he nodded to them to get back to work and, taking the count by the arm, led Falkes down the aisle. 'We'll let these men get on with their work, shall we?'

'But see here,' protested the count.

'Come, there is something I wish to show you,' said the abbot, surging ahead. 'The work is going well. We have years of construction still before us, of course, but the building will soon be serviceable. I'm contemplating a consecration ceremony on the eve of All Souls. What do you think of that?'

'I suppose,' agreed Falkes diffidently, 'although Baron de Braose will not be likely to attend. But see here, that carving in there . . .'

The abbot opened the door and stepped out. 'Why not?' he asked, turning back. He looped his arm through the count's and walked him into the market square. 'I would very much like the baron to attend. In fact, I insist. He must see what we have achieved here. It is his triumph as much as my own. He must attend.'

'I agree, of course,' said Falkes. 'However, the baron is away in France and not expected to return much before Christmas.'

'Pity,' sniffed the abbot, none too distraught. 'Then we will simply wait. It will give us time to finish more of the corbels and capitals.'

'That is what I wanted to speak to you about, Abbot,' said Falkes, who went on to explain that his treasury was all but depleted and there would be no more funds to pay the workers. 'I sent a letter to the baron – and it, like everything else, awaits his return from France.'

Abbot Hugo stopped walking. 'What am I to do until then? The men must be paid. They cannot wait until Christmas. The work must continue. The work must go on if we are ever to see the end of it.'

'That is as may be,' granted the count, 'but there is no money to pay them until the baron returns.'

'Can you not borrow from somewhere?'

'Do you really need cloth of gold to dress the altar?'

The abbot pursed his lips in a frown.

'You said you wished to show me something,' said Falkes.

'This way,' said the abbot. They walked across the empty market square to what was left of the former monastery of Llanelli, on whose ruins the town was being raised. The modest chapter house had been enlarged to provide adequate space for the abbot's needs – which, so it appeared to Falkes, were greater than his own, though he had a score of knights to house. Inside, what had been the refectory was now the abbot's private living quarters.

'I have drawn plans for the abbey garden and fields,' the abbot said, placing a rolled parchment in the count's hands. 'Some wine?'

'You are too kind,' said Falkes. Unrolling the skin, he carried it to the room's single window and held it to the light. The outline of the town was a simple square, and the fields, indicated by long narrow parallel lines, seemed to be some distance from the town and almost twice as large as Llanelli itself. 'What are you thinking of growing?'

'Flax mostly,' replied the abbot, 'and barley, of course. We will use what we need and sell the surplus.'

'With such a great extent of fields,' said the count, 'you will surely have a surplus. But I am wondering who will work these fields for you?'

'The monks.' Abbot Hugo handed him a cup of wine.

'How many monks do you reckon you will need?'

'As to that,' replied the abbot with a smile, 'I estimate that I can make do with no fewer than seventy-five, to begin.'

'Seventy-five!' cried Falkes. 'By the Virgin! If you had said thirty I would have thought that was fifteen too many. Why do you need so many?'

'To carry on the work of Saint Martin.' Falkes turned an incredulous gaze upon the abbot who, still smiling, sipped his wine and continued, 'It is ambitious, I confess, but we must begin somewhere.'

'Saint Martin's?'

'You cannot imagine,' said the abbot, 'that we would continue to call our new Norman abbey by its old heathen Welsh name. In fact, I have prepared a letter to the pope requesting a charter to be drawn up in the name L'Abbaye de Martin de Saint dans les Champs.'

At the mention of the pope, Falkes rolled up the parchment and handed it back to the abbot, saying, 'You would be well advised to hold onto that letter a little longer, Abbot.'

CHAPTER 8

King Raven's greenwood refuge served in most respects as a village for those forced to call it home. Deep in the forest, King Raven's flock had carved out a clearing below the protecting arm of a stony ridge. At great effort, they had extended the natural glade to include a pitiful little field for barley, a sorry bean patch, and one for turnips. They had dragged together bits of this and that for their huts and crude shelters, and the pens for their few scrawny animals. There was a patched-together tun which served as a granary for storing a scant supply of grain, and a seeping pool at the foot of the rock scarp that served them for a well.

In the days following the archery contest, I came to see the place in a little better light than had greeted me on first sight, but that en't saying much. For it did seem that a lorn and lonely air hung over the place – the vapour of suffering produced by the folk whose lives were bound to this perilous perch. No one was here who had hope of a better life elsewhere – saving, maybe, only myself. Now, a right fair forester like myself might find living in such a place no great hardship for a few weeks, or even months. But even I would be screaming to get free long before a year had come round. And these poor folk had endured it for more than a year — a tribute, I suppose, to Lord Bran and his ability to keep the flame of hope burning in their hearts.

I greatly wondered how they could keep such a place hidden, all the more since there was a bounty on Rhi Bran's head. The baron's reward had been set at a price, and it kept on creeping up, higher and higher as King Raven's deeds became more outrageous and damaging to the de Braose interests. The reward was enough to make me wonder how far some poor fella's loyalty might stretch before it snapped like a rotten rope. I also wondered how long it would be before one of the sheriff's search parties stumbled upon Cél Craidd.

Yet as I settled in amongst my new friends, I soon learned that the location was well chosen to confound discovery; to find it would take a canny and determined forester well trained to the March, which the baron did not possess. Beyond that, the folk worked hard to keep their home secret. They contrived everything from confusing the trails to sowing rumours specially concocted for Norman ears and sending spies among the folk of Elfael and Castle Truan. They kept perpetual watch on the King's Road and the forest approaches 'round about, marking the movements of all who came and went through the March.

Also call me tetched if you will — I came to believe there was something supernatural in it, too. Like in the old legends where the weary traveller comes upon a village hidden among the rocks on the seacoast. He sups there with the local folk and lays him down to sleep in a fine feather bed only to wake raw the next morn with sand in his eyes and seaweed in his hair, and the village vanished never to be found again . . . until it pleases its protectors to show itself to the next footsore wanderer.

I arrived at this odd belief after several curious encounters with Banfáith Angharad. They called her *hudolion* . . .

It means *enchantress*, Odo, thank you for interrupting.'

'Ah, it is the same as *hud*, no?' he says, the glint of understanding briefly lighting up his dull eyes. 'Enchant.'

'Yes, from the same word,' I tell him. 'And it is pronounced *hood*, so see you set it down aright.'

My leg is on fire again today. It pains me ferocious, and I am in no mind to suffer Odo's irritating ways. I watch as he bends his nose to the scrap of parchment and scratches away for a moment. 'So now,' I say, 'while we're about it, his name is not Robin, as you would have it. His name is Rhi Bran — that is, King Bran, to you.'

'*Rhi* is the word for *king*, yes, you told me already,' he intones wearily. 'And Bran — it is the same as Raven, no?'

'Yes, the word is the same. Rhi Bran — King Raven, see? It is the same. I will have you speaking like a Welshman yet, Odo, my lad.' I give him a pain-sharp smile. 'Just like a true-born son of the Black Country.'

Odo frowns and dips his pen. 'You were telling me about Angharad,' he says, and we resume our meandering march . . .

Indeed. Angharad was wise in ways beyond measure. Accomplished in many arts — some now all but lost — she could read signs and portents, and, as easily as a child tastes rain on the wind, she could foretell the shape of things to come long before they arrived. Old? She was ancient. Wreathed in wrinkles and bent low beneath the weight of years, she appeared to the unsuspecting eye merely one more old soul awaiting Elijah's chariot.

But the eyes in her head were bright as baubles. Her mind was quick and keen, restless as a wave on the strand and deep as that self-same sea. If she sometimes shuffled in her shapeless dress, her mind leapt light-footed and deerlike. Yet she never rushed, never strove, was never seen to be straining after anything. Whatever she needed seemed to come to her of its own accord. And if, betimes, their elders grew uncomfortable in her presence, the children always found peace and comfort in those stout arms.

She was, as I say, adept in all manner of curious arts. And it is through one of these or another that I suspect she purposed to keep Cél Craidd concealed from all intruders. How she did it, I have never yet discovered. But I know the old ones put great store in what they called the *caim* — a saining charm, you might say, useful for protection against many dangers, threats, and ills. Something like this must protect King Raven's roost. Then again, it may be I that am that big a fool and there is no such thing.

I soon came to regard our banfáith not as a doddering, spindle-shanked hag, but as the very life and spirit of Cél Craidd. Her soul was deep and gentle and blessed, her wisdom true as the arrow from Bran's unerring bow, her will resilient as heartwood and stronger than iron. From the flutter of the first dove of morning to the hushed feather-sweep of the midnight owl, nothing eluded her notice. The reach of her restless, searching senses ranged over her forest strong-hold and far, far beyond. At times, I do believe, they reached right into the very castles of the Norman barons.

One particular occasion taught me to respect her judgement, how-ever queer that judgement might seem at first blush. Well, a fine dry winter had set in. I had been some weeks with the forest tribe, learn-ing their ways and getting to know the folk right well. I helped in the fields to gather in the paltry root crop; I chopped firewood by the wagonload; I helped slaughter two of the three pigs, and salt and smoke the meat to keep over the winter. I also turned my hand at building two new huts – one for a family that had come a week or so earlier than myself, and one for a young widow and her wee daughter rescued from Count Falkes's marauders and their hounds.

Mostly, however, I went hunting with Iwan, Siarles, and one or two of the other men. Occasionally, Bran would join us; more often, Iwan led the party. Siarles, whose skills as a forester were greater even than my own, always served as guide since he knew the greenwood well: where the deer would be found, around which bend the pigs would appear, or when the birds would flock or fly. A good and worthy huntsman, uncanny in his own way, he made sure we rarely returned empty-handed from the chase. To be sure, it was desperate hunting – we brought back game or we went hungry.

In all these things, I was tested in small ways, and never openly. Still, through a word or gesture, or a glance exchanged, I soon came to understand that, while they accepted my presence among them, they did not wholly trust me yet. They were testing both my abilities and mettle, as well as my honour. This was only natural, I know, for a folk whose lives depended on remaining out of sight. The baron's spies were everywhere, and the abbot was a wily, relentless foe. King Raven lived or died on the loyalty of his flock, even as they lived or died with him.

So, they watched and they tested. Far from begrudging them their doubt, I welcomed every opportunity to prove myself.

'What's that, Odo? Strayed from the point, you say?' Lately, our Odo has taken to interrupting me whenever he thinks I have wandered too far afield and may not be able to make it back to the place of my departure. So he checks me with a word or two. 'Perhaps,' I allow, 'but it is all of a piece, you see.'

'That is as may be,' he says, rubbing his bald priest patch. 'But you were speaking of an incident that, ah' – he scans his scribbled scrip – 'taught you to trust Angharad's wisdom.'

'Right you are, Odo, lad. So I was. Well, then . . . where was I?'

'The days were growing dimmer and a fine dry winter had set in.'

He resumes writing, and we go on . . .

O ne morning a few days before Christmas, I heard the call of a raven, but thought nothing of it until I saw people hurrying to the bare circle of earth beneath the tree they called Council Oak. 'Will! Come, join us,' called Iwan. 'It is the summons!'

Angharad was there, wrapped head to foot in her cloak, although the day was mild enough for that time of year and the sun, low in the southern sky, was bright. Standing beside her was a small boy; I'd seen him before darting here and there about the place, always moving, never still. He seemed a clever, curious child, and a favourite of Bran's among the youngsters.

'Gwion Bach has news from Elfael,' she announced when Bran had taken his place. 'Count Falkes is expecting winter supplies from his uncle, the baron. The wagons are to arrive any day.'

'Is it known what is coming?' asked Bran.

'Grain and wine, cloth and such,' she replied, glancing at the boy, who gave a slight nod. 'And some things for the abbot's new church.'

'Any day,' mused Bran. 'Not much time.'

'None to lose,' agreed the hudolion.

'Then we must hurry if we are to make ready a warm welcome for them.' Bran was already moving towards his hut. 'Iwan! Siarles! To me!'

He paused in midstep, turned, and regarded me as if weighing the prudence of taking an untried hound a-hunting with the pack.

I sensed his reluctance and guessed what he was thinking. 'My lord, I stand ready to lend both hand and heart to whatever command you give me.' Indicating young Gwion Bach, who was following in his lord's footsteps, I said, 'But if even children serve you in this fight, then perhaps you would not deny a willing elder to aid you in your purpose.'

He nodded once, deciding it then and there. 'Come along, Will. Join us.'

'Rhi Bran!' Angharad called after him. 'One thing more – something else comes with the wagons.'

'Yes?'

'There will be snow,' she said, gathering her robe around her more tightly.

Bran accepted this without hesitation, but I had not yet learned to honour these utterances with unquestioning belief. Unable to help myself, I glanced up at the sky, bright and fine, and not the least smudge of a cloud to be seen anywhere. The amused expression on my face must have given me away, for as I stood looking on, Bran called to me. 'What, Will? Could it be that you doubt our good ban-fáith's word?'

'Nay, Lord,' I replied, softening his accusation. 'Let us rather say that it will be the first time I've seen snow from a clear blue sky.'

'Hmph!' sniffed Angharad, muttering as she stumped away, 'These old bones know snow when they feel it.'

I followed Bran to his hut and took my place alongside the other two. Iwan seemed comfortable enough with my presence, but Siarles did not appear to prize it much. Even so, I was there at the king's pleasure, so there was nothing to be said or done. 'It seems the baron in his boundless generosity is sending us a Christmas blessing,' Bran said. 'We must make ready to receive it with all good grace.'

The other two grinned at the thought, and all three began planning how best to greet the supply wagons when they passed through the forest on their way to Castle Truan. I listened to their talk, keeping my own counsel – as I was yet a little uncertain what manner of outlawry I had fallen into. Every now and then, the name *King Raven* arose in their discussion. It was the first time I had heard the name used among them in just this way. It was Bran himself they meant, and yet all three spoke of him as if it were someone else.

Finally, after this had gone on awhile, I asked, 'Pardon my ignorance, Lord, but are you not King Raven?'

'Of course,' replied Bran, 'as you already know.'

'To be sure,' I said, 'but why when you speak the name do you say, "he will go . . ." or, ". . . when he calls . . ." and the like, if it is yourself you mean?'

Bran laughed.

Iwan answered, 'It is Bran and not Bran. See?'

'Again, I must beg pardon. But that makes no sense to this dull head at all.'

'Bran is King Raven,' Siarles explained, giving me a superior smile, 'but King Raven is not Bran.'

'Sorry.' I shook my head. 'I may be slow of wit, God knows, but it still seems nonsense to me.'

Bran said, 'Then you'll just have to wait and see.'

Well, we spent most of the day planning the welcome for the baron's supply train. While they talked about all they would do, I still had little real idea what to expect save for my part in the proceedings, which amounted to little more than watching the road and being ready with a bow in case events did not fall out as predicted.

A few of the Grellon were involved, but not many, and none of them was given duty at the sharp end. Bran, Siarles, and Iwan assumed the greatest risk and made particular efforts to keep the people both out of sight and out of danger as much as possible.

Oh, but it would be dangerous. There was no avoiding that.

CHAPTER 9

I t was an odd thing: everyone scurrying around like ants in the rain – the children dragging wood into heaps near the door of each hut, and the women bundling foodstuffs, and the men drawing water and snugging the shelters – all labouring under a clear, bright sky to prepare for snow, the only hint of which was a twinge in an old woman's bones.

While the rest of us were taking such measures against the coming storm, Iwan and Siarles went to spy out the best place for the welcome. We did not know how many soldiers would come with the wagons, nor how many wagons there might be. But Iwan and Siarles knew the road and knew where an ambush might succeed.

They were gone all that short winter's day, returning at dusk. Upon arrival, they went directly to our lord's hut. Tired from the day's work, I settled by the common fire where a stew pot was bubbling, to warm myself and wait for the food to be served. 'You were busy all day,' observed a woman nearby.

'I was that.' I turned to see Mérian, bundled in her cloak, taking her place on the log beside me. 'My lady, I give you good greeting.'

'You didn't go with the others,' she observed.

'No, there was enough to be done here. They only went to see where the wagons might pass.'

'To see where the wagons might be attacked,' she corrected. 'That is what you mean.'

'Yes, I suppose that is my meaning.' She made a small tut of disapproval. 'You do not agree with the king in this?'

'Whether I agree or not makes no difference,' she replied crisply. 'The point is that Bran will never achieve peace with the baron if he insists on raiding and thieving. It only angers the baron and provokes him and the count to ever more cruel reprisals.'

'You are right, of course,' I agreed. 'But from where I stand, I don't see Rhi Bran making peace with the baron or the count, either one. He wants to punish them.'

'He wants the return of his throne,' she corrected crisply, 'and he will not achieve it by plundering a few supply wagons.'

'No, perhaps not.'

'There!' she said, as if she had won a victory herself. 'You agree. You see what must be done.'

'My lady?'

'You must talk to Bran and persuade him to change his mind about the raid.'

'Me?' I said. 'I cannot. I dare not.'

'Why?' she said, turning her large dark eyes on me.

'It is not my place.'

'I would have thought it the place of any right-thinking man to help his lord whenever he can. Certainly, if you saw him sticking his hand in a nest of vipers you would warn him.'

I regarded her closely before answering. 'My lady, please,' I said. 'I cannot do as you ask. Iwan might, and I daresay Siarles would risk it. But Will here cannot. I do beg your pardon.'

She lifted one slender shoulder and sighed. 'Oh, very well. It was worth a try. Do not think poorly of me, Will Scarlet. It is just that . . .' She paused to find the right word. 'I get so vexed with him sometimes. He will not listen to me, and I don't know what else to do.'

I accepted this in silence, stretching my hands towards the flames.

'I know he will get himself killed one day,' she continued after a time. 'If the sheriff catches him, or one of the baron's men, Bran is as good as dead before the sun sets.'

'You worry about him.'

'Truly, I do so worry,' she confided. 'I do not think I could bear losing him again.'

'Again?'

She nodded, growing pensive. 'It was just after the Ffreinc came to Elfael. The king – Bran's father, Lord Brychan – had been killed and all the warband with him. Only Iwan survived.' She went on to describe how Bran had been seized and taken hostage by Count Falkes, and how he had fled the cantref. 'He might have made good his escape, but he stopped to help a farmer and his wife who were being attacked by the count's rogues. He fought them off, but others came and gave chase. They caught him, and he was wounded and left for dead.' She paused, adding in a softer voice, 'Word went out that he had been killed . . . and so I thought. Everyone thought he had been killed. I only learned the truth very much later.'

She drew breath as if there was more she would say, but thought better of it just then, for she fell silent instead.

'How did Bran survive?' I asked after a moment.

'Angharad found him,' she explained, 'and brought him back to life. He has lived in the forest ever since.'

I considered this. It explained the curious bond I sensed between the old woman and the young man, and the way in which he honoured her. I thought on this for a time, content in the silence and the warmth of the flames.

'He won't always live in the forest,' I said, more to have something to say and so prolong our time together.

'No?' she replied, glancing sideways at me. She was kneading her fingers before the fire, and the flames made her eyes shine bright.

'Why, he intends to win back his throne. You said so yourself just now. When that happens, I expect we will all bid the forest a fond fare-thee-well.'

'But that will never happen,' she insisted. 'Does no one see? The baron is too strong, his wealth too great. He will never let Elfael go. Am I the only one who sees the truth?' She shook her head sadly. 'What Bran wants is impossible.'

'Well,' I said, 'I wouldn't be too sure. I have seen the lone canny fox outwit the hunter often enough to know that it matters little how many horses and men you have. All the wealth and weapons in the world will not catch the fox that refuses to be caught.'

She smiled at that, which surprised me. 'Do you really think so?'

'God's truth, my lady. That is exactly what I think.'

'Thank you for that.' She smiled again and laid her hand on my arm. 'I am glad you are here, Will.'

Just then, the first fresh flakes of snow arrived. One brushed her forehead and caught on her dark eyelashes. She blinked and looked up as the snow began to fall gently all around. God help me, I did not look at the snow. I saw only Mérian.

Is she?' Odo wants to know. His question brings me out of a reverie, and I realise I've drifted off for some moments.

'Is she what, lad?' I ask.

'Is she very beautiful – as beautiful as they say?'

'Oh, lad, she is all that and more. It is not her face or hair or fine noble bearing – it is all these things and more. She is a right fair figure of a woman, and I will trounce the man who slanders her good name. She was born to be a queen – and if there is a God in heaven, that is what she will be.'

'Pity,' sniffs Odo. 'With men like you to protect her, I wouldn't give a rat's whisker for her chances. Most likely, she'll share the noose with your Rhi Bran.'

Oh, this makes me angry. 'Listen, you little pus pot of a priest,' I say, my voice low and tight. 'This en't finished yet, not by a long walk. So, if you have any other clever ideas like this, keep 'em under your skirt.' Tired of him, of my confinement, sick of the pain that burns in my wounded leg, I lean back on my filthy pallet and turn my face away.

Odo is silent a moment, as well he should be, then says, 'Sorry, Will, I did not mean to offend you. I only meant—'

'It makes no matter,' I tell him. 'Read back where we left off.'

He does, and we go on.

The snow fell through the night. We awoke to a thick layer of white fluff over the forest. Branches dragged down and saplings bent low beneath the weight of cold, wet snow. Our little village of low-roofed huts lay almost hidden beneath this shroud. Early yet, the sun was just rising as we gathered our gear and made our final preparations.

73

After a quick meal of black bread, curds, and apples, we gathered to receive our marching orders.

'Here,' said Siarles, handing me what appeared to be a bundle of rags covered with bark and twigs and leaf wrack, 'put this on.'

Taking the bundle, I shook it out and held it up before me. 'A cloak?' I asked, none too certain of my guess. Long, ragged, dun-coloured things with all manner of forest ruck sewn on, they looked like the pelt of some fantastical woodland creature born of tree and fern.

'We wear these when moving about the forest,' he said, pulling a similar garment around his shoulders. 'Good protection.'

Folk — whether two-legged or four — are difficult enough to see in dense wood. This, any forester will tell you for nothing. Wearing these cloaks, a fella would be well-nigh impossible to see even for eyes trained in tracking game along tangled pathways through dense brush in the dim or faulty light that is the forest. Nevertheless, bless me for a dunce, I saw a flaw in the plan. 'It has snowed,' I said.

'You noticed,' replied Siarles. 'Oh, you're a shrewd one, no mistake.' He indicated a basket into which the others were digging. 'Get busy.'

The basket was filled with scrags of sheep's wool, birch bark, and scraps of bleached linen and such which we fixed to the distinctive hooded cloaks of the Grellon, quickly adapting them for use in the snow.

One of the men, Tomas — a slender, light-footed little Welshman — helped me with mine, then set it on my shoulders just right and adjusted the hood as I drew the laces tight. I did the same for him, and Iwan passed among us with bow staves, strings, and bags of arrows. I tucked the strings into the leather pouch at my belt and slung the bag upon my back. At Bran's signal, we fell in behind Iwan and tried our best to keep up with his great, ground-covering stride; no easy chore in the best of times, it was made more difficult still by the snow.

After a while we came to a place beneath the great overhanging limbs of oak and ash and hornbeam where the path was wide and still mostly dry. I found myself walking beside Tomas. 'Once in Hereford, a man told me a tale about Abbot Hugo losing his gold candlesticks to King Raven,' I said, opening a question that had been rumbling around in my skull for some time now. 'Is it true at all?'

'Aye, 'tis true,' Tomas assured me. 'Mostly.'

'Which part? Pardon my asking.'

'What did you hear?' he countered.

'There were twenty wagons full of gold and silver church treasure, they said – and all of it under guard of a hundred mounted knights and men-at-arms. They say King Raven swooped down, killed the soldiers with his fiery breath, and snatched away the gold candlesticks to use in unholy devil rites,' I told him. 'That's what I heard.'

'We did stop the wagons and help lighten the load,' replied the Welshman. 'And there was some gold, yes, and the candlesticks – that's true enough. But there were never a hundred knights.'

'Twenty, more like,' put in Siarles, who had overheard us talking.

'Aye, only twenty,' confirmed Iwan, joining in. 'And there weren't but three oxcarts. Still, we got more than seven hundred marks in that one raid, not counting the candlesticks.'

'And how much since then?' I asked, thinking I had come into a most gainful employment.

'A little here and there,' said Siarles. 'Nothing much.'

'Only some pigs and a cow or two now and then,' put in Iwan.

'Aye, any that wander too close to the forest,' said Tomas. 'Them's ours.'

'But the way people talk you'd think the raids were ten-a-day.'

'You can't help the way people talk,' Iwan said. 'We might stop the odd wagon betimes to remind folk to respect King Raven's wood, but there was only the one big raid.'

'What did you do with all the money?'

'We gave it away,' said Tomas, a note of pride in his voice. 'Gave it to Bishop Asaph to build a new monastery.'

'All of it?'

'Most of it,' agreed Iwan placidly. 'We still have a little kept by.'

'Thing is,' said Siarles, 'silver coin isn't all that useful in the forest.'

'We give out what is needful to the folk of Elfael to help keep body and soul together.'

I had heard this part of the tale, too, but imagined it merely wishful thinking on the part of those telling the story. It seemed, however, the generosity of Rhi Bran the Hud was true even if the greater extent of his notorious activities was not.

'Just the one big raid? Why so?'

'Two good reasons,' Iwan replied.

'It is flamin' dangerous,' put in Siarles.

'To be sure,' said Iwan. 'It does no one any good if we are caught or killed in a needless fight. Neither did we want the Ffreinc to become so wary they would make the escorts too large to easily defeat . . .'

'Or change the route the wagons followed,' Siarles said. The slight edge to his tone suggested that he did not altogether agree with the caution of his betters.

'As a result,' continued Iwan, 'the Ffreinc have grown lax of late. Because they have passed through the forest without trouble these many months, they think they can come and go at will now. Today, we will remind them who allows them this right.'

Such prudence, I thought. They would not spend themselves except for great and certain gain, nor kill the goose that laid the silver eggs. Meanwhile, they watched and waited for those chances worthy of their interest.

'Am I to take it that today's supply train is of sufficient value to make a raid worth the risk?'

'That is what we shall soon discover.' Iwan surged on ahead, and it was all we could do to keep up with him.

Finally, as the unseen sun stretched toward midday, we came in sight of the King's Road. Here we stopped, and Bran addressed us and delivered his final instructions. My own part was neither demanding nor all that dangerous so long as things went according to plan. I was to work my way along the road to a position a little south of the others, there to lie in wait for the supply train. I was to keep out of sight and be ready with my bow if anything went amiss.

Just before he sent us to our places, Bran said, 'Let no one think we do this for ourselves alone. We do it for Elfael and its long-suffering folk, and may God have mercy on our souls. Amen.'

CHAPTER 10

'Amen!' We pledged our lives with our king's, and then stood for a moment, listening to the hush of a woodland subdued beneath the falling snow. And there was that much to goad a fella to reflection. Some or all of us might be dead before the day's journey had run, and there's a thought to make a man think twice.

'You heard him, lads. Be about your work,' said Iwan, and we all scattered into the forest.

I moved a few dozen paces along the roadside and found a place behind the rotting bole of a fallen pine. It lay atop the slight rise of a bank overlooking the road below with a clear view ahead to the place where our rude welcome would commence. Trying not to disturb the snow too much, I cleared me a place and heaped up some dry leaves and pine branches, and lay my bowstave lengthwise along the underside of the pine trunk, where it would be somewhat protected from the snow and ready to hand. Then I hunkered down amongst the boughs and bracken. I need not have worried about leaving too many telltale signs, for the snow kept falling, gradually becoming heavier as the morning wore on. By midday the tracks we'd made had been filled in, removing any traces of disturbance. All the world lay beneath a clean, unbroken breast of glimmering white.

I sat and watched the flakes spin down, snow on snow, and still it fell. The day passed in silence, and aside from a few birds and squirrels, I saw no movement anywhere near the road. All remained so quiet I began to think that the soldiers guarding the supply train had thought better of continuing their journey and decided to lay up somewhere until the snow stopped and travel became easier. Maybe little Gwion Bach had it wrong and the wagons were not coming at all.

The daylight, never bright, began to falter as the snow fell thicker and faster. Warm as a cock in a dovecot under my cloak, I dozed a little the way a hunter will, alert though his eyes are closed, and passed the time in my half-sheltered nook . . .

. . . and awakened to the smell of smoke.

I looked around. Nothing had changed. The road was still empty. There was no sign of anyone passing or having passed; the snow was still falling in soft, clumping flakes. The light was dimmer now, the winter day fading quickly into an early gloom.

And then I heard it: the light jingle of a horse's tack.

I fished a dry string from my pouch and was rigging the bow before the sound came again. I shook the snow off from the bag of arrows and opened it. Bless me, there were nine black arrows inside – black from crow feather to iron tip. I placed four of them upright along the trunk of the tree in front of me, and blew gently on my hands to steady and warm them.

Oh, a fella can get a bit cramped waiting in the snow. I tried to loosen my stiff limbs a little without making too much commotion.

The sound came again and, again, the faint whiff of smoke. I had no time to wonder at this, for at that same instant two riders appeared.

79

The snow softened all sound but the jingle of the tack as they rode, and the hooves of their horses breaking a path in the snow. Big men — knights — they loomed larger still in their padded leather jerkins and long winter cloaks which covered their mail shirts. Helmeted and gauntleted, their shields were on their backs and their lances were tucked into the saddle carriers; their swords were sheathed.

They passed quietly up the road and out of sight. I counted slow beats until those following them should arrive. But none came after.

I waited.

After a time, the first two returned, hastening back the way they had come. When they reached a place just below my overlook, one of the riders stopped and sent the other on ahead while he tarried there.

Scouts, I thought. Wary, they were, and right prudent to be so.

The soldier below me was so close, I could smell the damp horse-hair scent of his mount and see the steam puff from the animal's nostrils and rise from its warm, sodden rump. I kept my head low and remained dead still the while, as would a hunter in the deer blind. In a moment, I heard the jingle of horse's tack once more and the second rider reappeared. This time, eight mounted soldiers followed in his wake. All of them joined the first knight, who ordered the lot to take up positions along either side of the road.

So now! These were not complacent fools. They had identified the hollow as potentially dangerous and were doing what they could to pare that danger to a nub. As the last soldier took his place, the first wagon hove into view. A high-sided wain, like that used to carry hay and grain, it was pulled by a double team of oxen, its tall wheels sunk deep in the snow-covered ruts of the King's Road. And though the wagon bed was covered against the snow, it was plain to a blind man by the way the animals strained against the yoke that the load was heavy indeed. Within moments of the first wain passing, a second followed.

The oxen plodded slowly along, their warm breath fogging in the chill air, the falling snow settling on their broad backs and on their patient heads between wide-swept horns.

No more appeared.

The ox-wains trundled slowly down between the double ranks of mounted knights, and that hint of smoke tickled my nostrils again – nor was I the only one this time, no mistake. The soldiers' horses caught the scent too, and came over all jittery-skittery. They tossed their fine big heads and whinnied, chafing the snow with hooves the size of bleeding-bowls.

The soldiers were not slow to notice the fuss their mounts were making; the knights looked this way and that, but nothing had changed in the forest 'round about. No danger loomed.

As the first wain reached the far end of the corridor, I caught a flicker of yellow through the trees. A glimmering wink o' light. Just that quick and gone again. With it, there came a searing, screeching whine, like the sound an arrow-struck eagle might make as it falls from the sky.

The short hairs on my arms and neck stood up to hear it, and I looked around. In that selfsame moment, one of the scouts' horses screamed, and broke ranks. The stricken animal reared and plunged, its legs kicking out every direction at once. The rider was thrown from the saddle, and as he scrambled to regain control of his mount, the animal reared again and went over, falling onto its side.

The other knights watched, but held firm and made no move to help the fella. They were watching still when there came another keening shriek and another horse reared – this one on the other side of the long double rank. As with the first animal, the second leapt and plunged and tried to bolt, but the rider held it fast.

As the poor beast whirled and screamed, I chanced to see what none of the soldiers had yet seen: sticking from the horse's flank low behind the saddle was the feathered stub of a black arrow.

The knight yelled something to the soldier nearest him. My little bit of the Frankish tongue serves me well enough most times, but I could not catch hold of what he said. He flung out a beseeching hand as the horse beneath him collapsed. Another soldier in the line gave out a cry – and all at once his horse likewise began to rear and scream, kicking its hind legs as if to smite the very devil and his unseen legions.

Before a'body could say 'Saint Gerald's jowls,' three more horses – two on the far side of the road and one on the near side – heaved up and joined in that dire and dreadful dance. The terrified animals crashed into one another, bucking and lashing, throwing their riders. One of the beasts bolted into the wood; the others fell thrashing in the snow.

It was then one of the knights caught sight of what was causing all this fret and flurry: an arrow sticking out from the belly of a downed horse. With a loud cry, he drew his sword and called upon his fellows to up shields and hunker down. His shouts went unheeded, for the other knights were suddenly fighting their own mounts. The poor brutes, already frightened by the scent of smoke and blood and the sight of the other animals flailing around, broke and ran.

The soldiers could no longer hold their terrified mounts.

The wagon drivers, fearful and shaking in their cloaks, had long since halted their teams. The commander of the guard – one of the two fellas I had first seen – spurred his mount into the middle of the road and began shouting at his men. Black arrows cut his horse from under him just that quick, and he had to throw himself from the saddle to avoid being crushed.

Dragging himself to his feet, he shouted to his men once more, trying to rally them to his side. Then, over and above the shouts and confusion, there arose a cry from the wood the like of which I had never heard before: the tortured shriek of a creature enraged and in terrible agony, and it echoed through the trees so that no one could tell whence it came.

The sound faded into a tense and uneasy silence. The Norman soldiers put hands to their weapons, turning this way and that, ready to defend themselves against whatever might come.

The screech rang out again, closer this time – devilishly close – and, if possible, even louder and angrier.

Three more horses went down, and the last followed in turn. Now all the knights were afoot, their mounts dead or dying. Oh, but it was a sorrowful sight – those proud destriers flailing away in the bloodred snow. It fair brought a sorry tear to the eye to see such fine animals slaughtered, I can tell you.

The commander of the knights summoned his soldiers to him. They seized their lances and hastened to join their commander. Back-to-back, weapons drawn, they formed a tight circle and waited behind their long, pointed shields for the next flight of cursed black arrows.

For a moment, all was quiet save for the quick breathing of the men and the neighing of the wounded horses. And then . . .

I saw a clump of snow fall from an elm branch overhead, sending a glistening curtain of down upon the road. When the frozen dust settled, there he was: King Raven. Black as Satan's tongue from the crown of his head to booted feet, and covered all over with feathers, great wings outspread with long, curving claws on the ends. But the thing which gave him the look of the pit was the absolutely smooth, round skull-like face with its wide hollow eyes and unnaturally long sword of a beak.

King Raven – it could be none other.

The knights saw this phantom creature and shrank back at the sight. I forgave them their fright. I felt it, too. Indeed, it seemed as if the day, already cold and dim, grew cold and dark as the grave in the moment of his appearing.

That dread beak rose slowly until it pointed straight up toward the dense webwork of snow-laden branches and boughs. The creature loosed another of its horrific cries. As if in reply, I saw a bright flicker in the air, and a flaming brand landed in the snow midway between King Raven and the cowering knights. Another joined the first — more or less the same distance from the knights, but behind them. Then a third fell behind the second — to the left of the huddled body of knights this time. A fourth fell among the others, on the opposite side of the third. I saw it arc high through the surrounding trees, and before it had even touched the ground, three more were in the air.

The knights, stunned and lifeless with disbelief, were ringed about with fire. The torches sputtered in the snow, sending thick black smoke boiling up through the down-drifting flakes.

So far, all had fallen out as planned, and I imagined we would escape clean away with the goods. But bad luck has a knack for catching a fella when he least can abide it. Even as our numb fingers reached for victory, ill fortune arrived in the person of Abbot Hugo. Dressed in a white satin robe with white leather boots and a woollen cloak of rich dark purple, he appeared more king than cleric as he came galloping into the clearing. With him was Marshal Guy de Gysburne, commanding a small company of oafish louts spoiling for a fight.

Truth be told, at the time I did not know who these men might be, though I would be learning soon enough. All I knew was that they had come to the banquet as guests uninvited, and had to be driven off before one or another of our folk got hurt.

Well, they burst into the clearing, weapons drawn, ready to start lopping heads and making corpses. Eight soldiers not counting the abbot broke into the ring of torches. Guy, all in mail and leather, greaves and gorget, charged ahead on a pale grey destrier. He took one look at the black-feathered phantom, reared up in the saddle, and let fly with his lance.

King Raven darted lightly to the side as the spear sailed past, easily evading the throw, even as I nocked one of the black arrows onto the string and, holding my breath, drew and aimed at the marshal.

Someone else had the same idea.

Out from the brushwood beside the trail streaked an arrow. It blazed across the clearing, struck Guy, and slammed him backwards in the saddle as he reached to draw his sword.

That reaching saved his life, I think. The arrow pierced the steel rings of his hauberk at the fleshy part of his upper arm and stuck there. If he had been more upright in the saddle, he'd have had it in his bonnet. As it was, he dropped the sword and called his men to shield themselves as the arrows began falling thick and fast.

Three men went down before they could unsling their shields, and a fourth took an arrow in the back the instant he swung it around to protect his chest. They fell like stones dropped in a well.

Abbot Hugo, shouting in Ffreinc, drove into the clearing, heedless of the missiles flying around him. Well, I suppose killing a priest is serious business – Norman or no – and Hugo maybe felt safe even with men falling all around him. Or, it may be he is that brave or stupid. Even so, he was urging the knights and men-at-arms to throw off their fear and attack, but that showed no understanding of the nature of the assault. A fella afoot cannot strike what he cannot see, and a warrior on a horse cannot charge into the brush and brake if he hopes to live out the day.

The soldiers on foot drew together, trying to form a shield ring to give them protection from the whistling death all around. I loosed two, and made good account of myself so that, by now, any soldier still in the saddle threw himself to the ground even as his horse was slaughtered beneath him. Those who somehow escaped being skewered with an oaken shaft scuttled on hands and knees to join the others as arrow after arrow slammed into the shield wall, splintering the wood, ripping the leather-covered panels apart, striking with the force of heavy hammers. I sent two more arrows to join those of the others.

The commander of the knights showed heart, if not brains. He struggled to his feet and, shield thrown high to protect his head, broke ranks, charging off in the direction of the main attack. He made but four steps from the ring before an arrow found him. There was a thin whisper as it cut through the snow-clotted air. I caught the dull glimmer of the metal head – and then the knight was lifted off his feet and thrown back a pace by the shock of the oaken missile driving into his chest.

He was dead before his heels came to rest in the snow.

Marshal Guy, clutching his arm with the slender shaft sticking out both sides of the wound, gave his thumping great warhorse his head, and the animal charged the black-cloaked phantom standing in the trail at the far end of the clearing.

King Raven stood motionless for a moment, allowing the beast and wounded rider to come nearer, lifting his long, narrow beak to the sky as if taunting them. As the horse closed the distance between them, Guy released his bloody arm and drew the dagger from his belt, making a clumsy swipe with his left hand.

The phantom ducked under the stroke. As the big horse sped by, he gave a last wild shriek and turned, wings spread wide, retreating not into the wood, as anyone might expect, but straight down the centre of the road – the way the wagons had come.

Abbot Hugo, seeing his adversary on the run, reined up and

screamed for the soldiers to give chase, but they remained cowering behind their shields. Crying down heaven on their craven heads, the abbot threatened strong punishment for any and all who disobeyed. The soldiers looked around, and when they saw King Raven fly, they did what Norman soldiers always do when an enemy retreats: they followed.

The soldiers, weighed down by their long mail shirts and shields and heavy cloaks and what have you, lurched through the snow after King Raven, who was swift and nimble as a bird. The abbot and marshal charged after them, guarding the rear. That soon, all of them disappeared from my view; I waited, wondering what would happen next. The drivers must have wondered, too, for they stood on the wagon benches and gazed into the murk after the departing soldiers. One of them shouted for the guardsmen, calling them back; but no reply was returned.

He did not shout again. Before he could draw breath, four cloaked figures swarmed out of the forest and onto the wain; I saw Tomas and Siarles leading the flock, two men to each wagon. While one of the Grellon threw a cloak over the head of the driver and pulled him off his bench, the other took up the ox goad and began driving the team.

The two wagons were taken up the road a little way to a place where the track dipped into a dell. Upon reaching the dingle, wonder of wonders, the wall of bush and brush beside the road parted and the oxen were led off the track and into the wood. As the second wagon followed the first into the brake, four more of the Grellon appeared and began smoothing out the tracks in the snow with pine branches.

The two drivers were bound in their cloaks, dragged to the side of the road, and each one left beside a dead horse where, I suppose, they might stay a mite warmer for a while. Frightened out of their wits, they lay still as dead men, offering only the occasional soft whimper to show the world they were still alive.

New snow was carried in reed baskets and spread lightly over any remaining tracks, and then the Grellon departed, flitting away into the gloaming, vanishing as quickly and quietly as they had appeared.

CHAPTER 11

I waited for a time, listening, but heard only the whispering hush of falling snow. I did not know what would happen next, and wondered if the attack was over and I should now begin making my way back to Cél Craidd. The wood was growing dark, and if I did not leave soon it would be a lonely slog on a frozen night for old Will.

Nothing moved in the forest or on the ground, save the lone wounded man who had taken the arrow in his back. He lay with the dead, moaning and trying now and then to rise, but lacking the strength. I felt that sorry for the fella, I thought that if someone did not come back for him soon, I might risk putting him out of his misery. But my orders were to watch and wait, so that is what I would do until told otherwise. I kept my eyes sharp and bided my time.

Winter twilight deepened the shadows, and the snow had been steadily melting into my cloak; the icy damp was spreading across my shoulders. As night came on, I knew I would have to leave my post soon or freeze there with the corpses on the trail.

As I was pondering this, I heard someone approaching on the road from the dingle where the wagons had disappeared in the direction of Elfael. In a moment, a man on horseback emerged from the gathering gloom. Not a tall man, he sat his saddle straight as a rod, his head high. Across his legs was folded a deerskin robe; his hat had a thin, folded brim which was pointed in front like the sharp prow of a seagoing ship. Heavily swaddled against the winter storm, he wore a monk's cloak of brown coarse-woven cloth secured at the throat with a thick brooch of heavy silver. Even from a distance in the failing light, I could tell he was more devil than monk: something about that narrow hatchet-shaped nose and jutting chin, the cruel slant of those close-set eyes, gave me to know that Richard de Glanville was happier with a noose in his hand than a rosary.

He reined up at the carcase of the first dead horse, regarded it, and then slowly swept his eyes across to one of the dead knights. He observed the arrows jutting rudely from the corpses and, after due contemplation, let out a shrill whistle. I've heard the same when falconers call their hawks to roost and, quick enough, four riders emerged from the gloaming to join him on the road . . .

'Yes, Odo, this was the first time I laid eyes on the sheriff,' I tell him. My monkish friend knows well of whom I speak. Our sheriff is a right sharp thorn of a man and that nasty – a man who thinks frailty a fatal contagion, and considers mercy the way most folk view the Black Death.

'If it was the first time,' says my scribe, 'how did you know it was the sheriff?'

'Well,' says I with a scratch of my head, 'the authority of the man could not be mistaken.'

'Even in a snowstorm?' asks Brother Odo with the smarmy smile he uses when he thinks he has caught me decorating the truth a little too extravagantly for his taste.

'Even in a snowstorm, monk,' I tell him. 'Anyway, it was the same with Abbot Hugo and Marshal Guy — if I did not know their names right off the first I saw them, I knew them well enough before the day was over. More's the pity, Odo, my friend. More's the pity.'

Odo grunts in begrudging agreement, and we stumble on . . .

The sheriff's men quickly dismounted and began searching among the dead men and horses for survivors. De Glanville remained in the saddle; he did not deign to get his fine boots wet, I reckon.

Well, they found the bundled-up wagon drivers, untied them, and brought them to stand before the sheriff. The drivers were still quaking from fright and gawking around as if they expected to be swooped upon by the phantom bird again. Under the sheriff's stern questioning, however, they soon lost their fear of the great preying bird. The sheriff had them now, and he was flesh-and-blood fiercer than any phantom or host of unseen archers.

I could tell from the way the ox handlers were gesturing and squawking that they were filling the sheriff's ears with their weird and wonderful tale. Oh, yes! And I could tell by the way the sheriff's scowl deepened by the moment that he was having none of it. He listened to them prate a while, and then cut off their mewling with a shout that travelled through the silent wood like a clap. Wheeling his mount, he cantered down the King's Road in the direction the abbot and soldiers had gone, passing so close to my perch I could have reached down and plucked that absurd hat from his pointy head.

He rode on, leaving his men and the ox drivers behind. Meanwhile, I studied hard to see what they might find, but was relieved to see that the snow had mostly filled in the tracks of men and beasts and wagon wheels; the only disturbance now to be seen was that left by the sheriff and his men themselves.

Soon enough, de Glanville returned. Close on his heels came Abbot Hugo and the marshal and the surviving soldiers. The fighting men were that weary and out of breath, they could hardly hold their weapons upright. King Raven had led them a wild chase right enough. Their snow-caked feet dragged, and their hair was stringy wet beneath their steel caps; they looked as cold and damp and limp as their own soggy cloaks.

They assembled in the road, gawking at the dead horses and knights, casting many a sideways glance into the wood lest the phantom catch them unawares. After a brief word with the sheriff, Marshal Guy sent his knights and the remaining soldiers and wagon drivers down the road. It would be a long, frozen walk to Count de Braose's castle, and I did not envy them the welcome they would likely receive. The wounded soldier, clinging to life, was taken up behind one of the sheriff's men, and they all clattered off with a rattle of tack and weapons.

Thoughts of home fires and welcomes put me in mind of a nice steaming bowl of something hot, and I was that close to quitting my post and finding my way back home . . . but glanced back to see that the sheriff had not yet departed. He simply sat there on his horse, alone, in the middle of the road, waiting. I could in no wise leave before he did, so I stayed put.

Good thing, too.

For as winter twilight settled over the forest, out from the undergrowth stumbled a man with two fat hares slung on a snare line over his neck, and another in his hand. I did not recognise the fella and supposed he was from Elfael – a farmer, out to get a little meat for his table.

'You there!' shouted the sheriff, his voice loud in the quiet glade. Startling as it was, it took a moment before I realised old rat face was speaking English. 'Stand where you are!'

The poor man was so surprised he dropped the hare in hand and turned to run. The sheriff was that quick; he spurred his mount forward to catch the poacher. The fleeing man lunged for the brush at the side of the road, but was caught and hauled back by the hood of his cloak.

The fella gave out a yelp and tried to struggle free of the cloak. The sheriff, well used to catching folk this way, pulled him off his feet. He hung there at the side of the sheriff's saddle, feet dangling off the ground, swinging his fists, and yelling to be released. When the sheriff drew his knife and put it to his squirming captive's neck, I reckoned the affair had gone far enough. Easing myself from my place, I tucked three arrows in my belt, put another on the string, and moved down onto the road as quickly and quietly as stiff muscles would allow.

Creeping like a shadow, I came up behind the sheriff's horse and, with an arrow already on the string, drew and took aim. 'Let him go,' I said, in my best English. 'Or wear this arrow to your wake.'

The sheriff's head spun around so fast I thought his neck would snap. He gaped at me and at the bow in my hand, opened his mouth, then thought better and closed it.

'You might be thinking your little knife will save you,' I said, 'but I think it won't. If you want to find out, just you hold on to that Welshman.'

De Glanville recovered himself then, and said, 'I am sheriff of the March. This thief is caught poaching in the king's forest, and unless you want a share of what is coming to him, turn aside and go your way.'

'Bold words, Sheriff,' I replied. 'But it is myself who holds the bow, and my fingers on this string are getting tired.'

I gave my arm a jiggle to sharpen my point, as it were, whereupon the sheriff dropped our man. 'Pick up the hare,' I told the farmer, 'and light out.' He scrambled to his feet, snatched up his prize, and dived into the wood.

'You cannot hope to gain anything by this,' the sheriff informed me. 'I have marked you for a felon. You will not escape the king's justice.'

'The king's justice!' I hooted. 'Sir, the king's justice is rough, to be sure, but it is fickle and inconstant as a flirty milkmaid. I will gladly take my chances.'

'Fool!' cried the sheriff, suddenly angry. Heedless of the arrow, he spurred his horse at me so as to run me down. I stepped lightly aside, and he made a wild, looping slash at me with his small blade as he passed.

He wheeled the horse at once. A beast well trained to war, it turned so fast the sheriff's long cloak flung out behind him. I saw it flying like a dull flag against the dark bulwark of an oak bole as he made to drive me down, and loosed the shaft.

The arrow whined through the air, catching the heavy cloak and pinning it to the oak as he passed. The cloak snapped taut, the horse charged on, and de Glanville was jerked clean from the saddle.

The sound of ripping fabric cut sharp in the little glade, but the cloth and arrow held fast. Sheriff de Glanville was strung up like a ham in a chimney to dangle with his feet a few inches from the snowy ground. Oh, he squirmed and wriggled and cursed me up one side and down t'other. But I was not ready to let him go so easy, so I sent two more arrows into the trunk to better nail my captive to the tree.

Red-faced and foamin' with rage, if that fella coulda spit poison, he would have. No mistake. Instead, he swung there, ripening the air with his rage. I calmly trained an arrow at the centre of his chest.

I was this close to loosing the shaft when I felt a hand on my shoulder. 'Put up,' said a familiar voice in my ear. 'The sheriff's men are returning. It is time to fly.'

'I have him,' I insisted. 'I can take him and save the world a load of trouble.'

'It may bring more trouble than it saves. Another day. We have what we came for – and now we must fly.'

With that, Bran pulled me into the brushwood at the side of the road and we were away.

No sooner in the wood and on the path than we heard the sheriff shouting behind us, 'After them! Through there! Ten marks to the man who brings them back!'

Immediately, we heard the crack and snap of branches as the soldiers searched for our trail. In less time than it takes to tell, they found it and were onto us.

So now, here was a bother: fleeing through the woods over snow-covered pathways and no way to cover our tracks. Those fellas would have no difficulty at all seeing where we went. The first clearing we came to, I stopped to make a stand. 'We can take them here, my lord,' I said. 'I'll drop the first one, you take the second.'

'I don't have a bow, Will,' said Bran. 'So, tonight, we let them live.'

'They will not pay us the same coin if they catch us,' I replied. 'That is a fair certainty.'

'True enough,' Bran allowed. Gone was the feathered cloak and the long-beaked headpiece; dressed in his customary black tunic and trousers, he shivered slightly with the cold. 'Consider it just one of the many things that makes us better men than they are.'

Our pursuers could be heard thrashing through the wood, coming closer with every heartbeat.

Bran smiled and winked his eye, his face a disembodied shape floating in the gloom. 'But that does not mean we cannot have a little fun at their expense.' Turning lightly on his heel, he said, 'Come, Will, let's give them something to talk about when they join their comrades at Castle de Braose.'

With that, he flitted away. I glanced over my shoulder, then followed him into the forest. I caught up with him a few dozen paces down the path, where he had stopped beside an ancient oak and was tugging on a bit of ivy vine. 'This is where we start,' he said, as the end of a rope snaked down from a branch above. 'Stand where you are and make no more tracks,' he instructed.

I did as I was told. Bran wound the end of the rope around one wrist and gave it a tug. The rope snapped taut. He tugged again and the end of a rope ladder dropped from the limb overhead.

'Up you go, Will,' he said, passing the ladder to me. 'I will hold it for you, but be quick.'

Slinging my bow, I grasped the highest rung I could reach and swung myself up, climbing the ladder with no little difficulty as it twisted and turned like an angry serpent under my weight. I gritted my teeth and hung on. After some tricksy rope climbing, I gained the limb of the oak at last. 'Pull up the ladder!' hissed Bran in an urgent whisper. The sheriff's men were that close he could not speak more loudly or risk being overheard.

'There is time,' I whispered back. 'Take hold and I'll pull you up.'

But he was already gone.

CHAPTER 12

I hauled up the ladder as fast as I could and crouched in the crux of the largest bough to wait. Within five heartbeats the sheriff's men burst into the clearing we had just left. A few more steps along our trail carried them to the base of the oak, where our tracks became slightly confused. Although I could no longer see the path below, and was not fool enough to risk looking down, I could well imagine what they were seeing: the well-formed footprints of two fleeing men set in deep, undisturbed snow, and then . . . one set of footprints vanishing.

Only a solitary track continued along the path, and they were not slow to mark this.

They paused to catch a breath beneath my hiding place. I could hear them puffing hard as they stood below, searching, trying to find where the second pair of tracks had gone. One of them muttered something in French – something about the futility of catching anything in this accursed forest. And then another voice called from the trail, and they moved on. From my perch, I caught a fleeting glimpse of three soldiers in dark cloaks barely visible in the winter twilight.

No doubt they were loath to return to the sheriff empty-handed, and seeing only a single set of footprints leading away, they had no choice but to follow them. So, panting and cursing, off they went to continue the pursuit. When they had gone, I settled myself more securely on the branch to wait for whatever would happen next. The night was not getting any warmer, nor my cloak any drier; folding my arms across my chest to keep warm, I prayed to Saint Christopher that they would not be pulling my frozen corpse from the oak come Christmas.

Twilight deepened to night and the wind sharpened, kicking up gusts to drive the snow. I wrapped myself tight in my cloak and had just closed my eyes beneath my hood when I heard the creak and clatter of tree limbs nearby as if something big was moving among the branches. My first thought was that all the fuss and fury had awakened a bear or wildcat asleep in its treetop bower. Peering around, Lord bless me, but I saw a great dark shape walking toward me along the very bough I had chosen.

The thing came closer. 'Get back!' I hissed, fumbling beneath my damp cloak for my knife.

'Hush!' came the whisper. 'You'll bring them back.'

'Bran?'

'Who else?' He laughed lightly. 'Heavens, Will, you look like you were ready to take wing.'

'I thought you were a bear,' I told him.

'Follow me,' he said, already turning away. 'They will be coming back this way soon, and it is best we are not here.'

Teetering on the bough, I edged after him, sliding one cautious, slippery foot at a time while clinging to a branch overhead. The bough narrowed as it went out from the trunk but, at the place where it would have begun to bend under our weight, I discovered another stout limb had been lashed into place to make a bridge, of sorts, on which to cross the gap between trees. This makeshift bridge spanned the trail below, linking two big oaks together.

And this was not all! No fewer than four trees were likewise linked in a mad squirrel-run through the treetops. We worked our way along this odd walkway until we came to another rope ladder, and so at last climbed down to a completely different forest track.

'You knew we would be chased,' I said the moment I set foot on solid ground once more.

'Aye,' he replied, 'King Raven can see the shapes of all things present and yet to come,' he told me.

'Peter and Paul on a donkey, Bran!' I gasped. 'Then you must have seen the sheriff and—'

'Peace, Will,' he said, chuckling at his jest. 'Angharad might be blessed with such a gift on occasion, but I am not.'

'No?' I said, none too certain.

'Listen to you,' he said. 'It does not take the Second Sight to know that any time you take arms against a company of Norman knights you might soon be running for your life.'

'True,' I allowed, feeling stupid for being taken in so easily. 'That's a fact, right enough. Still and all, it was a canny piece of luck they chased you the way you wanted to go.'

'Not at all,' he said, moving lightly away. 'I led them. This way or another it makes no difference. We have worked all summer to prepare such deceptions. There are ladders and treewalks scattered all over the forest, and especially along the King's Road.'

'Treewalk,' I said, enjoying the word. I hurried after him.

'Ladders and limbs and such,' he said. 'It makes for easier escape if you can move from tree to tree.'

'I agree. But do the Normans never see them?'

'The Ffreinc only ever view the world from the back of a horse,' Bran declared. 'They rarely dismount, even in dense forest, and almost never look up.' He shook his head again. 'I should have told you about all that, but I confess I did so want to see your face the first time we used it.'

This revelation stopped me in my tracks. 'I hope it gave you enjoyment, my lord,' I said, the complaint sharp in my voice. 'I live to provide amusement for my betters.'

'Oh, do not take on, Will. No harm done.'

'I thought you were a bear, I did.'

He laughed. 'Come. Iwan and Siarles will be wondering what has become of us.'

He hurried off along the darkened path, and it was all I could do to keep up with him. His long legs carried him by fast strides – and his sight, even in the dark, led him unerringly along a path that could no longer be seen. I struggled along, slipping and sliding in his footsteps, trying to avoid the branches and twigs that whipped back in my face. After a time, Bran slowed his pace; the trees were closer here, the wood more dense and the snow less deep on the path. We moved along at a much improved pace until we arrived at a place far from the road and where we had last seen the sheriff's men.

Bran paused and put his hand back to halt me. He hesitated, and then I heard Iwan's voice murmur something, and Bran stepped from the trail and into a small, snug clearing that had been hewn from the dense undergrowth beside the trail. A fire burned brightly in the centre of this bower and, aside from Iwan and Siarles, there were five of the Grellon huddled close around the flames. They all rose when Bran stepped through the brush, and welcomed him. They made room for us by the fire, but before Bran sat down, he spoke to each one personally, telling them how pleased he was of their accomplishments this day.

Aside from the men, there were two women from Cél Craidd. They had prepared barley cakes and a little mulled ale to help draw the chill from our bones, so while Bran spoke to the others, I sat down and soon had my frozen fingers wrapped around a steaming jar. 'We were getting worried,' said Siarles, settling down beside me. 'I might have known there would be trouble.'

'A little,' I confessed. 'The sheriff turned up and took it into his head to have us give some of his men a run through the wood.'

'The sheriff? Are you certain?'

'Oh, aye, it was himself. I challenged him, and he tried to talk me into giving myself up for a hanging.' I sipped my hot ale. 'Tempting as it was, I declined the offer and made one of my own. I decorated his fine cloak with arrow points.'

Siarles regarded me in the firelight with a look approaching appreciation. 'Did you kill him, then?'

'I drew on him, but did not loose.'

'Weeping Judas, why not?'

'King Raven prevented me,' I replied. 'He appeared just as I was about to let fly, and we've been running ever since. And now that I think of it, why did no one tell me about the treewalks and ladders?'

Siarles grinned readily. 'Oh, that — well, it's a secret we like to keep to ourselves as much as possible. A man's life could depend on it.'

'As my own did this selfsame night. It would have cheered me no end to know I wasn't about to end my days with a Norman spear in my back.'

'So, now you know.'

'Now I know,' I agreed. 'One of these days, I'll thank you to show me which of the other trails have been prepared this way and which trees.'

'Oaks,' replied Siarles, taking the jar from me and helping himself to a sip.

'Oaks,' I repeated, taking the cup back.

'It's always oak trees,' Iwan confirmed. 'Look for a dangling vine. As for the trails, we'll show you next time we come out. But that won't be for a while now. We will let the trail grow cold.'

'It is plenty cold now,' I said, quaffing down a hearty gulp. 'If the snow keeps up, by morning you won't be able to tell anyone passed this way at all.'

Iwan nodded and stood abruptly. 'Nóinina!' he called. 'A dry cloak for our man here.'

One of the women turned away from the fire and withdrew a bundle from a wicker basket they had brought. She came around the ring to where I sat, untied the bundle, and shook out a clean, dry cloak. 'Oooh,' she cooed gently, 'let me get that cold wet thing off you before you take a death.'

Leaning over me, she deftly untied the laces and lifted off the wet garment; the cold air hit my damp clothes and I shivered. She spread the dry cloak over my shoulders and rubbed my back with her hands so as to warm me. 'There now,' she said, 'you'll be warm and dry that soon.'

'Many thanks,' I said, craning my head around to see her better. It was the woman who had come to Cél Craidd after being rescued from the Ffreinc. As it happens, I had helped build a hut for her and her wee daughter. 'Nóinina, is it?' I asked, though I knew well and good that it was.

'Aye, that's me.' She gave me a fine smile, and I realized that she was a right fetching woman. Now, it might have been the heat of the fire after a long, cold day, or then again, it might have been something else, but I felt a certain warmth spread through me just then. 'You're called Will.'

'That I am.'

She lingered close, gazing down at me as I sat with my cup on my knees. 'I helped build the hut for you and the little 'un,' I told her.

'I know.' She smiled again and moved off. 'And for that I'll give you a barley cake.'

She was back a few moments later with a jug of warm ale and a barley cake fresh from the griddle stone. 'Get that into you and see if you don't warm up.'

'I'm feeling better already,' I told her. 'Much better.'

It didn't last long. As soon as we all had a bite and drained our cups, Iwan put out the fire and we were away. Oh, but it was a long, slow trek back to the settlement through deep-drifting snow. We tried to walk in one another's footsteps as much as possible so as not to disturb the snow overmuch, but that was tedious and taxing. We were fair exhausted by the time we reached Cél Craidd, and the night was far gone. Even so, our folk had built up a big, bright fire and were waiting for us with hot food and drink. They let out a great cheer when first we tumbled through the hedgewall and slid down the bank.

Well, our trials were forgotten just that quick, and we all gathered round the fire to celebrate our victory. There was still a thing or two needin' done – the oxen and wagons had been secured for the night, but the wagons would have to be unburdened and the oxen would require attention before another day had run. Our work was far from finished. Even so, the cares of tomorrow could fend for themselves a little while; this night we could celebrate.

The mood was high. We had fought the Ffreinc and delivered a blow they would not soon forget. As soon as we took our places at the fire, cups were pressed into our hands and meat set to roast on skewers. We drank the first of many healths to one and all, and I was that surprised to find myself standing beside the widow woman once more.

'Hello again, Nóinina,' I said, my clumsy half-Saxon tongue attempting the lilt she had given it. 'It's a good night that ends well even with the snow.'

'Call me Nóin,' she said. Indicating my cup with a quick nod of her head, she said, 'Your jar big enough for two?'

'Just big enough,' I replied, and passed it to her.

She raised it to her lips and drank deep, wiping her mouth with the back of her hand as she returned the jar. 'Ah, now, that is as it should be – hale and hearty and strong, with a fine handsome head.' She leaned near, and her lips curved with sweet mischief as she added, 'Just like our man here himself.'

Oh, my stars! It had been long since any woman had spoken to me with such invitation in her voice. My heart near leapt out of my throat, and I had to look at her a second time to make sure it was ol' Will Scarlet she was talking about. She gave me a wink with the smile, and I knew my fortunes had just improved beyond all reason. 'Do not be leaving just yet,' she said, and skipped away.

'I'll keep a place for you right here,' I called after her.

She returned with another jar and two skewers of meat for us to roast at the fire. We settled back to share a stump and a cup, and watch the snow drift down as the meat cooked. Sweet Peter's beard, but the flames that warmed my face were nothing compared to the warmth of that fine young woman beside me. An unexpected happiness caught me up, and my heart took wing and soared through a winter sky ablaze with stars.

I was on the point of asking her how she came to be in the forest when Lord Bran raised his cup and called for silence around the fire ring. 'Here's a health to King Raven and his mighty Grellon, who this night have plucked a tail feather from that stuffed goose de Braose!'

'To King Raven and the Grellon,' we all cried, lofting our cups, 'mighty all!'

When we had drunk and recharged our cups, Bran called again, 'Here's a health to the men whose valour and hardihood has the sheriff and his men gnashing their teeth in rage tonight!'

We hailed that and drank accordingly, swallowing down a hearty draught at the happy thought of the sheriff and count smarting from the wallop we'd given them.

'Hear now!' Bran called when we had finished. 'This health is for our good Will Scarlet who, heedless of the danger to himself, snatched a poor man from the sheriff's grasp. Thanks to Will, that man's family will eat tonight and him with them.' Raising his cup, he cried, 'To Will, a man after King Raven's heart!'

The shout went up, 'To Will!' And everyone raised their jars to me. Ah, it was a grand thing to be hailed like that. And just to make the moment that much more memorable to me, as the king and all his folk drank my health, I felt Nóin slip her hand into mine and give it a squeeze — only lightly, mind, but I felt the tingle down to my toes.

CHAPTER 13

Eiwas

The journey to Wales seemed endless somehow. Although only a few days from his castle in England's settled heart, Bernard Neufmarché, Baron of Hereford and Gloucester, always felt as if he had travelled half a world away by the time he reached the lands of his vassal, Lord Cadwgan, in the Welsh cantref of Eiwas. The country was darker and strangely uninviting, with shadowy wooded keeps, secret pools, and lonely rivers. The baron thought the close-set hills and hidden valleys of Wales mysterious and more than a little forbidding – all the more so in winter.

It wasn't only the landscape he found threatening. Since his defeat of Rhys ap Tewdwr, a well-loved king and the able leader of the southern Welsh resistance, the land beyond the March had grown decidedly unfriendly to him. Former friends were now hostile, and former enemies implacable. So be it. If that was the price of progress, Neufmarché was willing to pay. Now, however, the baron made his circuits more rarely and, where once he might have enjoyed an untroubled ride to visit his vassal lords, these days he never put foot to stirrup in the region unless accompanied by a bodyguard of knights and men-at-arms.

Thus, he was surrounded by a strong, well-armed force. Not that he expected trouble from Cadwgan – despite their differences, the two had always got along well enough – but reports of wandering rebels stirring up trouble meant that even old friends must be treated with caution.

'Evereux!' called the baron as they came in sight of Caer Rhodl perched on the summit of a low rock crag. 'Halt the men just there.' He pointed to a stony outcrop beside the trail, a short distance from the wooden palisade of Cadwgan's fortress. 'You and I will ride on together.'

The marshal relayed the baron's command to the troops and, upon reaching the place, the soldiers paused and dismounted. The baron continued to the fortress gate – where, as expected, he was admitted with prompt, if cold, courtesy.

'My lord will be informed of your arrival,' said the steward. 'Please wait in the hall.'

'But of course,' replied the baron. 'My greetings to your lord.'

The Welsh king's house was not large, and Neufmarché had been there many times; he proceeded to the hall, where he and his marshal were kept waiting longer than the baron deemed hospitable. 'This is an insult,' observed Evereux. 'Do you want me to go find the old fool and drag him here by the nose?'

'We came unannounced,' the baron replied calmly, although he was also feeling the slight. 'We will wait.'

They remained in the hall, alone, frustration mounting by the moment, until eventually there came a shuffle in the doorway. It took a moment for the baron to realise that Lord Cadwgan had indeed appeared. Gaunt and hollow-cheeked, a ghastly shadow fell across his face; his clothes hung on his once-robust form as upon a rack of sticks. His skin had an unhealthy pallor that told the baron his vassal lord had not ventured outdoors for weeks, or maybe even months.

'My lord baron,' said Cadwgan in the soft, listless voice of the sickroom. 'Good of you to come.'

His manner seemed to suggest that he imagined it was he who had summoned the baron to his hall. Neufmarché disregarded the inapt remark, even as he ignored the sharp decline evidenced in Cadwgan's appearance. 'A fine day!' the baron declared, his voice a little forced and overloud. 'I thought we might make a circuit of your lands.'

'Of course,' agreed Cadwgan. 'Perhaps once we have had some refreshment, my son could accompany you.'

'I thought you might ride with me,' replied the baron. 'It has been a long time since we rode together.'

'I fear I would not be the best of company,' said Cadwgan. 'I will tell Garran to saddle a horse.'

Unwilling to press the matter further, the baron said, 'How is your lady wife?' When the king failed to take his meaning, he said, 'Queen Anora – is she well?'

'Aye, yes, well enough.' Cadwgan looked around the empty room as if he might find her sitting in one of the corners. 'Shall I send someone to fetch her?'

'Let it wait. There is no need to disturb her just now.'

'Of course, Sire.' The Welsh king fell silent, gazing at the baron and then at Evereux. Finally, he said, 'Was there something else?'

'You were going to summon your son, I think?' Neufmarché replied.

'Was I? Very well, if you wish to see him.'

Without another word the king turned and padded softly away.

'The man is ill,' observed the marshal. 'That, or senile.'

'Obviously,' replied the baron. 'But he has been a useful ally, and we will treat him with respect.'

'As you say,' allowed Evereux. 'All the same, a thought about the succession would not be amiss. Is the son loyal?'

'Loyal enough,' replied the baron. 'He is a young and supple reed, and we can bend him to our purpose.'

A few moments later, they were joined by the young prince himself who, with icy compliance, agreed to ride with the baron on a circuit of Eiwas. The baron spoke genially of one thing and another as they rode out, receiving nothing but the minimum required for civility in return. Upon reaching a stream at the bottom of the valley, the baron reined up sharply. 'Know you, we need not be enemies,' he said. 'From what I have seen of your father today, it seems to me that you will soon be swearing vassalage to me. Let us resolve to be friends from the beginning.'

Garran wheeled his horse and came back across the stream. 'What do you want from me, Neufmarché? Is it not enough that you hold our land? Must you own our souls as well?'

'Guard your tongue, my lord prince,' snarled Evereux. 'It ill becomes a future king to speak to his liege lord in such a churlish manner.'

The prince opened his mouth as if he would challenge this remark, but thought better of it and glared at the marshal instead.

'Your father is not well,' the baron said simply. 'Have you sent for a physician?'

Garran frowned and looked away. 'Such as we have.'

'I will send mine to you,' offered the baron.

'My thanks, Baron,' replied the prince stiffly, 'but it will be to no purpose. He pines for Mérian.'

'Mérian,' murmured the baron, as if searching his memory for a

109

face to go with the name. Oh, but not a day had passed from the moment he first met her until now that he did not think of her with longing, and stinging regret. Fairest Mérian, stolen away from his very grasp. How he wished that he could call back the command that had sealed her fate. A clumsy and ill-advised attempt to capture the Welsh renegade Bran ap Brychan had resulted in the young hellion taking the lady captive to make good his escape from the baron's camp. Neufmarché had lost her along with any chance he might have had of loving her.

Mistaking the baron's pensive silence, Prince Garran said, 'The king thinks her dead. And I suppose she is, or we would have had some word of her by now.'

'There has been nothing? No demand for ransom? Nothing?' asked the baron. His own efforts to find her had been singularly unsuccessful.

'Not a word,' confirmed Garran. 'We always knew Bran for a rogue, but this makes no sense. If he only wanted money, he could have had it long since. My father would have met any demand – as well he knows.' The young man shook his head. 'I suppose my father is right; she must be dead. I only hope that Bran ap Brychan is maggot-food, too. '

Following Mérian's kidnapping, the baron had sorrowfully informed Mérian's family of the incident, laying the blame entirely at Bran's feet while failing to mention his own considerable part in the affair. All they knew was what the baron had told them at the time: that a man, thought to be Bran ap Brychan, had come riding into the camp, demanding to speak to the baron, who was in council with two of his English vassals. When the Welshman's demands were denied, he had grown violent and attacked the baron's knights, who fought him off. To avoid being killed, the cowardly rebel had seized the young woman and carried her away. The baron's men had given chase; there

was a battle in which several of his knights lost their lives. In all like-
lihood, the fugitives had been wounded in the skirmish, but their fate
was unknown, for they escaped into the hills, taking Lady Mérian with
them.

'Her loss has made my father sick at heart,' Garran concluded
gloomily. 'I think he will not last the winter.'

'Then,' said the baron, a tone of genuine sympathy edging into his
voice, 'I suggest we begin making plans for your succession to your
father's throne. Will there be any opposition, do you think?'

Garran shook his head. 'There is no one else.'

'Good,' replied Neufmarché with satisfaction. 'We must now look
to the future of Eiwas and its people.'

CHAPTER 14

Odo wants to know why I have never mentioned Nóin before. 'Some things are sacred,' I tell him. 'What kind of priest are you that you don't know this?'

'Sacred?' He blinks at me like a mole just popped from the ground and dazzled by a little daylight. 'A sacred memory?'

'Nóin is more than a memory, monk. She's a part of me forever.'

'Is she dead, then?'

'I'll not be telling the likes of you,' I say. I am peeved with him now, and he knows it. Nóin may be a memory, but even so she is a splendid pearl and not to be tossed to any Ffreinc swine.

Odo pouts.

'I meant no disrespect,' he says, rubbing his bald spot. 'Neither to you, nor the lady. I just wanted to know.'

'So you can run off and tell the blasted abbot?' I shake my head. 'I may be crow food tomorrow, but I en't a dunce today.'

My scribe does not understand this, and as I look at him it occurs to me that I don't rightly understand it, either. I protect her however I may, I suppose. 'So now!' I slide down the rough stone wall and assume my place once more. 'Where was I?'

'Returned to Cél Craidd,' he says, dipping his pen reluctantly. 'It is the night after the raid and it is snowing.'

'Snowing, yes. It was snowing,' I say, and we press on . . .

It snowed all night, and most of the next day, clearing a little around sunset. Owing to Angharad's timely warning, we were well prepared and weathered the storm in comfort – sleeping, eating, taking our ease. To us, it was a holy day, a feast day; we celebrated our victory and rare good fortune.

Around midday, after we'd had a good warm sleep and a little something to break our fast, Lord Bran and those of us who had helped in the raid crowded into his hut to view the spoils. In amongst the bags of grain and beans, sides of smoked meat, casks of wine, and bundles of cloth that made up the greater part of the take, the Grellon had found two small chests. The heavier goods had been hidden in the wood not far from the road, to be retrieved later when the weather was better and the sheriff far away.

The wooden boxes, however, had been toted back to our snuggery. With a nod from Angharad, standing nearby to oversee the proceedings, Bran said, 'Open them. Let's see what our generous baron has sent us.'

Siarles, waiting with an axe in his hand, stepped forward and gave the oak chest a few solid chops. The lid splintered. A few more blows and the box lay open to reveal a quantity of small leather bags that were quickly untied and dumped on a skin beside the hearth around which we all stood. The bags were full of silver pennies, which was more or less to be expected.

'Again,' said Bran, and Siarles wielded the axe once more and the second chest gave way. In it were more leather bags full of coins, but also three other items of interest: a pair of fine white leather calfskin gloves, richly embroidered on the back with holy crosses and other symbols in gold braid; a thick square of parchment, folded, bound with a blue cord, and sealed with wax; and, in its own calfskin bag, a massive gold ring.

'A fine bauble, that,' said Siarles, holding up the ring. He handed it to Bran, who bounced it on his palm to judge the weight of gold before passing it on to Angharad.

'Very fine work,' she observed, holding the ring to her squint. She passed it along, saying, 'Much too grand for a mere count.'

Indeed, the ring looked like something I imagined an emperor might wear. The flat central stone was engraved with a coat of arms such as might be used by kings or other notables for imprinting their seal on important documents. Around the carved stone was a double row of glittering rubies — tiny, but bright as bird's eyes, and each glowing like a small crimson sun.

'A most expensive trinket,' replied Bran. Leaning close, he examined the engraving. 'Whose arms, I wonder? Have you ever seen them, Iwan?'

The big man bent his head close and then shook it slowly. 'Not English, I think. Probably belong to a Ffreinc nobleman — a baron, I'd say. Or a king.'

'I doubt if anyone in all Britain has ever worn the like,' said Siarles. 'Where do you think de Braose got it?'

'And why send it here?' asked Iwan.

'These are questions that will require some thought,' replied Angharad as Bran slipped the ring onto his finger. It was far too big, so he put it on his thumb, and even then it did not fit; so he took a bowstring, looped it through the ring, and tied it around his neck. 'It will be safe enough there,' he said, 'until we find out more.'

We counted up the silver, and it came to fifty marks – a splendid haul.

'The gloves might be worth twenty or thirty marks all by themselves,' Mérian pointed out. She had come in during the counting and stayed to see the result. Stroking the gauntlets against her cheek, she remarked that they were the sort of thing a high-placed cleric might wear on festal days.

'What about the ring?' wondered Iwan aloud. 'What would that be worth?'

No one knew. Various sums were suggested – all of them fancies. We had no more idea how much that lump of gold and rubies might be worth than the king of Denmark's hunting hound. Some said it must be worth a castle, a cantref, maybe even a kingdom. Our ignorant speculation ran amok until Angharad silenced us, saying, 'You would do better to ask why it is here.'

'Why indeed,' said Bran, his fingers caressing the bauble.

We fell silent gazing at the thing, as at a piece of the moon dropped from the sky. Why had it been sent to Elfael in the bottom of a supply wagon?

'Oh, aye,' said Angharad, her voice cracking like dry twigs, 'a treasure like this will bring swarms of searchers on its trail.' She tapped it with a bony finger. 'It might be as well to give it back.'

This dropped us in the pickle pot, I can tell you. With these words, the realisation of what we'd done began to break over us, and our triumph turned to ashes in our mouths. We each crept away to our beds that night full of foreboding. I hardly closed my eyes at all, I was that restless with it. God knows, it may be deepest sin to steal, and in ordinary times I would never take so much as a bean from a bag that was not mine. But this was different.

This was a fight for survival.

Rule of law . . . king's justice . . . these words are worth less to the

Ffreinc than the air it takes to breathe them out. If we steal from those who seek ever to destroy us, may the Good Lord forgive us, but we en't about to stop and we en't about to start giving things back. It does irritate the baron and his nephew no end, I can say. And the sheriff, it upsets him most of all on account of the fact that he's the one who is meant to prevent our raiding and thieving.

Shed no tears for Richard de Glanville. He is a twisted piece of rope if ever there was one. It is said he killed his wife for burning his Sunday pork chop in the pan — strangled her with his own bare hands.

Personally, I do not believe this. Not a word. In the first place, it means our Richard Rat-face would have had to get someone to marry him, and I heartily doubt there is a woman born yet who would agree to that. Even granting a marriage, impossible as it seems, it would mean that he had taken matters into his own hands — another fair impossibility right there. You might better claim the sun spends the night in your barn and get more people to believe you than that the sheriff of the March ever sullied his lily-whites with anything so black. See, Glanville never lifts a finger himself; he pays his men to do all his dirty deeds for him.

To the last man, the sheriff's toadies are as cruel and vengeful as the day is long; a more rancorous covey of plume-proud pigeons you never want to meet. God bless me, it is true.

The folk of Derby still talk of the time when Sheriff de Glanville and three of his men cornered a poor tinker who had found his way into mischief. The tale as I heard it was that one bright day in April, a farmwife went out to feed the geese and found them all but one dead and that one not looking any too hearty. Who would do a mean and hateful thing like that? Well, it came to her then that there'd been a tinker come to the settlement a day or two before hoping to sell a new pot or get some patchwork on an old one. Sharp-tongued daughter of Eve that she was, she'd sent him off with both ears burnin' for his trouble.

Now then, wasn't that just like a rascal of a tinker to skulk around behind her back and kill her prize geese the moment she wasn't looking? She went about the market with this news, and it soon spread all over town. Everyone was looking for this tinker, who wasn't hard to find because he wasn't hiding. They caught him down by the river washing his clothes, and they hauled him half-naked to the sheriff to decide what to do with the goose-killer.

As it happened, some other townsfolk had rustled about and found a serf who'd broken faith with his Norman lord from somewhere up north. He'd passed through the town a day or so before, and the fella was discovered hiding in a cow byre on a settlement just down the road. They bound the poor fella and dragged him to town, where the sheriff had already set up his judgement seat outside the guildhall in the market square. De Glanville was halfway to hanging the tinker when the second crowd tumbles into town with the serf.

So now. What to do? Both men are swearing their innocence and screaming for mercy. They are raising a ruck and crying foul to beat the devil. Well, the sheriff can't tell who is guilty of this heinous crime, nor can anyone else. But that en't no matter. Up he stands and says, 'You call on heaven to help you? So be it! Hang them both, and let God decide which one shall go to hell.'

So his men fix another noose on the end of the first rope, and it's up over the roof beam of the guildhall. He hangs both men in the market square with the same rope – one wretch on one end, and one on t'other. And that is Richard bloody de Glanville for you beginning and end . . .

What's that, monk?' I say. 'You think it unlikely?'

Odo sniffs and wrinkles his nose in disbelief. 'If you please, which one of them killed the geese?'

'Which one? I'd a thought that would be obvious to a smart fella like you, Odo. So now, you tell me, which one did the deed?'

'The tinker — for spite, because the farmwife refused to buy his pots or give him work.'

'Oh, Odo,' I sigh, shaking my head and tutting his ignorance. 'It wasn't the tinker. No, never him.'

'The serf then, because he . . .' He scratches his head. 'Hungry? I don't know.'

'It wasn't the serf, either.'

'Then who?'

'It was a sneak-thief fox, of course. See, Odo, a man can't kill a goose but that the whole world knows about it. First you gotta catch the bloody bird, and that raises the most fearsome squawk you ever heard, and that gets all the others squawking, too. By Adam's axe, it's enough to wake the dead, it is. But a fox, now a fox is nimble as a shadow and just as silent. A fox works quick and so frightens the flock that none of them lets out a peep. With a fox in the barn, no one knows the deed is done till you walk in and find 'em all in a heap of blood and feathers.'

Odo bristles at this. 'Are you saying the sheriff hanged two innocent men?'

'I don't know that they were innocent, mind, but de Glanville hanged two men for the same crime that neither could have done.'

Odo shakes his head. 'Hearsay,' he decides. 'Hearsay and slander and lies.'

'That's right,' I say. 'You just keep telling yourself that, priest. Keep on a-saying it until they find a reason to tighten the rope around your fine plump neck, and then we'll see how you sing.'

CHAPTER 15

The snow continued through the night and over the next days, covering all, drifting deep on field and forest, hilltop and valley throughout Elfael. As soon as the hard weather eased up a little, we fetched the captured spoils back to Cél Craidd, along with the four oxen kept in a pen not far from the road, trusting to the windblown snow to remove any traces of our passing. We kept a right keen watch for the sheriff and his scabby men, but saw neither hank nor hair of them, and so hurried about our chores. The wagons we dismantled where they stood, keeping only the wheels and iron fittings; the animals were more useful, to be sure. One we kept to pull the plough in the spring; the others would be given to farmers in the area to replace those lost in one way or another to the Ffreinc.

It was the same with the money. Bran did not keep what he got from the raid, but shared it out among the folk of his realm, helping those who were most in need of it — and there were plenty of them, I can tell you. For the Normans had been in Elfael going on two years by then, and however bad it was in the beginning it was much worse now. Always worse with that hell crew, never better. So, the money was given out, and those who received it blessed King Raven and his men.

Oh, but that great gold ring began to weigh heavy on the slender strap around Bran's princely neck. Worth a king's ransom it was, and we all stoked a secret fear that one day the Red King himself would come after it with an army. We were all atwist over this when Friar Tuck showed up.

I had heard his name by then, and some few things about him — how he had helped Bran in his dealings with the king and cardinal. But whatever I had heard did nothing to prepare me for the man himself. Part imp, part oaf, part angel — that is Friar Tuck.

His arrival was announced in the usual way: one of the sentries gave out the shrill whistle of a crake. This warned the Grellon that someone was coming and that this visitor was welcome. An intruder would have demanded a very different call. For those few who were allowed to come and go, however, there was a simple rising whistle. Well, we heard the signal, and folk stopped whatever they were doing and turned towards the blasted oak to see who would appear through the hedge. A few moments later, a fat little dumpling rolled down the bank, red face shining with a sheen of sweat despite the chill in the air, the hem of his robe hiked up and stuffed in his belt to keep it from dragging through the snow.

'Happy Christ-tide!' he called when he saw all the folk hurrying to greet him. 'It is good to see you, Iwan! Siarles! Gaenor, Teleri, Henwydd!' He called out the names of folk he knew. 'Good to see you! Peace to one and all!'

'Tuck!' shouted Siarles, hurrying to greet him. 'Hail and welcome! With all this snow, we did not think to see you again until the spring.'

'And where should I be at Christ-tide, but with my own dear friends?'

'No bag this time?'

'Bag? I've brought half of Hereford with me!' He gestured vaguely toward the trail. 'There's a pack mule coming along. Rhoddi met me on the trail and sent me on ahead.'

Bran and Mérian appeared then, and Angharad was not far behind. The little friar was welcomed with laughter and true affection; I glimpsed in this something of the respect and high regard this simple monk enjoyed amongst the Grellon. The king of England might receive similar adulation on his travels, I'll warrant, but little of the fondness.

'God with you, Friar,' said Mérian, stepping forward to bless our visitor. 'May your sojourn here well become you.' She smiled and bent at the waist to bestow a kiss on his cheek. Then, taking that same round red cheek between finger and thumb, she gave it a pinch. 'That is for leaving without wishing me farewell the last time!'

'A mistake I'll not be making twice,' replied Tuck, rubbing his cheek. He turned as Angharad pushed forward to greet him. 'Bless my soul, Angharad, you look even younger than the last time I saw you.'

Wise and powerful she may be, but Angharad was still lady enough to smile at the shameless compliment. 'Peace attend thee, friend friar,' she said, her wrinkled face alight.

'Brother Tuck!' cried Iwan, and instantly gathered the sturdy friar in a rib-cracking embrace. 'It is that good to see you.'

'And you, Wee John,' retorted the priest, giving the warrior a clip 'round the ear. 'I've missed you and all.' Iwan set him down, and the priest gazed at the ring of happy faces around him. 'Well, Bran, and I see you and your flock have fared well enough without me.' Adjusting his robe to cover his cold bare legs once more, he then raised his hands in a priestly benediction. 'God's peace and mercy on us all, and may our Kind Redeemer send the comfort of this blesséd season to cheer our hearts and heal our careworn souls.'

Everyone cried 'Amen!' to that, and when Tuck turned back to Bran, he said, 'Some new faces, I see.'

'One or two,' confirmed Bran. He grasped the priest's hands in his own, then presented the newcomers; I found myself last among them. 'And this one here,' he said, pulling me forward, 'is the newest member of our growing flock and as handy with a bow as King Raven himself.'

'That's saying something, that is,' remarked Tuck.

'Will Scatlocke, at your service,' I said, thrusting out my hand to him.

He took it in both his own and shook it heartily. 'Our Lord's abundant peace to you, Will Scatlocke.'

'And to you, Friar. See now, two Saxons fallen among Welshmen,' I said in English.

He cast a shrewd eye over me. 'Is that the north country I hear in your voice?'

'Oh, aye,' I confessed. 'Deny it, I'll not. Your ear is sharp as Queen Meg's needle, Friar.'

'Born within sight of York Minster, was I not? But tell me, how did you come to take roost among these strange birds?'

'Lost my living to William Rufus – may God bless his backside with boils! – and so I came west,' I told him, and explained quickly how, after many months of living rough and wandering, Bran had taken me in.

'Enough!' cried Bran. 'There is time for all that later. We have Christmas tomorrow and a celebration to prepare!'

Ah, Christmas . . . how long had it been since I had celebrated the feast day of Our Sweet Saviour in proper style? Years, at least – not since I had sat at table in Thane Aelred's hall with a bowl of hot punch between my hands and a huge pig a-roasting on the spit over red-hot coals in the hearth. Glad times. I have always enjoyed the Feast of Christ – the food and song and games . . . everything taken together, it is the best of all the holy days, and that is how it should be.

I did not know how the Cymry hereabouts celebrated the Christ Mass, and nursed the strong suspicion that if Friar Tuck had not arrived when he did, King Bran's pitiable flock would have had little with which to make their cheer. But when his pack mule arrived a short while later, it was clear that the friar had brought Christmas with him.

Within moments, he seemed to be everywhere at once, kindling the banked coals of the forest-dwellers' hearts – a word of greeting here, a song there, a laugh or a story to lift the spirits of our down-cast tribe. Bless him, he fanned the cold embers of joy into a cracking fine blaze.

Although they have adopted some of the more common Saxon practices, the Britons appeared not to observe the trimming of pine boughs, so it fell to Tuck and me to arrange this part of the festivi-ties. The day had cleared somewhat, with bright blue showing through the clouds, so the two of us walked into the nearby wood to cut some suitable branches and bring them back. This we did, talking as we worked, and learning to know one another better.

'What we need now,' declared Tuck when we had cut enough greenery to satisfy tradition, 'is a little holly.'

'As good as got,' I told him, and asked why he thought it needful.

'Why? It is a most potent symbol, and that is reason enough,' the priest replied. 'See here, prickly leaves remind us of the thorns our dear Lamb of God suffered with silent fortitude, and the red berries remind us of the drops of healing blood he shed for us. The tree remains green all the year round, and the leaves never die – which shows us the way of eternal life for those who love the Saviour.'

'Then, by all means,' I said, 'let us bring back some holly, too.'

123

Shouldering our cut boughs of spruce and pine, we made our way back to the village, pausing to collect a few of the prickly green branches on the way. 'And will we have a Yule log?' I asked as we resumed our walk.

'I have no objection,' the friar allowed. 'A harmless enough observance, quite pleasant in its own way. Yes, why not?'

Why not, indeed! Of all the odd bits that go to make up this age-old fest, I hold the Yule log chief among them and was glad our friar offered no objection. The way some clerics have it, a fella'd think it was Lucifer himself dragged into the hall on Christmas day. For all, it's just a log – a big one, mind, but a log all the same.

As Thane Aelred's forester, it always fell to me to find the log. We'd walk out together, lord and vassal, of a Christmas morn – along with one of the thane's sons or daughters astride a big ox – and drag the log back to the hall, where it would be pulled through the door and its trimmed end set in a hearth already ablaze. Then, as the end burned, we'd feed that great hulk of wood inch by inch into the flame. Green as apples, that log would sputter and crack and sizzle as the sap touched the flame, filling the hall with its strong scent. We always chose a timber too green to burn any other time for the simple reason that, so long as that log was a-roast, none of the servants had to lift a finger beyond the simple necessities required to keep the celebration going.

A good Yule log could last a fortnight. I suspect it was the idleness of the vassals that got up so many priest's noses. They do so hate to see anyone taking his ease. Then again, there was the ashes. See, when the feasting was over and the log reduced to cold embers, those selfsame ashes were gathered up to be used in various ways: we sprinkled some on cattle to ensure health and hearty offspring; we scattered some in the fields to encourage abundant crops; and, of course, sheep had their fleece dusted to improve the quality of their wool. A little was mixed with the first brewing of ale for the year to aid in warding off sickness and ill temper, and so on. In all, the ashes of a Yule log provided a useful and necessary commodity.

Over time, a good few of the Britons took up the Yule log tradition, just like many of the Saxons succumbed to the ancient and honourable Celtic rite of eating gammon on Christ's day. To be sure, a Saxon never requires much encouragement where the eating of pigs is at issue, less yet if there is also to be drinking ale. So, naturally, a great many priests try to stamp out the practice of burning Yule trees.

'Well now,' said Tuck, when I remarked on his obvious charity towards a custom most of his ilk found offensive, 'they have their reasons, do they not? But I tell the folk who ask me that the fire provided is the flame of faith, which burns brightest through the darkest nights of the year, feeding on the log – which is the holy, sustaining word of God, ever new and renewed, day by day, year by year. The ashes, then, are the dust of death, the residue of our sins when all has been cleansed in the Refiner's fire.'

'Well said, Brother.'

'You seem a thoughtful sort of man, Will,' the cheerful cleric observed.

'I hope I am,' I replied.

'And dependable?'

'It would please me if folk considered me so.'

'And are you a loyal man, Will?'

I stopped walking and looked at him. 'On my life, I am.'

'Good. Bran has need of men he can trust.'

'As do we all, Friar. As do we all.'

He nodded and we resumed our walk. The light was fading as the short winter day dwindled down.

'You said you lost your living,' he said after a moment. 'I would hear that tale now, if nothing prevents you.'

'Nothing to tell you haven't heard before, I'll warrant,' I replied, and explained how I had been in service to Thane Aelred, who ran afoul of King William the Red during the accession struggle. 'As punishment, the king burned the village and claimed the lands under Forest Law.' I went on to describe how I had wandered about, working for bread and bed and, hearing about King Raven, decided to try to find him if I could. 'I found Iwan and Siarles first, and they brought me to Cél Craidd, where Bran took pity on me. What about you, Tuck? How did an upright priest like yourself come to have a place in this odd flock?'

'They came to me,' he replied. 'On their way to Lundein, they were, and stopped for a night under the roof of my oratory.' He lifted a palm upward. 'God did the rest.'

By the time we returned to the settlement, the first stars were peeking through the clouds in the east. A great fire blazed in the ring outside Bran's hut, and there was a fine fat pig a-sizzle on a spit. A huge kettle of spiced ale was steaming in the coals; the cauldron was surrounded by spatchcocks splayed on willow stakes, and the savory scent brought the water to my mouth.

With the help of some of the children, Tuck and I placed pine branches over the doors of the huts and around the edge of the fire ring itself. At Bran's hut and those of Angharad and Mérian, and Iwan and Siarles, we also fixed a sprig or two of the holly we had cut. A few of the smaller girls begged sprigs for themselves and plaited them into their hair.

As soon as the ale was ready, everyone rushed to the fire ring with their cups and bowls to raise the first of a fair many healths to each other and to the day. As wives and husbands pledged their cups to one another, I lofted my cup to Brother Tuck. *'Was hale!'* I cried,

Ruddy face beaming, he gave out a hearty, 'Drink hale!' And we drank to one another.

Bran and Mérian, I noticed, shared a most cordial sip between them, and the way those two regarded one another over the rim of the cup sent a pang of longing through me, sharp and swift as if straight from the bow. I think I was not the only one sensing this particular lack, for as I turned around I glimpsed Nóin standing a little off to one side, watching the couples with a wistful expression on her face.

'A health to you, fair lady,' I called, raising my cup to her across the fire.

Smiling brightly, she stepped around the ring to touch the rim of her cup to mine. 'Health and strength to you, Will Scarlet,' she said, her voice dusky and low.

We drank together, and she moved closer and, wrapping an arm around my waist, hooked a finger in my belt. 'God's blessing on you this day, and through all the year to come.'

'And to you and yours,' I replied. Glancing around, I asked, 'Where is the little 'un?'

'Playing with the other tads. Why?'

'There will be no keeping them abed tonight,' I suggested, watching the excited youngsters kicking up the snow in their games.

'Nor, perhaps, their elders,' Nóin said, offering me a smile that was both shy and seasoned. Oh, she knew the road and where it led; she had travelled it, but was a mite uncertain of her footing just then. It opened a place in my heart, so.

Well, we talked a little, and I remembered all over again how easy she was to be near, and how the firelight flecked her long, dark hair with red, like tiny sparks. She was the kind of woman a man would find comfortable to have around day in, day out, if he should be so fortunate.

I was on the point of asking her to join me at table for the feast when Friar Tuck raised his voice and declared, 'Friends! Gather around, everyone! Come, little and large! Come fill your cups. It is time to raise a health to the founder of the feast, our dear Blesséd Saviour — who on this night was born into our midst as a helpless infant so that he might win through this world to the next and, by his striving, open the gates of heaven so that all who love him might go in.' Lofting his cup, Tuck shouted, 'To our Lord and Eternal Master of the Feast, Jesus!'

'To Jesus!' came the resounding reply.

Thus, the Feast of Christ began.

The devil, however, is busy always. Observing neither feast nor fest, our infernal tormentor is a harsh taskmaster to his willing servants. The moment we dared lift cup and heart to enjoy a little cheer, that moment the devil's disciples struck.

And they struck hard.

CHAPTER 16

The first sign of something amiss came as our forest tribe gathered to share the festal meal. We drank the abbot's wine and savoured the aromas of roasting meat and fresh bread, and then Friar Tuck led us in the Christ Mass, offering comfort and solace to our exiled souls. We prayed with our good priest and felt God's pleasure in our prayers.

It was as we were singing a last hymn the wind shifted, coming around to the west and bringing with it the scent of smoke.

'Yes, Odo.' I sigh at his interruption. 'It is not in any way unusual to smell smoke in a forest. In most forests there are always people burning things: branches and twigs to make charcoal, or render lard, clear land . . . what have you. But the Forest of the March is different from any other forest I've ever known, and that's a fact.'

My monkish friend cannot understand what I am saying. To him, a forest is a forest. One stand of trees is that much like another. 'See

here,' I say, 'Coed Cadw is ancient and it is wild — dark and dangerous as a cave filled with vipers. The Forest of the March has never
been conquered, much less tamed.'

'You would call a forest tame?' He wonders at this, scratching the
side of his nose with his quill.

'Oh, aye! Most forests in the land have been subdued in one way
or another, mastered long ago by men — cleared for farmsteads, harvested for timber, and husbanded for game. But Coed Cadw is still
untouched, see. Why, there are trees that were old when King Arthur
rallied the clans to the dragon flag, and pools that have not seen sunlight since Joseph the Tin planted his church on this island. It's true!'

I can see he doesn't believe me.

'Odo, lad,' I vouch in my most solemn voice, 'there are places in
that forest so dark and doomful even wolves fear to tread — believe
that, or don't.'

'I don't, but I begin to see what you mean,' he says, and we move
on . . .

Well, as I say, we are all of us in fine festive fettle and about to
sit down to a feast provided, mostly, at Abbot's Hugo's
expense, when one of the women remarks that something has caught
fire. For a moment, she's the only one who can smell it, and then a few
more joined her, and before we knew it, we all had the stink of heavy
timber smoke in our nostrils. Soon enough, smoke began to drift into
the glade from the surrounding wood.

In grey, snaking ropes it came, feeling its way around the boles of
trees, flowing over roots and rocks, searching like ghost fingers, touching and moving on. Those of us seated at the table rose as one and
looked to the west, where we saw a great mass of slate-black smoke

churning up into the winter sky. Even as we stood gaping at the sight, ash and cinders began raining down upon us.

Someone gave out a cry, and Bran climbed onto the board. He stood with hands upraised, commanding silence. 'Peace!' he said. 'Remain calm. We will not fear until there is cause to fear, and then we will bind courage to our hearts and resist.' Turning to the men, he said, 'Iwan, Siarles, fetch the bows. Will, Tomas, Rhoddi, follow me. We will go see what mischief is taking place.' To the others he said, 'Those who remain behind, gather supplies and make ready to leave in case we must flee Cél Craidd.'

'Be careful, Will,' said Nóin, biting her lip.

'A little work before dinner,' I replied, trying to make my voice sound light and confident although the smoke thickening and ash raining down on our heads filled me with dread. 'I'll be back before you know it.'

Iwan and Siarles returned and passed out the bows and bundles of arrows. I slung the strung bow over my chest and tied a sheaf of arrows to my belt. Leaving the folk in the care of Angharad and the friar, we departed on the run. We followed the drift of the smoke as the wind carried it from the blaze, and with every step the darkness grew as the smoke clouds thickened. Before long, we had to stop and wet the edges of our cloaks and pull them fast around our faces to keep from breathing the choking stuff.

We pressed on through the weird twilight and soon began to see the flicker of orange-and-yellow flames through the trees ahead. The fire produced a wind that gusted sharply, and we felt the heat lapping at our hands and faces. The roar of the blaze, like the surge of waves hurled onto the shore, drowned out all other sound.

'This way!' urged Bran, veering off the track at an angle towards the wall of fire.

Working quickly and quietly, we came around to a place where the fire had already burned. And there, standing on the charred, still-smouldering earth stood a body of Ffreinc soldiers – eight of them, loitering beside a wagon pulled by two mules and heaped with casks of oil. Some of them carried torches. The rest held lances and shields. All were dressed for battle, with round steel helmets and swords strapped to their belts; their shields leaned against the wagon bed.

We dropped to the ground and wormed back out of sight behind the screen of smoke and flames.

'Sheriff's men,' spat Siarles.

'Trying to burn us out,' observed Tomas, 'and on Christmas day, the sots. Not very friendly, I'd say.'

'Shall we take them, Bran?' asked Rhoddi.

'Not yet,' Bran decided. 'Not until we know how many more are with them.' Turning to me and Rhoddi, he said, 'You two go with Iwan. Siarles and Tomas come with me. Go all the way to the end and take a good look' – he pointed off into the wood where the wall of flame burned brightest—'and then come back here. We will do the same.'

Rhoddi and I fell into step behind Iwan, and the three of us made our way along the inside of the fiery wall, as it were, until, after a few hundred paces, we reached the end. Keeping low, to better stay out of the smoke, we crawled on hands and knees to peer around the edge of the flames. Ten Ffreinc soldiers were working this end of the blaze – two with torches and three with casks of oil they were sprinkling on the damp underbrush. Five more stood guard with weapons ready.

Iwan pointed out the one who seemed to be the leader of the company, and we withdrew, hurrying back to the meeting place. Bran and Iwan spoke briefly together. 'We will take the first group here and now,' Bran told us, unslinging his bow. 'Then we will take the others.'

Iwan drew three arrows from the cloth bag. 'Fan out,' he told us, indicating the spread with three jerks of his hand, 'and loose on my signal.'

We all drew three shafts and crept into position, halting at the edge of the flame wall. The Ffreinc were still watching the fire, their faces bright. When I saw Iwan fit an arrow to the string, I did likewise. When he stood, I stood. He drew, and so did I . . .

'Now!' he said, his voice low but distinct.

Six shafts streaked out from the wood, crossing the burned clearing in a wink. Four soldiers dropped to the ground.

The two remaining men-at-arms had no time to wonder what had happened to the other fellas. Before they could raise their shields or look around, winged death caught them, lifted them off their feet, and put them on their backs – pierced through with two shafts each.

Then it was a fleet-footed race to the further end of the flame wall. The fire was burning hotter as more of the underbrush and wood took light, drawing wind to itself and spitting it out in fluttering gusts. The smoke was heavy. We clutched our cloaks to our faces and made our way as best we could, stumbling half-blind through the murk to take up new positions.

The flames were now between us and the Ffreinc. We could see the soldiers moving as through a shimmering curtain. Imagine their surprise when out from this selfsame curtain flew not frightened partridges to grace the Christmas board, but six sizzling shafts tipped with stinging death.

Four of the arrows found their marks, and three Marchogi toppled into the snow. A fifth shaft ripped through a soldier's arm and into the cask in the hands of the fella behind him. The amazed soldier dropped the cask, dragging down his companion, who was now securely nailed to the top of the cask.

'Ready . . . ,' said Iwan, placing another arrow on the string and leaning into the bow as he drew and took aim. 'Now!'

Six more arrows sped through the high-leaping flames, and four more Ffreinc joined the first four on the ground. The remaining two, however, reacting quickly, threw themselves down, pulling their shields over them, thinking to protect themselves this way. But Iwan and Siarles, pressing forward as far as the flames would allow, each sent a shaft pelting into the centre of the shields; one glanced off, taking the edge of the shield with it. The other shaft struck just above the boss and penetrated all the way through and into the neck of the soldier cowering beneath it.

The last fella, crouching behind his shield, tried to back away. Bran knelt quickly and, holding the bow sideways, loosed a shaft that flashed out of the flames, speeding low over the ground. It caught the retreating soldier beneath the bottom edge of the shield, pinning the man's ankles together. He fell screaming to the snow and lay there moaning and whimpering.

We held our breath and waited.

When no more soldiers appeared, we began to imagine it safe to leave.

'What are we to do about the fire?' I asked.

'We cannot fight it,' Siarles replied. 'We'll have to let it go and hope for the best.'

'We will watch it,' Iwan said. 'If it spreads or changes direction, we should know.'

Bran looked back through the curtain of flame towards the fallen soldiers. 'I did not see the sheriff.' Turning to us, he said, 'Did anyone see the sheriff?'

No one had seen him, of course, for just as the question had been spoken there came a shout and, from the night-dark wood behind us, mounted knights appeared, lances couched, crashing up out of the brush where they had been hidden.

CHAPTER 17

I saw the spearheads gleam sharp in the firelight and the fire glow red on the helmets of the knights and chamfers of the horses as they clattered up out of the brake. I tried to count and made it eight or ten of them, closing fast.

They were that near we had time but to pull once and loose.

In less time than it takes to catch a breath, our arrows streaked out, the stinging whine followed by a slap and crack like that of a whip as steel heads met padded leather jerkin and then ring mail, piercing both. The force of the blow lifted two hard-charging riders from the saddle and sent a third backwards over the rump of his horse.

Before the onrushing knights could check their mounts, we each had another shaft on the string. Iwan took the foremost knight, and I took the one behind him. Bran changed his aim at the last instant and sent a shaft into the breast of a charger that had already lost its rider. The oncoming horse's legs tangled and it stumbled, taking down the two horses behind it as well. The knights tried to quit the saddle before their steeds rolled on them, but only one avoided the crush. The other was lost in a heap of horseflesh and churning hooves.

I pulled another arrow from my sheaf and nocked it, but did not have time to aim. I threw myself to the ground as a lance blade swept the place lately occupied by my head. As I scrambled to my feet, a trumpet sounded. I looked to the sound as at least eight more knights came bounding from the wood with Marshal Gysburne leading the charge.

Slow cart that I am, it was only then that I understood we had been caught in a neatly spread net and the ends were about to close on us.

Bran had already seen it. 'Fall back!' he shouted.

But there was nowhere to flee.

Behind us was a wall of burning trees and brush, ahead a swarm of angry soldiers — each one in a blood-rage to take our heads.

The trumpet sounded again, and there he was: Sir Richard de Glanville, the devil himself, looking powerfully pleased with his surprise. He swept out of the darkness flanked by two knights holding torches, and I do believe he imagined that at the very sight of him the fight would go out of us. For as he emerged from the dark wood he called out in English.

The others looked to me. 'He says we must surrender, but that quarter will be given.'

Siarles spat and put an arrow on the string. Iwan said, 'We ask no quarter.'

Raising his bow, Siarles said, 'Shall I make reply, Lord?'

Bran nodded. 'Give him our answer.'

Before Bran had even finished speaking, the shaft was on its way. The sheriff, anticipating such a response, was ready.

Having faced a Welsh bowman before, he had provided himself with a small round shield clad in iron plate. As Siarles' arrow seared across the flame-shot distance, de Glanville threw his heavy round shield before him, taking the blow on the iron boss. There was a spark as metal struck metal, and the sturdy oak shaft shattered from the impact.

There was no time for a second flight, for at that moment a second body of knights charged in on the flank. I could not count them. I saw only a rush out of the darkness as the horses appeared.

We all loosed arrows at will, sending as fast as we could draw. Three knights were despatched that quick, and two more followed before the first were clear of the saddle. Then, with the horses on top of us, it was time to flee.

'This way!' cried Bran, edging back and back towards the burning trees and brush – a place even the best-trained Norman horses would not willingly go. 'Through there,' said Bran, already starting towards a gap between two burning elm trees. Pulling his cloak over his head, he darted through the narrow, fire-filled space as through a flaming arch.

Siarles and Rhoddi followed. Iwan, Tomas, and I made good their escape, sending another shaft each into the mounted soldiers as they wheeled and turned to get a good run at us. Then it was our turn to face the fire.

Pulling my cloak over my head, I bent low and ran for the flames, diving headlong between the two elms. I felt the heat lick out, scorching the cloth of my cloak, and then I was through to the other side. Tomas was not so fortunate. He got a little too close and his cloak caught fire. He came through in a rush, shouting and crying that he was burning alive. I grabbed him and threw him down on the ground, rolling him until the flames were out. He was singed, and his cloak was blackened a little along the hem in the back, but he was unharmed.

'To me!' shouted Bran. Through the flames, he had seen the Marchogi regrouping. As I took my place beside him, I could hear the sheriff rallying his men on the other side of the flame wall. 'Take the horses!'

With that, he sent a shaft through the shimmering flames into the indistinct shapes that were the Ffreinc knights and their horses. The arrow found a target, for at once a knight gave out a cry. Soon we were all at it, braving the heat and smoke, to stand and deliver death and havoc from out of the flames. Again and again, I drew and loosed, working in rhythm with the others.

We made good account of ourselves, I think – though it was hard to be sure as we could not always see where our shafts went. But by the time the soldiers had regrouped and come charging around the end of the flame wall, there were far fewer than there had been just moments before.

'Away!' shouted Bran, pointing to the wood behind us. Siarles was already disappearing into the scrub at the edge of the clearing. Bran followed on his heels.

'Time to run for it,' said Iwan. Loosing one last shaft, he turned and fled.

I slung my bow and pushed Tomas ahead of me, saying, 'Go! Run! Don't lose them!'

We crossed the smouldering ground, leaping over the bodies of the soldiers we had killed before the sheriff had tipped his hand. While Tomas dived into the underbrush, I cast a glance over my shoulder as the knights came pounding into the clearing.

By the time Sheriff de Glanville took command of the field, he found it occupied only by his own dead men-at-arms, lying where they'd fallen in the melted snow. His voice sounded sharp in the cold night air. I fancied I could hear the disappointment and frustration as he began calling for his men to start searching the area for our tracks.

That much I got, anyway. The luck of Cain to 'em, I thought. The ground was that chewed up — what with the soldiers setting fires and all — I did not think they'd be able to find our trail in a month of Christmases, but we did not wait to find out. From the cover of the wood, we sent some more arrows into them, killing some, wounding others. The sheriff, realising the battle was now beyond winning, called the retreat. They fled back the way they had come and, since our arrows were mostly spent, we let them go.

'They might return,' Bran said, and ordered us all to scatter and work our way around the blaze. 'Confuse your trail and make certain you are not followed. Then fly like ravens for the roost.'

I put my head down and lit out through the dark winter wood. Keeping the blaze on my left, I worked my way slowly and carefully around until I'd coursed half the circle, then faded back along a deer run that took me near to the bottom of the ridge protecting Cél Craidd. After a time picking my way carefully through a hedge of brambles and hawthorn, I reached the foot of the ridge and paused to listen, kneeling beside a rock to rest a moment before continuing.

I heard nothing but the night wind freshening the tops of the larches and pines. The fire still stained the night sky, tinting the smoke a dull rusty red, but it was less fierce now; already the blaze was dying out. Overhead, there were patches of winter sky showing through the clouds, and stars glimmering bright as needle pricks. The air was cold and crisp. As I started up the snow-covered slope it came to me that this attack signalled a change in our fortunes. We had beaten the sheriff this time, but it was just the beginning. Next time he would come with more men, and still more. There would be no stopping him now.

CHAPTER 18

In the bleak heart of midwinter, with the snow deep and white, the air cold and still, it seemed as if the greenwood awaited the coming of the new year with breath abated. We of the Raven Flock held our breath, too, waiting and watching through the night and all the next day. Bran doubled the number of watchers on the road, and set others in a surrounding ring around Coed Cadw. But the sheriff and his men did not return.

The evening of the day after the attack, Lord Bran summoned his advisors to his hut. Wary and uncertain still, we gathered. Iwan, Siarles, Mérian, Tuck, and myself took our places around the small hearth in the centre of his hut. 'We have rattled the hornets in their nest,' Iwan pointed out as we settled to discuss what had happened the night before and what it might mean.

'That much is plain as your big feet,' replied Siarles.

'Where is Angharad?' wondered Mérian. 'She should be with us.'

'So she should,' agreed Bran. 'But she has begged leave to absent herself.'

'Not like her,' observed Iwan. 'Not like her at all.'

'Is she well?' asked Tuck. 'I could go see her.'

'She is well,' replied Bran, adding, 'but the raid last night has disturbed her mightily. She did not foresee it.'

'Nor did any of us,' pointed out Tuck.

'No, but our *hudolion* feels she should have sensed it. She is going to her cave to learn the reason and' — he lifted the ring on its string around his neck — 'to learn more of this lovely trinket.' The gold shone with a fine lustre, and the jewels gleamed even in the dim light of the hut.

Tuck took one look at the heavy gold bauble and cried, 'Lord have mercy! Where did you get that?'

Bran explained about the raid on the supply train. Tuck sucked his teeth, shaking his head all the while. 'I do not wonder Angharad is distressed. You have called down the wrath of Baron de Braose upon your silly heads, my friends.' Tapping the ring with a finger to watch it swing, he added, 'He wants it back, and now you have made it worth his while to find you.'

'This wasn't all,' said Iwan. 'Show him the rest.'

Mérian fetched a small box, which she opened, drawing out the richly embroidered gloves and passing them to the friar.

'Well, well, lookee here,' chirped the priest, 'what a fine pair of mittens.' Seizing them, he pulled them tightly over his chubby hands and held them up for all to see. 'Goatskin, if I'm not mistaken,' he said, 'and made in France, I shouldn't wonder.' He withdrew his hands and stroked the leather flat again. 'Someone will be missing these sorely.'

'Aye, but who?' asked Bran. 'Abbot Hugo?'

'For him?' wondered Tuck. 'Possibly. It would not surprise me that he holds himself so highly. But see here—' he indicated the cross on the right hand and, on the left glove, a curious symbol shaped something like a cross, but with two extra arms and a closed loop at its head. 'That is the Chi Rho,' he told us, 'and most often seen on the vestments of high priests of one kind or another.' He passed the gloves back to Mérian. 'If you asked me, I'd say these were made for a prince among priests – an archbishop or cardinal, at least.'

'Then what are they doing here?' asked Iwan.

'Perhaps our humble abbot has more exalted ambitions,' replied Bran.

'Was there ever any doubt?' quipped Tuck. His smooth brow wrinkled with thought. 'Ring and gauntlets,' he mused. 'It must mean something. But for the love of Peter, I cannot think what it might be.'

'We were hoping you would have an idea,' sighed Mérian.

'Nay, lass,' replied the friar. 'You will have to find a better and wiser man than the one that sits before you to get an answer.'

'There is one other thing,' said Bran. Reaching into the box, he brought out the square of parchment and passed that to the priest.

In the hurly-burly of the feast and later attack, I had mostly forgotten all about that thick folded square of lambskin. I looked at it now – I think we all did – as the very thing needed to explain the mystery to us.

'Why didn't you say you had this?' said Tuck. He turned it over in his hands. 'You haven't opened it.'

'No,' answered Bran. 'You may have the honour.'

We all edged close as the friar's stubby fingers fumbled with the blue cord. When he had untied it, he laid it in his lap and looked around at the circle of faces hovering above him. 'If we break this,' he said, fingering the wax seal, 'there is no going back.'

'Break it,' commanded Bran. 'It has already cost the lives of a score of men or more. We will see what it is that the abbot and sheriff value at such a high price.'

Drawing a breath, Tuck cracked the heavy wax seal and carefully unfolded the parchment, spreading it before him on the rush-strewn floor of the hut.

'What is it?' asked Iwan.

'What does it say?' said Siarles.

'Shh!' hissed Mérian. 'Give the man a chance.' To Tuck she said, 'Take your time.' Then, when he appeared to do just that, she added, 'Well, what does it say?'

Lifting his face, he shook his head.

'Bad news?' wondered Bran.

'I don't know,' replied the priest slowly.

Bran leaned close. 'What then?'

'God knows,' Tuck lifted the parchment to pass around. 'It is written fair enough, but not in Latin. I cannot read the bloody thing.'

'Are you certain?'

'I think so. I read little enough Latin, to be sure. But I cannot make out a word of that.' He shook his round head. 'I don't know what it is.'

We passed the parchment hand to hand, and as it came to me, I saw the entire surface covered with a fine, flowing script in dark brown ink. As I had never acquired the knack of reading – not English, nor Latin either – I had nothing to say about it. But it seemed to me that the words were well formed, the letters long and graceful – it put me in mind of ivy and how it loops and curls around all it touches. The skin was fine-grained and well prepared; there were hardly any grease smudges or ink spatters at all.

'I think it is Ffreinc,' Mérian decided, holding it up to the light and bending her head close. 'I can speak it well enough, but I have only seen it written once or twice, mind.' She concluded, 'It looks very like Ffreinc to me.'

'Yes, well, that would make sense,' mused Tuck, taking back the parchment. The two of them proceeded to examine it closely, tracing various letters with their fingers and muttering over it. 'See, here that is a *D*,' said Tuck, 'and that an *I* followed by *E* and *U*.' He paused to string together what he'd found. 'Dee-a-oo,' he said.

'God!' exclaimed Mérian. '*Dieu* means God.' She put her finger on a letter. 'What is that?'

Tuck peered hard at the script. 'I think it might be an *S*,' he said. 'With an *A* . . . *F* . . . ah, no that might be an *L* . . . *U* . . . *T* . . .' He continued picking out letters one by one and uttered the word as he did so. I followed some of this, but my small store of Ffreinc was of the more rough and ready sort spoken in the market, not the court or church, and it soon left me trailing far behind.

'*Salutations!*' said Mérian before he finished. "Greetings!'' She beamed happily. '*Salutations dans Dieu*,' she said. "Greetings in God' — that must be it.'

Tuck agreed. 'I think so.'

'That would be expected,' said Iwan. 'What else?'

The two continued, trying to scry out the letters and make words of them that Mérian knew. And though they succeeded in guessing several more, they fell far short of the mark and were forced to give up in the end, leaving us little the wiser for the effort. 'We know it is Ffreinc, at least,' said Bran. 'That is something.'

'Well, whatever is in that letter,' said Tuck, tapping the sheepskin with his finger, 'you can be sure the baron will be missing it. I think de Braose wants his treasures back.'

'Oh, aye,' affirmed Iwan, 'and he's willing to risk good men to get them.'

Tuck nodded thoughtfully. 'Mark me, there is a dread mystery here. You would be wise to return these things as soon as possible,' he concluded, 'before any more blood is shed.'

'That I will not do,' declared Bran. 'At least, not until I know what it is we have found. If de Braose considers it worth an army to recover' – he smiled suddenly – 'perhaps it is worth more.'

'A castle!' suggested Siarles.

'Perhaps,' allowed Bran. 'Maybe even a kingdom.'

And, no, Odo, I say with a sigh, 'I cannot read. Not even my own name when it is writ. Then again, Thane Aelred couldn't read a whit, either, nor any of his vassals, saving the monks at the abbey, and he was a towering oak of a man, bless him.'

'Oh,' smirks he, 'but there is nothing to it once you have the learning. I could teach you,' he says, hopeful as a puppy.

'Well then, Odo, me lad,' I tell him, 'one day when I have the leisure of a cleric, as you most certainly do, I shall let you teach me to read. Now, where was I?'

'Bran considered the ring of great value,' replies Odo. I lick my lips and rumble on . . .

The next day, when Angharad learned what Tuck had revealed about the parchment, she thanked Bran for telling her, gave him a few words of advice, and took her leave. Pulling on her cloak, she bunged a few leftovers from our truncated feast into a leather bag slung on her back, took up her staff, and departed Cél Craidd then and there.

Some of us saw her leave. 'Is she angry?' Tomas asked. 'She seems fair put out with the world.'

'I don't know,' I replied. 'Maybe.'

'Where is she going?'

'She has a cave somewhere in the greenwood,' said Huw, one of the elder Grellon. 'She goes there of a time to think.'

Well, the sheriff's attack had cast a shadow of gloom over our none-too-happy home, I can tell you. As soon as Angharad left, Bran hived himself in his hut with Iwan and Tuck to decide what to do next.

'God with you, Will,' said Mérian, coming to stand beside me.

'And with you, my lady,' I answered.

She rubbed her hands to warm them. 'I wonder what they will decide.'

'Difficult to say. Weighty decisions require patience and pondering aplenty.'

'Do you think it dangerous, this ring?'

'I think it valuable, and that is usually danger enough.' I nodded towards the hut. 'I think Tuck is right when he says there is a dread mystery in the thing.'

As we were talking, I caught sight of someone out of the corner of my eye. I looked across the clearing to see Nóinina disappearing between two huts; she cast a last look over her shoulder as she moved from view. Something about her expression as she passed out of sight gave me to think she had been watching Mérian and me and did not approve, not one tiny little scrap.

It was just the merest glimmer of a glance, to be sure. Still, it gave me a curious warmth that lasted throughout the day.

The king and his advisors emerged a short time later. 'What was decided?' I asked Iwan as he came out to join us.

'We will take the treasure to Saint Tewdrig's for safekeeping as Angharad has advised,' he told me. 'We will also show the letter to Bishop Asaph. Perhaps he or one of his monks can read it and tell us something about how and why this ring has come to Elfael.'

'That sounds a sensible plan,' Mérian remarked.

I nodded my agreement. 'Good,' I said.

'I'm glad you approve, Scarlet,' he answered, turning on his heel and walking backwards a step or two. 'Because it's you that's going.'

CHAPTER 19

In less time than it takes a fella to lace up his boots, I was on my way. I suppose others reckoned that, as a half-Saxon with a snip of Ffreinc under my belt, I could more easily pass among the Normans as a wandering labourer – which is what I was until joining King Raven's flock.

This decision did not sit well with at least one member of our band. Siarles got it into his thick head that I was more affliction than remedy and asked to be allowed to accompany me. After a brief discussion, it was agreed that Siarles, who had been to the monastery before and knew the way, would go with me to act as guide. We were given a deerskin bundle containing the ring and gloves, and the parchment in its wrap, which we were to take to the bishop at Saint Tewdrig's and learn whatever we could from the monks – they, being men of learning, might know how to read the letter and could be trusted to hold their peace about whatever there was that might be gleaned. The rest of the treasure was to be placed with them for safekeeping.

'If the sheriff or any of his men catch you with these things,' Bran warned, the flat of his hand on the parcel as he handed it to Siarles, 'they will hang you for thieves — and that is the least they will do. Stay sharp, and hurry back with all speed.'

'My lord,' I replied, 'this skin of mine may be poor quality as some would judge, but it is my own and I have grown to love it. Rest assured, I will not risk it foolishly.' I might have added that Nóin also had a definite interest in seeing me return hale and whole.

'There is yet one thing more,' said Tuck. He had been standing beside Bran, listening to the instructions. 'Hear me, if you will. Hear me, everyone.'

'Silence!' called Bran. 'Friar Tuck will speak.'

When all had quieted, he said, 'The ring has value and therefore power, does it not? It may be that God has given it to us to aid in the redemption of Elfael. Brothers and sisters all, we must hold tight to this hope and guard it with a mighty strength of purpose. Therefore, know that this is a solemn charge that has been laid upon you, Will and Siarles.' He regarded Siarles and me with a commanding stare. 'You take our lives in your hands when you leave this place. See you do nothing that would endanger them, or there will be hell to pay. Is this understood?'

We nodded our assent, but he would have more. 'Say it,' he insisted. 'Pledge it on your honour.'

This we did, and Tuck declared himself satisfied. He turned to Bran and said, 'We have done what we can do. Now, it is for God to do as he will do.' Raising his hands high, he said, 'I pray the Lord of Hosts to send an army of angels to guard you every step of the way, to smooth your path in the rough world and bring you safely home. Amen and God with you.'

'Amen!'

Nóin and I shared a kiss of farewell. She clutched me tight, and whispered, 'Come back to me, Will Scarlet. I have grown that fond of you.'

'I will come back, Nóin, never fear.'

With that, we took leave of our king and rode out, taking a path that was only rarely used by the Grellon. The trail, which was tangled and overgrown in many places, would lead us north a fair distance where, once well away from Cél Craidd, we would double back to the Norman lands of the south and east. It was decided that we should stay off the King's Road so as to avoid any travellers, especially Norman soldiers. For two days we made our slow way through the winterland and shivered in a frosty silence as we moved through a world bleached white by the snow and cold – the stark, bloodred berries of holly and the deep green strands of ivy twining round boles of elm and oak the only hues that met our colour-starved eyes.

The Forest of the March seemed to slumber beneath its thick mantle, although here and there we saw the tracks of deer and pigs, sometimes those of wolves and other creatures – the long slashing strides of the hare, and the light skittery tracings of mice and squirrels. Overhead we heard the creak and crack of cold boughs and branches, and the occasional twit and chirp of birds interested in our passing. But these were the only things to relieve the dull sameness of the slumbering greenwood.

Nor was Siarles the easiest companion a man might choose. Short-tempered and quick to judge; easily stirred to anger or despair; in character, steadfast; in mood as changeable as water – he is Cymry through and through, Siarles is. Poor fella, he is one of God's creatures that is happiest when most miserable. And should he lack sufficient cause for misery, an imaginary source is all too easily conjured. For some reason he had taken against me from that first day I dropped out of the tree.

By day's end, I reckoned I had endured enough of his rudeness. 'Siarles, my friend, there is a boil of contention between us as wants lancing.'

'So you say.'

'I do say it. You act like a fella with bees in his breeches every time we meet. For the life of me, I cannot think why that should be. Nevertheless, I know an unhappy man when I see one, and here I have one in my eye.'

'I am not unhappy,' he said, his whole face puckered in a petulant scowl.

'I think you are. Or, if not unhappy, then displeased. Tell me what you've got caught in your craw, and I will do my best to help you.'

He glared at me, then turned away. 'Finish saddling your horse. It is time we were on our way.'

'No,' I replied. 'Not until you tell me what is wrong with you.'

He turned on me with sudden anger. 'With me?' he said, almost shouting. 'You find fault with me when it is yourself you should be chiding.'

'Me! What have I done?'

He made a sound like the growl of a frustrated dog and turned away again.

'Well, this is going to be a long day a-standin' here,' I told him. 'I'm not moving until I know your mind.' He glared at me balefully, and I thought he would not speak.

'Well? What is it to be? Either we make peace between us, or stand here and glower at one another like two stubborn roosters in a yard.'

He snarled again, his frustration boundless, and I could not help but laugh at the hopelessness of the situation. 'See here, Siarles, my contrary friend. You're going to have to give me something more than grunts and growls if we are to get to the meat of the matter. So you might as well tell me and get it done.'

'I don't like Englishmen,' he grimaced through gritted teeth. 'Never have. Never will.'

'Half an Englishman only,' I corrected. 'My mother was a Briton, mind. As was your own if you had one.'

'You know what I mean. Bran had no business taking you in.'

'No? It seems to me that a lord can take a vassal of any fella willing to swear fealty to him. I bent the knee to Bran right gladly, and my word holds fast through fair or foul,' I declared. 'You wanted to come along because you don't trust me. You thought I'd steal the ring and fly away as soon as I got out of sight.'

He glowered at me, and I could see I'd hit near the mark. 'You don't know what I think,' he muttered at last.

'Yes, I do,' I told him. 'You had a cosy little nest in the greenwood and then along comes this big ol' Englishman, Will Scarlet, stomping all over your tidy garden with his great boots, and you're afraid he's going to squash you like a bug.' Siarles frowned and climbed into the saddle. 'But, see here, I en't about squashing you or anybody else, nor usurping 'em from their rightful place. Neither am I leaving my sworn liege lord just because you don't like the cut of my cloth. Lord Bran's dealings are his own, and if that sticks in your gizzard, then talk to him. Don't punish me.'

He turned his mount and rode away. I followed a few paces behind, giving him space and time, hoping he would come 'round to a better humour sooner or later. But though I tried my best to cheer him along and show him I bore no ill feelings over his churlishness, his mood did not improve. I resolved to ignore his sour disposition and get on with the chore at hand.

Saint Tewdrig's in the north is but a short distance beyond the border of Elfael – a new monastery tucked in the curving arm of a valley across the river close on the border of the cantref. I counted five buildings, including a small church, all of timber arranged in a loose square and surrounded by a low whitewashed wall. Small fields – flat squares of snow with barley stubble showing through like an unshaved chin – flanked the monastery. We crossed one of these and arrived at the gate and pulled the braided bell cord hanging at the gatepost. A light, clinking ring sounded in the chill air, and presently a small door opened within the larger. '*Pax vobiscum*. How can I help you?' asked the porter. He looked blandly at me, and then at Siarles, and his eyes lit with recognition. 'Silidons! Welcome! Come in. Come in! I will tell Father Asaph you are here.' He turned and hurried off across the yard, leaving us to stand outside with our mounts, which could not pass through the small door.

'Silidons?' I said. 'What is that?'

'It was Bran's idea,' he said. 'He thought it would be better for the monks if they did not know our real names.'

True enough, I reckoned, for if the Normans suspected the monks knew anything to help them find us, they would be in danger deep and dire. 'Nor can they sell us out,' I considered.

'Not likely, that.'

'You must have a high opinion of priests. I've known one or two that would not spare a moment's thought to trade their mothers to the Danes for a jug of ale and two silver pennies.'

'The priests you know may be rogues,' he said, 'but the brothers here can be trusted.'

'How do you know they won't go running to the sheriff behind our backs?'

'Lord Bran built this monastery,' he explained simply. 'That is, our Bran gave the money so that it could be built. Asaph was the bishop of Llanelli, the monastery at Caer Cadarn before the Ffreinc took it and drove the monks out and turned the place into a market town. Asaph accepts the patronage without asking who gives it.'

I was not really concerned, but if I'd had any fear of betrayal, meeting Bishop Asaph removed even the most niggly qualm. The man was like one of those saints of old who have churches named after them. White haired and wispy as a willow wand, the old man pranced like a goat as he swept us into the holy precinct of the monastery, arms a-fly, bare heels flashing beneath his long robe, welcoming us even as he berated the porter for leaving us loitering at the gate.

'God's peace, my friends. All grace and mercy upon you. Silidons! It is good to see you again. Brother Ifor, how could you leave our guests standing outside the gate? You should always insist they wait inside. Come in! Come in!'

'Bishop Asaph,' said Siarles, 'I present to you a friend of mine' – he hesitated a moment, and then said – 'by the name of . . . Goredd.'

O do has stopped to scratch his head. He is confused. 'Yes,' I tell him, 'Siarles and Silidons are one and the same. The monks know him as Silidons, see? They know me now as Goredd. Can we get on?'

'Just one question, Will . . .'

'One?'

'Another question, then. This monastery you speak of in Saint Tewdrigs? Where would that lie, specifically?'

'Why, it lies exactly on the spot where it stands, not a foot's breadth to the north nor to the south.'

Odo frowns. 'I mean to say it sounds a pagan name. Would you know the French?'

I let my temper flare at him. 'No – I would not! If the Ffreinc will insist on renaming every village and settlement willy-nilly, it is unreasonable of them to expect honest men such as myself to commit them all to memory and recite them at the drop of a hat! If your good abbot wishes to visit the place, I suggest that he begin further enquiries in hell!'

Odo listens to this with a hurt, doglike expression. As I finish, his hurt gives way to wryness. 'Honest men such as you?' he asks.

'There is more honesty in me than there is in a gaggle of Norman noblemen, let us not be mistaken.'

Odo shrugs and dips his quill. After allowing me to cool for a moment, he repeats the last line written, and we trudge on . . .

Long robes flapping around his spindly shanks, the old bishop led us across the yard. For all his joy at seeing us, a doleful mood seemed to rest heavy on the place, and I wondered about it.

The brother stabler took our horses away to be fed and watered, and the bishop himself prepared our rooms, which, I believe, had never been used. They were spare and smelled of whitewash, and the beds were piled with thick new fleeces. 'I see they don't get many visitors,' I observed to Siarles when Asaph had gone.

'The monastery is new still,' he allowed, 'and since the Ffreinc came to Elfael not many people travel this way anymore.'

One of the brothers brought a basin of water and some soap for us to wash away the last few days of travel. Siarles and I took turns splashing our faces and rinsing our hands in the basin before joining the bishop for refreshment in his quarters above the building they called a refectory.

'We eat a meal after evening prayers,' Asaph informed us, 'but travel is hungry work.' He stretched a hand towards the table that had been prepared for us. 'So please, my friends, take a little something to keep body and soul together until then.'

We thanked him and filled our wooden bowls from the fare on offer: boiled eggs and sliced sheep's cheese and cold mutton. There was some thin ale – no doubt the best they had – and fresh butter-milk. We sat down to eat, and the bishop drew his chair near the table. 'You must tell me the news,' he said, his tone almost pitiful. 'How does our benefactor fare?'

'Never better,' Siarles answered. 'He looks forward to the day when he can visit you himself. And he sends me with this token of his earnest goodwill for your work here.' With that, Siarles produced a small leather bag of coins from his purse, and placed it on the table before the cleric.

The bishop smiled and, thanking God and us both, opened the bag and poured out a handful of silver pennies. 'Tell your lord that this will go far towards easing the burden of the poor hereabouts. The Ffreinc press everyone so very hard . . .' Here he faltered and looked away.

'Father?' I said. 'You look like a fella who has just bit his tongue rather than speak his mind. Why not tell us what is wrong?'

'Things are bad just now – worse than ever before.'

'Indeed?' asked Siarles. 'What has happened?'

Asaph tried to talk, but could not. Siarles passed him a cup of the watery ale, and said, 'Drink some of that down and maybe it will help loosen the words.'

He drank and placed the cup carefully on the table before him as if he was afraid it might shatter. 'I do not know how it came about,' he said when he had found his voice again, 'but something of great value to the count has gone missing. They are saying it was stolen by the creature called King Raven.'

'We have heard of this,' I told him, to encourage him and keep him talking now that he had begun. 'What has the count done?'

'He has taken prisoners – men and boys – pulling them out of their beds in the dead of night. A decree has gone out. He says he will start hanging them on Twelfth Night . . .'

'The great steaming pile!' exclaimed Siarles.

The bishop turned large, sad eyes on us. 'One man or boy each day at sunset until what was stolen is returned. That is what Count de Braose has said. How this will end, God only knows.'

So that was it. When their attempt to burn us out failed, the cowardly Ffreinc turned to those unable to defend themselves. 'How many?' I asked. 'How many has he taken?'

'I don't know,' said the bishop. 'Fifty or sixty, they say.' The ageing cleric drew both hands down his face and shook his head in despair. 'God help us,' he murmured.

'You know what they say,' Siarles told him. 'King Raven only takes back what was stolen in the first place. No doubt it is the same with whatever was taken this time . . .'

What is that, Odo? Did the old bishop know that King Raven was his mysterious benefactor?' I give him a fishy smile. 'Do I look such a fool that you think you can trap me so easily? Think again, my scribbling friend. Will cannot be drawn.' I regard him with his smooth-shaved pate and his ink-stained fingers. 'What do you think?'

'I think he must have known,' Odo says. 'A man knows whose largess keeps him.'

'Does he now?' I crow. 'Do you know who keeps you, monk?'

'God keeps me,' replies the monk, his sanctimony nigh insufferable.

'Ha! It's Abbot Hugo keeps you, priest – and you're as much a captive as Will Scarlet ever was. Hugo owns you as much as he owns the food you put in your mouth and the bed you sleep in at night – don't think he doesn't. See here, our Bishop Asaph is not a stupid man. Only a right fool would pry into things that could bring ruin if all was known.'

'Then he is a sinner,' concludes Odo loftily.

'A sinner,' I repeat. 'How so?'

'Receiving the benefit of money acquired by theft makes a thief of any who accept it.'

'Is that right?' I say. 'Is that what they teach in the monkery?'

'It is.' Oh, he is so smug in his righteousness, sometimes I want to throttle him with the belt around his sagging middle.

'Well,' I allow, 'you may be right. But tell me which is the greater theft – stealing a man's purse, or his homeland?'

'Stealing is stealing,' he replies smoothly. 'It is all the same in God's eyes.'

'God's eyes! I will give you God's eyes, Odo! Get out! We are finished. I will speak no more today.' He looks at me with a hurt expression. 'Out with you,' I roar. 'Leave me.'

He rises slowly and blows on the parchment and rolls it. 'You take offence where none was offered,' he sniffs. 'I merely point out the church's position in the matter of theft, which – as we all know, is a mortal sin.'

'Well and good, but this is war, you scurvy toad. And war makes thieves of all good men who would oppose the cruel invader.'

'There is no war,' declares my weak-eyed scribe. His sanctimony is boundless. 'There is only rebellion to the established rule.'

'Out!' I cry, and pick up a handful of mouldy straw from the damp floor of my cell. I fling the clump at him. 'Out! And do not come back.'

He turns to go, showing as much haste as I have ever seen in him. But at the door he hesitates. 'If I do not return, the hangman comes the sooner.'

'Let him come!' I shout. 'I welcome him. I would rather listen to him raising his gibbet than you telling me about the established rule. For the love of the Holy Virgin, Odo! It is a rule established in blood on a stolen throne. So now! Who is the saint and who the sinner?'

He ducks his head as he steps through the ironclad door of my cell and slinks away into the darkness. I lie back and close my eyes. *Sweet Lord Jesus,* I pray, *let my enemies kill me, or set me free!*

CHAPTER 20

Odo has not come today, and I begin to think that he has taken me at my word. Perhaps he has gone to our false abbot with my rantings and Hugo has decided to be done with me at last. If Odo does not come tomorrow, I will send for him and make my shrift. A lame piece of priesthood he may be, but in truth I do not trust anyone else in this nest of vipers to hear my confession. Odo can do that, at least, and though he riles me no end, I know he will see me right.

I hear from my keeper, Gulbert — or is it Gibbert? — that the wet weather has passed and the sun has returned. This is good news. It may be that my damp pit will dry out a little — not that ol' Will plans to wear out the world much longer. Even without my bone-headed outburst, the abbot's patience must be growing thin as his mercy. From all accounts, he was never a fella to suffer long to begin with.

So now, my execution day must be drawing nigh.

But, what is this?

There is a muffled scrabbling in the corridor beyond my cell . . . hushed voices . . . and then the familiar slow, shuffling footfall.

161

'Good day, Will Scarlet,' says Odo as he appears at the door. 'God with you.' His voice is that much strained as if addressing a stroppy stranger.

'This day is almost done, my friend,' I say to put him at ease. Well, he is the closest thing to a friend I have in this forsaken place. 'I'll say good evening and God bless.'

He makes no move to open the door, but stands in the narrow stone corridor. 'Are you coming in, then?' I ask.

'No, it will be dark soon, and I could not get any candles.'

'I see.'

'The abbot does not know I am here. He has forbidden me to listen to you.'

'He has had enough of my ravings and ramblings, I suppose.'

'Oh, no,' Odo is quick to assure me, 'it is that he has gone and does not want me talking to you while he is away.'

'Gone? Where has he gone?'

'I am not to say,' Odo replied, but continued anyway. 'There is an envoy from Rome visiting some of the towns hereabouts – a Spaniard, a Father Dominic. Abbot wishes him to visit, so he has ridden out to find him.'

'I see.' I suck my teeth and give him a shrug to show I will not try to pry any more out of him. 'Well, then . . .'

Odo bites his lip. He has something more to tell me, but cannot yet trust himself to speak. So I fish a little and see if I can tickle him into my net. 'How long will the abbot be away?'

'I cannot say, my lord,' says Odo, and I smile. He does not know what he has said yet. Give him time.

He blushes as it comes to him. 'Will, I mean . . .'

I chuckle at his small mistake. He has begun to think of me as a nobleman, and his superior. 'No harm, monk,' I tell him.

'It is just that there are a few things I do not understand.'

'Only a few?' I laugh. 'Then you are a better man than I.'

'In your story, I mean.'

'It is not a story, Odo,' I tell him. 'It is a man's life – I'm telling my life. And we both know how it's going to end. See you remember that.'

He looks at me, blinking his big, soft eyes. 'Well, the abbot has said we are not to pursue our tale any further just now.'

'Ah, I see.'

'So, I should be on my way.' He stands flat-footed and hunched in the cramped corridor.

He says he cannot stay, and yet he will not leave. Something holds him here.

'Well, perhaps,' I suggest lightly, 'the abbot would not mind if you spent a little time stalking the understanding that eludes you. It is for the abbot's benefit, after all.'

Odo brightens at once. 'Do you think so?'

'Oh, aye. Who else cares about the ravings of a wild outlaw?'

'This is exactly what I was thinking,' says he. 'It would do no harm to clarify a few of the details – clear up any misunderstandings for the abbot's benefit.'

'For the abbot's benefit, of course.'

Odo nods, making a firm decision for once in his soft pudding of a life. 'Good. I will come tomorrow.' Then he smiles; pleased with himself and revelling in this milk-mild defiance. He turns to go, but lingers. 'God's peace this night, Will.'

'And also with you,' I reply as off he scuttles.

There may be hope for Odo yet, please God.

Although the ending is in sight, there is, of course, much more of this tale, this life, to be told. How I came to be in this pinch, for one – but I will not tell this to Odo. Not yet. Distraction may be my best weapon just now -- indeed, my only weapon. I must distract our ambitious abbot as long as I can to buy King Raven time to work and achieve his purpose. And it is all to do with that blasted ring and infernal letter.

Job's bones! I would not be here now if not for that stupid, bloody treasure. It will be the death of me, beyond a doubt. Truth be told, I fear it will be the death of many before this dreadful tale is done.

CHAPTER 21

Vale of Elfael

Marshal Guy de Gysburne leaned against the freshly daubed wall of Saint Martin's new tax house, and took in his first sight of the latest arrivals sparring at the edge of the square. Seven soldiers – three knights and four men-at-arms – they were the first muster of Abbot Hugo's personal army. Arguing that no abbot worthy of the name could long exist without a bodyguard to protect him as he performed his sacred office in a blighted wilderness full of hostile and bloodthirsty barbarians, Abbot Hugo had prevailed upon Baron de Braose to send troops for his protection and, Gysburne had no doubt, prestige. Indeed, the abbot seemed determined to create his own fiefdom within Elfael, right under de Braose's long, aristocratic nose.

Having arrived while Gysburne was away visiting his father in the north country, the seven newcomers had spent the last few days practising and idling in the town's market square. As Sir Guy watched them now, he found little to dislike. Though they were young men, judging from the way each deftly lunged and parried all were skilled in their weapons. Guy supposed that they had received their training in

Aquitaine or Angevin before being recruited to join the baron's forces. Indeed, they reminded him of himself only a few short years ago: keen as the steel in their hands for a chance to prove themselves and win advancement in the baron's favour, not to mention increased fortune for themselves.

All the same, it would have surprised Guy if any of the newcomers had ever drawn human blood with their painstakingly oiled and sharpened blades, much less fought in a battle.

God willing, that would come. Just now, however, it was time to make the acquaintance of his new army. On a whim, Guy decided to take them hunting; a day in the saddle would give him a chance to see what manner of men they were, and it would do the fresh soldiers good to learn something of the territory that was their new home.

He walked out to meet his men in the square.

'To me!' he called, using the rally cry of the commander in the field. The soldiers stopped their practice and turned to see the lanky, fair-haired marshal striding across the square.

'Lord Gysburne!' shouted one of the knights to his fellows. 'Put up! Lord Gysburne has returned.'

The others stopped their swordplay and drew together to meet their commander. 'At your service, Lord,' said the foremost knight, a bull-necked, broad-shouldered youth who, like the others, had the thick wrists and slightly bowed legs of one who has spent most of his short life on the back of a horse, with a sword in his hand. The others, Guy noted, seemed to defer to him as leader of the band and spokesman.

'The sergeant said you were away,' the young knight explained. 'I thought best to keep our blades busy until you returned.' He smiled, the sun lighting his blue eyes. 'Jocelin de Turquétil at your service.'

'My best regards, Jocelin,' replied Guy. 'And to you all,' he said, turning to the others. 'Welcome to Elfael. Now then, if any of the rest of you have names, let's hear them.'

They proceeded to introduce themselves around the ring: Alard, Osbert, Warin, Ernald, Baldwin, and Hamo. They spoke with the easy exuberance of men for whom the day held only possibilities, never disappointment. As Guy had surmised, two came from Angevin and three from the baron's lands in Aquitaine; the others had been born in England, but raised in Normandie. This was their first sojourn in Wallia, but all had heard of the ferocity of the native Britons and were eager to try their strength at arms against them.

Sergeant Jeremias appeared in the yard just then and, seeing the marshal, hurried to greet him. 'God be good to you, my lord. We've been expecting you these last days. I trust you had a peaceful journey.'

'Entirely uneventful,' replied Guy.

'And your father is well?'

'He thrives.' Regarding the soldiers gathered around him, he said, 'It seems our ranks have grown in my absence.'

'As you see, Lord Marshal,' agreed Jeremias. 'And, if I may say so, they are second to none. The abbot is well pleased.'

'Then who am I to disagree with the abbot?' remarked Guy, and ordered his new cohort to saddle their horses and prepare for a day's hunting. The soldiers hurried off to ready their mounts, leaving the marshal and sergeant in the yard.

'See all is ready,' instructed Guy. 'I must go inform the abbot that I have returned.'

'Ah,' said the sergeant, 'no need. He is away and not expected back before Saint Vincent's Day.'

'Well, then, we will just have to struggle on as best we can,' said Guy, his heart lifting at the thought of not having to pay court to the abbot for a spell. Truth be told, he did not care much for Abbot Hugo

— Guy respected him, and obeyed him, and had vowed to serve him to the best of his ability . . . but he did not like the arrogance, vanity, and ever-more-insistent demands that were becoming a burden.

He owed Hugo a great deal for taking his part and saving him following that first disastrous encounter with King Raven — as the abbot was ever swift to point out. The baron would have had the young marshal horsewhipped and driven from his ranks if not for Hugo's intervention. Guy knew it was not out of sympathy or compassion for himself that the power-grasping cleric had acted but, as with the newly acquired soldiers, it was all part of a carefully devised scheme to gain a force of men who answered to no one but Abbot Hugo alone.

Guy, the abbot's commander, was liking the circumstances of his service less and less. In fact, the reason for braving the cold journey to the North Riding was to see if there might be some place for him in his father's retinue. Sadly, the state of affairs that had sent him south and forced him to link his fortunes with Baron de Braose remained unaltered. There was no living to be had in the north and, as he had long ago discovered, it was too far away from the dance of power and influence attending the king and his court — which was the only hope of the landless lord for advancement, or even a living.

Marshal Guy de Gysburne still needed the abbot because he still needed the baron and ultimately the king. But he was determined that when a better situation presented itself, he would not hesitate to seize it. For now, however, the prospect of commanding a new company of men was an agreeable development and one he determined to bend to his own advantage.

After taking a few mouthfuls of wine and some bread, the knights mounted their horses and rode out, striking north from the town towards the shaggy hills and great encircling arms of the forest. The day was brisk and the sky speckled with grey-edged clouds which passed as shadows over the smooth green snow-spattered hillsides before them. The soldiers, glad for a chance to explore the unfamiliar territory of their new home, galloped through the long grass, exulting in the strength of the horses beneath them.

They reached the edge of the forest, found the entrance to a game run, and entered the long, dim, tree-lined tunnel. The path was wide and they rode easily along, each with a spear ready in case they caught a glimpse of a stag or doe, or some other creature to give them a good chase. But, though they followed the trail as it coursed deeper into the heart of the greenwood, the would-be hunters found nothing worthy of their sport, and as the day began to wane, Guy signalled to Jocelin, riding ahead, that it was time to turn toward home.

Loath to come away without bloodying his spear, Jocelin suggested, 'My lord, let us ride on to the top of the ridge just there. If we haven't found any fresh tracks by then, we will turn back.'

'The trail is cold today,' Guy replied, 'and I am getting hungry. Leave it,' he said, turning his mount to begin the ride back, 'and save a stag or two for another day.'

The soldiers followed reluctantly, and as soon as they had quit the forest once more, the ride became a race. Letting their horses have their heads, they flew over the low hills towards the low-sinking sun. Guy, unwilling to restrain their high spirits any longer, let them go.

'Shall I call them back?' asked Jeremias, reining in beside the marshal as the last of the soldiers disappeared over the crest of the hill.

'No, Sergeant, it would serve no purpose,' Guy answered. 'They will have their ride and feel better for it.'

The two proceeded at an easy trot until, reaching the place where they had seen the last rider, they heard shouts and cries echoing up from the valley below. Little more than a crease between two slopes, the valley angled away towards the south and east, broadening slightly before ending in a rocky outcrop. There, in the centre of this close-set defile, was a Welsh herdsman with his cattle.

The soldiers had the man and his few forlorn beasts surrounded and were attempting to separate them from each other. Darting this way and that, their horses wheeling and plunging, they charged and charged again as the frantic Welshman tried to keep his frightened cows together.

As Marshal Guy and his sergeant watched, one of the terrified animals broke from the herd and ran bawling along the valley floor. Jocelin gave out a wild whoop and set out after the beast. He quickly closed on his quarry and, with a quick thrust of his lance, drove the spearhead into the cow's side. The poor creature bellowed the more as the soldier speared it again, and yet again.

The cow crashed to its knees and, still bawling, rolled onto its side as the soldier galloped past. Wheeling his mount, the knight returned to deliver the killing blow with a quick thrust between the dying cow's ribs and into its heart.

Seeing this was all the fun to be had, the other knights followed their comrade's example. Ignoring the shouts and cries of the herdsman, the Ffreinc soldiers quickly cut another cow from the herd and drove it screaming down the valley to its eventual slaughter. The third, a young bullock, gave a good account of itself, turning on its attacker and raking its horns along the pursuing horse's flanks and causing the soldier to abandon the saddle before being killed where it stood by the uninjured but angry knight.

'I shall stop this, my lord, before it goes too far,' said Jeremias as a fourth cow was cut out and just as swiftly slaughtered. He lifted the reins and made to ride on.

'Hold,' said Guy, putting out a hand to restrain him. 'There is little enough harm in it, and they are almost finished. It is the only sport they've had since they came out here.'

The herdsman, beside himself at what was happening to his cattle, happened to glimpse the marshal and sergeant watching from the hilltop and decided to take his appeal to them. He started up the slope, shouting and waving his arms to be recognized. One of the Ffreinc knights saw the farmer starting away and rode him down. The Welshman tried to evade his pursuer, but the knight was quicker. Turning his spear butt first, he struck the fleeing herdsman from behind, knocking him to the ground, where he squirmed in pain until the knight gave him a solid thump on the head and he lay still.

When the last animal had been slaughtered, Lord Guy rode down to join his troops. '*Bon chance,*' he said, regarding the carnage: seven head of cattle lay dead on the valley floor, along with a stunned herdsman who was holding his head and moaning gently. 'It would seem our hunt has provisioned a feast after all. Jeremias, you and the men gut that young bullock and we'll take it back with us.' He pointed to another young animal, 'And that heifer as well. I'll ride ahead and tell the cook to prepare the roasting pit. We will eat good Welsh beef tonight.'

Jeremias looked around at the dead cattle and their wounded herdsman. 'What about the Welshman, my lord?'

'What about him?'

'He might make trouble.'

'He is in no condition to make trouble.'

'That never seems to stop them, my lord.'

'If he persists, then I am certain you will deal with him accordingly.' Marshal Guy turned and rode back up the hillside, leaving his sergeant and men to their work.

Later, Gysburne sat on a stump behind the abbey cookhouse watching the bullock turn slowly on the spit while the cook and kitchener's boy basted the roasting meat with juices from the basin nestled in the glowing embers below the carcase. The smell of the meat filled the air and made his mouth water. He lifted his jar and drank down another healthy draught of new ale. Yes, he thought, at times like this he could almost forget that he was stranded in a backward no-account province awaiting the pleasure of the abbot to advance or deny him.

Although it might have been the ale making him feel benevolent and expansive, Guy considered that, despite his frustration and disappointment, perhaps life in the March was not so bad after all.

At that moment, if only then — as the blue winter twilight deepened across the Vale of Elfael and the voices of the knights chorused rough laughter beneath the glow of a rising moon — that was true.

CHAPTER 22

I am explaining about Bishop Asaph and our visit to Saint Tewdrig's monastery and here is Odo, frowning. It is the ring he wants to hear about, only the ring.

'What's wrong now, monk?' I ask him, sweet and innocent as a milk-maid's smile. 'You look like a fella that mistook a bolt of vinegar for ale.'

'I am certain that this bishop of yours is every bit as kind and holy as you claim,' he complains in that irritating whine that he uses when he thinks he is being long-suffering.

'Well then?'

'How did the bishop know about the stolen ring?'

'How did he know?' I say. 'Odo, you dullard, the good bishop did not know the first thing about it.'

'Then why did you go to see him?'

'We went to find out what he knew,' I say, 'and to show him the letter, and give him the stolen goods for safekeeping.' I spread my hands wide. 'In the end, he knew nothing about the ring, he could not read the letter, and would not agree to keep the treasure for us.'

'Then you discovered exactly nothing,' concludes Odo. 'A wasted journey.'

'God's mill grinds slowly, my monkish friend, but it grinds exceedingly fine. Our ways are not his ways, and there's a rare fact.'

Odo makes a sour face. 'Then why tell—'

'All will come 'round in good time,' I say, squashing his objection in the egg.

Brother Scribe sighs like a broken bellows, and we trudge on . . .

Well, as we were alone in the bishop's private quarters, we soon got down to showing the churchman the letter. He confirmed that it was indeed written in Ffreinc.

'Can you tell us what it says?' asked Siarles hopefully.

'I am sorry, my friend,' said the cleric with a thin smile. 'That skill has defied this old head, I'm afraid.'

'Can you make nothing of it?' I said, annoyed and more than a little disappointed at having risked so much to come so far for no purpose.

The old man bent his head to the square of parchment and studied it once more, his nose almost touching the surface. 'Ah, yes! Here,' he said, stabbing at a word in the middle of the page, 'that is *carpe diem*.'

'Latin?' I said.

Asaph nodded. 'It means "seize the day" – you might say an exhortation to be about your work, perhaps, or to make the most of your present opportunity.' He shrugged. 'Something like that, anyway.'

So, aside from another scrap or two of Latin, we were no better off for our trouble save in one respect only: we knew that Count de Braose was that anxious for the return of his stolen goods that he would dare to hang the population of Elfael to get it.

'Is there nothing else you can tell us?' asked Siarles.

'I am sorry,' replied the old man as the bell sounded for evening prayers. 'No one here can read Ffreinc, either.' He brightened with a thought. 'Perhaps one of the monks at Saint Dyfrig's could help you.'

But, having learned about de Braose's cruel plans for the men and boys of Elfael, Siarles and I were loath to waste even so much as a day extending a chase that might not succeed. 'We must move on at once,' my companion told him. 'Could you take it, Father?'

The old man did not like the idea. Who could blame him? It was a cold and dangerous errand we were asking. But he was too much in his benefactor's debt to say no outright. His pale eyes pleaded to be excused, and my heart went out to the old fella. Yet there was no other way. Even if we'd had the time to spare, neither of us knew anyone at Saint Dyfrig's, nor which of them might be trusted. Bishop Asaph saw this too, I think, for in the end he allowed himself to be persuaded to take the letter for us. But, having agreed to that, he would not in any wise agree to hold the rest of the treasure in safe-keeping at the monastery.

This he had decided, even though we had not yet shown him the parcel containing the ring and gloves. It made no difference; the old man would not be moved. 'I don't know what you have, or whence it came.' Siarles opened his mouth to tell him, but Asaph held up his hand to prevent him speaking. 'Nor do I wish to know. But if something happened and any of those things were found here, my monks and those few forlorn souls under my care would suffer for it.' He shook his head, his mouth firm. 'As shepherd of my flock, I cannot in good conscience allow it.'

That was that.

So we ate a hearty supper and took a little nap, resting ourselves as well as our horses. We were awake again at midnight and lit out under a cold winter moon for Cél Craidd. The Twelfth Night observance was six days away. We had only that much time and no more before the hangings began.

CHAPTER 23

The sun was already down and a freezing mist was rising with the moon in the east by the time we reached our forest hideaway at Cél Craidd. We had pushed the horses hard all the way, and they were almost spent. Yet the Welsh breed a hardy little beast, as everyone knows, and they lifted their dragging feet once we came in sight of the greenwood, because they knew they were almost home.

The Grellon greeted our return with keen interest, assembling before the Council Oak as we rode into the glade. I swung down from the saddle, searching for the face I suddenly wanted to see above all others and, before I could find it, was taken by the shoulder and spun around.

'Nóin, I——' was all I got out before I was immediately folded into a sweetly robust embrace.

She kissed me once, very hard, and then again. 'I have missed you, Will Scarlet.' She put her cheek against mine as she held me close. I could feel her shivering beneath her cloak, and thought it was not merely from the cold. 'I was afraid something might happen to you.'

'Ah, now, nothing that a good night's sleep won't cure,' I replied lightly, clutching her tight to me.

'Siarles! Will!' Bran cried, striding across the clearing to greet us. Tuck, Iwan, and Mérian followed, slipping in the well-trodden snow. 'What news?'

Without wasting a breath, Siarles told Bran and all the others about the hangings. 'Fifty or sixty stand to forfeit their lives if we do not act quickly. It is for us to save them.'

This caused an outcry among the Grellon, who raised a clamour to be allowed to march on Castle Truan and free the prisoners. 'That we will not do,' Bran said, raising his voice above the shouting. He called his council to attend him and for food and drink to be brought to help revive the travellers, and we all trooped off to join him in his hut.

This began a lengthy session of rumination about what we had learned, what it might mean, and what might be done about it. 'Asaph refused to accept the ring and gloves for safekeeping,' Siarles explained, returning the leather-wrapped bundle to Bran. 'Nor could he read the letter.'

'But we prevailed upon him to take the parchment to the abbey to see if someone there might help us,' I offered. 'We would have taken it ourselves, but seeing as the abbot means to start hanging half of Elfael, we thought best to hightail it home.'

'You did well,' Bran said. 'It is, no doubt, what I would have done.'

Iwan and the others agreed, and they began to discuss the hangings and what could be done to prevent them. I endured as long as I could, but soon the warmth of the hearth and the food combined to club me over the head and pull me down. Bran noticed my yawning and, thanking me for my diligence in bringing the news so quickly, ordered me to go and get some rest.

Creeping from Bran's hearth, I went to Nóin and found her waiting at her own small fire in her hut. Little Nia was asleep on her mat in the corner, and Nóin was idly feeding twigs into the flames. She turned and smiled as I entered. 'They kept you long,' she said.

'They did, but I am here now.' I settled on the roebuck hide beside her. 'Ah,' I sighed, 'there is nothing like a warm fire and a roof over your head at the end of the day.'

'And you a brave forester,' she chided lightly, lifting a warm hand to my face. 'Well, rest yourself, Will Scarlet.' She paused and smiled. 'You need not stir until tomorrow's light if that is what you wish.'

We kissed then and she nestled in my arms. We talked a little then – but, try as I might, I could not keep my eyes open. I fell asleep with Nóin in my embrace.

I awoke the next morning wrapped in her cloak. When I sat up who should be watching me but little Nia, her pixie face shining with some sort of happiness known only to herself. 'Hello, blossom,' I said, rolling up onto my elbow. 'Where has your mam gone?'

The little darling giggled and pointed to the door. 'Come here, sprite,' I said, holding my arms out to her. She needed no coaxing. Up she jumped and dashed into my arms, her bare feet slapping the beaten earth. I gave her a hug and settled her in my lap. We sat together and broke branches and bits of bark into the coals on the hearth to build up the fire again. By the time we had a small blaze going, Nóin returned with freshly baked loaves of barley bread, a knob of new butter, and a jar of honey. She planted a kiss on my rough cheek, then busied herself preparing the food to break our fast.

'I must have fallen asleep,' I said as she spread a cloth on the floor next to the hearth, 'but I don't remember.'

'I'm not surprised,' she replied. 'You were already halfway gone when you sat down. It did not take much to send you on your way.'

'I'm sorry.'

'How so? You were near worn through from your journey.' Nóin smiled, more to herself than to me. 'I have no cause to blame you, Will, nor do I.'

That was good enough for me. She broke open a steaming loaf, slathered it with butter, and dribbled honey over it. 'You know,' I said, trying to sound as if I had just thought of it, 'you are a right fine woman who needs a man, and I am a fella without a wife. If we got married that would fell two birds with a single stone.'

'Oh, would it now?' she said, turning to regard me with a look I could not quite read. She folded her hands in her lap. 'What makes you think I care to get married?'

'Well, I . . . I don't know. Do you?'

She said nothing, but tore off a bit of the prepared half loaf and passed it to Nia, handing the remaining portion to me.

'Nóin, I'm asking you to be my wife if . . . if you'll have me, that is.'

'Shush! Will I have you? Do you have to ask?' She smiled and began buttering the second half of the warm loaf. 'Was I not thinking the same thing the moment I laid eyes on you?'

This was news to me. 'Were you?'

'If you're a man of your word, Will Scarlet, our friar could marry us tomorrow.'

'He could,' I agreed, my head swimming a little at the turn this conversation had taken.

'I've already spoken to him. We talked while you were gone.'

'And?' I asked, thinking this was all happening far faster than I could have imagined.

'He said he could not do it,' she replied just like that. 'He said that he would give up Holy Orders before he allowed the likes of you to tie the knot.'

'What? He said that?' I started up, climbing to my feet. 'He has no cause to——'

'Oh, sit down, you big ox.' She laughed. 'What do you think he said?'

'Well, knowing him,' I conceded, 'it might be anything.'

'He said he would be honoured to do it. We have but to name the day and it is good as done.' She handed me the bread. 'So? What day shall we tell him?'

'Tomorrow it is,' I said.

'Tomorrow,' said Nóin, and now the doubt crept into her voice. 'Are you certain that is what you want?'

'No, of course not. Today! That is better still.'

'William!' she cried. 'It can't be today.'

'Why not?' I reached for her and pulled her close. 'The sooner the better, I say.'

'There are things to be done!' she exclaimed, pushing me away. 'Eat your bread and stop talking nonsense.'

'Tomorrow, then.' I reached down and cupped Nia's face in my hand. 'What do you say, snowdrop? Shall your mam and me get married tomorrow?'

The little mite laughed and hid behind her mother's shoulder.

'See? She likes the idea. I'm going to go hunt the biggest stag in the forest for our wedding supper – and a boar or two, as well.'

'Listen to you,' Nóin said, beaming with pleasure at my bold talk. 'Eat.' She pushed a chunk of honeyed bread into my mouth and kissed the sweetness on my lips.

'One day more, then,' I murmured, drawing her close, 'and we will be together always.'

Oh! Would that I had said anything but that, for the bread and honey was still warm in my mouth when Iwan appeared at the door. 'Will Scarlet? Are you in there, Will?'

'Aye, I am,' I called in reply. 'Come in if you can. We have bread and honey if you're hungry.'

He opened the narrow plank door and put his head into the hut. I don't know what he expected to find. 'Oh,' he said when he saw Nóin, 'beg pardon, I——' He lowered his eyes with embarrassment. 'I must pull Will away. Lord Bran has summoned a council of war.'

'That sounds right dire,' said I, taking another bit of bread as I rose to follow him. 'Soldiers never rest,' I sighed, and bent to steal another kiss.

'Go,' she said, sending me on my way with a quick peck, 'the sooner to return.'

Outside, I fell into step beside Iwan. 'A handsome woman there,' he said thoughtfully. 'You're that much a lucky man, Will.'

'And I know it. Pray God, I never forget.'

'There's some as would have plucked that flower for themselves.'

'Aye,' I allowed, 'Siarles for one, I think. But do you mean you would have done likewise?'

'The thought occurred to me,' he confessed. 'But, no, no . . . ,' he sighed. 'I am too old.'

'Too old?' I scoffed. 'Job's bones! Where did you ever pick up a two-headed notion like that? Have you been listening to Siarles?'

'Something like that.'

'Well, it is a wicked falsehood, Iwan, my friend. Stop up your ears to such odious blather; it will fair addle what little is left of the brain God gave you.'

The others were already gathered in Bran's hut by the time we arrived, and we entered to take our places around the hearth. Angharad had not returned from her sojourn in the cave, but Tuck took her place on Bran's right hand, with Mérian at his left. I found a place beside the door and waited to see what the others would decide.

When we were all settled, Bran nodded to Tuck, and he began a long invocation.

Tilting his round face towards the unseen heavens, he said, 'Eternal Encompasser, Fair Redeemer, Holy Friend the All-Wise Three in One, hear our prayer! Our enemies are many, and their strength is mighty. Bless our deliberations on this fairest of mornings that we may search your will for us in the days to come, and searching, find, and finding, make fast. Protect us from the foul deceptions of the evil one, and from the weapons of all who wish us harm. Be our fortress and our shield in the hour of our sorest trial . . .' His lips moved a moment longer, but his voice could no longer be heard.

In the silence of the moment, Bran said, 'By the power just bespoken, we seek justice for our people and freedom from the usurper and all who would oppress. We ask the Almighty Lord, who is ever swift to aid his children, to guide us in the task before us and grant us assurance of victory.'

We all added our *amens* to that. And then Bran smiled.

Oh, he could change quick as water! That smile was dark as the fearsome gleam in his eye. He was steeped in mischief as any imp, and itching to begin spreading discord and disorder among our enemies. He was that keen, I felt my own blood warm to the chase just the same as if we'd been out tramping the forest runs and spotted a fine, big stag to bring home.

'There is much we do not know about this,' he said, pulling up the loop on which the ring hung around his neck, 'but I am persuaded that we will not learn more by keeping it here in the forest. It has already caused death and destruction; I will not stand by and let it harm the people of Elfael more than it has already.'

'Hear him! Hear him!' boomed Iwan heartily. No doubt, it had chafed him to remain behind while Siarles and I were away, and disappointed as we were that our journey had been for naught. Now that there was a prospect of something to be done, he was for it, every British scrap of him.

'Well and good,' affirmed Tuck. 'And what do you propose to do?'

'We will give back the treasures taken in the raid.'

'Give 'em back!' cried Siarles. 'My lord, think what you are saying!'

Bran silenced him with a glance. 'I propose to return them before the sheriff hangs anyone.' Siarles huffed and rolled his eyes, but Bran's smile deepened. 'See here, we still have five days until Twelfth Night — five days before we give up the treasure,' he said. 'Five days to learn why the Ffreinc place such high value on it.'

'Good,' said Mérian. 'That is the most sensible thing I have heard since Christmas. But if anyone thinks the sheriff will just let you walk into the castle and hand it over, you best think again.' She regarded us with a high and haughty glance. 'Well, does anyone have any idea how to give back what was stolen without getting hung for a thief? Does anyone have a plan?'

Bran heard the iron in her tone and said, 'You are right to remind us of the danger, my lady. And have you conceived such a plan?'

'As it happens,' she answered, her satisfaction manifest, 'I have.'

'And will you yet tell us this plan?'

'Gladly,' she answered, lowering her shapely head a little in deference to him. Turning again to those of us gathered around the king's hearth, she added, 'However, I am certain that once you have heard what I have to say, you will contrive an even better banquet on the bare boards I lay before you . . .'

What did she say?' asks Odo. He raises his head and rubs the side of his nose in anticipation.

'That,' I say with a great, gaping yawn, 'must wait until tomorrow.'

'Oh!' he whines. 'You did that deliberately to spite me.'

'We have talked long, brother monk, and I am tired,' I reply, drawing a hand down my face. 'Leave me to my rest.'

'You are a mean and spiteful man, Will Scarlet,' grumps Odo as he gathers up his inkpot and parchment.

I roll onto my side and face the damp stone wall. 'Close the door behind you,' I tell him as if already half asleep. 'It does get cold down here of a night.'

He hesitates at the door and says, 'God with you this night, Will.' He shuffles off and I listen until his slow footfall has died away. Then I am alone in the dark with my thoughts once more.

CHAPTER 24

W hat did she say?' demands Brother Odo as he bustles breathless into my cell. He is that much like an overgrown puppy – all feet and foolish fervour – it makes me smile.

It seems to me that my dull but amiable scribe is as much a prisoner of Abbot Hugo's devices as Will Scarlet ever was. Here he sits most days, scribbling away in this dim, dank pit with its mud and mildew, the reek of piss and stagnant water in his nostrils, dutifully fulfilling his office, never complaining. What an odd friendship has grown between us. I wonder what it can hold, yes, and how much it can bear.

'God with you this morning, Odo,' I reply.

He settles himself in his place, the short plank balanced on his knees, and begins paring a new quill. 'What did she say?'

'Who?'

'Mérian!' he shrieks, impatience making his soft voice shrill as an old fishwife's. 'You remember – do not pretend otherwise. We were talking about King Raven's council.'

'Soup and sausages,' I sigh, shaking my head in weary dismay. 'Are you certain that's what we were talking about? I must have slept the memory right out of my head. I have no recollection of it at all.'

'I remember!' he cries. 'Lord Bran called a council, and Mérian volunteered a plan she had devised.'

'Yes? Go on,' I urge him. 'What next?'

'But that's all I know,' he cries. He is that close to throwing his inkhorn at me. 'That is where you stopped. You must remember what happened next.'

'Peace, Odo,' I say, trying to placate him. 'All is not lost. Remind me of what you have written, and we'll see soon enough if that stirs the pot.'

Odo busies himself with unrolling his scrap of parchment and unstopping his inkhorn.

'Read it out,' I say, as he smoothes the sheepskin beneath his podgy palms. 'Perhaps that will help me remember.'

He begins, and I hear once again how he nips and crimps my words, giving them all a monkish cast. He bleeds them dry, and makes them all grey and damp like the greenwood in the grip of November. Still and all, he gets the gist of it, and renders my ramblings rather more agreeable than many would find them.

What his high-nosed infernal majesty Abbot Hugo makes of all this, I cannot say.

'. . . the captive Lady Mérian begged leave to reveal a plan she had made. The rebels fell silent to hear what she would say . . .' He stops here and looks up expectantly. 'That is where we ended for the night.'

'If you say,' I tell him, shaking my head slowly. It is all I can do to keep from laughing. 'But my head is a cup scoured clean this morning.'

Odo makes a face and grinds his teeth in frustration. 'Well, then, what *do* you remember?'

'I remember something . . .' I pause and reflect a little. Ah, yes, how well I remember. 'See now, monk, when the council finished I returned to Nóin's hut,' I tell him, and we go on . . .

Nóin was not in her hut when I returned, nor was Nia. The council had taken the whole of the morning, and they had gone out to do some chores; so I went along to find them and lend a hand. The snow still lay deep over our ragtag little settlement, and the day, though bright, was cold. Many of King Raven's rag-feathered flock were at work chopping and splitting wood for the many hearth fires needed to keep warm. I could hear their voices sharp in the crisp air, chirping like birds as they toiled to fill their baskets and drag bundles of cut wood back to their huts. I saw this now, as I had seen such work countless times since coming to Cél Craidd, but this time something had changed.

Maybe it was only ol' Will Scarlet himself, but I did see the place in a different way, and did not much like what I saw. It put me in an edgy, uneasy mood, and I did not know why. Perhaps it was only to do with the bad news I had just now to deliver.

Oh, it was that, to be sure, but perhaps there was something else as well.

Even so, thinking to make the bitter draught a little easier to swallow, I put a big smile on my face and tried to take cheer in the sight of my beloved. But my heart was weighty and cold as a stone in a mountain stream. I saw Nóin bending low to pick up a split branch, and thought how I would love nothing more than to carry her away this instant to leave this place and its demands and duties, to flee far away from the bastard Normans and their overbearing ways. Alas, there was no longer such a place in all Britain. It made me sad and angry and disappointed and frustrated all at the same time, because I did not know what to do about it and feared nothing could be done.

I gathered my thoughts and, swallowing my disappointment, strode to where Nóin was working. 'Here, my love,' I said, 'let me carry that basket for you. Heap it high now, so you won't have to fetch any more today.'

She stood and turned with a smile. 'Ah, Will,' she began, then saw something in my face I was not able to hide. 'What is it, love?'

She looked at me with such tender concern, how could I tell her?

'The council has decided . . . ,' I said, hearing my voice as from the bottom of a well. 'We have come to a decision.'

Nóin's smile faded; she grew sombre. 'Well, what is it, Will? Speak it out.'

I bent my head. 'I have to leave again.'

'Is that all?' She fairly shouted with relief. 'Mother Mary, I was afraid it was serious.'

'I thought you would be unhappy.'

'Oh, I am right enough,' she replied, balling her fist on her hip. 'But I would be more unhappy if I thought you had changed your mind about marrying.'

'But I do want to marry you, Nóin. I do.'

'Then all is well between us.' She turned as if to go back to her work, but paused. 'When do you go?'

'As soon as all can be made ready,' I said.

'Go, then and help them see it through. We will fare as best we can while you are away,' she said, lifting a hand to my face, 'and count the days until your return.'

'I will bring our friar back with me if I have to carry him on my back, and we will be wed the day I return.' This I told her, kissing the palm of her hand. We talked about our wedding day and the plans I had to build her a new house on my return — with a big bed, a table, and two chairs.

So it was, the five of us were set to leave the next morning: Friar Tuck and myself; Bran, of course; Iwan, because we could use another pair of hands and eyes on the road; Mérian because the plan was her idea entire, and she would in no wise stay behind in any event.

However, this notion was not without difficulties of its own and, though I was loath to do it, the chore fell to me to point this out. 'Forgive me, my lord, if I speak above myself,' I began, 'but is it wise for a hostage — begging your pardon, my lady — to . . . well, to be allowed to enter into affairs of such delicacy?'

'You doubt my loyalty?' challenged Mérian, dark eyes all akindle with quick anger. 'I thought I knew you better, William Scatlocke.'

'I do heartily beg your pardon, Lady,' I said, raising my hands as if to fend off blows of her fists. 'I only meant—'

'Here's the pot calling the kettle black!' she fumed. 'That is rich indeed, my friend!'

Siarles smiled to see me handed my head so skilfully. But Bran waded into the clash. 'Mérian, peace. Will is right.'

'Right!' she snapped. 'He is a fool, and so are you if you believe for even one heartbeat that I would ever do anything to endanger—'

'Peace, woman!' Bran said, shouting down her objection. 'If you would listen for a moment, you would consider that Will has raised a fair point.'

'It is not,' she sniffed. 'It is silly and insulting — I don't know which the more.'

'No, it is neither.' Bran shook his head. 'It goes to the heart of things between us. The time has come for you to decide, Mérian Fair.'

'Decide what?' she asked, her eyes narrowing with suspicion.

'Are you a hostage, or are you one of us?'

She frowned. 'You tell me, Bran ap Brychan. What am I to you?'

'You know that right well. I would call you queen if you would but hear it.'

Her frown deepened, and a crease appeared between her brows. She was caught on the thorns this time, no mistake – and she knew it. 'See here!' she snapped. 'Do not think to make this about that.'

'Say what you will, my lady. It comes 'round to the same place in the end – either you stand with us, join us in heart and spirit or . . .'

'Or?' she replied, haughty in her indignation. 'Or what will you do?'

'Or you must stay here like a good little hostage,' Bran replied, 'while we enact your plan.'

'That I will not do,' she snipped.

'Then?'

Those of us who stood 'round about found other places to look just then, so as not to be drawn into what had become the latest clash in a royal battle of tempers and wills.

Mérian glared at Bran. She did not like having her loyalty questioned, but even she could see the problem now.

'What will you do?' Bran pressed. 'We are waiting.'

'Oh, very well!' she fumed, giving in. 'I will forswear my captivity and pledge fealty to you, Bran ap Brychan – but I'll not marry you.' She smiled with sour sweetness at the rest of us. 'There! Are we all happy now?'

'I accept your pledge,' replied Bran, 'and release you from your captivity.'

'Then I can go with you?' inquired Mérian, just to make sure.

'My lady, you are a free woman,' granted Bran gently, and I could see how much the words cost him. 'You can go with us, or you can simply go. Should you choose to stay, you will be in danger – as you already know.'

'I am not afraid,' she declared. 'It is my plan, remember, and I will not have any clod-footed men mucking it up.'

She was not finished yet, for as we gathered to depart, Mérian spied a woman named Cinnia, a slender, dark-eyed young widow a few years older than herself, Mérian's favourite amongst the forest dwellers – another of the Norman-widowed brides of which there were so many. My lady asked Cinnia to join us. She would serve as a companion for Mérian, who explained, 'A woman of rank would never travel alone in the company of men. The Ffreinc understand this. Cinnia will be my handmaid.'

We loaded our supplies and weapons – longbows and sheaves of arrows rolled in deer hides – onto two packhorses. When we were at last ready to depart, Tuck said a prayer for the success of our journey, although he could have no idea what he was praying. Thus blessed, we took our leave. Angharad was still gone, so Tomas and Rhoddi were charged with keeping watch over Cél Craidd and Elfael while Lord Bran was away, and to reach us with a warning if the sheriff got up to anything nasty.

Thus, on a splendid winter's day, we rode out to beard the sleeping lion in his den.

What is that, Odo? I have not told what we planned to do?' My weak-eyed scribe thinks I have skipped too lightly over this important detail. 'All in good time,' I tell him. 'Patience is also a virtue, impetuous monk. You should try it.'

He moans and sighs, rolls his eyes and dips his pen, and we go on . . .

CHAPTER 25

Coed Cadw

Richard de Glanville watched the forest rising before him like the rampart of a vast green fortress, the colours muted and misty in the pale winter light. Just ahead lay the stream that ran along the valley floor at the foot of the rise leading to the forest. He raised his hand and summoned the man riding behind him to his side. 'We will stop to water the horses, Bailiff,' he said. 'Tell the men to remain alert.'

'Of course,' replied the bailiff in a voice that suggested he had heard the command a thousand times and it did not bear repeating.

The man's tone of dry irritation piqued his superior's attention. 'Tell me, Antoin,' said the sheriff, 'do you think we will catch the phantom today?'

'No, Sheriff,' replied the bailiff. 'I do not think it likely.'

'Then why did you come on this sortie?'

'I came because I was ordered thus, my lord.'

'But of course,' allowed Sheriff de Glanville. 'Even so, you think it a fool's errand. Is that so?'

'I did not say that,' replied the soldier. He was used to the sheriff's dark and unpredictable moods, and rightly cautious of them. 'I say merely that the Forest of the March is a very big place. I expect the phantom has moved on.'

The sheriff considered this suggestion. 'There is no phantom, Bailiff. There are only a devil's clutch of Welsh rebels.'

'However that may be,' replied Antoin blandly, 'I have no doubt your persistence and vigilance has driven them away.'

De Glanville regarded his bailiff with benign disdain. 'As always, Antoin, your insights are invaluable.'

'King Raven will be caught one day, God willing.'

'But not today – is that what you think?'

'No, Sheriff, not today,' confessed the soldier. 'Still, it is a good day for a ride in the greenwood.'

'To be sure,' agreed the sheriff, reining up as they reached the fording place. The water was low, and ice coated the stones and banks of the slow-moving stream. Sir Richard did not dismount, but remained in the saddle, swathed in his riding cloak and leather gauntlets, his eyes on the natural wall of bare timber rising on the slope of the ridge before him. Coed Cadw, the locals called it; the name meant 'Guardian Wood,' or 'Sheltering Forest,' or some such thing he had never really discovered for certain. Whatever it was called, the forest was a stronghold, a bastion as mighty and impenetrable as any made of stone. Perhaps Antoin was right. Perhaps King Raven had flown to better pickings elsewhere.

When the horses had finished drinking and his soldiers had taken their saddles once more, the sheriff lifted the reins and urged his mount across the ford and up the long slope. In a little while, he and the four knights with him passed beneath the bare, snow-covered boughs of elm trees on either side of the road and entered the greenwood as through an arched doorway.

The quiet hush of the snowbound forest fell upon him, and the winter light dimmed. As he proceeded along the deep-shadowed track into the wood, the sheriff's senses pricked, wary to a presence unseen; his sight became keen, his hearing more acute. He could smell the faint whiff of sour earth that told him a red deer stag had passed a short while earlier, or was lying in a hidden den somewhere nearby.

After a fair distance, they came to a place where a narrow animal trail crossed their own. Here the sheriff paused. He sat for a moment, looking both ways along the ground. The tracks of pigs and deer lay intertwined in the snow and, here and there, the spoor of wolves – and all were old. Just as he was about to move along, his eye caught the sign that had no doubt caused him to stop in the first place: the slender double hoofprint of a deer and, behind and a little to one side, a slight half-moon depression. Without a word, he climbed down from the saddle and knelt for a better look. The half-moon print was followed by another a short stride length away.

'You have found something, Sire?' asked Bailiff Antoin after a moment.

'It seems our ride is to be rewarded today,' replied de Glanville.

'Deer?'

'Poacher.'

Antoin raised his eyes and peered down the tunnel formed by the overhanging branches. 'Better still,' he replied.

The sheriff resumed his saddle and, with a gesture to silence the chattering soldiers, turned onto the narrow trail and began following his quarry. The trail led up a low rise and then down into a dell with a little rock-bound rill trickling along the bottom. There in the soft mud were a half dozen depressions – including the mark of a knee where a man had knelt to drink.

De Glanville raised a gauntlet to halt those coming from behind.

He caught the sheen of a damp glimmer where water had splashed onto a rock. 'He was here not long ago,' observed the sheriff. Turning in the saddle, he singled out two of his men. 'Stay here and be ready should he double back before we catch him.'

He lifted the reins and urged his mount across the brook, up the opposite bank, and into a thicket of elder that formed a rough hedge along the streambed. Once beyond the hedge, the trail opened slightly, allowing the sun to penetrate the dense tangle overhead. Shafts of weak winter light slanted down through the naked branches above. A few hundred paces further along, the sheriff could see that the track entered a snow-covered glade. He reined up and, pointing to the clearing ahead, motioned Antoin and the remaining knights to dismount and circle around on foot. When they had gone from sight, Sir Richard proceeded on alone, pausing again as he entered the clearing. There, across the snowy space, kneeling beside the sleek, ruddy stag he had just brought down, was a swarthy Welshman. Knife in hand, he stooped to begin butchering his kill. In a glance the sheriff saw the hunter, the knife, and the longbow leaning against the trunk of a fallen birch a few paces from the crouching man.

Drawing his sword silently from its sheath with his left hand, de Glanville unslung his shield with his right. Tightening his grip on the pommel of his sword, he drew a deep breath and called across the glade, 'In the name of the king!'

The shout rang clear in the chilly air, shattering the quiet of the glade.

The startled Welshman lurched and spun. 'Throw down your weapons!' shouted de Glanville. The hunter dived for his bow. In the time it took the sheriff to swing his shield into place, the hunter had an arrow on the string. 'Halt!' cried the sheriff as the poacher drew and loosed.

The arrow struck home with a jolt that rocked the sheriff in his high-cantled saddle. The arrow point pierced the solid ashwood planking that formed the body of the shield, the iron point protruding a finger's width below the sheriff's eye.

The man's quickness was impressive, but ultimately futile. Before he could nock another arrow, two knights rushed into the clearing from either side. The hunter whirled and loosed at the nearest of the two, but the arrow merely grazed the top of the soldier's shield and careered away. Desperate, the Welshman swung the bow at the second knight and turned to flee. The two soldiers captured him in a bound, subduing him with a few skull-crushing blows before dragging him to where Sheriff de Glanville sat watching from his horse.

'Poaching deer in the king's forest,' the sheriff said, his voice loud in the sanctuary of the glade, 'is an offence punishable by death. Do you have anything to say before you are hanged?'

The hunter, who clearly did not understand the language of the Ffreinc, nevertheless knew the fate he faced just then. He gave out a cry and, with a mighty heave, tried to shake off the two soldiers clinging to him. They hung on, however, and showered blows upon his head until he subsided once more.

'Bailiff Antoin,' said the sheriff, 'you profess some proficiency in the tongue of these brutes. Ask him if he has anything to say.'

The bailiff, clinging to the man's right arm, informed him of the charge against him. The Welshman struggled and shouted, pleading and cursing as he flailed helplessly in the grasp of his captors until he was silenced with blows to the head and stomach. 'It appears he has no defence,' Bailiff Antoin declared.

'No, I wouldn't think so,' remarked the sheriff. The three remaining knights burst into the glade just then. 'The rope, Bailiff,' de Glanville ordered, and Antoin reached into the bag behind the sheriff's saddle and drew out a coiled length of braided leather.

The Welshman saw the rope and began shouting and struggling again. The sheriff ordered his knights to haul the man to the nearest tree. The rope was lofted over a stout bough and the quickly fashioned noose pulled tight around the wretch's neck.

'By order of His Majesty, King William of England, in whose authority I am sworn, I sentence you to death for the crime of poaching the king's deer,' said the sheriff, his voice low and languid, as if pronouncing such judgement was a dreary commonplace of his occupation. He directed Bailiff Antoin to repeat his words in Welsh. The bailiff struggled, lapsing now and again into French, and finished with a shrug of indifference.

The sheriff, satisfied that all had been done in proper order, said, 'Carry out the sentence.'

The knight holding the end of the rope was joined by two others and the three began pulling. The leather stretched and creaked as the victim's weight was lifted from the ground. The poor Welshman scrabbled with his hands as the noose tightened around his neck and his dancing feet swung free, toes kicking up clods of snow.

Then, as the suffocated choking began, the sheriff seemed to reconsider. 'Hold!' he said. 'Let him down.'

Instantly the rope slackened, and the man's feet touched ground once more. The wretch collapsed onto his knees, and his hands tore at the constricting leather band around his neck, his breath coming in great, grunting gasps.

When the colour had returned to the Welshman's face, the sheriff said, 'Inform the prisoner that I will give him one more chance to live.'

Antoin, standing over the gasping man, relayed the sheriff's words. The unfortunate looked up, eyes full of hope, and grasped the bailiff's leg as might a beggar beseeching a would-be benefactor.

'Tell him,' continued de Glanville, 'that I will let him go if he will but tell me where King Raven can be found.'

The bailiff duly repeated the offer, whereupon the Welshman rose to his feet. Speaking slowly and with care, aware of the dire consequence of his reply, the hunter folded his hands in supplication to the sheriff and delivered himself of an impassioned speech.

'What did he say?' asked the sheriff when the hunter finished.

'I cannot be certain,' began the bailiff, 'but it seems that he is a poor man with hungry children – five in number. His wife is dead – no, ill, she is ill. He says his cattle were killed by soldiers of the marshal. They have nothing.'

'That is no excuse,' replied de Glanville. 'Does he know that? Ask him.'

The bailiff repeated the sheriff's observation, and the Welshman retorted with an impassioned plea.

'He says,' offered Antoin, 'that they are starving. The loss of his cattle has driven him to take the deer. This, he grieves, ah, no, regrets – but always when hunger drove him to the wood, he could take a deer with his lord's blessing.'

The sheriff considered this, and then said, 'The law is the law. What about King Raven? Make him understand that he can walk free, and take the deer with him, if he tells me where to find that rebel and thief.'

This was told to the prisoner, who replied in the same impassioned voice. The bailiff listened, then answered, 'The poacher says, if it is a crime to be hungry, then a guilty man stands before you. But if there be a thing such as mercy under heaven, then he pleads to you before God to let him go for the sake of mercy. He calls upon Christ to be his witness, for he knows nothing of King Raven or where he might be found.'

The sheriff listened to this, impressed as he occasionally was with the Welsh facility with expression. If talking could save them, they had nothing to fear. Alas, words were but empty things, devoid of power and all too easily broken, discarded, and forgotten. 'I will ask one last time,' said the sheriff. 'Tell me what I want to know.'

When the sheriff's words had been translated, the captive Briton drew himself up full height and gave his answer, saying, 'Release me, for the sake of Christ before whom we all must stand one day. But know this, if it lay in my power to know the wiles and ways of the creature you call King Raven, I would not spare so much as a breath to tell you.'

'Then save your breath for dying,' replied the sheriff when the captive's reply had been relayed. 'Hang him!'

The three knights began hauling on the end of the rope. The Welshman's feet were soon kicking and his hands clawing at the noose once more. His strangled cries were swiftly choked off, and his face, now purple and swollen, glared his dying hatred for the sheriff and all Ffreinc invaders.

In a few moments, the victim's struggles ceased and his hands fell limp to his sides, first one and then the other. The sheriff leaned on the pommel of his saddle, watching the poacher's body as it swung, twisting gently from side to side. After a time, the bailiff said, 'He is dead, Sire. What do you want us to do with the body?'

'Let it swing,' said the sheriff. 'It will be a warning to others of his kind.'

With that, he turned his mount and started from the clearing, mildly satisfied with the day's work. True, he was no closer to finding King Raven, but hanging a poacher was always a good way to demonstrate his authority and power over the local serfs. A small thing, perhaps, as some would reckon, but it was, after all, in the exercise of vigilance and attention to such small details that power was maintained and multiplied.

Richard de Glanville, Sheriff of the March, knew very well the ways and uses of power. He would find the rebel known as King Raven one day, and on that day all Elfael would see how traitors to the crown were punished. Justice might be delayed, but it could not be escaped. King Raven would be caught, and his death would make that of the hanged poacher seem like a child's game. He would not merely punish the rebel, he would destroy him and snuff out his name forever. That, he considered, would be a delight to savour.

CHAPTER 26

We rode hard for Glascwm and passed through the gates of Saint Dyfrig's as a wet winter storm closed over the valleys. Rain, stinging cold, spattered into the hard-packed yard as the monks scurried to pull the horses into the stable and bundle us soggy travellers into the refectory where they could spoon hot soup into us. They did not yet know who it was they entertained – not that it would have made a difference, I reckon, for the abbey yard was already full of local folk who, having fled the Ffreinc, sought sanctuary within the walls of the abbey.

Wet and wretched, battered and beaten down, they stood slump-shouldered in the rain before the low huts they had built in the yard, watching us with the mute, dull-eyed curiosity of cattle as we trotted through the gate. Forlorn and past caring, they huddled before their hovels, shivering as the rain puddled in the mud at their bare feet. The monks had made a fire in the middle of the yard to warm them, but the damp fuel ensured that it produced more smoke than heat. Most were thin, half-starved farmers by the look of them; and more than a few bore the signs of Norman justice: here a missing hand, or chopped-off foot, there an eye burned out by a red-hot poker.

Oh, the Ffreinc love lopping bits off the poor folk. They are tireless at it. And when a Norman noble cannot find good excuse to maim some unfortunate who wanders across his path . . . why, he'll concoct a reason out of spit and spider silk.

As soon as we dismounted, the ladies were taken to the guest lodge where they could dry their clothes, but the rest of us foreswore that comfort for a hot meal instead. The abbot, a stiff old stick with a face like a wild pig's rump, huffed and puffed when he saw our lord and his rough companions puddling up his dining hall. 'Bran ap Brychan!' he cried, bursting into the long, low-beamed room. 'They told me you were killed dead a year ago or more.'

'I am as you see me, Father,' replied Bran, standing to receive Abbot Daffyd's blessing. 'I hope we find you well.'

'Well enough. If the Ffreinc would leave off harrowing the valleys and driving decent folk from their homes, we would fare that much better. I hope you do not plan on staying – we are stretched tight as a drum head with caring for those we have already.'

'We will not trouble you any longer than necessary,' Bran assured him.

'Good.' The old man did not waste words. His forthright manner made me smile. Here was a fella who would listen to reason, and give back the same. 'I'm glad you're not dead. What are you doing here?'

'And here I was thinking you would never ask,' replied Bran. Iwan and Siarles chuckled, but Bran silenced them with a stern glance. 'A few days ago, a letter was brought to you by Bishop Asaph.'

'That is so,' answered the abbot, folding his hands over his chest. His frown suggested he suspected grave mischief, and he was not wrong. 'What is that to you, my son – if I may be so bold?'

'Be as bold as you like,' answered Bran. 'Only tell me that you have that letter.'

'I do.'

'And have you read it, Father?'

'I have not,' said Daffyd. 'But another has.'

'I hope he is a trustworthy man.'

'If he was not, I would not have given him the task.'

'Come, then.' He put a hand to the abbot's shoulder and turned him around. 'We will hear it together.'

'You're soaking wet!' remarked the abbot, shrugging off Bran's hand. 'I'll not have you shaking water all over my abbey. Stay here and finish your soup. I will bring the letter here.'

I began to appreciate the abbot right well. He was a bluff old dog whose bark concealed the fact that he would never bite. Bran returned to his place on the bench with a rueful smile. 'He knew me as a boy,' he explained, 'when he was under Asaph at Llanelli.'

The abbot returned as we were finishing our soup and bread. He brought the folded square of parchment clutched tight in both hands, as if he thought it might try to wriggle free; with him was a dark-haired, slender monk of middling years with a long face, prominent nose, and skin the colour of good brown ale.

'This is Brother Jago,' announced the abbot. 'He was born in Genoa and raised in Marseilles. He speaks Ffreinc far better than any-one here in the abbey. He has read the letter.'

The slender monk dipped his head in acknowledgement of his superior's wishes. 'I am happy to serve,' he said, and I discerned in his speech a lightly lisping quality I'd never heard before. He turned to the abbot, who still stood holding the parchment bundle. 'Father?' he said, extending his hand.

Abbot Daffyd gazed at the letter and then at Bran. 'Are you certain you wish to proceed with this?'

Bran nodded.

The abbot frowned. 'I will not be a party to this. You will excuse me.'

'I understand, Abbot,' replied Bran. 'No doubt, it is for the best.'

Placing the bundle in Brother Jago's hands, the abbot turned and left the room. When the door had closed again, Bran nodded to the monk. 'Begin.'

Jago untied the blue cord and carefully unfolded the prepared skin. He stood for a moment, gazing at it, then placed it on the board in front of him and, leaning stiff-armed on his hands, began to read in a slow, confident voice.

'I, William, by the grace of God, Baron of Bramber and Lord of Brienze, to the greatly esteemed and reverend Guibert of Ravenna. Greetings in God, may the peace of Christ, Our Eternal Saviour, remain with you always. Pressed——' Jago paused. 'Ah, no, rather . . . urged by faith, we are obliged to believe and to maintain that the Church is one: Holy, Catholic, and also Apostolic. We believe in Her firmly and we confess with simplicity that outside of Her there is neither Salvation nor the remission of Sins, and She represents one sole mystical Body whose Head is Christ and the Head of Christ is God.'

Although we understood little enough of what he said, the musical quality of his speech drew us near; as he continued to read, we gathered around to hear him better.

'In all our Realms and whatsoever lands exist under our rule, granted by God, we venerate this Church as one. Therefore, of the one and only Church there is one Body and one Head, not two heads like a monster; that is, Christ and the Vicar of Christ, Peter and the successor

205

of Peter, since the Lord speaking to Peter Himself said: "Feed my sheep," meaning, my sheep in general, not these, nor those in particular, whence we understand that He entrusted all to this same Peter, entrusting to him and him alone, the Keys of the Kingdom . . .'

Well, I never would have believed it – that Bloody Baron de Braose should preach so about the nature of the church and whatnot – well, it passed understanding.

'. . . Therefore, if anyone should say that they are not belonging—' Jago broke off, read to himself for a moment, then raised his head and said, 'I am sorry. It has been some time since I read French like this.'

'You are doing well,' Bran said. 'Pray, continue.'

'Ah . . . that they are not *under the authority* of Peter and his successors, they must confess not being the Sheep of Christ, since Our Lord says in the Gospel of John "there is one sheepfold and one Shepherd." Therefore, whoever resists this power thus ordained by God, resists the ordinance of God, unless he invent like Manicheus two beginnings, which is false and judged by us heretical, since according to the testimony of Moses, it is not "in the beginnings" but "in the beginning" that God created Heaven and Earth. Furthermore, we declare, we proclaim, we define that it is absolutely necessary for Salvation that every human creature be subject to the Roman Pontiff . . .'

When Jago broke off once more to collect himself, Iwan said, 'What is the old rascal talking about?'

'Shh!' hissed Tuck. 'Let him read on and we will see.'

Jago resumed his reading. '. . . Be it known to all sons of our Holy Church present and future that we have heard the Spirit's admonition to seize the day of Peace, and have ordained this concord to be made between William and Guibert, formerly Archbishop of Ravenna . . .'

Mérian and Cinnia, given dry robes by the monks, entered just then. 'You started without us!' Mérian said, her voice sharp with disapproval.

'Shh!' said Bran. 'You have missed little enough.' He gestured to Jago. 'Go on.'

'. . . attendant with very Sacred vows to uphold His Holiness, the Pope, and bind our Powers to the Throne of Saint Peter and the One Church Universal, recognizing him as Pontiff and Holy Father, forsaking all other Powers, henceforth holding only to the Authority invested in His Holiness, the Patriarch of Rome. May the Divinity preserve you for many years, most Holy and Blessed Father.

'Given at Rouen on the third day of September, before these witnesses: Roger, Bishop of Rheims; Reginald des Roches, Bishop of Cotillon; Robert, Duke of Normandy; Henry Beauclerc; Joscelin, Bishop of Véxin; Hubert de Burgh, Justiciar of King Philip; Gilbert de Clare, Count of Burgundy and Argenton; Ralph fitzNicholas, our seneschal; Henry de Capella, Baron of Aquitaine; and others in most Solemn and August Assembly.'

Jago glanced up quickly and, seeing all eyes on him, concluded. 'Written by the hand of his servant Girandeau, scribe to Teobaldo, Archbishop of Milan.'

Well, I won't say I gleaned the full meaning of that letter just then. Then again, no one did. Indeed, we all sat looking a little perplexed at what we'd heard. Iwan spoke for us all, I think, when he said, 'That was worth a man's life on Christmas day?'

'There is something in it we cannot yet see,' replied Bran.

'If we only knew where to look,' sighed Tuck. 'For all its folderol, it is only a simple offer of support for the pope. I confess, I make nothing of it.'

Jago straightened and turned a thoughtful gaze to Bran. 'Pray, how did you come by this, my lord?' he asked, his voice quiet in the silence.

'It was with some other items taken in a raid,' Bran said simply.

Jago nodded, accepting this without comment. 'These other items – may I see them?'

Bran considered for a moment, then turned to Tuck. 'Show him.'

Tuck rose and turned his back to one and all and, from a hidden pocket in his robe, produced a roll of cloth tied with a horsehair string. He untied the string and unrolled the cloth on the table to reveal the ruby-studded ring and the finely embroidered gloves.

Jago took one look at the ring and picked it up; he held it between thumb and forefinger, turning it this way and that so that the light glinted on the gold and ring of tiny rubies. 'Do you know whose crest this is?'

'That of a Ffreinc nobleman,' replied Iwan.

'Beyond that?' said Bran. 'We know nothing.'

Jago nodded again. Replacing the ring, he picked up the gloves, lifting them to his nose to take in the scent of the fine leather. Almost reverently, he traced the heavy gold thread of the cross and the looped whorl of the Chi Rho with a respectful fingertip. 'I have seen gloves like this only once in my life – but once seen, it is never forgotten.' He smiled, as if recalling the memory even then. 'They were on the hands of Pope Gregory. I saw him as a boy when he passed through the village where I was born.

'But,' he said, replacing the gloves, 'I fear this does little to help you. I am sorry I could not be of better service.' He placed the palm of his hand on the parchment. 'I agree with the friar. There is something in the letter that the baron does not wish known to a wider world.'

Well, you could have knocked us down with a wren feather. We all looked at each other, the mystery deeper now than when we had begun.

Lady Mérian found her voice first. 'Nevertheless, it goes back. Whether we discover what it means or not,' she declared, 'it must be returned – all of it – as we agreed.'

CHAPTER 27

W hat do you want me to do?' asked the abbot, when, after Jago had been dismissed, he returned to see if we would like to join the monks for vespers.

Bran pressed the folded parchment into Daffyd's hands. 'Make a copy of this,' he commanded. 'Letter for letter, word for word. Make it exactly the same as this one.'

'I cannot!' gasped the abbot, aghast at the very suggestion.

'You can,' Bran assured him. 'You will.'

'Leave it to me,' said Tuck, stepping boldly forward. 'This is an abbey, is it not?' He took the abbot by the elbow, turned him, and led him to the door. 'Then let us go to your scriptorium and see what can be done.'

O do is frowning again. He does not approve of our King Bran's high-handed ways. My scribe has put down his quill and folded his hands across his round chest. 'Copying a stolen letter – you had no right.'

This makes me laugh out loud. 'Hell's bells, Odo! That is the least of the things we have done since this whole sorry affair began, and it en't over yet.'

'You should not have done that,' he mutters. 'It is a sin against the church.'

'Well, I suppose you could hold to that if you like,' I tell him, 'but your friend Abbot Hugo was willing to burn defenceless folk in their beds to get that letter. He sent men to their deaths to reclaim it, and was only too willing to send more. Seems to me that if we start totting up sins, his would still outweigh the lot.'

In his indignation, my podgy scribe has forgotten this. He makes his sour face and pokes out his lower lip. 'Copying a stolen letter,' he says at last. 'It's still a sin.'

'Perhaps.'

'Undoubtedly.'

'Very well,' I concede. 'I suppose you have never stood on a battleground naked and alone while the enemy swarms around you like killing wasps with poison in their stings.'

'No!' he snorts. 'And neither have you.'

I grant him that. 'Maybe not. But we are sorely outmanned in this fight. The enemy has all the knights and weapons, and he has already seized the high ground. Whatever small advantage comes our way, we take it and thank God for it, too.'

'You stole the letter!' he complains.

Oh, Odo, my misguided friend, takes what refuge can be found in dull insistence. Well, it is better than facing the truth, I suppose. But that truth is out now, and it is working away in him. I leave it there, and we roll on . . .

There were but four days remaining before Twelfth Night, when the hangings would commence. At Bran's insistence, and with Tuck's patient cajoling, the monks of Saint Dyfrig's abbey prepared a parchment the same size and shape as that of the baron's letter; they then proceeded to copy the letter out exact, matching pen stroke to pen stroke. If they had been archers, I'd have said they hit the mark nine times for ten and the tenth a near miss — which is right fair, considering they didn't know what they were scribing. True, they were not able to use the same colour brown ink as the original; the ink they made for their use at the abbey had a more ruddy appearance when it dried. Still, we reasoned that since none of the Ffreinc in Elfael had ever seen the original, they would not know the difference.

While the monks toiled away, Bran and Iwan undertook to carve a seal of sorts out of a bit of ox bone. Working with various tools gathered from around the abbey — everything from knife points to needles — they endeavoured to copy the stamp that made the seal that was affixed to the letter. And, while they laboured at this, Mérian and Cinnia made a binding cord, weaving strands of white satin which they then dyed using some of the ruddy ink and other stuff supplied by the abbey.

It took two days to finish our forgery, and a fine and handsome thing it was, too. When it was done, we placed the letters side by side and looked at them. It was that difficult to tell them apart, and I knew which was which. No one who had not seen the genuine letter would be able to tell the difference, I reckoned, and anyone who did not know, would never guess.

Abbot Daffyd held a special Mass of absolution for the monks who had worked on the parchment and for the monastery itself for its complicity in this misdeed; he sought the forgiveness of the High Judge of the world for the low crimes of his followers. I held no such qualms about any of this myself, considering it a right fair exchange for the lives of those who awaited death in the count's hostage pit.

When the service was finished, Bran ordered everyone to make ready to ride to Castle Truan to return the stolen goods to the count. 'And just how do you intend to do that?' asked Daffyd; if his voice had been a bodkin, it could not have been more pointed. I suppose he imagined he had caught Bran in a mistake that would sink the plan like a millstone in a rowboat. 'If you are caught with any of this, the sheriff will hang you instead.'

'Good abbot,' replied Bran, 'your concern touches me deeply. I do believe you are right. Yet, since we have no interest in providing fresh meat for the hangman, we must make other arrangements.'

Warned by the devious smile on Bran's face, Daffyd said, 'Yes? And those would be?'

'*You* shall return the treasures to the count.'

'Me!' cried the abbot, his face going crimson in the instant. 'But see here! I will do no such thing.'

'Yes,' Bran assured him, 'I think you will. You must.'

Well, the abbot was the only real choice. When all was said and done, he was the only one who could come and go among the Ffreinc as neatly as he pleased without rousing undue suspicion.

'This will not do at all,' the abbot fumed.

'It will,' countered Bran. 'If you listen well and do exactly as I say, they will hail you as a champion and drink your health.' Bran then explained how the stolen goods would be returned. 'Tomorrow you will awaken and go to the chapel for your morning prayers. And there, on the altar, you will find a bag containing a box. When you open the box you will find the letter and the ring and the gloves. You will recognize them as the very items Count de Braose is missing, and you will take them to him, telling him precisely how you found them.'

'It hardly serves the purpose if they hang me instead,' Daffyd pointed out.

'If you can contrive to have the sheriff and abbot present when you hand over the goods,' continued Bran, 'that would be better still. De Glanville was there. He knows you could not have been involved in the theft; therefore you will remain above suspicion. And since you did not see who left the bundle on the altar, they cannot use you to get at us.'

The abbot nodded. 'It would all be true,' he mused.

'You would not have to lie to them.'

'But it would pare the truth very narrowly, my lord,' humphed Abbot Daffyd.

'Narrow is the gate,' chuckled Tuck, 'and strait is the way. Do as Rhi Bran says, and they will sing your praises.'

'And I will give you silver enough to feed the hungry in your yard.'

The abbot twisted and turned like a worm on a griddle, but even he had to admit that it was the only way. He agreed to do it.

'Stay long enough to see the prisoners released,' added Bran. 'Once the abbot and count have received the goods, they should set the captives free as promised.'

'I am not an imbecile,' sniffed the abbot. 'I fully appreciate why we're going to all this trouble.'

'As you say,' replied Bran. 'Please do not take offence, Abbot; I just wanted to make sure we were all working to the same end. It is the lives of those men and boys we are saving. Lest anyone forget.'

While the others worked on preparing the forged letter, I had not been idle. I had been gathering bits of this and that from the abbey's stores and supplies. Tuck, Mérian, and the others had helped, too, when they could, and on the Eve of Twelfth Night all was nearly ready.

We slept little that night, and dawn was a mere rumour in the east when we departed the abbey. There was no one about in the yard, and I do not think we were observed. But if any of the poor asleep in their miserable hovels had looked out, they would have observed a far different group of travellers leaving than that which arrived.

CHAPTER 28

Saint Martin's

Richard de Glanville sat at table with a knife in one hand and a falcon on the other. With the knife he hacked off chunks of meat from the carcase before him, which he fed to the fledgling gyrfalcon — one of two birds the sheriff kept. He had heard from Abbot Hugo that falconry was much admired in the French court now that King Philip owned birds. De Glanville had decided, in the interest of his own advancement, to involve himself in this sport as well. It suited him. There was much in his nature like a preying bird; he imagined he understood the hawks, and they understood him.

The day, newly begun, held great promise. The miserable wet weather of the week gone had blown away at last, leaving the sky clean scoured and fresh. A most impressive gallows had been erected in the town square in front of the stable, and since there had been no communication on the part of the thieves who had stolen the abbot's goods, all things considered it was a fine day for a hanging.

He flipped a piece of mutton to the young bird and thought, not for the first time in the last few days, how to direct the executions for best effect. He had made up his mind that he would begin with three. Since it was a holy day there was a symbolic symmetry in the number three and, anyway, more than that would certainly draw the disapproval of the church. Count Falkes De Braose insisted on waiting until sundown rather than sunrise, as the sheriff would have preferred, but that was a mere trifle. The count clung doggedly to the belief that the threat of the hangings would yet bring results; he wanted to give the thieves as much time as possible to return the stolen treasure. In this, the sheriff and count differed. The sheriff held no such delusions that the thieves would give up the goods. Even so, just on the wild chance that the rogues were foolish enough to appear with the treasure, he had arranged a special reception for them. If they came – and somewhere in the sheriff's dark heart he half hoped they would ride into Saint Martin's with the treasure – none of them would leave the square alive.

When he finished feeding the hawk, he replaced it on its perch and, drawing on his riding boots, threw a cloak over his shoulder and went out to visit his prisoners. Though the stink of the pit had long since become nauseating, he still performed this little daily ritual. To be sure, he wanted the wretches in the pit to know well who it was that held their lives in his hands. But the visits had another, more practical purpose. If, as the death day lurched ever nearer, any of the prisoners suddenly remembered the whereabouts of the outlaw known as King Raven, Sheriff de Glanville wanted to be there to hear it.

He hurried across the near-empty square. It was early yet, and few people were about to greet the blustery dawn. He let himself into the guardhouse and paused at the entrance to the underground gaol where, after waking the drowsy keeper, he poured a little water on the hem of his cloak. Holding that to his nose, he descended the few steps and proceeded along the single narrow corridor to the end, pausing only to see if anyone had died in either of the two smaller cells he passed along the way. The largest cell of the three lay at the end of the low corridor, and though it had been constructed to hold as many as a dozen men, it now held more than thirty. There was not enough room to lie down to sleep, so the prisoners took turns through the day and night; some, it was said, had learned to sleep on their feet, like horses.

At first sight of the sheriff, one of the Welsh prisoners let out a shout and instantly raised a great commotion, as every man and boy began crying for release. The sheriff stood in the dank corridor, the edge of his cloak pressed to his face, and patiently waited until they had exhausted their outcry. When the hubbub had died down once more – it took less time each day – the sheriff addressed them, using the few words of Welsh that he knew. 'Rhi Bran y Hud,' he said, speaking slowly so that they would understand. 'Who knows him? Tell me and walk free.'

It was the same small speech he made every day, and each time produced the same result: a tense and resentful silence. When the sheriff finally tired of waiting, he turned and walked away to a renewed chorus of shouting and wailing the moment his back was turned.

They were a stubborn crowd, but de Glanville thought he could detect a slight wearing down of their resolve. Soon, he believed, one of his captives would break ranks with the others and would tell him what he wanted to know. After a few of them had hanged, the rest would find it increasingly difficult to hold their tongues.

It was, he considered, only a matter of time.

The sheriff did not care a whit about retrieving Abbot Hugo's stolen goods, despite what Hugo told him about the importance of the letter. It was the capture of King Raven he desired, and nothing short of King Raven would satisfy.

After his morning visit to the gaol, the sheriff returned to the upper rooms of the guardhouse to visit the soldiers and speak with the marshal to make certain that all was in order for the executions. It was Twelfth Night and a festal day, and the town would be lively with trade and celebration. Sheriff de Glanville had not risen to his position by leaving details to chance.

He found Guy de Gysburne drinking wine with his sergeant. 'De Glanville!' called Guy as the sheriff strolled into the guardhouse. A fire burned low in the grate, and several soldiers lolled half-asleep on the benches where they had spent the night. Empty cups lined the table and lay on the floor. *'Une santé vous, Shérif!'* Gysburne cried, raising his cup. 'Join us!'

As the sheriff took a seat on the bench, the marshal poured wine into an empty cup and pressed it into de Glanville's hands. They drank, and the sheriff replaced his cup after only a mouthful, saying, 'I will expect you and your men to be battle-sharp today.'

'But of course,' replied Guy carelessly. 'You cannot think there will be any trouble?' When the sheriff did not reply, he adopted a cajoling tone. 'Come, de Glanville, the rogues would never dare show their faces in town.'

'I bow to your superior wisdom, Lord Marshal,' he replied, his voice dripping honey. 'I myself find it difficult to forget that a little less than a fortnight ago we lost an entire company of good men to these outlaws.'

Guy frowned. 'Nor have I forgotten, Sheriff,' he said stiffly. 'I merely see nothing to be gained by wallowing in the memory. Then again,' he added, taking another swig of wine, 'if it was my plan that had failed so miserably, perhaps I would be wallowing, too.'

'Bâtard,' muttered de Glanville. 'You're rotten drunk.' He glared at the marshal and then at the sergeant. 'You have until sundown to get sober. When you do, I will look for your apology.'

Marshal Guy mouthed a curse and took another drink. The sheriff rose, turned on his heel, and strode from the room. 'There was never but one *bâtard* in this room, Jeremias,' he muttered, 'and he is gone now, thank God.'

'I thought I smelled something foul,' remarked Sergeant Jeremias, and both men fell into a fit of laughter.

In truth, however, the sheriff was right: they were very drunk. They had been drinking most nights since that disastrous Christmas raid. Most nights they, along with the rest of the soldiers in the abbot's private force, succeeded in submerging themselves in a wine-soaked stupor to forget the horror of that dreadful Christmas night. Alas, it was a doomed effort, for with the dawn the dead came back to haunt them afresh.

Upon leaving the guardhouse, the bell in the church tower rang to announce the beginning of Mass. The sheriff walked across the square to the church, pushed open the door, and entered the dim, damp darkness of the sanctuary. A few half-burnt candles fluttered in sconces on the walls and pillars, and fog drifted over the mist-slick stones underfoot. De Glanville made his way down the empty aisle to take his place before the altar with the scant handful of worshippers. As he expected, one of the monks was performing the holy service, his voice droning in the hollow silence of the near-empty cave of the church; the abbot was nowhere to be seen.

He watched as the Mass moved through its measured paces to its ordained finish and, with the priest's benediction ringing in his ears, left the church feeling calm and pleasantly disposed towards the world. There were more people about now. A few merchants were erecting their stalls, and some of the villagers carried wood for the bonfire which would be lit in the centre of the square. He stood for a moment, watching the town begin to fill up, then looked to the sky. The sun was bright, but there were dark clouds forming in the west.

There was nothing he could do about that, so he hurried on, pausing now and again to receive the best regards of the townsfolk as he progressed across the muddy expanse, visiting some of the stalls along the way. There were a few provisions he needed to procure for his own Twelfth Night celebration. Odd: he was always ravenously hungry following a public execution.

He spent the rest of the morning going over the preparations with his men. There were but four of them now – the others had been killed in the raid – and de Glanville was concerned about the survivors falling into melancholy. They had been caught off guard in the forest, for which the sheriff took the blame; he had not anticipated the speed with which the outlaws had struck, nor the devastating power of their primitive weapons. Tonight's executions would provide some redress, he was sure, and remove some of the lingering pain from the beating they had taken.

When he had determined that all was in order, the sheriff returned to his quarters for a meal and a nap. He ate and slept well, if lightly, and rose again late in the day to find that the sun had begun its descent in the west and the threatened storm was advancing apace. It would be a snowy Twelfth Night. He buckled his sword belt, drew on his cloak and gloves, and returned to the town square, which was now filled with people. Torches were being lit, and the bonfire was already ablaze. Judging from the sound alone, most had already begun their celebrations. Spirits were high, with song and the stink of singed hair in the air; someone had thrown a dead dog onto the bonfire, he noted with distaste. It was an old superstition, and one he particularly disliked.

He proceeded across the crowded square to the guardhouse to deliver final instructions to the marshal and his men. Out of the corner of his eye, he noticed a group of travelling merchants setting out their wares. The fools! The feast about to begin and here they were, arriving when everyone else was finishing for the day and making ready to celebrate. Two women he had never seen before lingered nearby, attracted, no doubt, by the possibility of a bargain from traders desperate to make at least one sale before the hangings began.

At the guardhouse, he delivered his message to the sergeant, who seemed sober enough now. That done, he proceeded to the abbot's quarters to share a cup of wine while waiting for the evening's festivities to begin. 'So!' said Abbot Hugo as de Glanville stepped into the room. 'Gysburne came to see me. He doesn't like you very much.'

'No,' conceded the sheriff, 'but if he would learn to follow simple commands, we might yet achieve a modicum of mutual accord.'

'Mutual accord – ha!' Abbot Hugo snorted. 'You don't like him, either.' He splashed wine into a pewter goblet and pushed it across the board towards de Glanville. 'Personally, I do not care how you two get on, but you might at least accord me the respect of asking my permission before you begin ordering around my soldiers as if they were your own.'

'You are right, of course, Abbot. I do beg your pardon. However, I would merely remind you that I am aiding your purpose, not the other way around – and with the king's authority. I require things to be done properly, and the marshal has been lax of late.'

'Tut!' The abbot fanned the air in front of his face, and frowned as if he smelled something rancid. 'You pretty birds get your feathers ruffled and pretend you have been ill used. Drink your wine, de Glanville, and put these petty differences behind you.'

They began to discuss the evening's arrangements when the porter interrupted to announce the arrival of Count Falkes, who appeared a moment later wrapped head to heel in a cloak of double thickness, thin face red after the ride from his castle, his pale hair in wind-tossed disarray. In all, he gave the impression of a lost and anxious child. The abbot greeted his guest and poured him a cup of wine, saying, 'The sheriff and I were just speaking about the special entertainment.'

An expression of resigned disappointment flitted across Count Falkes's narrow features. 'Then you think there is no hope?'

'That the stolen items will be returned?' countered the sheriff. 'Oh, there is hope, yes. But I think we must stretch a few British necks first. Once they learn that we are in deadly earnest, they will be only too eager to return the goods.' The sheriff smiled cannily and sipped his wine. 'I still do not know what was in those stolen chests that is so important to you.'

Abbot Hugo saw Falkes open his mouth to reply, and hastily explained, 'That, I think, is for the baron to answer. The count and I have been sworn to secrecy.'

The sheriff pursed his lips, thinking. 'Something the baron would prefer to remain hidden — a matter of life and death, perhaps.'

'Trust that it is so,' offered the count. 'Even if it were not at first, it is now. We have *you* to thank for that.'

The sheriff, quick to discern disapproval, stiffened. 'I did what I thought necessary under the circumstances. In fact, if I had not antici-pated the wagons, we would not have had any chance of catching King Raven at all.'

'You still maintain that it was the phantom.'

'He is no phantom,' declared the sheriff. 'He is flesh and blood, whatever else he may be. Once word reaches him that we have hung three of his countrymen, he'll be only too eager to return the baron's treasure.'

'Three?' wondered the count. 'Did you say three? I thought we had agreed to execute only one each day.'

'Yes, well,' answered de Glanville with a haughty and dismissive flick of his head, 'I thought better to start with three tonight – it will instil a greater urgency.'

'Now, see here!' objected the count. 'I must rule these people. It is difficult enough without you—'

'Me! We would not be in this quagmire if you had—'

'Peace! There is enough blame for all to enjoy a healthy share,' said the abbot, breaking in. Holding the wine jar, he refreshed the cups. 'I, for one, find this continual acrimony as tiresome as it is futile.' Turning to Falkes, he said, 'Sheriff de Glanville has responsibility for controlling the forest outlaws. Why not trust him to effect the return of our goods in his own way?'

The count finished his wine in a gulp and took his leave. 'I must see to my men,' he said.

'A good idea, Count,' said Abbot Hugo. Turning to the sheriff, he said, 'You must also have much to do. I have kept you from your business long enough.'

In the square outside, Gulbert, the gaoler, had assembled the prisoners – sixty men and boys in all – at the foot of the gallows. They were chained together and stood in the cold, most of them without cloaks or even shoes, their heads bowed – some in prayer, some in despair. Marshal Guy de Gysburne, leading his company of soldiers, established a cordon line to surround the miserable group and keep any from escaping – as if that were possible – but also to keep townspeople from interfering with the proceedings in any way. A few of the wives and mothers of the Cymry captives had come to plead for the release of their sons or husbands, and Sheriff de Glanville had given orders that no one was to have even so much as a word with any of the prisoners. Guy, nursing a bad headache, wanted no trouble this night.

To a man, the Ffreinc knights were helmed and dressed in mail; each carried a shield and either a lance or naked sword; and though none were expecting any resistance, all were ready to fight. Count Falkes had brought a dozen men-at-arms, and these all carried torches; additional torches had been given to the townsfolk, and two large iron braziers set up on either side of the gallows — along with the bonfire — bathed the square in a lurid light.

The mostly Ffreinc population of Saint Martin's had gathered for the Twelfth Night spectacle, along with the residents of Castle Truan and the merchants who had traded in town that day. Abbot Hugo appeared, dazzling in his white satin robe and scarlet cloak; two monks walked before him — one carrying a crosier, the other a gilt cross on a pole. Fifteen monks followed, each carrying a torch. The crowd shifted to accommodate the clerics.

Richard de Glanville, Sheriff of the March, stepped up onto the raised platform of the gallows. An expectant hush swept through the crowd. 'In accordance with the Rule of the March, and under authority of King William of England,' he called, his voice loud in the silence of fluttering torches, 'we are come to witness this lawful execution. Let it be known to one and all, here and henceforth, that refusal to aid in the capture of the outlaw known as King Raven and his company of thieves will be considered treason towards the crown, for which the punishment is death.'

The sheriff glanced up as the wind gusted, bringing the first frigid splash of the promised rain. He took a last look around the square — at the bonfire, the torches, the soldiers armed and ready, the close-gathered crowd. It occurred to him to wonder what had become of those late-arriving merchants, who seemed to have disappeared. Finally, satisfied that all was as it should be, de Glanville gave the order to proceed. Stepping to the edge of the platform, he turned his gaze upon the cringing victims. None dared raise their heads or glance up to meet his eye, for fear of being the one singled out.

He raised his hand and pointed to an old man who stood shivering in a thin shirt. Two soldiers seized the man and, as they were removing the wretch's shackles, the sheriff's finger came to rest over another. 'Him, too,' said the sheriff.

This victim, shocked that he should have been chosen as well, gave out a shout and began struggling with the soldiers as they removed his chains. The man was quickly beaten into submission and dragged to the platform.

One more. From among the younger captives, de Glanville chose a boy of ten or twelve years. 'Bring him.' The youngster, dazed by his captivity, was too brutalized to put up a fight, but some of the men nearest him began pleading with their captors, offering to take the lad's place. Their desperate protests went unheeded by soldiers who did not speak Welsh, and did not care anyway.

Excitement fluttered through the crowd as the captives were dragged onto the platform and the spectators realized they would be feted to three hangings this night.

Ropes were produced and the ends snaked over the strong beam of the gallows arm; sturdy nooses were looped around the necks of the three Cymry – one old, one young, and one in his prime – whose only real crime under heaven was having been captured by the Normans.

As the nooses were being tightened, there came a shout from the crowd. 'Wait! Stop the execution!'

Those gathered in the square, Ffreinc and Welsh alike, heard the cry in priestly Latin and, upon turning towards the commotion, saw a company of monks in dull grey robes pushing their way through the throng to the front of the gallows. 'Stop! Release these men!'

The sheriff, his interest piqued, called for the crowd to let them through. 'Dare you interrupt the execution of the law?' he asked as they came to stand before him. 'Who are you?'

'I am Abbot Daffyd of Saint Dyfrig's near Glascwm!' he called in a loud voice. 'And I have brought the ransom you require.'

The sheriff cast a quick glance at Abbot Hugo, whose plump round face showed, for once, plain wide-eyed astonishment. On the ground, Count Falkes shoved his way towards the newly arrived monks. 'Where is it?' he demanded. 'Let us see it.'

'It is here, Lord Count,' said Daffyd, his face glistening with sweat from the frantic scramble to reach the town. 'Praise Jesu, we have come in time.' He turned to one of the priests behind him and took possession of a small wooden box, which he passed to the count. 'Inside this casket, you will find the items which were stolen from you.'

'Here! Here!' cried Abbot Hugo. 'Make way!' He pushed through the crowd to the count's side. 'Let me see that.'

Seizing the chest from the count's hands, he opened the lid and peered inside. 'God in heaven!' he gasped, withdrawing the gloves. He took out the leather bag and, shoving the casket into the count's hands, fumbled at the strings of the bag, opened it, and shook the heavy gold ring into his hand. 'I don't believe it.'

'The ring!' said the count. Looking up sharply, he said, 'Where did you get this?'

'These are the things that were stolen in the forest raid at Christ-tide, yes?' Daffyd asked.

'They are,' confirmed Count Falkes. 'I ask again, where did you get them?'

'With God and the whole Assembly of Heaven bearing witness, I went to the chapel for prayers this morning, and the box was on the altar. When it was left there, no one knows. We saw no one.' Raising his arm, the Welsh abbot pointed to the gallows. 'Seeing that the goods have been returned and accepted, I beg the release of all prisoners.'

For the benefit of the Cymry hovering at the edges of the crowd, he repeated his request in Gaelic; this brought a cheer from those brave enough to risk being identified by the count and sheriff as potential troublemakers.

Abbot Hugo, still examining the contents of the box, withdrew the carefully folded bundle of parchment. 'Here it is – the letter,' he said, holding it up so he could see it in the torchlight. 'It is still sealed.' Looking to the count, he said, 'It is all here – everything.'

'Excellent,' Falkes replied. 'My thanks to you, Abbot. We will now release the prisoners.'

'Not so fast, my lord,' said Hugo. 'I think there are still questions to be answered.' He turned with sudden savagery on the Welsh abbot. 'Who gave these things to you? Who are you protecting?'

'My lord abbot,' began Daffyd, somewhat taken aback by his fellow churchman's abrupt challenge. 'I do not th—'

'Come now, you don't expect us to believe that you know nothing about this affair? I demand a full explanation, and I will have it, by heaven, or else these men will hang.'

Daffyd, indignant now, puffed out his chest. 'I resent your insinuation. I have acted in good faith, believing that box was given to me so that I might secure the release of the condemned men – doomed, I would add, through no fault of their own. It would seem that your threat reached the ears of those who stole these things and they contrived to leave the box where it would be found so that I might do precisely what I have done.'

The abbot frowned and fumed, unwilling to accept a word of it. Count Falkes, on the other hand, appeared pleased and relieved; he replied, 'For my part, I believe you have acted in good faith, Abbot.' Turning towards the gallows, where everyone stood looking on in almost breathless anticipation, he shouted, '*Relâcher les prisonniers!*'

Marshal Guy turned to the gaoler and relayed the command to

release the prisoners. As Gulbert proceeded to unlock the shackles that would free the chain, Sheriff de Glanville rushed to the edge of the platform. 'What are you doing?'

'Letting them go,' replied Gysburne. 'The stolen goods have been returned. The count has commanded their release.' He gave de Glanville a sour smile. 'It would appear your little diversion is ruined.'

'Oh, is it?' he said, his voice dripping venom. 'The count and abbot may be taken in by these rogues, but I am not. These three will hang as planned.'

'I wouldn't—'

'No? That is the difference between us, Gysburne. I very much would.' He turned and called to his men. 'Proceed with the hanging!'

'You're insane,' growled the marshal. 'You kill these men for no reason.'

'The murder of my soldiers in the forest is all the reason I need. These barbarians will learn to fear the king's justice.'

'This isn't justice,' Guy answered, 'it is revenge. What happened in the forest was your fault, and these men had nothing to do with it. Where is the justice in that?'

The sheriff signalled the hangman, who, with the help of three other soldiers, proceeded to haul on the rope attached to the old man's neck. There came a strangled choking sound as the elderly captive's feet left the rough planking of the platform.

'It is the only law these brute British know, Marshal,' remarked the sheriff as he turned to watch the first man kick and swing. 'They cannot protect their rebel king and thumb the nose at us. We will not be played for fools.'

He was still speaking when the arrow sliced the air over his shoulder and knocked the hangman backwards off his feet and over the edge of the platform. Two more arrows followed the first so quickly that they seemed to strike as one, and two of the three soldiers hauling on the noose rope simply dropped off the platform. The third soldier suddenly found himself alone on the scaffold. Unable to hold the weight of the struggling prisoner, he released the rope. The old man scrambled away, and the soldier threw his hands into the air to show that he was no longer a threat.

The sheriff, his face a rictus of rage, spun around, searching the crowd for the source of the attack as an uncanny quiet settled over the astonished and terrified crowd. No one moved.

For an instant, the only sound to be heard was the crack of the bonfire and the rippling flutter of the torches. And then, into the flame-flickering silence there arose a horrendous, teeth-clenching, bone-grating shriek — as if all the demons of hell were tormenting a doomed soul. The sound seemed to hang in the cold night air; and as if chilled by the awful cry, the rain, which had been pattering down fitfully till now, turned to snow.

De Glanville caught a movement in the shadows behind the church. 'There!' he cried. 'There they go! Take them!'

Marshal Gysburne drew his sword and flourished it in the air. He called to his men to follow him and started pushing through the crowd towards the church. They had almost reached the bonfire when out from its flaming centre — as if spat from the red heat of the fire itself — leapt the black feathered phantom: King Raven.

One look at that smooth black, skull-like head with its high feathered crest and the improbably long, cruelly pointed beak, and the Cymry cried out, 'Rhi Bran!'

The soldiers halted as the creature spread its wings and raised its beak to the black sky above and loosed a tremendous shriek that seemed to shake the ground.

Out from behind the curtain of flame streaked an arrow. Guy, in the fore rank of his men, caught the movement and instinctively raised his shield; the arrow slammed into it with the blow of a mason's hammer, knocking the ironclad rim against his face and opening a cut across his nose and cheek. Gysburne went down.

'Rhi Bran y Hud!' shouted the Cymry, their faces hopeful in the flickering light of the Twelfth Night bonfire. 'Rhi Bran y Hud!'

'Kill him! Kill him!' screamed the sheriff. 'Do not let him escape! Kill him!'

The shout was still hanging in the air as two arrows flew out from the flames, streaking towards the sheriff, who was commanding the gallows platform as if it was the deck of a ship and he the captain. The missiles hissed as they ripped through the slow-falling snow. One struck the gallows upright; the other caught de Glanville high in the shoulder as he dived to abandon his post.

Suddenly, the air was alive with singing arrows. They seemed to strike everywhere at once, blurred streaks nearly invisible in the dim and flickering light. Fizzing and hissing through the snow-filled air, they came — each one taking a Ffreinc soldier down with it. Three flaming shafts arose from the bonfire, describing lazy arcs in the darkness. The fire arrows fell on the gallows, kindling the post and now-empty platform.

Count Falkes, transfixed by the sight of the phantom, stood as arrows whirred like angry wasps around him. He had heard so much about this creature, whom he had so often dismissed as the fevered imaginings of weak and superstitious minds. Yet here he was — strange and terrible and, God help us all, magnificent in his killing wrath.

The last thing Falkes de Braose saw was Sheriff de Glanville, eyes glazed, clutching the shaft of the arrow that had pierced his shoulder, passed through, and protruded out his back. The sheriff, staggering like a drunk, lurched forward, dagger in his hand, struggling to reach the phantom of the wood.

Count Falkes turned and started after the sheriff to drag him back away and out of danger. He took but two steps and called out to de Glanville. The word ended in a sudden, sickening gush as an arrow struck him squarely in the chest and threw him down on his back. He felt the cold wet mud against the back of his head and then . . . nothing.

CHAPTER 29

'See now, Odo,' I tell my dull if dutiful scribe, 'we did not plan to attack the sheriff and his men – we were sorely outmanned, as you well know – but we came ready to lend muscle to Abbot Daffyd's demand to stop the hangings.'

'But you killed four men and wounded seven,' Odo points out. 'You must have known it would come to a fight.'

'Bran suspected the sheriff would betray himself, and he wanted to be there to prevent the executions if it came to that. As it happens, he was right. So, if you're looking for someone to blame for the Twelfth Night slaughter, you need look no further than Richard de Glanville's door.'

Odo accepts this without further question, and we resume our slow dance towards my own appointment with the hangman.

Bran was angry. Furious. I'd never seen him so enraged – not even in the heat of battle. When fighting, an icy calm descended over him. With swift but studied motion, he bent the belly of the bow and sent shaft after shaft of winged death to bite deep into enemy flesh. He did not exult; neither did he rage. But this! This was something different – a black, impenetrable fury had swept him up, and he shook with it as he stalked around the fire ring in his hut, his face twisted into a rictus of ferocity. Like a terrible, monstrous beast, anger had consumed him completely.

Seeing him now, a body would not have known him as the same man from the night before. For as we stood in the town square on Twelfth Night and the realisation broke upon us that Sheriff Bloody de Glanville would hang those three men even after recovering the treasure, Bran simply turned to us as we gathered close about and said in a low voice, 'String your bows.'

Then he calmly set about the destruction of our enemies.

As I said to Odo, it was no great surprise that the vile sheriff would betray his own promise. Truth be told, we fairly expected it. That is why we had hurried from the abbey to the town ahead of Abbot Daffyd to ensure that the sheriff would release the captives once the stolen goods were returned. I reckon that each of us, in some corner of our hearts, knew it was all too likely de Glanville would show his true colours that grim night.

Now that it was over, however, Bran had stewed and fretted and worked himself into a towering rampage. 'The man is a craven butcher,' spat Bran, pacing around the hearth. Fleeing the town, we had ridden all night to reach Cél Craidd; none of us had slept, nor could we. Though exhaustion heaved heavy rollers upon us, we sat around the low-flickering fire and listened to our lord give voice to his anger.

In the time I had been among the Grellon, I had picked up hints and suggestions that our Lord Bran sometimes suffered from black, unreasoning rages. But I had never seen it for myself . . . until now.

'He must be stopped,' snarled Bran, smashing his fist against his thigh with each word. 'God as my witness, he will be stopped!'

'De Glanville had no intention of keeping his word,' Iwan pointed out. 'He meant to kill as many as he could from the start. I'd like to see him dance on the end of that leather rope.'

'It may be too late for that,' said Tuck quietly. As everyone turned toward him, he yawned hugely and said, 'He may be dead already. I saw him struck, did I not?'

'It's true,' I affirmed. 'I saw it, too.'

'He took an arrow maybe,' allowed our incensed lord. 'But I won't rest until I've seen his head on a pole.'

'For a certainty,' Tuck insisted, 'I saw him go down.'

'He might have been struck, but was he killed?' Bran glared around at us as if we were a troop of enemy soldiers sprung up to surround him. 'Was he killed?' Bran demanded, his voice aquiver with passion. 'Is he dead?'

There was no way for any of us to know that beyond a doubt; when the time came to flee, we had all cleared off like smoke. We had done what we could do, the few of us, and were in danger of overstaying our welcome. So with the confusion at its height, we used the chaos in the town square to cover our retreat.

'I was not counting bodies,' remarked Iwan; he glanced around, somewhat defiantly. 'Nor did I see anyone else with a tally stick.'

'De Glanville must have been killed,' said Mérian. 'If he took an arrow, he must be dead by now. Bran, calm yourself. It is over and done. You saved those men, and the Ffreinc have been dealt a blow. Be satisfied with that.'

Bran regarded her with a look of cruel disdain, but he held his tongue. When he could trust himself to speak again, he said, 'Dead or alive, we must know beyond a doubt. One way or the other, we must find out.'

'We'll know soon enough,' pointed out Tuck. 'Word will spread.'

'Aye, but late in coming here,' suggested Siarles.

'Unless someone went to Llanelli to find out,' said Bran, using the Welsh name for the place. Like all true sons of Elfael, our Bran refused to dignify the Norman name of Saint Martin's by uttering it aloud.

'None of us can go,' Iwan said. 'They know us now. We'd be caught and strung up on sight.'

'Someone who has never been there, then,' said Tuck, thinking aloud.

'Or,' added Bran, glancing up quickly, 'someone who goes there all the time . . .' Turning to Siarles, he said, 'Fetch Gwion Bach. We have a chore for him.'

Well, before anyone could gainsay the plan, the boy was found and brought to sit with the council. A quick, intelligent lad, he is, as I say, a mute and such a furtive little sneak that he easily flits from place to place with no one the wiser, and so quiet folk don't often know he's around. The townsfolk had long since grown used to seeing him here and there, and it is a fair bet that no one thought anything of it when he appeared the evening following what the alarmed citizens of Saint Martin's are now calling the Twelfth Night Massacre.

Iwan and I walked him to the edge of the forest and beyond as far as we dared go, then left him to hurry on his way into town. It was long past dark by the time we returned. Gwion stayed in town overnight, God knows where, and returned to Cél Craidd late the next day. The winter sun was almost down when he appeared, red-cheeked from his run through the frosty air. Bran had food and drink ready and waiting for him, but the boy would not sit down, less yet touch a bite, until he had delivered his charge. He fairly danced with excitement at being included in the plans of his elders.

'Good lad, good,' said Bran, kneeling down in front of him. 'Did you learn what we want to know?'

Gwion nodded so hard, I thought his head might fall off.

'Is the sheriff alive?' asked Iwan, unable to restrain himself.

Bran gave the big man a perturbed glance, and said, 'Is he alive, Gwion? Is the sheriff still alive?'

The boy nodded again with undimmed enthusiasm.

'And the count?' asked Tuck. 'He was hit, too? Did the count survive?'

The boy turned wide eyes towards the friar and lifted his shoulder in an elegant shrug. 'You don't know?' asked Mérian.

The boy shook his head. He did not know how the count fared, but the sheriff, it seemed, had indeed survived.

Bran thanked the boy with a hug, and dismissed him to his supper with a pat on the head and chuck under the chin. 'So now!' he said, when Gwion had gone. 'It seems the sheriff lives. I think we must invite him to Cél Craidd and arrange a suitable welcome for him when he arrives.'

The anger, which I had allowed myself to imagine had burned itself out between times, leapt up – renewed, refreshed, and just as poisonous as before – all in that blinding instant. I saw the darkness draw a veil across his eyes and his grin become malicious, frightening. 'Hear me now,' he said, his voice a smothered whisper, 'this is what we are going to do . . .'

When he had delivered his demands to us, we were allowed to go rest and eat, and prepare ourselves for the fight ahead. I walked by Nóin's hut, and although it was early yet, could discern no light from a welcome fire in the hearth. I reckoned she had given up waiting for me and gone to sleep. I was that tired myself that I left her and the mite to their rest and took myself off to my own cold bed.

Thus, I did not see Nóin until the next day. She had heard all about the Twelfth Night battle, of course, and was that heartily glad we had freed the captives and lived to tell the tale. She was not best pleased, however, to learn that we could not be wed just yet on account of Lord Bran's plan to host a visit by the sheriff.

'And how do you imagine the sheriff will agree to come?' she asked in all innocence.

'I do not imagine for one moment that old Richard Rat-face will agree to anything we say or do,' I replied.

'Then how — ,' she protested.

'Shh!' I laid a fingertip to her lips, and then kissed them. 'Enough questions now. I cannot tell you any more than I have.'

'But—'

'It is a secret until all is in order. I've said too much already,' I whispered. 'Let us talk of something else.'

'Very well,' she agreed with grudging reluctance, 'let us talk of our wedding. Tuck is here now, and I've been thinking that—'

She must have seen my face fall just then, for she said, 'Now what is the matter? What have I said?'

'Nothing,' I replied. 'All is well, truly, love. It is just that we cannot be married yet.'

'And why not?' Nóin frowned dangerously, warning me that my explanation had better be good enough to save a hiding.

In the end, since I could not tell her what Bran was planning, I simply replied, 'It seems I must go away again.'

'Go?' she asked. 'Where this time?'

'Not far,' I said. 'And it will only take a day or so — but we are leaving at once.'

She sighed and tried to smile. 'Ah, well, I suppose I should be grateful you bothered to come back at all.'

Before I could think what to say to that, she rose. 'Come back to me when you can stay, Will Scarlet,' she said. I saw the sheen of tears in her eyes as she turned away.

'Nóin, please don't.'

But she was already gone.

Iwan found me a short time later. 'Ready, Will?'

'It makes no matter,' I grumbled.

'Then let us be about our work.'

Our work was to reassemble the wagons we had taken apart in the Christmas raid. Bran's plan was simple, but required a little preparation. While Iwan, Tomas, Siarles, and I carried our tools and fittings into the wood and set about putting the wains back together, some of the other Grellon gathered the other items we would need in order to make Bran's plan succeed.

In all, it took most of the day to make the wagons serviceable once more and fortify the woodland alongside the road. When we finished, Bran inspected the work and declared that all was ready. Early the next morning, as the others made their way to the wagons leading the oxen, I enjoyed a warm dip-bath and a change of clothes – I was to pass as the servant of a Saxon merchant – and then, armed with only a knife in my belt, I lit out for Saint Martin's.

After a brisk ride, I approached the town on the King's Road and entered the square as the bell in the church began tolling. At first I imagined it was some kind of alarm, and braced myself to ride away again in retreat. But it was only the summons to midday prayers; it drew few worshippers and no soldiers at all. Plucking up my courage, I dismounted, walked to the guardhouse, and knocked on the door.

After a few moments standing in the cold, the door opened and a young soldier looked out. Seeing no one but a rough Saxon standing before him, he said, '*Quel est? Que voulez-vous, mendiant?*'

This was spoken rudely, as one would speak to a bothersome dog. I do not think he even expected an answer, for before I could make a reply, he began to shut the door. '*Arrêter, s'il vous plaît! Un moment.*'

Hearing his own language spat back at him like that, he paused and opened the door once more. 'Please, Sire,' I said, feeling the French words strange in my mouth, 'I was told I would find the sheriff here.'

'You were told wrong,' he said, then pointed to a large house across the square. 'He lives there.'

I thanked the soldier for his trouble and walked across the town square. So far, the plan was holding together. Now that I knew where the sheriff could be found and that I could trust myself in marketplace Ffreinc it was time to get down to business. I knocked on the door that opened onto the street. 'A word, if you please,' I said to the man who answered. He appeared to be a servant only — whoever he was, I knew it was not the sheriff. 'I have come to see the sheriff on an urgent matter.'

'What would that be?' inquired the fella.

'It is a matter for His Honour, the sheriff, himself alone,' I said. 'Are you Sheriff de Glanville?'

'No, I am his bailiff.' Without another word, he opened the door wider and indicated that I was to come inside. 'This way,' he said. Closing the door behind him, he led me up stone steps to the single large room which occupied the upper floor. A fire burned in a stone fireplace and, near it, a heavy table had been set up. Richard de Glanville sat in a big, thronelike chair facing the fire, his legs and feet covered by a deerskin robe. There was a young gyrfalcon perched on a wooden stand next to him.

'What?' he said without taking his gaze from the fire. 'I told you I was not to be disturbed, Antoin.' I noticed his voice was thick in his throat.

239

'Please, my lord sheriff,' I said, 'I have come from Hereford with a message from my master.'

'I do not care if you have come from hell with a message from the devil,' he snarled with unexpected savagery. 'Go away. Leave me.'

The bailiff called Antoin gave me a half shrug. 'As you see, he is not feeling well. Come back another time, maybe.'

'Is he injured?' I asked, trying to determine if, in fact, he had been wounded in the skirmish as Tuck believed.

'No,' replied Antoin. 'Not that way.'

'Bailiff!' growled the sheriff from his chair. 'I said to leave me alone!' He did not turn from staring at the fire.

'It would be best to come back another time,' Antoin said, turning me toward the door once more.

'This is not possible,' I said. 'You see, my master is a gold merchant. He and some other merchants are on the way to Saint Martin's today. He has sent me to beg soldiers to help us through the forest.' I lowered my voice and added, 'We have been hearing worrisome tales about a, ah, phantom of the wood, this King Raven, no? We beg protection, and we can pay.'

Antoin frowned. I could see him wavering.

'My master has said he will gladly pay anything you ask,' I told him. 'Anything reasonable.'

'Where is your master now?'

'They were already entering the forest when I left them on the road.'

'How many?'

'Four only,' I answered, 'and two wagons.'

He considered this a moment, tapping his chin with his finger. Then he said, 'A moment, please.'

Leaving me by the door, he walked to where the sheriff was seated and knelt beside the chair. They exchanged a brief word, and Antoin rose quickly and returned to me. 'He has agreed to provide you with an escort. See to your horse and wait for me in the square outside. I will summon the men and meet you there.'

'Very well, Sire,' I said, ducking my head like a dutiful vassal. 'Thank you.'

I returned to the square and watered my mount in a stone trough outside the guardhouse, then waited for the sheriff and his soldiers to appear. While I waited, I observed the square, searching for any signs of the battle that had taken place only a few nights before.

There were none.

Aside from a few hoofprints in the churned-up mud and, here and there, a darker stain which might have been made by blood, there was nothing at all to suggest anything more than a Twelfth Night revel had taken place. Even what was left of the gallows had been removed.

I wondered about this. Why take away the gibbet? Was it merely that it was not needed now that the captives would not be executed? Or was there more to it – an end to the sheriff's hanging ways, perhaps?

I determined to find out if I could. When Bailiff Antoin appeared a short time later, I found my chance. Quickly scanning the double rank of knights, I did not see the one man I wanted. 'Where is Sheriff de Glanville?' I asked.

'He has asked me to lead the escort,' said Antoin.

Just like that our deception was dashed to pieces.

'Will he come later?' I asked, climbing into the saddle. Mind whirling like a millwheel in the race, I tried my best to think how to rescue our shattered plan.

'No,' replied the bailiff, 'he will remain here and await our return. Ride on; lead the way.'

That is how I came to be leading a company of six knights, a bailiff, and three men-at-arms into the forest – and myself to my doom.

CHAPTER 30

Ogof Angharad

I t had taken far longer to reach the cave than she hoped. The deep
snow underfoot made for slow going, and now, as Angharad toiled
up the long steep track leading to the rock cave, she wished she had
left Cél Craidd earlier. Already, there were stars peeping between the
clouds to the east; it would be dark before she could get a fire going.
Exhausted, she paused and sat on the cracked bole of a fallen tree to
rest for a moment and catch her breath for the final climb up to the
cave entrance.

She listened to the silence of the forest, keen ears straining for
wayward sounds. All she heard was the tick of branches settling in
the evening air and, far off, the rasping call of a rook coming in to
roost. The distant, lonely sound moved her unexpectedly. She loved
the winter and the night. She loved the forest, and all its wonders –
just one of innumerable gifts bestowed by a wildly benevolent
Creator.

'Before Thee, may I be forever bowing, Kindly King of All
Creation,' sighed Angharad, the prayer rising gently upward with the

visible mist of her breath. And then, leaning on her staff, much more heavily than before, she continued on her way.

Upon reaching the small level clearing halfway up the hill, she paused again to catch her breath. The day would come when she would no longer have the strength to climb up to her *ogof*, her cave house.

The snow lay undisturbed, deep and crisp and white before the open black entrance. All was as it should be, so she moved quickly inside, throwing off her tuck bag and cloak at the threshold. Then, gathering the dry kindling from its place by the cave mouth, she carried it to the fire ring. Working in utter darkness, her deft fingers found the steel and flint and wisps of birch bark, and soon the rosy bloom of a fire was spreading up through the mass of broken twigs. With patience born of long practice, Angharad shepherded the flames, slowly feeding in larger branches until the fire spread its rosy glow over the interior of the cave.

Rising from her knees, she removed her shoes and her wet, cold robe and drew the undershift over her head, then hung the damp garments from hooks set in the rock walls of the cave so that they could dry. She unrolled her favourite bearskin nearer the still-growing fire and lay down. Closing her eyes, she luxuriated in the blessèd warmth seeping into her ancient bones.

After a time, she roused herself, and, wrapping herself in a dry cloak she kept in a basket in the cave, she began to prepare a simple meal, singing as she worked. She sang:

O Wise Head, Rock and Redeemer,
In my deeds, in my words, in my wishes,
In my reason, and in the fulfilling of my desires, be Thou.
In my sleep, in my dreams, in my repose,

In my thoughts, in my heart and soul always, be Thou.
And may the promised Son of Princely Peace dwell,
Aye! in my heart and soul always.
May the long-awaited Son of Glory dwell in me.

Taking the stone lid from a jar, she placed a double handful of barley meal into a wooden bowl, adding a splash of water from the stoup and a bit of lard from the leather tuck bag she had brought with her. She kneaded the dough and set it aside to rest while she filled her kettle and put it on the fire to boil. Next she formed the dough into small cakes and set them on the rounded stones of the fire ring.

Then, while waiting for the water to boil and the cakes to bake, she resumed her song . . .

In my sleep, in my dreams, in my repose,
In my thoughts, in my heart and soul always, be Thou.
Thou, a bright flame before me be,
Thou, a guiding star above me be,
Thou, a smooth path below me be,
And Thou a stout shield behind me be,
Today, tonight, and ever more.
This day, this night, and forever more
Come I to Thee, Jesu —
Jesu, my Druid and my Peace.

She rested, listening to the fire as the flames devoured the fuel and the water bubbled in the kettle. When the water reached the boil, she roused herself and turned the cakes. Then she rose and, taking a handful of dried herbs and roots from another of her many jars and baskets, she cast the stuff into the steaming bath, removing the kettle from the fire to allow the mixture to steep and cool.

When it was ready, she poured some of the potion into a wooden bowl and drank it, savouring the mellow, calming effect of the brew as it eased the stiffness in her old muscles. She ate a few of the cakes, and felt her strength returning. The warmth of the fire and food, combined with the exertions of the last days, made her drowsy.

Yawning, she rose and carried some more wood to the hearth so that it would be close to hand. Then, banking the fire for the night, she lay down to sleep. She stretched out on the bearskin, and pulled her cloak over her and along with it a covering made from the downy pelt of a young fallow deer. There was no special significance to these but, like the wise women of old who esteemed the hides of the red ox for qualities friendly to dreams and visions, Angharad had always had good luck with this particular combination.

At once, exhaustion from her long walk overwhelmed her and dragged her down into the depths of unknowing. She fell asleep with the words of her song still echoing through her mind and heart . . .

In my sleep, in my dreams, in my repose,
In my thoughts, in my heart and soul always, be Thou.
Thou, a bright flame before me be,
Thou, a guiding star above me be,
Thou, a smooth path below me be,
And Thou a stout shield behind me be,
Today, tonight, and ever more.

She had come to her cave to dream. She had come to think, and to spend time alone, away from Bran and the others, in order to discern the possible paths opening before them into the future. Following the last raid, the feeling had come upon her that Bran stood at a crossing of the ways.

It may have been the appearance of the baron's odd gifts – the gold ring and embroidered gloves and mysterious letter – which filled her with sick apprehension. But the count's swift retaliation in burning the forest indicated that the theft was far more damaging than any of them had yet suspected.

This did seem to be the case. Whatever value those particular objects possessed was far beyond silver or gold; it was measured in life and death. This is what concerned Angharad most of all. Not since the coming of King Raven to the greenwood had anything like this happened; she did not know what it meant, and not knowing made her uneasy. So she had come to her snug ogof to seek an answer.

All along the way, as she trudged through the deep-drifted snow, she had turned this over in her mind. As her aged body stumped along, her agile mind ranged far and wide through time and realms of ancient lore, searching out the more obscure pathways of knowledge and knowing, means now largely forgotten.

As a child, sitting at the feet of Delyth, her people's wise hudolion, little Angharad had seen how the old woman had cast a pinch of dry herb powder into the flames as she stirred her porridge. Taking a deep breath, she had announced that the hunting party that had been away for three days was returning.

'Go, Bee.' That was her nickname for young Angharad. 'Go tell the queen to fill the ale vat and fire the roasting pit, for her husband will soon arrive.' Angharad knew better than to question her banfáith, so she jumped up and darted off to deliver the message. 'Three pigs and four stags,' Delyth called as the youngster scampered away. 'Tell her we will be entertaining strangers as well.'

Before the sun had quartered the sky, the hunting party rode into the settlement leading pack animals bearing the dressed carcases of three big boars and four red deer stags. With them, as the banfáith had said, were strangers: three men and two boys from Penllyn, a cantref to the north, who were to be their guests.

That was not the first or last time she had witnessed such fore-telling of events, but it was the time she asked how the banfáith gained this knowledge. 'Knowledge is easy,' the old woman told her. 'Wisdom is hard.'

'But how did you know?' she persisted. 'Was it in the smoke?'

Banfáith Delyth smiled and shook her head. 'When something happens, little one, it is like casting a rock into a pool – it sends ripples through the subtle currents of time and being.' Her fingers lightly bounced as if tracing such ripples. 'If you know how, you can follow all the rings back to where they began and see the rock that made them.'

'Can you teach me?' she had said, blissfully ignorant of what she was asking.

Banfáith Delyth had cupped her small face in her wrinkled hand and gazed deep into her eyes for a long time. 'Aye, yes, little Bee. I think I can.' In that moment, Angharad's life and destiny had been decided.

The cave had been Delyth's ogof, and that of the hudolion before her, and so on. Now, a lifetime or two later, she was about to call on those same skills she had first learned from her wise teacher so many, many years ago.

It would take all her considerable skill and experience to succeed. Events which had happened so far away were much more difficult to discern; their ripples – she still thought of it that way – were faint and diffused by the time they reached Angharad's cave in the forest. She would have to be on her best mettle to learn anything useful at all. But if she was right in thinking that the appearance of the baron's curious gifts signalled an event of great significance, the ripples cast in the pool of time and being would be more violent, and she still might be able to learn something about what, and who, had caused them.

She slept and rose early, but rested. The herbal tincture had done its restorative work, and she felt clearheaded and ready to proceed. She built up the fire from coals smoored the night before, and set about making some porridge on which to break her fast. It was dark outside yet; the sun would be late rising. So she lit a few of the clay candle pots she had scattered around the cave, and soon the dark interior was glowing with soft, flickering light. She had brought a bit of cooked meat with her, and decided to warm it up, too. If all went well, she would need a little flesh to carry her through until she could eat again.

After she had eaten, Angharad went outside, knelt in the snow, and as a pale pink sun broke in the east, she lifted her hands in a morning prayer of thanksgiving, guidance, and protection. When she finished, she walked to an alcove deeper in the cave and took up the hide-wrapped bundle there — her harp. Returning to the hearth, she settled herself on her three-legged stool and began to play, stroking the strings, tuning them as needed, limbering up fingers that were no longer as supple as they had once been.

After a time, the music began to work its ancient magic. She could feel her body relax as her mind began to drift on the music, as a leaf drifts on the river's flow. She felt all around her the dip and swirl of time, like the tiny flutters of butterfly wings causing minute eddies in the air. She imagined herself standing to her thighs in a wide, slow-flowing stream and resting her fingertips lightly on the surface of the water so as to feel each tiny wave and ripple as it passed. Each of these, she knew, was some small happening in Elfael or beyond.

It was always the same picture in her mind: the broad easy-moving water, dense with the myriad particles of random happenstance, glowing like pale gold beneath a sky of sunset bronze in the time-between-times. She moved deeper into the warm wash and felt the water surge around her, gently tugging against legs and gown as she stood there — head held to one side as if listening, her face intent, but calm — touching the sliding skin of the river as it flowed.

After a time, her hands fell from the harp strings and found their way to a small jar she had placed beside her stool. She withdrew a pinch of a pungent herb and dropped it into the flames, just as Delyth had done so long ago. The smoke rose instantly — a clean, dry, aromatic scent that seemed to sharpen her inner sight and touch. She imagined she could feel the ripples more easily now as her fingers played among them.

There were so many, so very many. She shrank within herself to see how many there were and each one connected in some way to another and to many others. It was impossible to know which of all those flowing ripples bore significance for her. She lifted her fingers to the strings and began strumming the harp once more, holding in her mind an image of the ring and the gloves, demanding of the flowing stream to bring her only those waves and ripples where the ring and gloves could be felt.

It took monumental patience, and ferocious concentration, but at last the river seemed to change course slightly — as when the tide, which has been rising all the while, suddenly begins to ebb. This it does between one wave and the next and, while there is nothing to signal the change, it is definite, inexorable, and profound. The flow of time and being changed just as surely as the tide, and she felt the inescapable pull of events flowing around her — some definite and fixed, others half-formed and malleable, and still others whose potential was long since exhausted. For not everything that happened in the world was fixed and certain; some events lingered long as potentialities, influencing all around them, and others were more transient, mere flits of raw possibility.

As a child might dangle its fingers in the water to attract the tiny fish, Angharad trailed her fingers through the tideflow of all that was, and is, and is yet to be. She imagined herself strolling through the water, feeling the smooth rocks beneath her bare feet, the shore moving and changing as she walked until she came to a familiar bend. She had dabbled here before. Taking a deep breath, she stretched out her hands, tingling with the pulse of possibility.

There!

She felt a glancing touch like the nibble of a fish that struck and darted away. An image took shape in her mind: A host of knights past numbering, all on the march, swarming over the land, burning as they advanced, crushing and killing any who stood in their way. Black smoke billowed to the sky where they had passed. At the head of this army she saw a banner – bloodred, with two golden lions crouching, their claws extended – and carrying the banner, a man astride a great warhorse. The man was broad of shoulder and gripped the pole of the banner in one hand and a bloody sword with the other; he bestrode his battle horse like a champion among men. But he was not a mere man, for he had flames for hair and empty pits where his eyes should be. The vast army arrayed behind this dread, implacable lord carried lances upraised – a forest of slender shafts, the steel heads catching the livid glimmer of a dying sun's rays.

Inwardly, she shrank from this dread vision, and half turned away. Instantly, another image sprang into her mind: a broad-beamed ship tossed high on stormy waves, and a rain-battered coastline of a low, dark country away to the east. There were British horses aboard the ship, and they tossed their heads in terror at the wildly rocking deck. This image faded in its turn and was replaced by another: Bran, bow in hand, fleeing to the wood on the back of a stolen horse. She could feel his rage and fear; it seared across the distance like a flame. He had killed; there was blood behind him and a swiftly closing darkness she could not penetrate — but it had a vague, animal shape, and she sensed a towering, primitive, and savage exultation.

The image so shocked her that she opened her eyes.

The cave was dark. The fire had burned out. She turned towards the cave entrance to see that it was dark outside. The whole day had passed, maybe more than one day. She rose and began pulling on her dry clothes, dressing to go out. She wished she had thought to prepare something to eat; but she had rested somewhat, and that would have to keep her until she reached Cél Craidd.

If she left at once and walked through the night, she could be there before nightfall tomorrow. Knowing she was already too late to prevent whatever had taken place — something terrible, she could feel it like a knife in her gut — she nevertheless had to go now, if only to tend the wounded and gather up the broken pieces.

CHAPTER 31

Well, here I was twixt hammer and anvil, no mistake. I had little choice but to carry on as best I could, hoping all the while that when we reached the meeting place in the forest I might alert Bran to the disaster before the trap was sprung. Our plan to capture the sheriff when he arrived to escort the merchant's wagons depended wholly on de Glanville's eagerness to catch King Raven. Not one of us had foreseen the possibility that he would choose to stay home.

As I led those knights and soldiers into the wood on that clear bright day, I felt as if I was leading them to my own funeral . . .

Odo thinks this is funny. He stifles a chuckle, but I see his sly smirk. 'Tell me, monk,' says I, 'since you know so much – which is funnier, a man about to die speaking of funerals? Or a priest laughing at death while the devil tugs at his elbow?'

'Sorry, my lor—' He catches himself again, and amends his words. 'Sorry, Will, I didn't mean anything. I thought it amusing, is all.'

'Well, we live to entertain our betters,' I tell him. 'The condemned must be a constant source of pleasure for you and your bloody Abbot Hugo.'

'Hugo is not my abbot.' This he says in stark defiance of the plain facts. 'He is a disgrace to the cloth.'

How now! There is a small wound a-festering, and I poke it a little, hoping to open it more.

'Odo,' I say, shaking my head, 'is that any way to talk about your spiritual superior?'

'Abbot Hugo is not my spiritual superior,' he sniffs. 'Even the lowest dog in the pack is superior to him.'

This is the first time I'd ever heard him dishonour the abbot, and I cannot help but wonder what has happened to turn this dutiful pup against his master. Was it something I said?

'I do believe you are peevish, my friend,' I say. 'What has happened to set your teeth on edge?'

Odo sighs and rolls his eyes. 'It is nothing,' he grunts, and refuses to say more. I coax but, stubborn stump that he is, Odo will not budge. So, we go on . . .

We followed the King's Road up from the Vale of Elfael and into the bare winter wood. Bailiff Antoin was more than wary. He was not a fool, mind. He knew only too well what awaited him if King Raven should appear out of the shadows. Yet, give him his due, he showed courage and good humour riding into the forest to offer protection to the merchants. All the soldiers did, mind, and most were eager to take arms against the phantom.

I was the Judas goat leading these trusting sheep to the slaughter.

True, I did not know what Bran would do when he saw that the sheriff was not with us. The bailiff noticed my fretful manner and tried to reassure me. 'You're worrying for nothing,' he said. 'The raven creature will not attack in daylight. He only comes out at night.'

Where he had picked up this notion, I have no idea. 'You would know best, Sire,' I replied, trying to smile.

The road rose up the long slope into the wood, eventually following the crest a short distance before beginning the long descent into the Valley of the Wye. The soldiers maintained an admirable wariness; they talked little and kept their eyes moving. They were learning: if not to fear the wood and its black phantom, then at least to show a crumb of respect.

The road is old and descends below deep banks for much of the way; here and there it crosses streams and brooks that come tumbling out of the greenwood. Little humps of snow still occupied the shadows and places untouched by the sun. The going is slow at the best of times, and on that winter day, with the weak sunlight spattered and splayed through bare branches, little puffs of mist rising from the rocks or roots warmed by the sun, eternity seemed to pass with every dragging step. The men grew more quiet the deeper into the wood we went. I was thinking that we must be near to meeting the wagons when I heard the low bellow of an ox and the creaking of wooden wheels. I raised myself in the saddle to listen.

A moment later, the first wagon hove into view. I saw Iwan walking beside the lead ox, holding a long goad. In his merchant's clothing — a long wool cloak, tall boots, and a broad belt to which a fat purse was attached — he seemed only slightly more tame than usual. He was shaved, and his hair had been trimmed to make him appear more like a merchant, or the guard of a travelling trader. The other wagon was some distance behind, and I could only just make it out as it lumbered toward us, bumping along the rutted road.

I did not wait for Bailiff Antoin to make the first move. 'There they are!' I called. 'This way!'

With a slap of the reins, I rode on ahead, leaving the Ffreinc to come on at their own pace. I wanted a word with Bran before they arrived.

Rhi Bran was sitting in the second wagon, which was being led by Siarles. I rode directly to Bran. He smiled when he saw me and raised his hand in greeting, but the smile quickly faded. 'Trouble?'

'De Glanville is not with us,' I said. 'He would not come, and sent his bailiff instead.'

Bran's eyes narrowed as his mind began to work on the problem. Iwan joined us just then, and I explained what I had just told Bran. 'Do you think he suspected a trap?'

I shook my head. 'He is sick, I think – maybe from the wound he took on Twelfth Night. He would not leave his chamber.'

Iwan cast a glance at the advancing soldiers. We had but a moment more before a decision would be needed.

Siarles said, 'We cannot send them back, I suppose.'

Said I, 'Maybe you could go explain to them that they are no longer needed.' Siarles frowned and gave a snort of derision, then turned to Bran to see what he would say.

We were all looking at Bran by then. It was time to decide.

'Well, my lord?' I asked. 'What will you do?'

'We will go on.' Bran smiled and raised his hand as the bailiff came riding up. 'Come back and speak to me when we reach the town.'

'All is well,' I told Antoin in my broken French. 'They say there has been no sign of the phantom of the wood.'

'We will not see that black coward today,' the bailiff declared, but I noticed he cast a hasty glance 'round about just to make certain he had not spoken too soon. He called a command for some of his men to fall in behind the last wagon and guard the rear. 'If you are ready,' he said, wheeling his horse, 'we will move along. We must hurry if we are to reach Saint Martin's by nightfall.'

'Lead the way, my lord,' I said, and accompanied him to the front of the train.

'Only two wagons?' asked Antoin as we began the return journey.

'Only two,' I confirmed. 'Why do you ask?'

He shrugged. 'I thought it would be more. Where are they from?' he asked.

'From the north country,' I told him. The southern Ffreinc knew little about anything beyond the Great Ouse. 'It is a hard winter up there. Trading is easier in the south this time of year.'

Antoin nodded as if this were well known, and we made our way up the slope to the crest of the ridge once more, the wagons rumbling slowly behind us. Every now and then the bailiff would ride off to one side and look back to reassure himself that all was as it should be. As we started down into the Vale of Elfael, I wondered what Bran was thinking, and how we would make good the deception. We might have posed as the traders we professed to be, but we had no goods to trade; we had a few pelts and some other odds and ends, but that was only for show. Once we reached the market square, we would be discovered for the rascals we were.

Now and again I found a chance to look back, but Bran was too far behind and I could not see him. I tried slowing down so as to drop back to speak to him, but the bailiff kept everyone moving, saying, 'Step up! Step up! Don't fall behind. We want to reach the town before dark.'

Indeed, the sun was well down by the time we left the forest. Clouds were drifting in from the west, and the wind was picking up – a wild night in the offing. We came to the fording place where the road crossed the stream that cuts through the floor of the valley. 'The animals need water,' I called. Before the bailiff could say otherwise, I slid down from the saddle and gave my horse to drink. One by one, the others joined us at the ford. While the oxen drank, I sidled over to where Bran was standing.

'What are we to do?' I asked, smiling and nodding as though we talked of nothing more consequential than the weather.

'It will be almost dark by the time we reach the square,' he said. 'So much the better. Tell the bailiff we mean to make camp for the night behind the church, and that we will set out our wares in the morning. I'll explain the rest when they've left us alone.'

I nodded to show I understood, and then felt his hand on my shoulder. 'Nothing to fear, Will,' he said. 'We'll just have a little further to ride when we snatch de Glanville – nothing more. All will be well.'

I nodded again, and then walked back to my mount.

Bailiff Antoin called to his men to move the wagons on, and we were soon rolling again: down and down, into the valley, leaving the protection of the forest behind. The clouds thickened and the wind sharpened. The sun set as the first wagon passed Castle Truan, the old caer, Bran's former home. Though we were that close we could almost reach out and touch the wooden palisade, Bran gave no sign that he knew the place. As we passed, one of Count De Braose's men came out to meet us on the road, and I feared he might make trouble. He and Antoin exchanged a brief word and he rode back up to the fortress; we continued on to the town, which we could see in the near distance.

The wind fell away as we rounded the foot of the fortress mount. A silvery pall of smoke hung over the town. Folk were expecting a cold night and had already built their fires high. I could well imagine the warmth of those flames burning brightly on the hearth and longed to stretch my cold bones beneath a tight roof. The soldiers, seeing we were within sight of the town and there were no bandits lurking on the hilltops, asked to be relieved of duty. The bailiff turned to me and said, 'The town is just there. You are safe now.'

I thanked him for his good care and said, 'We will make camp behind the church and offer trade tomorrow. Pray, do not trouble yourself any longer on our account.'

'Then I will bid you good night,' said Antoin. He made no move to leave until I dipped my fingers into the leather purse at my belt and drew out some silver. I dropped the coins into his palm and his fist closed over them. Without a word, he signalled to the others; his men put spurs to their mounts and they all galloped for home.

I wheeled my mount and hurried back to the second wagon. 'They're away home,' I told Iwan in the first wagon as I passed him. 'Keep moving.' Reining in beside Bran, I said, 'They've gone on ahead to town. I thanked them and explained that we'd make camp behind the church. I don't think they suspect anything.'

'Good,' said Bran. 'We should have some time to work.' Rising in his seat, he turned and looked back the way we'd come. I thought he was looking at the fortress, but he said, 'Now where did those other soldiers get to?'

'Other soldiers?' I asked. 'They all returned to Saint Martin's.'

'All but three,' said Bran. 'There were five behind us, and only two rode on.'

Now I looked back along the trail to see if I might catch sight of the missing three. I saw nothing but a dull grey mist rising with the oncoming night. 'I don't see anyone.'

'It would be good to know what happened to them.'

'Could they have stopped at the caer?' I wondered.

Bran shrugged. 'More likely stopped to pee.' He turned around again, and said, 'Lead on, Will. Let's get to the church.'

It was well and truly dark by the time we reached the little town square. No one was about. The mud underfoot had hardened with the cold and crunched under the heavy wagon wheels. A single torch burned outside the guardhouse, and it fluttered in the rising wind. Of our escort of soldiers, there was no sign. No doubt, they had already stabled their horses and gone in to their supper. The thought of a hot meal brought the water to my mouth and made my stomach gurgle.

As we passed the stone keep of the guardhouse, a burst of laughter escaped into the square. It was the sound of soldiers at their drink – a fella has only to hear that once to know it whenever he hears it again. Crossing the square, we passed the church and made our way to the little grove behind. We put the wagons in the grove, unhitched the oxen, and led them to the wall of the church, where they might get some shelter from the wind. We tethered them so they might graze, and left them. 'Gather round,' said Bran, and we formed a tight circle around him as he explained how we were to proceed. 'But before we go any further, we must get some horses,' he concluded.

'Leave that to me,' said Iwan. 'Siarles and I will get them.'

Bran nodded. 'Then Will – you and I will fetch the sheriff. Tomas,' he said, turning to the young Welshman, 'you wait here and ready our weapons. Pray, all of you, that we don't need them.'

We all crept to the corner of the church and looked across to the stables. 'God with you,' said Bran.

'And you,' said Iwan; then he and Siarles moved out into the square. They walked quickly, but without seeming to hurry.

A half-moon sailed high overhead, shining down through rents in the low clouds. They reached the stables and let themselves in. Bran turned to me, his smile dark and sinister. 'Ready, Will?'

I nodded, and told him what to expect inside the sheriff's house. 'Maybe I should lead the way.'

We hurried along the wall of the church and then passed in front of the entrance. I thought I could hear the monks praying inside as we moved off towards the sheriff's house. We paused at the door, and as I put my hand to the latch, Bran eased the sword from where it had been hidden beneath his cloak. 'Sick or not, I do expect de Glanville to come along quietly,' he said. 'But I would prefer not to kill him.'

'It may come to that,' I said. Pushing open the door, we began to climb the stairs to the upper floor as quietly as we could. Even so, de Glanville heard us. '*Cela vous, Antoin?*' he called out in Ffreinc, his words slurred in his mouth.

I hesitated and glanced at Bran. 'Answer him,' he whispered.

'Antoin?' the sheriff called again.

'*Oui, c'est,*' I replied, speaking low, trying to make my voice sound as much like the bailiff's as I could – easier to do, I discovered, in Ffreinc than Saxon.

'*Venir,*' he said, '*le vin de boisson avec moi.*'

'*Un moment,*' I called. To Bran, I whispered, 'I think he wants us to come drink with him.'

'Right friendly of him,' whispered Bran. 'Let us not keep him waiting.'

We started up the stairs; I let my feet fall heavily on the wooden treads to cover the sound of Bran's lighter steps behind me.

We entered together, pausing in the doorway to take in the room, which was deep in shadow; the only light came from the fire in the hearth, which had burned low. The sheriff was still sitting wrapped in his deerskin robe before the hearth; the remains of a meal lay scattered over the nearby table.

'*Remettre votre manteau,* Antoin,' said de Glanville, '*et dessiner une chaise près du feu.*'

'Take him now!' whispered Bran in my ear. I felt his hand on my back urging me forward as he sprang past me into the room.

De Glanville sensed the sudden surge towards him, but made no move to prevent us or call out. He simply turned his head as we rushed to his chair, Bran on one side and myself on the other. He did not seem especially surprised to see us, but when he languidly raised his hand as if to fend us off with backward flick of his wrist, I saw that he understood something of the danger descending upon him.

'Drunk as a bishop,' I said. 'He's probably been sucking the bottle all day.'

A lazy smile spread across the sheriff's narrow rat face. '*Vous n'êtes pas Antoin,*' he said, the wine rank on his breath. '*Où est Antoin?*'

'Look at him,' I said, shaking my head with disgust. 'Doesn't even know who we are.'

'Good,' replied Bran. 'It makes our chore that much easier.' Taking de Glanville's arm, he pulled the sheriff to his feet, where he stood swaying like a willow wand in a gale.

'He can't walk,' I said. 'We'll have to carry him.'

'Take his feet.' Bran allowed the sheriff to topple gently backwards and caught him under the arms. Stooping, I grabbed his ankles, and together we slung him between us and started hauling him down the stairs and out the door. De Glanville, unresisting, allowed himself to be rough handled all the way to the bottom. He revived somewhat as we stepped outside and the cold air hit him. He moaned and rolled his head from side to side.

We started out across the square and, as we passed in front of the church, the door opened and out came a gaggle of monks carrying torches. Prayers finished, I suppose they were returning to the abbey and were brought up short by the sight of two men makin' off with a third.

'Tell them he's drunk and we're taking him home,' Bran said. 'Quick, Will, tell them!'

I did as he commanded, and that might have succeeded — as indeed we thought for a fleeting moment that it had — but for the knights that appeared out of the night. We heard the sound of hooves and turned to see the three missing soldiers pounding into the square.

There we were, Bran and Will Scarlet with Sheriff de Glanville slung between us like a bag of wet corn — thieves caught with the plunder in hand.

'*Arrêt! Vous, arrêtez là-bas!*' shouted the foremost knight.

'He says we are to halt,' I told Bran.

'I got that. Keep going,' urged Bran. 'We'll lose them when we get to the horses.'

'*Ils ont tué le shérif!*' shouted another.

I might have misunderstood, but that brought me up short. 'They've recognised the sheriff,' I gasped. 'They think we've killed him.'

'Tell them they're wrong,' said Bran. 'Tell them he's a friend of ours fallen drunk. But for God's sake, keep moving!'

I shouted back as Bran commanded, but the knights came on regardless. As they drew nearer, I saw that one of them carried a bulky bundle across the back of his horse. As the knight passed into the torchlight, I saw a dark head of hair and small arms hanging limply down and knew at once what they had captured.

'Bran!' I hissed, dropping the sheriff's heels. 'They've got Gwion Bach!'

CHAPTER 32

T he knights rode on, drawing their weapons as they came. One of them shouted for us to halt. *'Arrêt! Arrêt!'* Bran released the sheriff's shoulders. De Glanville landed heavily on the frozen ground, which seemed to revive the fella somewhat. He grunted and rolled over.

We streaked down the side of the church, shouting to Iwan and Siarles that we were attacked. We rounded the corner to discover that those two had not yet returned from the stables. But Tomas was there, waiting with longbows strung and swords unsheathed. We each grabbed a bow and a handful of arrows and spread out, keeping the wall of the church behind us.

The soldiers did not stop to help the sheriff — no doubt they thought him dead already — but came pounding around the corner of the church and into a sharp hail of arrows. We loosed at will. One rider was struck high in the chest and thrown over the rump of his mount.

The two remaining knights tried to swerve out of the way, but horses are far from the nimblest creatures afoot. As they slowed to turn, we drew and loosed again. A second knight went down, and the third – the one with Gwion bound to his saddle – threw his hands high in surrender.

'Get the horses!' shouted Bran. Tomas and I ran to catch the two riderless mounts, and Bran took care of the third. He gestured with a strung arrow for the knight to dismount and lay down flat on the ground, then ever so gently lifted the head of the boy. 'Gwion? Gwion, wake up.'

The lad opened his eyes, saw Bran, and began to cry. Bran untied him double quick, lifted him down from the horse, and began rubbing the warmth back into the little 'un's hands and feet. 'Will!' he shouted as I came running back. 'Go see what has happened to Iwan and Siarles.'

I skittered down the side of the church towards the square. The sheriff still lay where we had dropped him, sound asleep again in his drunken stupor. The square was empty; the monks had disappeared – either back into the church or, more likely, they'd scurried off to the abbey. I ran to the stables and quietly pulled open the door. First to meet my eye were three Ffreinc grooms lying on the floor of the stable, dead or unconscious, I could not tell. Iwan and Siarles were cinching the saddle straps of the last two mounts.

'Hsst!' I said, putting my head through the gap in the door. 'What is taking so long?'

Iwan glanced around as he pulled the strap tight. 'We had to put some fellas to sleep,' he said. 'We're ready now.'

'Then hurry!' I said. 'We've been attacked.'

'How many?' asked Siarles, gathering the reins of two fresh horses.

'Three knights,' I said. 'Two are down and the other surrendered. Hurry!'

I pulled open the stable doors, allowing Iwan and Siarles to lead the saddled horses out; they headed down the short ramp and into the quiet square. All was silent and dark.

Just as we started across to the church, however, the door to the guardhouse opened and out swarmed six knights or more. 'Bloody blazes!' I said. 'The monks must have told them. Fly!'

The Ffreinc saw us with the horses and cried for us to stop. Iwan leapt into the saddle of his mount and lit out for the church across the square, with Siarles right behind. I paused to loose an arrow at the soldiers, thinking to take at least one down. I missed the mark, but the arrow buried itself in the door frame. One fella, who was still inside, slammed the door hard, which briefly prevented any more Ffreinc from spilling out.

That was the last of my arrows, so I turned and hightailed it after the others. I ran but a half dozen strides and my leg buckled under me and I fell. In the same instant, a pain like no other ripped through the meaty part of my thigh. Reaching down, I felt the shaft of a lance. The spear had hit the ground and caught me as it bounced up. Even as I lay clutching the wound, with blood streaming through my fingers, I thought, *That was lucky. I could have been killed.* Hard on the heels of this thought came the next: *Will, you bloody fool! Get up or they'll be carving your dull head from your shoulders.*

I got to my feet and staggered forward; my injured leg felt like a lump of wood on fire, but I limped on. Bran and Iwan, mounted now, came charging from around the back of the church, bows in hand. Both loosed arrows at my pursuers, and two soldiers fell, screaming and rolling on the hard winter ground. Siarles, cradling Gwion in the saddle before him and holding the reins of one of the big Ffreinc horses, rode out to meet me. 'Time to go,' he said, tossing the reins to me.

I caught the traces and tried to haul my foot to the stirrup, but could not lift my leg. I tried once and missed. The Ffreinc were almost upon us. 'Go on! Ride!' I said. 'I'm right behind you.'

Siarles wheeled his mount and galloped away without a backward glance as I tried once more to get my clumsy foot into the stirrup. I did catch the bar with my toe, but the horse, frightened by the noise and confusion, jigged sideways. My hands, slippery with blood, could not hold, and the reins slipped from my grasp. Unbalanced on one leg, I fell on my back, squirming on the frozen ground. I was still trying to get my feet under me when the Ffreinc rushed up and laid hold of me.

I glimpsed a swift motion above me, and the butt of a spear crashed down on my poor head . . .

So that, Odo, is how they caught me,' I tell him. He lifts his ink-stained hand from the page and looks at me with his soft, sad eyes. I shrug. 'All the rest you know.'

'The others got away,' he says, and the resignation in his voice is that thick you could stuff it in your shoe.

'They did. Got clean away,' I reply. 'Fortunate for me that the sheriff was sleeping like the drunken lump he was, or I would have been strung high long since. By the time he woke up, Abbot Hugo already had me bound hand and foot and was determined to have his wicked way with me.'

Odo scratches the side of his nose with the feathered end of his quill. He is trying to think of something, or has thought of something and is trying to think how to say it. I can see him straining at the thought. But as I have all the time God sends me, I do not begrudge him the time it takes to spit it out.

'About that night,' he says at last. 'Did Siarles leave you behind on purpose?'

'Well, I've asked myself the same thing once and again. Truth is, I don't know. Could he have helped me get away? He did bring the horse, mind. Could he have helped me more than he did? Yes. But remember, he had Gwion Bach with him, and any help he could have offered me would have risked all three of us. Could he have told Iwan or Bran to come back for me? Yes, he could have done that. For all I know, maybe he did. But then again, the Ffreinc were on me that quick, I don't think anyone could save me getting captured.' I spread my hands and give him a shrug. 'He did, more or less, what I would have done, I suppose.'

'You would have made sure he got away, Will,' Odo asserts.

'Why, Odo, what a thing to say,' I reply. 'A fella'd think you cared what happened to ol' Will here.'

He makes a worm face and looks down at his scrap of parchment. 'You have to remember that it was dark and cold, and everything was happening very fast,' I say. 'I doubt anyone could have done more than they did. It was bad luck, is all. Bad luck from the beginning if you ask me.' I pause to reflect on that night. 'No,' I conclude, 'the only regret I have is that we didn't kill the sheriff when we had the chance.'

'Why didn't you kill him?'

'We had some idea of holding him to justice,' I say, and shake my head. 'I suspect Bran wanted to make him answer before the king. God knows how we would have brought that about. Bran had a way, I guess. He has a way for most things.'

Odo nods. He is thinking. I can see the tiny wheels turning in his head. 'What about the ring and the letter?' he wants to know.

'What about them?'

'Well,' says he, 'who were they for?'

'Now, I've thought about that, too. The letter was addressed to the pope, so I suppose they were for him.'

'Which pope?'

I stare at him. 'The pope – head of the Mother Church.'

'Will, there are two popes.'

Dunce that he is, some of the most fuddling things come out of his mouth. 'There are *not* two popes,' I tell him.

'There are.'

He seems quite certain of this.

I hold up two fingers — my bowstring fingers — and repeat, 'Two popes? I'll wager a whole ham on the hoof that you didn't mean that just now. It cannot happen.'

'It can,' he assures me. 'It happens all the time.'

'See now, Odo, have you been staring at the sun again?' I shake my head slowly. 'Two popes! Whoever heard of such a thing? Next you'll be tellin' me the moon is a bowl of curds and whey.'

Odo favours me with one of his smug and superior smirks. 'I do not know about the moon, but it happens from time to time that the church must choose between two popes. So it is now. I do not wonder that, living in the forest as you do, you might not have heard about this.'

'How in the name of Holy Peter, James, and John has it come about?'

I have him now. A wrinkle appears on Odo's smooth brow. 'I do not know precisely what has happened.'

'Aha! You see! You think to play me for a fool, monk, but I won't be played.'

'No, no,' he insists, 'there are two popes right enough.' It is, he contends, merely that the facts of such an event taking place so far away are difficult to obtain, and more difficult still to credit. All that can be said for certain is that there has been some kind of disagreement among the powers governing the Holy Church. 'Papal succession came under question,' he tells me. 'How it fell out this time, I cannot say. But kings and emperors always try to influence the decision.'

'Now that I can believe, at least.' Indeed, this last did not surprise me overmuch. It is all the same with kings of every stripe; nothing they get up to amazes me anymore. But as Odo spoke, I began to discern the glimmering of suspicion that this strange event and the appearance of the ring and letter in Elfael might in some way share a common origin, or a common end. Find the truth of one, and I might well discover the truth of the other.

'No doubt this is what has caused the rift this time.'

'Go on,' I tell him. 'I'm listening.'

'However it came about, the disagreement has resulted in a dispute in which the two opposing camps have each chosen their own successor who claims to be the rightful pontiff.'

'Two popes,' I mutter. 'Will wonders never cease?'

Odo has been toying with the scrap of parchment before him. 'This is what made me think of it,' he says, and holds up the ragged little shred. There, in one corner of the scrap, someone has drawn a coat of arms. I glance at it and make to hand it back. My hand stops midway, and I jerk back the parchment. 'Wait!'

I study the drawing more closely. 'I've seen this before,' I tell him. 'It is on the ring. Odo, do you know whose arms these are?'

'The arms of Pope Clement,' he says. 'At least, that is what the abbot has said.'

'Abbot Hugo told you that?'

Odo nods.

I regard him with an excitement I have not felt for months. Odo has never lied to me. That is, perhaps, his singular virtue. I think about what he has said before speaking again. 'But see here,' I say slowly, 'it is not Clement we recognise as head of the church. It is Urban.'

'This is the difficulty,' he replies. 'Some hold with Urban, others with Clement.'

'Yes, as you say. Now, Odo, my faithful scribe, tell me the truth.'

'Always, Will.'

'Which Pope does Baron de Braose support?'

He answers without hesitation, his tone flat, almost mocking. 'Clement, of course.'

I hear that in his tone which strikes a tiny spark of hope in my empty heart. 'The way you say it, a fella'd think you didn't entirely approve.'

'It is not for me to approve or disapprove,' he counters.

'Perhaps not,' I allow slowly, desperate to keep alive that wee spark. 'Perhaps not, as you say. Probably it is better to let the kings and nobles fight it out amongst themselves. No doubt they know best.'

Odo yawns and stretches. He gathers his inkhorn and his penknife, stands, and shuffles to the door of my cell, where he hesitates. 'God with you, Will,' he says, almost embarrassed, it seems.

'God with you, Odo,' I reply. When he has gone I lie awake listening to the dogs bark, and thinking that there is something very important in all this two popes business . . . if this dull head of mine could only get a grip on what it might be.

CHAPTER 33

Coed Cadw

The damage was done. In a single ill-advised, ignorant stroke, Bran had dashed Angharad's carefully considered design for defeating the Ffreinc invaders and driving them from Elfael. In a mad, impulsive rush he had destroyed months of subtle labour and, she could well imagine, stirred the ire of the enemy to white-hot vengeance. For this and much else, the hudolion blamed Bran – but, more, she blamed herself. Angharad had allowed herself to believe that she had weaned Bran away from that unreasoning rage that he had possessed when she first met him, that she had at long last extinguished the all-consuming fire of an anger that, like the *awen* of the legendary champions of old, caused the lord of Elfael to forget himself, plunging him into the bloodred flames of battle madness – a worthy attribute for a warrior, perhaps, but unhelpful in a king. No mistake, it was a king she wanted for Elfael, not merely another warrior.

Alas, there was nothing for it now but to pick up the pieces and see if anything could be salvaged from the wreckage of that disastrous attempt to capture the sheriff.

What she had seen in the cave while testing the onrushing stream of time and events had caused her to return to Cél Craidd with as much haste as she could command. Her old bones could not move with anything near their former speed, and she had arrived too late to prevent Bran from acting on his ludicrous scheme. The small warband had already departed for Saint Martin's, and the die was cast.

The wise hudolion was waiting when the raiders returned. Dressed in her Bird Spirit cloak, she stood beneath the Council Oak and greeted them when they returned. 'All hail, Great King,' she crowed, 'the people of Elfael can enjoy their peace this night because you have gained for them a mighty victory over the Ffreinc.' As the rest of the forest tribe gathered, she said, 'I see a riderless horse. Where is Will Scarlet?'

'Captured,' Bran muttered. There was a stifled cry from the crowd, and Nóin rushed away from the gathering.

'Captured, is he?' the hudolion cooed. 'Oh, that is a fine thing indeed. Was that in your plan, Wise King?'

Heartsick over his failure, he knew full well that he had made a grave and terrible mistake and was not of a mood to endure her mockery — deserved as it might be. 'Silence, woman! I will not hear it. We will speak of this tomorrow.'

'Yes,' she croaked, 'the rising sun will make all things new, and the deeds done in darkness will vanish like the shadows.'

'You go too far!' Bran growled. Weary, and grieving the loss of Will, he wanted nothing more than to slink away to his hut and, like the beaten hound he was, lick his wounds. 'See here,' he said, pointing to Gwion Bach as Siarles eased the lad down from his mount. 'We rescued the boy from the Ffreinc. They would have killed him.'

'Oh? Indeed?' she queried, her eyes alight with anger. 'Has it not yet occurred to you that the boy was caught only because he was following you?'

Bran drew breath to reply but, realizing she was right, closed his mouth again and turned away from her scorn.

When Bran did not answer, the old woman said, 'Too late you show wisdom, O King. Too late for Will Scarlet. Go now to your rest, and before you sleep, pray for the man whose trust you have betrayed this night. Pray God to keep him and uphold him in the midst of his enemies.'

That is exactly what Bran did. Miserable in his failure, he prayed the comfort of Christ for Will Scarlet, that the All-sustaining Spirit would keep his friend safe until he could be rescued or redeemed.

The next morning, Lord Bran gathered the Grellon and formally confessed his failure: they had not succeeded in taking the sheriff, and Will Scarlet had been captured instead. Nóin, who already knew the worst, did not join the others, but remained in her hut taking consolation with Mérian. Bran went to her to beg forgiveness and offer reassurance. 'We will not rest until we have secured Will's release,' he promised.

Angharad soon learned of the vow and cautioned, 'The sentiment is noble, but word and deed are not one. It will be long ere this vow is fulfilled.'

'Why?' he asked. 'What do you know?'

'Only that wishing does not make doing easier, my impetuous lord. If our Will is to be rescued, then you must become wiser than the wisest serpent.'

'What does that mean?'

By way of reply, Angharad simply said, 'I will tell you tonight. When the sun begins to set, summon the Grellon to council.'

So as twilight claimed the forest stronghold, the men stoked the fire in the fire ring, and the people of Cél Craidd gathered once more to hear what their wise banfáith had to say.

As Angharad took up her harp, the children crowded close around her feet, but their elders, apprehensive and fearful now, did not join them in their youthful eagerness. Will's fate cast a pall over everyone old enough to understand the likely outcome of his capture, and every thought was on the captive this night.

Looking out upon her audience, Angharad saw the faces grim in the reflected fire glow; and they seemed to her in this moment not faces at all, but empty vessels into which she would pour the elixir of the song which was more than a song. They would hear and, God willing, the story would work in their hearts and minds to produce its rare healing fruit.

As silence descended over the beleaguered group, she began to strum the harp strings, letting the notes linger and shimmer in the air, casting lines of sound into the gathering darkness – lines by which she would ensnare the souls of her listeners and draw them into the story realm where they could be shaped and changed. When at last she judged the fortuitous moment had arrived, she began.

'After the Battle of the Cauldron, when the men of Britain conquered the men of Ireland,' she began, her voice quavering slightly, but gathering strength as she sang, 'the head of Bran the Blesséd was carried back to the Island of the Mighty and safely buried on the White Hill, facing east, to protect forever his beloved Albion.'

Recognition flickered among some of the older forest dwellers as the familiar names of long ago tugged at the chords of memory. Angharad smiled and, closing her eyes, began the tale known as 'Manawyddan's Revenge.'

As the warriors made their farewells and departed for their homes, Manawyddan, chief of battle, gazed down from the hill upon the muddy village of Lundein, and at his companions, and gave a sigh of deepest regret. 'Woe is me,' said he. 'Woe upon woe.'

'My lord,' said Pryderi, a youth who was his closest companion, 'why do you sigh so?'

'Since you ask, I will tell you,' replied Manawyddan. 'The reason is this: every man has a place of his own tonight except one only – and that one happens to be me.'

'Pray do not be unhappy,' answered Pryderi. 'Remember, your cousin is king of the Island of the Mighty, and although he may do you wrong, you have never asked him for anything, though well you might.'

'Aye,' agreed the chieftain, 'though that man is my kinsman, I find it somewhat sad to see anyone in the place of our dead comrade, and I could never be happy sharing so much as a pigsty with him.'

'Then will you allow me to suggest another plan?' asked Pryderi.

'If you have another plan,' answered Manawyddan, 'I will gladly hear it.'

'As it happens, the seven cantrefs of Dyfed have been left to me,' said young Pryderi. 'It may please you to know that Dyfed is the most pleasant corner of our many-coloured realm. My mother, Rhiannon, lives there and is awaiting my return.'

'Then why do we linger here, feeling sorry for ourselves, when we could be in Dyfed?'

'Wait but a little and hear the rest. My mother has been a widow for seven years now, and grows lonely,' explained the youth. 'I will commend you to her if you would only woo her; and wooing, win her; and winning her, wed her. For the day you wed my mother, the sovereignty of Dyfed will be yours. And though you may never possess more domains than those seven cantrefs, there are no cantrefs in all of Britain any better. Indeed, if you had the choice of any realm in all the world, you would surely have chosen those same seven cantrefs for your own.'

'I do not desire anything more,' replied Manawyddan, inspired by the generosity of his friend. 'I will come with you to see Rhiannon and this realm of which you boast so highly. Moreover, I will trust God to repay your kindness. As for myself, the best friendship I can offer will be yours, if you wish it.'

'I wish nothing more, my friend,' Pryderi said. And the next morning, as the red sun peeped above the rim of the sea, they set off. They had not travelled far when Manawyddan asked his friend to tell him more about his mother.

'Well, it may be the love of a son speaking here,' said the young warrior, 'but I believe you have never yet met a woman more companionable than she. When she was in her prime, no woman was as lovely as Queen Rhiannon; and even now you will not be disappointed with her beauty.'

So they continued on their way, and however long it was that they were on the road, they eventually reached Dyfed. Behold! There was a feast ready for them in Arberth, where Cigfa, Pryderi's own dear wife, was awaiting his return. Pryderi greeted his wife and mother, then introduced them to his sword brother, the great Manawyddan. And was it not as Pryderi had said? For, in the battle chief's eyes, the youth had only told the half: Rhiannon was far more beautiful than he had allowed himself to imagine — more beautiful, in fact, than any woman he had seen in seven years, with long dark hair and a high, noble forehead, lips that curved readily in a smile, and eyes the colour of the sky after a rain.

During the feast, Manawyddan and Rhiannon sat down together and began to talk, and from that conversation the chieftain's heart and mind warmed to her, and he felt certain that he had never known a woman better endowed with beauty and intelligence than she. 'Pryderi,' he said, leaning near his friend, 'you were right in everything you said, but you only told me the half.'

Rhiannon overheard them talking. 'And what was it that you said, my son?' she asked.

'Lady,' said Pryderi, 'if it pleases you, I would see you married to my dear friend Manawyddan, son of Llyr, an incomparable champion and most loyal of friends.'

'I like what I see of him,' she answered, blushing to admit it, 'and if your friend feels but the smallest part of what I feel right now, I will take your suggestion to heart.'

The feast continued for three days, and before it had ended the two were pledged to one another. Before another three days had passed, they were wed. Three days after the wedding, they began a circuit of the seven cantrefs of Dyfed, taking their pleasure along the way.

As they wandered throughout the land, Manawyddan saw that the realm was exceedingly hospitable, with hunting second to none, and fertile fields bountiful with honey, and rivers full of fish. When the wedding circuit was finished, they returned to Arberth to tell Pryderi and Cigfa all they had seen. They sat down to enjoy a meal together and had just dipped their flesh forks into the cauldron when suddenly there was a clap of thunder, and before anyone could speak, a fall of mist descended upon the entire realm so that no one could see his hand before his face, much less anyone else.

After the mist, the heavens were filled with shining light of white and gold. And when they looked around they found that where before there were flocks and herds and dwellings, now they could see nothing at all: neither house, nor livestock, nor kinfolk, nor dwellings. They saw nothing at all except the empty ruins of the court, broken and deserted and abandoned. Gone were the people of the realm, gone the sheep and cattle. There was no one left in all Dyfed except the four of them, and Pryderi's pack of hunting dogs, which had been lying at their feet in the hall.

'What is this?' said Manawyddan. 'I greatly fear some terrible tribulation has befallen us. Let us go and see what may be done.'

Though they searched the hall, the sleeping nooks, the mead cellar, the kitchens, the stables and storehouses and granaries, nothing remained of any inhabitants, and of the rest of the realm they discovered only desolation and dense wilderness inhabited by ferocious beasts. Then those four bereft survivors began wandering the land; they hunted to survive and banked the fire high each night to fend off the wild beasts. As day gave way to day, the four friends grew more and more lonely for their countrymen, and more and more desperate.

'God as my witness,' announced Manawyddan one day, 'we cannot go on like this much longer.'

'Yet unless we lie down in our graves and pull the dirt over our own heads,' pointed out Pryderi, 'I think we must endure it yet a while.'

The next morning Pryderi and Manawyddan got up to hunt as before; they broke fast, prepared their dogs, took up their spears, and went outside. Almost at once, the leader of the pack picked up the scent and ran ahead, directly to a small copse of rowan trees. As soon as the hunters reached the grove, the dogs came yelping back, all bristling and fearful and whimpering as if they had been beaten.

'There is something strange here,' said Pryderi. 'Let us see what hides within that copse.'

They crept close to the rowan grove, one trembling step at a time, until they reached the border of the trees. Suddenly, out from the cover of the rowans there burst a shining white boar with ears of deepest red. The dogs, with strong encouragement from the men, rushed after it. The boar ran a short distance away, then took a stand against the dogs, head lowered, tusks raking the ground, until the men came near. When the hunters closed in, the strange beast broke away, retreating once more.

After the boar they went, chasing it, cornering it, then chasing it again until they left the familiar fields and came to an unknown part of the realm, where they saw, rising on a great hill of a mound in the distance, a towering caer, all newly made, in a place they had seen neither stone nor building before. The boar was running swiftly up the ramp to the fortress with the dogs close behind it.

Once the boar and the dogs had disappeared through the entrance of the caer, Pryderi and Manawyddan pursued them. From the top of the fortress mound the two hunters watched and listened for their dogs. However long they were there, they heard neither another bark, nor whine, nor so much as a whimper from any of their dogs. Of any sign of them, there was none.

'My lord and friend,' said bold Pryderi, 'I am going into that caer, to recover our dogs. You and I both know we cannot survive without them.'

'Forgive me, friend,' said Manawyddan, leaning on his spear to catch his breath, 'but your counsel is not wise. Consider, we have never seen this place before and know nothing about it. Whoever has placed our realm under this enchantment has surely made this fortress appear also. We would be fools to go in.'

'It may be as you say,' answered Pryderi, 'but I will not easily give up my dogs for anything – they are helping to keep us alive these many days.'

Nothing Manawyddan could say would divert Pryderi from this plan. The young warrior headed straight for the strange fortress and, reaching it, looked around quickly. He could see neither man, nor beast, nor the white boar, nor his good hunting dogs; neither were there houses, or dwellings, or even a hall inside the caer. The only thing he saw in the middle of the wide, empty courtyard was a fountain with marble stonework around it. Beside the fountain was a golden bowl of exquisite design, attached by four chains so that it hung above the marble slab; but the chains reached up into the air, and he could not see the end of them.

Astonished by the remarkable beauty of the bowl, he strode to the fountain and reached out to touch its lustrous surface. As soon as his fingers met the gleaming gold, however, his hands stuck to the bowl and his two feet to the slab on which he was standing. He made to shout, but the power of speech failed him so he could not utter a single word. And thus he stood, unable to move or cry out.

Manawyddan, meanwhile, waited for his friend outside the entrance to the caer, but refused to go inside. Late in the afternoon, when he was certain he would get no tidings of Pryderi or his dogs, he turned and, with a doleful heart, stumbled back to camp. When he came shambling in, head down, dragging his spear, Rhiannon stared at him. 'Where is my son?' she asked. 'Come to that, where are the dogs?'

'Alas,' he answered, 'all is not well. I do not know what happened to Pryderi, and to heap woe on woe, the dogs have disappeared, too.' And he told her about the strange fortress and Pryderi's determination to go inside.

'Truly,' said Rhiannon, 'you have shown yourself a sorry friend, and fine is the friend you have lost.'

With that word she wrapped her cloak around her shoulders and set off for the caer, intending to rescue her son. She reached the place just as the moon rose, and saw that the gate of the fortress was wide open, just as Manawyddan had said; furthermore, the place was unprotected. In through the gate she walked, and as soon as she had entered the yard she caught sight of Pryderi standing there, his feet firmly planted to the marble slab, his hands stuck fast to the bowl. She hastened to his aid.

'Oh, my son! Whatever are you doing here?' she exclaimed.

Without thinking, she put her hand to his and tried to free him. The instant she touched the bowl, however, her two hands stuck tight and her feet as well. Queen Rhiannon was caught, too, nor could she utter a single cry for help. And as they stood there, night fell upon the caer. Lo! There was a mighty peal of thunder, and a fall of shining mist so thick that the caer disappeared from sight.

When Rhiannon and Pryderi failed to return, Cigfa, daughter of Gwyn Gloyw and wife of young Pryderi, demanded to know what had happened. Reluctantly, Manawyddan related the whole sorry tale, whereupon Cigfa grieved for her husband and lamented that her life to her was no better than death. 'I wish I had been taken away with him.'

Manawyddan gazed at her in dumb disbelief. 'You are wrong to want your death, my lady. As God is my witness, I vow to protect you to my last breath for the sake of Pryderi and my own dear wife. Do not be afraid.' He continued, 'Between me and God, I will care for you as much as I am able, as long as God shall wish us to remain in this wretched state of misery.'

And the young woman was reassured by that. 'I will take you at your word, Father. What are we to do?'

'As to that, I have been thinking,' said Manawyddan, 'and as much as I might wish otherwise, I think this is no longer a suitable place for us to stay. We have lost our dogs, and without them to help in the hunt we cannot long survive, however hard we might try. Though it grieves me to say it, I think we must abandon Dyfed and go to England. Perhaps we can find a way to support ourselves there.'

'If that is what you think best, so be it,' Cigfa replied through her tears; for she was loath to leave the place where she and Pryderi had been so happily married. 'I will follow you.'

So they left the comely valleys and travelled to England to find a way to sustain themselves. On the way, they talked. 'Lord Manawyddan,' said Cigfa, 'it may be necessary while among the English to labour for our living. If that be so, what trade would you take?'

'Our two heads are thinking as one,' replied Manawyddan. 'I have been contemplating this very thing. It seems to me that shoe-making would be as good a trade as any, and better than some.'

'Lord,' the young woman protested, 'think of your rank. You are a king in your own country! Shoe-making may be very well for some, and as good a trade as others no doubt deserve, but it is far too lowly for a man of your rank and skill.'

'Your indignation favours me,' replied Manawyddan ap Llyr. 'Nevertheless, I have grown that fond of eating that it does me injury to go without meat and ale one day to the next. I suspect it is the same with you.'

Lady Cigfa nodded, but said nothing.

'Therefore, I have set my sights on the trade of making shoes,' he said, 'and you can help by finding honest folk to buy the shoes I shall make.'

'If that is what you wish,' said the young woman, 'that is what I will do.'

The two travelled here and there, and came at last to a town where they felt they might settle for a spell. Manawyddan took up his craft and, though it was harder than he had imagined, he persevered – at first making serviceable shoes, then good shoes and, after much diligence and hard labour, fashioning the finest shoes anyone in England had ever seen. He made buckle shoes with gilt leather and golden fittings, and boots of red-dyed leather, and sandals of green with blue laces. He made such wonderful shoes that the work of most other cobblers seemed crude and shabby when compared to his. It was soon voiced aloud through all England that as long as either a shoe or boot could be got from Manawyddan the Welshman, no others were worth having. With lovely Cigfa to sell his wares, the nobles of the realm were soon refusing to buy from anybody else.

Thus, the two exiles spent one year and another in this way, until the shoemakers of England grew first envious and then resentful of their success. The English cobblers met together and decided to issue a warning for the Welshman to leave the realm or face certain death, for he was no longer welcome among them.

'Lord and father,' said Cigfa, 'is this to be endured from these ill-mannered louts?'

'Not the least part of it,' Manawyddan replied. 'Indeed, I think it is time to return to Dyfed. It may be that things are better there now.'

The two wayfarers set off for Dyfed with a horse and cart, and three good milk cows. Manawyddan had also supplied himself with a bushel of barley, and tools for sowing, planting, and harvesting. He made for Arberth and settled there, for there was nothing more pleasant to him than living in Arberth and the territory where he used to hunt: himself and Pryderi, and Rhiannon and Cigfa with them.

Through the winter, he fished in the streams and lakes, and despite the lack of dogs, was able to hunt wild deer in their woodland lairs. When spring rolled around, he began tilling the deep, rich soil, and after that he planted one field, and a second, and a third. The barley that grew up that summer was the best in the world, and the three additional fields were just as good, producing grain more bountiful than any seen in Dyfed from that day to this.

Manawyddan and Cigfa peacefully occupied themselves through the seasons of the year. When harvest time came upon them, they went out to the first hide and behold, the stalks were so heavy with grain they bowed down almost to breaking. 'We shall begin reaping tomorrow,' said Manawyddan.

He hurried back to Arberth and honed the scythe. The following day, in the green light of dawn, he went out to begin the harvest. When he arrived at the field he discovered, to his shock and dismay, nothing but naked stalks. Each and every stalk had been broken off and the ear of grain nipped clean away, leaving just the bare stem.

It fair broke his heart to see it. 'Who could have done this?' he wailed, thinking it must have been English raiders because there were no countrymen near, and no one else around who could have accomplished such a feat in one night. Even as he was thinking this, he hurried on to examine the second field; and behold, it was fully grown and ready to harvest.

'God willing,' said he, 'I will reap this tomorrow.'

As before, he honed the scythe and went out the next morning. But upon reaching the field, he found nothing except stubble.

'O, Lord God,' he cried in anguish, 'am I to be ruined? Who could do such a thing?' He thought and thought, but reached only this conclusion: 'Whoever began my downfall is the one who is completing it,' he said. 'My enemy has destroyed my country with me!'

Then he hurried to examine the third field. When he got there, he was certain no one had ever seen finer wheat fully grown and bending to the scythe. 'Shame on me,' he said, 'if I do not keep guard tonight, lest whoever stripped the other fields will come to carry off this one, too. Whatever befalls, I will protect the grain.'

He hurried home and gathered his weapons, then went out and began guarding the field. The sun went down and he grew weary, but he did not cease from walking around the borders of the grain field.

Around midnight, the mighty lord of Dyfed was on watch when all of a sudden there arose a terrific commotion. He looked around, and lo, there was a horde of mice – and not just a horde, but a horde of hordes! So many mice it was not possible to count or reckon them, though you had a year and a day to do it.

Before Manawyddan could move, the mice descended upon the field, and every one of them was climbing to the tip of a barley stalk, nipping off the ear, and bearing it away. In less time than it takes to tell, there was no stalk untouched. Then, as quickly as they had come, the mice scurried off, carrying the ears of grain with them.

A mighty rage gripped the warrior. He lunged out at the fleeing mice. But he could no more catch them than he could catch the birds in the air – except for one that was so fat and heavy Manawyddan was able to spring upon it and snatch it up by the tail. This he did and dropped it inside his glove; then he tied the end of the glove with a string. Tucking the glove in his belt, he turned and started back to where Cigfa was waiting with a meal for the hungry guardsman.

Manawyddan returned to the simple hut where he lived with Cigfa, and hung the glove on a peg by the door. 'What have you there, my lord?' asked Cigfa, brightening the fire.

'A marauding thief,' replied mighty Manawyddan, almost choking on the words. 'I caught him stealing the food from our mouths.'

'Dear Father,' wondered Cigfa, 'what sort of thief can you put in your glove?'

'Since you ask,' sighed Manawyddan, 'here is the whole sad story.' And he told her how the last field had also been destroyed and the harvest ruined by the mice that had stripped it bare, even as he was standing guard.

'That mouse was very fat,' he said, pointing to the glove, 'so I was able to catch it, and heaven and all the saints bear witness, I will surely hang that rascal tomorrow. Upon my oath, if I had caught any more of the thieves I would hang them all.'

'You may do as you please, for you are lord of this land and well within your rights,' replied the young woman. 'However, it is unseemly for a king of your high rank and nobility to be exterminating vermin like that. It can avail you little to trouble yourself with such a creature. Perhaps you might better serve your honour by letting it go.'

'Your words are wise counsel, to be sure,' answered Manawyddan. 'But shame on me if it should become known that I caught any of those thieving rascals only to let them go.'

'And how would this become known?' wondered Cigfa. 'Is there anyone else, save me, to know or care?'

'I will not argue with you, my daughter,' answered Manawyddan. 'But I made a vow, and since I only caught this one, I will hang it as I have promised.'

'That is your right, Lord,' she replied. 'You know, I hope that I have no earthly reason to defend this creature, and would not deign to do so except to avoid humiliation for you. There, I've said it. You are the lord of this realm; you do what you will.'

'That was well said,' granted Manawyddan. 'I am content with my decision.'

The next morning, the lord of Dyfed made for Gorsedd Arberth, taking the glove with the mouse inside. He quickly dug two holes in the highest place on the great mound of earth, into which he planted two forked branches cut from a nearby wood. While he was working, he saw a bard coming towards him, wearing an old garment, threadbare and thin. The sight surprised him, so he stood and stared.

'God's peace,' said the bard. 'I give you the best of the day.'

'May God bless you richly!' called Manawyddan from the mound. 'Forgive me for asking, but where have you come from, bard?'

'Great lord and king, I have been singing in England and other places. Why do you ask?'

'It is just that I haven't seen a single person here except my dear daughter-in-law, Cigfa, for several years,' explained the king.

'That is a wonder,' said the bard. 'As for myself, I am passing through this realm on my way to the north country. I saw you working up there and wondered what kind of work you might be doing.'

'Since you ask,' replied Manawyddan, 'I am about to hang a thief I caught stealing the very food from my mouth.'

'What kind of thief, Lord, if you don't mind my asking?' the bard wondered. 'The creature I see squirming in your hand looks very like a mouse.'

'And so it is.'

'Permit me to say that it poorly becomes a man of such exalted station to handle such a lowly creature as that. Thief or no, let it go.'

'I will not let it go,' declared Manawyddan, bristling at the suggestion. 'I caught this rascal stealing, and I will execute the punishment for a thief upon it – which, as we all know, is hanging.'

'Do as you think best, Lord,' replied the bard. 'But rather than watching a man of your rank stooping to such sordid work, I will give you three silver pennies that I earned with song if you will only pardon that mouse and release it.'

'I will not let it go – neither will I sell it for three pennies.'

'As you wish, mighty lord,' said the bard. And taking his leave, he went away.

Manawyddan returned to his work. As he was busy putting the crossbeam between the two gallows posts, he heard a whinny and looked down from the mound to see a brown-robed priest riding towards him on a fine grey horse.

'Pax vobiscum!' called the priest. 'May our Great Redeemer richly bless you.'

'Peace to you,' replied Manawyddan, wondering that another human being should appear so soon. 'May the All Wise give you your heart's desire.'

'Forgive my asking,' said the priest, 'but time moves on and I cannot tarry. Pray, what kind of work occupies you this day?'

'Since you ask,' replied Manawyddan, 'I am hanging a thief that I caught stealing the means of my sustenance.'

'What kind of thief might that be, my lord?' asked the cleric.

'A low thief in the shape of a mouse,' explained the lord of Dyfed. 'The same who, with his innumerable comrades, has committed a great crime against me – so great that I have now no hope of survival at all. Though it be my last earthly act, I mean to exact punishment upon this criminal.'

'My lord, rather than stand by and watch you demean yourself by dealing so with that vile creature, I will redeem it. Name your price and I will have it.'

'By my confession to God, I will neither sell it nor let it go.'

'It may be true, Lord, that a thief's life is worthless. Still, I insist you must not defile yourself and drag your exalted name through the mud of dishonour. Therefore, I will give you three pounds in good silver to let that mouse go.'

'Between me and you and God,' Manawyddan answered, 'though it is a princely sum, the money is no good to me. I want no payment, except what this thief is due: its right and proper hanging.'

'If that is your final word.'

'It is.'

'Then you do as you please.' Picking up the reins, the priest rode on.

Manawyddan, lord of Dyfed, resumed his work. Taking a bit of string, he fashioned a small noose and tied the noose around the neck of the mouse. As he was busy with this, behold, he heard the sound of a pipe and drum. Looking down from the *gorsedd* mound, he saw the retinue of a bishop, with his sumpters and his host, and the bishop himself striding towards him. He stopped his work. 'Lord Bishop,' he called, 'your blessings if you please.'

'May God bless you abundantly, friend,' said the satin-robed bishop. 'If I may be so bold, what kind of work are you doing up there on your mound?'

'Well,' replied Manawyddan, growing slightly irritated at having to explain his every move, 'since you ask, and if it concerns you at all — which it does not — know that I am hanging a dirty thief which I caught stealing the last of my grain, the very grain which I was counting on to keep myself and my dear daughter-in-law alive through the coming winter.'

'I am sorry to hear it,' answered the bishop. 'But, my lord, is that not a mouse I see in your hand?'

'Oh, aye,' confirmed Manawyddan, 'and a rank thief it is.'

'Now see here,' said the bishop, 'it may be God's own luck that I have come upon the destruction of that creature. I will redeem it from its well-deserved fate. Please accept the thirty pounds I will give you for its life. For, by the beard of Saint Joseph, rather than see a lordly man as yourself destroying wretched vermin, I will give that much and more gladly. Release it and retain your dignity.'

'Nay, Lord Bishop, I will not.'

'Since you will not let it go for that, I will give you sixty pounds of fine silver. Man, I beg you to let it go.'

'I will not release it, by my confession to God, for the same amount again and more besides. Money is no use to me in the grave to which I am going since the destruction of my fields.'

'If you free the mouse,' said the satin-robed one, 'I will give you all the horses on the plain, and the seven sumpters that are here, and the seven horses that carry them.'

'I do not want for horses. Between you and me and God,' Manawyddan replied, 'I could not feed them if I had them.'

'Since you do not want that, name your price.'

'You press me hard for a churchman,' said the lord of Dyfed. 'But since you ask, I want, more than anything under heaven, the return of my own dear wife, Rhiannon, and my good friend and companion, Pryderi.'

'As I live and breathe, and with God alone as my witness, they will appear the moment you release that mouse.'

'Did I say I was finished?' asked Manawyddan.

'Speak up, man. What else do you want?'

'I want swift and certain deliverance from the magic and enchantment that rests so heavily upon the seven cantrefs of Dyfed.'

'That you will have also,' promised the bishop, 'if you release the mouse at once and do it no harm.'

'You must think me slow of thought and speech,' countered Manawyddan, his suspicions fully roused. 'I am far from finished.'

'What else do you require?'

'I want to know what this mouse is to you, that you should take such an interest in its fate.'

'I will tell you,' said the bishop, 'though you will not believe me.'

'Try me.'

'Will you believe me if I tell you that the mouse you hold is really my own dear wife? And were that not so, we would not be freeing her.'

'Right you are, friend,' agreed Manawyddan. 'I do not believe you.'

'It is true nonetheless.'

'Then tell me, by what means did she come to me in this form?'

'To plunder this realm of its possessions,' the bishop answered, 'for I am none other than Llwyd Cil Coed, and I confess that it was I who put the enchantment on the seven cantrefs of Dyfed. This was done to avenge my brother Gwawl, who was killed by you and Pryderi in the Battle of the Cauldron. After hearing that you had returned to settle in the land,' the false bishop continued, 'I turned my lord's war-band into mice so they might destroy your barley without your knowledge. On the first night of destruction the warband came alone and carried away the grain. On the second night they came too, and destroyed the second field. On the third night my wife and the women of the court came to me and asked me to transform them as well. I did as they asked, though my dear wife was pregnant. Had she not been pregnant, I doubt you would have caught her.'

'She was the only one I caught, to be sure,' replied Manawyddan thoughtfully.

'But, alas, since she was caught, I will give you Pryderi and Rhiannon, and remove the magic and enchantment from Dyfed.' Llwyd the Hud folded his arms across his chest and, gazing up to the top of the mound at Manawyddan, he said, 'There! I have told you everything – now let her go.'

'I will not let her go so easily.'

'Now what do you want?' demanded the enchanter.

'Behold,' the mighty champion replied, 'there is yet one more thing required: that there may never be any more magic or enchantment placed upon the seven cantrefs of Dyfed, nor on my kinfolk or any other people beneath my care.'

'Upon my oath, you will have that,' the Llwyd said, 'now, for the love of God, let her go.'

'Not so fast, enchanter,' warned Manawyddan, still gripping the mouse tightly in his fist.

'What now?' Llwyd moaned.

'This,' he said, 'is what I want: there must be no revenge against Pryderi, Rhiannon, Cigfa, or myself, ever, from this day henceforth, forever.'

'All that I promise and have promised, you shall get. And, God knows, that last was a canny thought,' the enchanter allowed, 'for if you had not spoken thus, all of the grief you have had till now would be as nothing compared to that which would have soon fallen upon your unthinking head. So if we are agreed, I pray you, wise lord, release my wife and return her to me.'

'I will,' promised Manawyddan, 'in the same moment that I see Pryderi and Rhiannon standing hale and hearty in front of me.'

'Look then, and see them coming!' said Llwyd the Hud.

Thereupon, Pryderi and Rhiannon, together with the missing hounds, appeared at the foot of the gorsedd mound. Manawyddan, beside himself with joy, hailed them and welcomed them.

'Lord and king, now free my wife, for you have certainly obtained all of what you asked for.'

'I will free her gladly,' Manawyddan said, lowering his hand and opening the glove so the mouse could jump free. Llwyd the Enchanter took out his staff and touched the mouse, and she changed into a charming and lovely woman once more – albeit a woman great with child.

'Look around you at the land,' cried Llwyd the Hud to the lord of Dyfed, 'and you will see all the homesteads and the settlements as they were at their best.'

Instantly, the whole of the country was inhabited and as prosperous as it had ever been. Manawyddan and Rhiannon and Pryderi and Cigfa were reunited, and, to celebrate the end of the dire enchantment, they made a circuit of all the land, dispensing the great wealth Rhi Manawyddan had obtained in his bargain with the enchanter. Everywhere they went, they ate and drank and feasted the people, and no one was as well loved as the lord of Dyfed and his lovely queen. Pryderi and Cigfa were blessed with a son the next year, and he became, if possible, even more beloved than his grandfather.

Here, Angharad stopped; she let the last notes of the harp fade into the night, then added, 'But that is a tale for another time.' Setting aside the harp, she stood and spread her hands over the heads of her listeners. 'Go now,' she said softly, as a mother speaking to a sleep-heavy child. 'Say nothing, but go to your sleep and to your dreams. Let the song work its power within you, my children.'

Bran, no less than the others, felt as if his soul had been cast adrift – all around him washed a vast and restless sea that he must navigate in a too-small boat with neither sail nor oars. For him, at least, the feeling was more familiar. This was how he always felt after hearing one of Angharad's tales. Nevertheless, he obeyed her instruction and did not speak to anyone, but went to his rest, where the song would continue speaking through the night and through the days to come. And although part of him wanted nothing more than to ride at once to Llanelli, storm the gaol, and rescue the captive by force, he had learned his lesson and resisted any such rash action. Instead, Bran bided his time and let the story do its work.

All through the winter and into the spring, the story sowed and tended its potent seeds; the meaning of the tale grew to fruition deep in Bran's soul until, one morning in early summer, he awoke to the clear and certain knowledge of what the tale signified. More, he knew what he must do to rescue Will Scarlet.

CHAPTER 34

I wake in the night all a-fever with the odd conviction that I know what it all means. The letter, the ring, the gloves – I know what this strange treasure signifies, and why it has come to Elfael. For the first time, I am afraid. If I am right, then I have discovered a way to save Elfael, and I fear I may not live to pass on this saving knowledge to those who can use it. Oh, Blesséd Virgin, Peter, and Paul, I pray I am not too late.

I sit in the cold dark and damp of my cell, waiting for daylight and hoping against hope that Odo will come early, and I pray to God that my scribe has true compassion in his heart.

I pray and wait, and pray some more, as it makes the waiting easier.

I am at this a long time when at last I see the dim morning light straggling along the narrow corridor to my cell. I hear Gulbert the jailer stumbling around as he strikes up a small fire to heat his room. I content myself with the sorry fact that our jailer lives only a little better than his prisoners. He is as much a captive of the abbot as I am, if not the more. At least I will leave this rank rat hole one day and he, poor fella, will remain.

Odo is long in coming. I shout for Gulbert, asking if the scribe has been seen, but my keeper does not answer me. He rarely does, and I remain a tightly wrapped bundle of worry until I hear the murmur of voices and then the scrape of an iron door against the stone flags of the corridor. In a moment, I hear the familiar shuffling footfall, and my heart leaps in my chest.

Easy now, Will me lad, I tell myself, *you don't want to scare the scribe; he's skittery enough as it is without you gettin' him up all nervous.* So to make it look like I have been doing anything but waiting for him, I lie back on my musty mat and close my eyes.

I hear the jingle of a key, and the door to my cell creaks open. 'Will? Are you asleep?'

I open one eye and look around. 'Oh, it is you, Odo. I thought it might be the king of England bringing my pardon.'

Odo smiles and shakes his head. 'No luck today, I fear.'

'Don't be too sure, my friend.' I sit up. 'What if I told you I knew a secret that could save our sovereign king from black treachery and murder, or worse.'

Odo shakes his head. 'I know I should be well accustomed to your japes by now . . .' The look in my eye brings him up short. 'I do begin to believe you are in earnest.'

'Aye, that I am, lad.'

I am pleased to see that he is in a mood to humour me this morning. He settles heavily into his accustomed place. 'How will you save King William?'

'I will tell you, my friend, but you must promise me a right solemn oath on everything you hold most sacred in the world – promise me that what I tell you will not pass your lips. You cannot write it down, nor in any other way repeat what I say to another living soul.'

He glances up quickly. 'I cannot.'

'You will, or I will not say another word.'

'Please, Will, you do not understand what you're asking.'

'See here, Odo, I am asking you to pledge your life with mine – no more, no less.' He would look away, but I hold him with the strength of my conviction. 'Hear me now,' I continue after a moment, 'if I am wrong, nothing will happen. But if I am right, then a great treachery will be prevented and hundreds, perhaps thousands of lives will be saved.'

He searches my face for a way out of this unexpected dilemma. All his natural timidity comes flooding to the fore. I can see him swimming in it, trying to avoid being swept away.

Fight it, Odo, boy. It is time to become a man.

'Abbot Hugo . . . ,' he begins, then quits. 'I could never . . . he would find out anything you said . . . he would know.'

'Has he the ears of the devil now? Unless you told him, he would never know.'

'He would find out.'

'How?' I counter. Here is where the battle will be fought. Is his desire to do right stronger than his fear of the black abbot?

After a moment, I say, 'Only the two of us will know. If you say nothing to him, then I fail to see how Hugo will ever know what I mean to tell you.'

He looks at me, his round face a tight-pinched knot of pain.

'It is life and death, Odo,' I tell him quietly. He is that close to fleeing. 'Life and death in your hands.'

He stands abruptly, scattering pen and parchment and spilling his inkhorn. 'I cannot!' he says, and bolts from the cell.

I hear his feet slapping the stones in the corridor; he calls Gulbert to let him out, and then he's gone.

Well, it was a risk doomed from the start. I should have known better than to think he could help. Now escape is my only hope, and it is such a starved and wretched thing it brings sad tears to my eyes. I tug at the chain on my leg and feel the lump in my throat as frustration bites. To hold the solitary answer to the riddle of the baron's treasure — to be entrusted with the key to free Elfael and to be unable to use it — that fair makes the eye-water roll down my whiskered cheeks.

I lie on my filthy bed and think how to get word to Bran, and my head — dull from these weeks and months of captivity — feels like a lump of useless timber. I think and think . . . and it always comes out at the same place. I can do nothing alone. I must have help.

Oh, God, if it is true that you delight in a heartfelt prayer, then hear this one, and please send Odo back.

CHAPTER 35

Odo returns, and so quickly that I am surprised. He has not shown such clear and ready resolve before. There is something on his mind – a blind man could see it – and he has come back with all the bluster of a fella who has made up his mind to embark on a dangerous journey, or a long-neglected chore that will get him mucked up from heel to crown. I do greatly wonder at the wild glint in his soft brown eyes. This is not the Odo I have come to know.

So, here is Odo, standing outside the door of my cell, like a faithful hound returning to a harsh master he would rather forgive than leave. I see he has his parchment and goose feather in one hand and inkhorn in the other as always; but the sharpness in his aspect gives me to know this is not like all the other times.

'Are you coming in, Odo?' I say. He has made no move to join me.

'I have to know something,' he says, glancing down the corridor as if he fears we might be overheard. Gulbert, if he hears anything from the cells at all, is long past caring. 'I have to know beyond all doubt that you will not betray me.'

'Odo,' I reply, 'have we known each other so long that you ask me that?'

'Swear it,' he insists. I hear in his voice what I have not often heard — a little bone and muscle, a little bit of iron. 'Swear it on your soul that you will not betray me.'

'As God is my witness, I swear on my everlasting soul that I will not betray you.'

This seems to satisfy him; he opens the door to my cell and takes his customary place. I see by the firm set of his soft mouth that he is chewing on something too big to swallow, so I let him take his time with it.

'It is the abbot,' he says at last.

'It usually is,' I reply. 'What has he done now?'

'He has been lying to me,' remarks Odo. 'Lying from the very beginning. I have caught him time and again, but said nothing.'

'I understand.'

'No, Will,' replies my scribe, 'you do not. I have been lying to him, too.'

I stare at him. 'Odo, you do amaze me.'

'That is why I rushed away. If I am to do as you ask, I had to make confession. If I am killed, I want to go to God with clean hands and a clean heart.'

'As do we all, Odo. But tell me more about this deception.'

He nods. 'I knew you would not give up Bran — not even to save yourself.'

'Truly, I never would.'

'When I saw that you were a man of honour, I decided to spin the abbot a tale that would keep us talking, but would tell him little.'

Astonished at this turn, I do not know what to say. It seems best to just let him talk as he will. 'Oh?'

'That is what I did. Some of what you said, I used, but most I made up.' He shrugs. 'It is easy for me. The abbot knows nothing of Mérian, or Iwan, Siarles, or Tuck, and what he knows of Bran is mostly fancy.' He allows himself a sly smile. 'The more you told me of the real Bran, the less I told the abbot.'

'Well, you have me, Odo. I don't know what to say.'

But Odo is not listening.

'Abbot Hugo has been lying to me from the beginning. Nothing he says can be trusted. He thinks I am stupid, that I cannot see through his veil of lies, but I have from the start.' He pauses to draw breath. I can see that he is working himself up to do the thing he has come to do. 'Like the letter Bran stole – abbot says it was nothing, a simple letter of introduction only. But if that was true then why was he so desperate to get it back?'

'And they were that desperate, I can tell you,' I said, recalling the Christmas raid. 'A good many men died that night to recover it. I think you can fair be sure it was far more than a letter of introduction.'

'What you said about treachery against the crown . . .' His voice falls to a creaky whisper. 'Knowing the abbot, I do not doubt it. Still, I cannot think what it might be.'

'Nor could I, Odo, nor could I – not for the longest time,' I tell him. 'But the answer was starin' me in the face all along. Blind dog that I am, I could not see it until you showed me where to look.'

'I showed you?' he says, and smiles.

'Oh, aye,' I tell him, and then explain how I tumbled to what the Bloody Baron and Black Abbot were up to at last. He listens, nodding in solemn agreement as I conclude, 'Fortunately, we are not without some tricks of our own.'

'Yes?' He nods and licks his lips, eager now to hear what I propose.

'But as you made me swear on my solitary soul, so must I hear your pledge, my friend. We are in this together now, and you can tell no one – not even your confessor.' This I tell him in a tone as bleak as the tomb which will certainly claim us both if he fails to keep his vow.

Odo hesitates; he knows full well the consequence of what I am about to ask him. Then, squaring his round shoulders, he nods.

'Say it, Odo,' I say gently. 'I must hear the words.'

'On my eternal soul, I will do exactly as you say and breathe a word to no one.'

'Good lad. You have done the right thing,' I tell him. 'It is not easy to go against your superior, but it is the right thing.'

'What do you want me to do?' he says, as if anxious now to get the deed done.

'We must get a message to Bran,' I say. 'We must let him know what is about to happen so he can move against it.'

Odo agrees. He unstops the inkhorn and pares his quill. I watch him as he spreads the curled edge of parchment beneath his pudgy hands – I have seen this countless times, yet this time I watch with my heart in my mouth. *Do not let us down, monk.*

He dips the pen and holds it poised above the parchment. 'What shall I write?'

'Not so fast,' I say. 'It is no use writing in Ffreinc, as no one in Cél Craidd can read it. Can you write in Saxon?'

'Latin,' he says. 'French and Latin.' He shrugs. 'That's all.'

'Then Latin will have to do,' I say, and we begin.

In the end, it is a simple message we devise, and when we finish I have him read it back to me to see if we've left anything out. 'See now, we must think what word to add to let Bran know that this has come from me, and no one else. It must be something Bran will trust.'

It takes me a moment to think of a word or two – something only Bran and I would know . . . about Tuck, or one of the others? . . . Then it comes to me. 'Odo, my fine scribe, at the end of the message add this: "The straw man was shaved twice that day: once by error, and once by craft. Will's the error, Bran's the craft. Yet Will took the prize." This Bran knows to be true.'

Odo regards me with a curious look.

'Write it,' I tell him.

He dips his quill and leans low over the parchment scrap, now all but covered with his tight script. 'What does it mean?'

'It is something known between Bran and myself, that is all.'

'Very well,' says Odo. He bends to the task and then raises his head. 'It is done.'

'Good,' I say. 'Now tuck that up your skirt, priest, and keep it well out of sight.'

'It is my head if I fail,' he says, and frowns. 'But how am I to find Rhi Bran?'

I smile at his use of the name. 'It is more likely that he will find you, I expect. All you have to do is start down the King's Road, and, if you do what I tell you, he'll find you soon enough.' I begin to tell him how to attract the attention of the Grellon, but he makes a face and I stop. 'Now what?'

'I am watched day and night,' he points out. 'I can't go wandering around in the forest. The abbot would catch me before I was out of sight of the town.'

He has a point. 'So, then . . .' I stare at him and it comes to me. 'Then we will look for someone in town – a Welshman. Despite everything, they must come to the market still.'

'Sometimes,' Odo allows. 'Would you trust a Welshman? Someone from Elfael?'

'Would and do,' I reply. 'All the more if the fella knew it was to serve King Raven and Elfael.'

'Tomorrow is a market day,' Odo announces, 'and with the snows gone now there will likely be traders from Hereford and beyond. That always seems to bring a few of the local folk into town. They don't stay long, but if I was able to keep close watch, I might entrust the message to someone who could pass it along.'

Bless me, Mother Mary, there are more things wrong with this plan than right. But in the end, we are left face-to-face with the plain ugly fact that we can do no better. I reluctantly agree, and tell Odo he is a good fella for thinkin' of it. This small praise seems to hearten him, and he hides the scrap of parchment in his robes and then stands to leave. 'I should like to pray before I go, Will,' he says.

'Another fine idea,' I tell him. 'Pray away.'

Odo bows his head and folds his hands and, standing in the middle of the cell, begins to pray. He prays in Latin, like all priests, and I can follow only a little of it. His soft voice fills the cell like a gentle rain and, if only for a moment, I sense a warming presence – and sweet peace comes over me. For the first time in a long time, I am content.

CHAPTER 36

I make it five days since Odo took the message out of the cell. He has not come back, and I fear he has been caught. A weak choice to begin with, true, but if the poor fella'd got even a thimble's worth o' luck he might have got a fair chop at it. I guess even that little was too much to hope for.

No doubt he did his best with the scant handful he was given, but Odo was not born to the outlaw life, like ol' Will, here. I do not hold him to blame.

Blame, now. There is a nasty black bog if ever there was one. If I think about it long enough I come 'round to the conclusion that if blame must be spooned out to anyone at all the Good Lord himself must take the swallow for making it so fiendishly easy for the strong and powerful to crush down the weak and powerless. Would that he had foreseen the host of problems arising from that little error. Oh, but that en't the world we got. I suppose we don't deserve a better one.

I close my eyes on that bitter thought and feel myself begin to drift off when ... what's this, now? I hear the door open at the far end of the corridor. I guess it is Gulbert bringing me some sour water and the scrag end of a mutton bone to gnaw on.

I roll over and look up as he comes to my cell and . . . it's Odo!

He's back, but one look at his pasty face and doleful eyes tells me all is not cream and cakes in the abbey.

'I feared they'd caught you, monk. I reckoned we'd be soon enough sharing this cell. Ah, but look at you now. A face like the one you're a-wearin' could bring clouds to a clear blue sky.'

'Oh, Will . . . ,' he sighs and his round shoulders slump even further. 'I am so sorry.'

'They found the message,' I guess. 'Well, I thought as much. At least they didn't lock you up.'

Odo is shaking his head. 'It's not that.'

'Then?'

'It's something else,' he moans, 'and it's bad.'

'Well, tell me, lad. Ol' Will is a brave fella; he can take the worst you got to give him.'

'They're going to hang you, Will.'

'That much I know already,' I say, giving him a smile to jolly him along a bit. 'If that's all, then we're no worse off than before.'

Odo will not look at me. He stands there drooping like a beaten dog. 'It's today, Will,' he breathes, unable to rise above a whisper.

'What?'

'They mean to hang you today.'

A dozen thoughts spin through my poor head at once, and it fair steals the warm breath from my mouth. 'Well, now,' I say when I have hold of myself once more, 'that is something new, I do confess.'

Odo lets loose another sigh and snivels a little. Bless him, he feels that bad for me.

'Why not tell me what's happened?' I say, for I would rather hear him talk than dwell on my predicament. 'But first, I have to know – did you get the message out? That is the most important thing anyway.'

He nods. 'It was not difficult,' he says, brightening a little as he remembers. 'The first Welshman I found was brother to one of those the sheriff meant to hang on Twelfth Night. He was only too happy to take the message for you.' The ghost of a smile brushes his lips. 'The farmer said we were not to worry. He said he'd get the message to Rhi Bran without fail.'

'Good,' I say, feeling a little of my ruffled peace returning. 'All is well then.' Another thought occurs to me. 'But that was five days ago, as I make it. Why did you not come to tell me sooner?'

'The abbot has returned and said I could not come here anymore. But the day before yesterday some important visitors arrived, and the whole town has gone giddy. Everyone is busy preparing a special reception and feast.'

Who, I wonder, could have come? Instead, I ask him, 'Then why did they let you come today?'

'I begged the abbot to be the one to tell you,' he says, and adds, ever so softly, 'and to shrive you.'

So now, my death is to be for the entertainment of important guests. Well, that is the Normans first and last. The devils can think of nothing better than a good hanging to impress their betters. The notion makes me right angry, it does.

'So, there it is,' I say. Odo cannot find his voice. He just stands there, suddenly miserable once more.

Aye, there it is. I could have wished it had all turned out better. I could have wished Nóin and me had got married, that I'd had the chance to love that good woman as she deserves, that little Nia had known a doting father, and on and on . . . but then a man can wish all he likes his whole life through and it's like flinging a raindrop into the raging sea, and just as much use.

'When is it to be?'

'Before the feast,' he says, and still will not look at me. 'At midday.'

Well, that takes some of the wind out of my sails, to be sure. 'At least,' I say, trying to swallow around the lump in my throat, 'I will not have long to think on it.' I offer a smile, but it is a thin, simpering thing. 'Sitting here dwellin' on a thing like that — why, a fella might lose heart.'

Odo smiles. As quickly as it comes, it is gone again. 'They will come soon. We should begin.'

'Will you come in and sit with me?'

'I was told not to,' he says.

'Odo, please,' I say, 'after all the days we've spent together. At least let us sit together one last time . . . as friends.'

He doesn't have it in him to disagree. He opens the door and steps in, but this time, judging by his mournful expression, it is as if he is entering a tomb. In a way, I suppose he is.

'I know I grumbled and growled like a bear with a sore head most days,' I tell him. 'But I did enjoy our talks. I did.'

'You did all the talking,' Odo points out.

'True,' I agree. 'I reckon a fella never knows what he's got stored up in his purse until it comes time to pay the tax man.'

He smiles again. 'Tax man?'

'We all owe a debt to nature, Odo, never forget. Pay we must.'

He nods sadly. I can see his feelings are running on a razor's edge. He's fighting to keep from melting into a puddle of grief on the floor.

'Shrive me, Odo. I don't want to go to meet our Maker filthy in sin and stinkin' of brimstone. Let's get it done so I can go in peace.'

He brings out a little roll he has tucked into his sleeve. It contains the proper words for a man's last rites. This makes me happier than I could have imagined. I knew I could trust him to see me right. I know our Black Abbot would never have troubled himself as much, and that's a fact. If left to him, I'd be knockin' at heaven's gates one dirty, naked sinner instead of standing in the clean white robe of a saint. Odo has ensured that will not happen now, and for that I am forever grateful.

Aye, and I am that close to forever.

Odo bends his round head and offers a prayer. His voice is gentle and humble as a priest's should be. Although he speaks to God in Latin, I hear that in it that puts me at ease. When he finishes, he says in English, 'God our Father, long-suffering, full of grace and truth, you create us from nothing and give us life. Man born of woman has but a short time to live. We have our fill of sorrow. We blossom like the lowly flowers of the field and wither away. We slip away like a shadow and do not stay. In the midst of life we are in death. Where can we turn for help? Only to you, Lord, who are justly angered by our sins.

'Though we are weak and easily led astray, you do not turn your face from us, nor cast us aside. When we confess, you are right glad to forgive. Hear, Loving God, the final confession of William Scatlocke . . .'
He glances up and says, 'Repeat the words as I say them.'

I nod, and we go on.

'Almighty and most merciful Father, maker of all things, judge of all people, like a poor lost sheep, I have wandered from your ways. I have followed too much my own will and ways. I have offended against your holy laws . . .'

Odo pauses at each hurdle – and I climb over after him. The words are simple and sincere, not like those most priests use, and I know he is trying his best to do right by me.

'We have left undone those things that we ought to have done; and we have done those things that we ought not to have done; and there is no righteousness in us,' he says, and I notice that he is including himself in my prayer now, and it makes me smile.

'We confess that we have sinned against you and our brothers. We acknowledge and confess the wickedness which so often ensnares us. O Lord, have mercy upon us sinners. You spare those who confess their faults. We earnestly repent, and are deeply sorry for all our wrong-doings, great and small. Eternal and merciful judge, both in life and when we come to die, let us not fall away from you. Do not abandon us to the darkness and pain of death everlasting.

'Have mercy upon us, Gracious Redeemer. Restore us as you have promised, and grant, O Merciful Father, that we may enter your peace. Hear us for the sake of your Son, and bring us to heavenly joy, in the name of Jesus Christ our Lord. Amen.'

I add my 'Amen' as he has directed, and then we sit in silence a moment. I feel the thing was squarely done. There is no more to be said, nor need be. I am content.

From down the corridor, I hear the grating whine of the iron door opening and know that my time has run its course. They are coming for me. My heart lurches at the thought, and I draw a deep breath to steady myself.

I have thought about this day every day since I was dragged into Black Hugo's keep. Truth to tell, I thought it would be different some-how, that I would meet the evil hour with a smile and a tip o' my hat. Instead, my bowels squirm and ache, and I feel death's cold hand rest-ing heavy on my shoulder.

There was so much I meant to do, and now the end has come. It is all done but the dyin', and that's a true fact.

CHAPTER 37

Saint Martin's: The Pavilion

'Look! Here he comes,' cried Count de Braose, his voice fluttering high with excitement as the shambling heap of a man appeared at the door of the guardhouse.

The count's visitors turned to see a number of Ffreinc soldiers spilling out of the keep. Armed with lances and led by Marshal Guy, they started across the market square, dragging a ragged wreck between them. The man's hands were bound and his legs were unsteady; he kept listing to one side as if the ground were constantly shifting beneath his feet.

'Oh, he is a rogue!' continued Count Falkes. 'You can tell that simply by looking at him.'

The count's words were directed to the visiting dignitaries, whose arrival two days before had surprised and thrilled the entire population of the emerging town of Saint Martin's. The count's words were translated and conveyed to the others by a priest named Brother Alfonso — a tall, sallow, somewhat sombre and officious monk in a new brown robe. While Count Falkes looked on, smiling, his guests exchanged a brief word amongst themselves. Being Spanish, they were strangers to England and to the rough ways of the March. Most of them bore the swarthy complexion of their countrymen, and the black hair and dark, inquisitive eyes. They professed to find everything fascinating and, in the brief time they had been with him, had shown themselves to be enthusiastic and appreciative guests. Then again, one might expect no less from the personal envoy of none other than Pope Clement himself.

The ambassador, Father Dominic, was far younger than the count would have imagined for one in such an important, nay exalted, position. Dark and slender in his impeccable black robes, he held himself with a solemn, almost melancholy reserve, as if the thoughts inside him bore on body and soul alike and he sagged a little beneath their weight. Though there was dignity and reverence in his glance, his natural expression was the pensive reflection of a man who, despite his youth, had seen and suffered much at the hands of an unrepentant world. His black hair was trimmed short and his tonsure newly shaved. He moved with deliberation, his steps measured and sure as he dispensed priestly blessings to those who looked on.

Attending Father Dominic were two servants – most likely lay brothers but of a hardy sort. Tall and strong and none too genteel, they had no doubt been chosen to protect the envoy on his journey. Besides the interpreter, Brother Alfonso, there were two young women: a young highborn woman of unmistakable nobility, and her maidservant. The lady was quiet, well-spoken, gracious, and possessed of a warm and winsome manner, but also, alas, undeniably plain, with poor skin, dull hair, and discoloured teeth. 'Drab as a farmyard drudge,' was Guy of Gysburne's assessment. 'I prefer her maid.' The sheriff had expressed a similar judgment, if in less kindly terms. Even so, Count Falkes found himself attracted to her despite her plainness and the difficulty imposed by the language divide. He even allowed himself to fancy that she regarded him with something more than passing affection.

'Oh!' gasped Lady Ghisella, averting her eyes at the sight of the condemned man. Her maid followed the lady's example.

'Never fear, my lady,' offered the count, mistaking her reaction. 'He cannot escape. You may rest assured, this one will soon trouble the world no longer.'

Unexpected visitors, their abrupt arrival had initially roused the count's suspicions. On second thought, however, it was more than reasonable given the circumstances: a small party travelling together without an extensive entourage of servants and courtiers might more easily pass unmolested through the countryside and, considering who they represented, would more easily elude the notice of the king. Such a group would not likely draw the unwanted attentions of rival factions and potential adversaries.

Abbot Hugo, who had been south with Count Falkes's uncle, Baron de Braose, at Bramber, had returned to find the dignitaries already established in his abbey. 'All well and good,' he had complained to Falkes, 'but we should have received word of their coming. This is awkward, to say the least.'

'It is nothing of the sort,' the count reassured him. 'You worry too much, Hugo.'

'And you not enough.'

'I suspect it is merely Clement's way of judging the faith and loyalty of those who have pledged to him, before . . . you know . . .' He let the rest remain unspoken.

Abbot Hugo fixed him with an ominous stare. 'No,' he replied stiffly, 'I do not know.'

'Before the fighting begins,' said the count. 'Must I shout it from the rooftop? Think, man. The king will have spies everywhere. It is open rebellion we are talking about.'

The abbot's frown deepened, but he held his tongue.

'See here,' offered Count Falkes, adopting a lighter tone, 'the envoy and his people will only be here another day or two. We will simply entertain them with good grace, reassure them of our intentions, and send them on their way. Where's the harm in that?'

'Why are they here?' demanded the abbot. 'That's what I want to know. His Holiness has given no indication of sending an envoy to England.'

'And does the pope now confide his every private thought to you, Abbot?' Falkes gave an airily dismissive wave of his hand; the movement caused a twinge of pain in his chest – a lingering reminder of the arrow wound that had nearly taken his life. 'All will be well. I propose that we host a feast in their honour and send them on their way.'

'A feast,' murmured Hugo. 'Yes, I think we might do just that. We could also hang that tiresome rogue for them – that should give them something to talk about.'

'Hang the rebel?' wondered Falkes. 'Are you finished with him, then?'

'Long since,' answered the abbot. 'It was folly to hope he would tell us anything worth hearing. It's all a morass of confusion and lies, and so tedious it makes my teeth ache.'

'Well, it cost us little enough to find out,' Falkes countered. 'In any event, it hurts nothing to try.'

'I suppose,' allowed the abbot. 'I should hang him twice over for wasting my time.'

'Well, you would have hanged him anyway in the end,' concluded Falkes. 'De Glanville and I had our disagreements over the Twelfth Night executions, God knows. But I cannot say I will be sorry to see this one dangle. The sooner we rid ourselves of these bandits, the better.'

Now, with the feast about to begin, they were all seated in a hastily erected pavilion facing the open ground behind the church, where some of Marshal Guy's knights and a few of the sheriff's men were performing mock battle manoeuvres. In a show of military might, the great, galloping destriers' hooves threw clots of turf high, churning up the soft earth. The glint of sword blade and lance head blazed like lightning strokes in the bright sunlight; the resounding crack of oak lance shafts, the clank of heavy steel, and the shouts of the soldiers lent excitement to an otherwise ordinary display. The feast-day crowd swarmed the square behind the canopy-covered platform, their voices filling the air with loud, if somewhat forced, levity as they bellowed rude songs and screamed with laughter at the antics of the wandering troupe of tumblers, minstrels, and storytellers the count and abbot had procured especially for the occasion.

At the entrance to Saint Martin's churchyard, a new gibbet had been erected from which to hang the criminal, whose execution was now to mark the occasion of the papal envoy's visit. One sight of the captive as he was escorted from the guardhouse sent the crowd scampering for places from which to view the spectacle. Some cheered, others blew their noses, and still others threw rotten apples and eggs at the bearded, dishevelled prisoner as he was hauled across the square on the arms of his guards.

As the wretch neared the pavilion, Father Dominic summoned his interpreter and whispered something into his ear. Brother Alfonso leaned close, nodded, then turned to the count and said, 'My Lord Count, the envoy says that he is most interested in this case. He would like to know what crime this unfortunate has committed.'

'Pray, tell His Eminence that he is a traitor to the crown,' the count explained. 'He, along with other desperate rebels, has sought to pervert the course of the king's justice, and has on numerous occasions attacked the king's men and prevented them from engaging in their lawful duties. He has incited rebellion against the crown. This, of course, is treason.'

'A very grave crime, indeed,' observed the envoy through his interpreter. 'Is that not so?'

'Indeed,' agreed the sheriff, intruding into the conversation. 'But if that was not enough, this criminal is also a thief. He has stolen money and other valuables from travellers passing through the forest.'

'A very rogue,' agreed the envoy.

'That and more,' said Count Falkes. 'We have good reason to believe that he was part of a gang of outlaws that have plagued this commot since we established our rule in this lawless region. Indeed, we have it from his own lips that he has violated Forest Law by killing the king's deer – also a capital offence.'

As these words were delivered to the envoy, the sheriff added, 'These murderers have been responsible for the deaths of many good men. They answer to one known as King Raven, who styles himself a phantom of the greenwood.'

At this, the special ambassador of Pope Clement turned suddenly, clapped his hands, and exclaimed, 'Rhi Bran y Hud!'

Both count and sheriff were taken aback by this unexpected outburst and regarded the priest with alarm. After a quick word with the ambassador, Alfonso, the interpreter, confided, 'His Eminence says that word of this phantom has reached him.'

'Truly?' wondered Count Falkes, greatly amazed.

'It must be the same,' said Father Dominic through his interpreter. 'There cannot be more than one, surely.'

'Surely not,' confirmed the sheriff. 'But never fear, Your Eminence.

These outlaws cannot elude us much longer. We will bring them to justice. They will all hang before another year is out.'

The condemned man was brought to stand before the nobles and dignitaries in the pavilion. He stared dull-eyed, his expression slack, hair and beard matted and filthy. The sheriff, splendid in his green velvet cloak and belt of gold discs, rose and held up a gloved hand for silence from the swiftly gathering crowd. 'Be it known,' he called out, his voice cutting through the chatter, 'that on this day, in accordance with the rule of law, the criminal William Scatlocke, also known as Scarlet, is put to death for crimes against the crown — namely treachery, rebellion, robbery, and the abuse of the king's sheriff, Richard de Glanville.' The sheriff's eyes narrowed. 'None other than myself.'

He paused to allow these words to be translated for the foreigners, then continued, saying, 'The hour of your death is upon you, thief and murderer. Have you anything to say before justice is served?'

The outlaw known as Will Scarlet glowered at the sheriff and spat. 'Do your worst, de Glanville,' he growled, his voice low. 'We all know who the real rogues are.'

With a disinterested flick of his hand, the sheriff said, 'Take him away.'

'It is said that the Welshmen are cunning archers,' observed Father Dominic as the prisoner was dragged away to the gibbet.

'So they would have their ignorant countrymen believe,' sneered the sheriff. 'Believe me, they are nothing more than a rabble — unruly as they are untrained.'

'Even so, I have heard a Welsh archer can put an arrow into the eye of a blackbird in flight.'

'Tales for children,' said Falkes, with a small, hollow laugh. 'Although, I daresay the Welsh appear to believe it themselves.'

316

'I understand,' replied the envoy through his interpreter. 'As it happens, I myself am an archer.'

'Indeed, my lord?' said Falkes, feigning interest.

'Oh, yes!' said the envoy, his enthusiasm plain, even through the remove of a translator. 'I count the days spent with a bow in my hand blessed. It helps ease the burden of my office, you see.'

'Well, I suppose,' granted the count, 'it must be pleasant for you.'

'It is the one secular pursuit I allow myself,' continued the envoy, confiding his observations to Alfonso, who dutifully passed them along. 'As a child, I myself often enjoyed hunting with a bow on my father's estate in Spain. I know well enough what such a weapon can do in the hands of one well schooled in its use. You are right to fear the rebels.'

'We do not fear them,' insisted the sheriff. 'It is merely that . . .' Unable to finish this assertion in a convincing way, he paused, then concluded lamely, 'They do not fight fairly.'

The prisoner was brought to stand beneath the gallows, and the rope was knotted and thrown over the short stout gibbet arm. The soldiers began tying the victim's legs with short bands of cloth.

'I see,' replied Father Dominic when the sheriff's words had been made clear to him. He shrugged, then smiled, turned to Lady Ghisella beside him and exchanged a brief word, whereupon the envoy suddenly announced, 'My cousin would like to see the Welshman ply the bow.'

'What!' asked the sheriff, looking around suddenly. The request caught him off guard.

'But that is not possible, Your Eminence,' said Count de Braose. 'A man like that' – he flung his hand towards the group at the gallows – 'must not be given a deadly weapon under any circumstances.'

'Ah, I understand,' said Father Dominic through his translator. 'It is that you fear him too greatly. I understand. Perhaps there is something in this children's tale you speak of after all, no?'

'No!' said Abbot Hugo, at the count's silent urging, 'Pray do not misunderstand. It is not that we fear him, but merely that it would be unwise to allow him to lay hands to the very weapon he has used to kill and maim our soldiers. He is a condemned man and must be executed according to the law.'

At this the papal envoy's ordinarily woeful features arranged themselves in a wide grin of pleasure. Brother Alfonso turned and announced, 'His Eminence wishes to assure you that he is looking forward to the execution as much as anyone, but suggests that there is good sport to be had before it takes place. These affairs are, after all, very short-lived, shall we say.' The sallow monk smiled at his wordplay. 'It is a commonplace in Italy and elsewhere, that wagers are placed on such things as how many kicks the condemned will produce, how long he will swing before he succumbs, or whether he will piss himself, things like this. A good wager heightens the enjoyment of the occasion, yes?'

'I see,' replied the count coolly. 'What sort of wager does your master think appropriate here?'

After a quick consultation, Brother Alfonso replied, 'His Eminence suggests that a demonstration of some sort would be amusing.'

'Perhaps,' granted the count. 'What sort of demonstration?'

'As an archer himself, Father Dominic is especially keen to see this prisoner's skill.'

'Well, I suppose something might be arranged,' Count Falkes conceded at last. 'If it is what our guest wants, I see no good reason to deny him.'

'No. Wager or no, it is impossible,' declared the sheriff. 'Out of the question.'

But the discussion had already moved on. 'His Eminence suggests that as his own skill with the bow is exceptional, he begs the boon of participating in an archery contest with the condemned, and that in accordance with the best tradition the prisoner be allowed to draw for his freedom.'

'What?' wondered the sheriff in slack-jawed dismay at the insane proposal.

Brother Alfonso continued, 'His Eminence says that the contest can have no meaning or excitement without consequences, and of course the only prize to rouse the poor wretch's interest would be the chance to draw for his life.'

'If His Eminence should fail, a dangerous criminal – one who has attacked me personally, mind! – would be spared the consequences of his crimes. Justice would be made a laughingstock.'

'The man has been in your dungeons for how long?'

'Five months or so,' replied the sheriff. 'Why?'

'Five months is a very great punishment in itself,' observed Brother Alfonso. 'Aside from that, Father Dominic will no doubt hold the advantage over the prisoner and wishes to assure you that the wretch will hang this day. Nevertheless, there must be a prize at stake – otherwise the sport is meaningless.'

It took a moment for the emissary's meaning to become absolutely clear. 'An archery contest,' considered Count Falkes carefully, 'with freedom of the prisoner as the prize.'

'It is what the pope's ambassador wants,' answered Brother Alfonso. 'Lady Ghisella would be much amused as well. They are certain to carry back a good report to His Holiness.'

Both sheriff and count appealed to Abbot Hugo, who had suddenly become very quiet and thoughtful. 'Well? Speak up!' hissed the sheriff. 'Tell His Eminence it is impossible. The rogue hangs here and now, and that is that.'

'But it is not,' whispered the abbot sharply in reply. 'Our guest seems determined to have his way, and Baron de Braose would not be pleased to hear that we refused the envoy any simple request it was in our power to grant.'

'Any simple request!' muttered the sheriff in a strangled voice. 'We cannot risk setting that rogue free.'

'Nor will we,' Hugo assured him. 'Let the pope's fool have his contest. All we need do is make certain the Welshman does not win.'

'He is right,' concluded Falkes. 'My uncle would not look kindly on anything that threatened his good favour with Clement. We must find a way to please His Eminence, however strange the request. Need I remind you that we are not in favour with the baron just now? Letting the legate have this ridiculous contest might be just what we need to return ourselves to the baron's good graces.'

The sheriff gazed at the other two as at men bereft of their reason.

'Find a bow, and let the contest begin,' commanded the count. 'Meanwhile, de Glanville, I think you should go' – he paused so the sheriff would not mistake his meaning – 'and *prepare* the prisoner.'

'Yes,' added the abbot. 'See to it nothing is left to chance.'

'Very well,' answered the sheriff, catching their meaning at last. 'I will attend the prisoner personally.'

Turning to his guests, Count Falkes adopted a grand and gracious air and announced, 'Please convey to His Eminence and his entourage that I am pleased to grant his request. I have therefore arranged for the contest to take place. However, I fear it may not be as entertaining as His Grace might wish. As we shall see, these bandits are not as skilled as they make out.'

'My thanks to you, Lord Count,' said the envoy, and immediately climbed down from the pavilion and began making his way across the grounds towards the gibbet.

'Wait! Your Eminence, a moment, if you please!' cried the count, hurrying after him. 'You must allow us to ready the contest.'

The papal envoy was led back to his place in the pavilion to be entertained by Abbot Hugo; meanwhile, the count hurried on to order a target to be made up, and a bow and arrows to be found and brought to the field.

'This is absurd!' growled Marshal Guy when Falkes explained what was going to take place. 'Is he insane?'

'No doubt,' remarked the count, 'but he has Pope Clement's ear and goodwill. We dare not upset him or give him cause to complain of his reception while he was here.'

The marshal glanced at the pavilion across the greensward. 'What do you want me to do?'

'Just make it look like a reasonable competition between two archers. The sheriff is taking measures to make certain our prisoner is in no way able to win this contest,' said the count, stepping away. 'Do your best to make it look fair, and all will be well.'

Guy de Gysburne looked across to the bound captive with the rope around his neck as he stood waiting beneath the gallows. 'Knowing the sheriff, the contest is well in hand.'

CHAPTER 38

Saint Martin's: The Green

To Will Scarlet, it seemed as if all of Elfael had turned out to see him swing. A bright and festive air hung over the little town, which was alight with flags and the coloured banners of a wandering troupe – the same that was performing tricks in the square to the bawdy laughter of the crowd. Of all those in attendance, only Will himself failed to rise to the full mirth of the occasion. He had other things on his mind as the soldiers half walked, half dragged him out of the guardhouse and across the thronging square. Only a few of the town's citizens left off their merrymaking to watch the condemned man hauled to his doom, and these few were Welshmen who dared come into town, braving the scorn and ridicule of the townsfolk, to witness the death of one of those who had risked his life to prevent the Twelfth Night hangings of their countrymen.

Will Scarlet did not notice the silent Britons looking on from the margins of the celebration. He did notice how very bright the sunlight was and how soft and impossibly fresh the breeze that bathed his shaggy features. How sad, really, that his last moments should be lived out on such a fine, hopeful day in direct opposition to the black gloom that filled his soul. Just his luck, he thought unhappily, to go down to the grave while all the rest of the world was awash in singing and dancing and the glad feast a-roast on the fire. Not to taste a lick of that handsome fare, nor a drop of the ale that would be served up in cups overflowing — now there was real pity.

As the rough procession passed along the side of the stone church, he saw that a platform had been set up for the visiting dignitaries, a pavilion with a splendid blue canopy from which the nobles and their guests could watch him kick his last as the cruel rope choked out his life. The idea of providing sport for these highborn scum roused a fleeting flame of anger he thought might sustain him in his last moments. Alas, this was not to be. For the moment the cold length of braided leather touched his neck and the soldiers began lashing his legs together, anger fled and was replaced by a stark, empty, bottomless fear. *Lord have mercy*, he thought, looking up at the gibbet arm and the clear blue boundless sky beyond. *Christ have mercy on my soul.*

This swift prayer had no sooner winged through his mind than Sheriff de Glanville was standing before him, his sharp features set in a malicious sneer. 'Untie him,' he commanded the soldiers. 'It seems we are to have a little sport before he hangs.'

Will, whose French stretched at least this far, understood from what the sheriff said that death had been delayed a little, and was grateful for even that little. He drew a deep breath as the noose was removed and the bands loosed. From behind the sheriff he saw two dark figures approaching — a tall, slender priest in long black robes, and another, a monk in brown, beside him. Behind these two came the count, hurrying to keep up with the black-robed priest's long, eager strides.

'This is your lucky day, traitor,' de Glanville told him in a low, menacing voice. 'Our guest desires an archery contest. Your life is the prize.' The sheriff eyed him closely. 'Do you understand?'

It took Will a moment to work out what the sheriff had said. There was to be a contest for his life. He nodded. 'I understand,' he replied in Ffreinc.

'Good,' said the sheriff. Taking Will's bound hands in his gauntleted fist, he seized the fingers of his right hand and began to squeeze.

'Just so there will be no mistake,' de Glanville added. Before Will knew what was happening, the sheriff gave his fingers a sudden, vicious twist. There was a pop and crack like that of dried twigs as his finger bones snapped. 'We will make certain you understand who is to win this contest.'

Pain streaked up his arm and erupted in a fiery blast that stole Will's breath away. Tears instantly welled up in his eyes, distorting his vision. He sank to his knees, whimpering with agony and struggling to remain conscious.

'There,' said de Glanville with a satisfied nod. 'Now there will be no surprises.'

The condemned man glowered up at the sheriff, mouthing a silent curse as he cradled his ruined fingers to his chest, tears streaming from his eyes.

He was jerked to his feet again and marched between two knights out onto the centre of the green. There he stood upright as best he could, shaking with the effort. He struggled to keep from weeping from the humiliation of being so easily bettered by his enemies – as much as from the physical pain itself.

While Will was trying to regain some small part of his composure, Marshal Guy of Gysburne appeared with a longbow and bag of arrows. The sight of the bow cast Will into a dismal, all-embracing despair. Here was the instrument of his salvation, now useless to him because of the sheriff's wicked ploy. He could no more draw a bow with broken fingers than he could have walked across the sea to Ireland.

But, what was this? Guy was handing the bow to the tall, dark priest.

Forcing the pain from his mind, Will brought all his concentration to bear on what was being said. Because the marshal's instructions had to be repeated for the visiting priest, Will could just about work out what was happening. They were each to loose three arrows in turn, and the closest to the mark would be declared the winner. The priest gave a sign that he understood and accepted the terms of the contest; no one asked Will if he understood, or accepted, anything.

Then, while a hastily constructed straw man was set up a hundred paces or so down the greensward, the two contestants walked out to take their places, followed by a large, excited crowd of onlookers. Two soldiers stood at Will's elbow, watching his every move. Guy, who was supervising the contest, handed the bow to the priest, saying, 'You will each use the same bow, Your Eminence. Here is the weapon.'

The young priest took the offered bow and tried the string, bending the bow tentatively: back stiff, elbows awry. The action, while not entirely awkward, lacked something of the confidence of great skill. Will, even in his agony, was not slow to see it, and the gesture kindled a flicker of hope in his woeful heart.

That hope leapt up the higher when the priest turned to him and offered the bow, indicating that he should try it as well. 'My thanks,' muttered Will through teeth clenched against the pain in his throbbing fingers.

Although it had been some time since he had held a bow, Will found the instrument balanced well enough; but the draw, when tested with his thumb, was far too loose. Clearly, this was a toy the Ffreinc had either made themselves or found somewhere; it was not the warbow of a Welshman. Still, it might serve for a simple contest; if both of them were to use it, there could be no advantage to either party.

Will made to pass the bow back to his smiling adversary, who waved him off and, taking an arrow from Guy, handed it to the captive and then stepped back to allow him the honour of loosing first.

Sweating now, his jaw clenched so hard he thought his teeth would shatter, Will tried to nock the arrow onto the string. But the injured fingers would not obey, and the arrow slipped from his grasp and fell at his feet. The priest was there in an instant to retrieve it for him. With a flourish of his hand and a smile to the sheriff and Marshal Guy, who stood looking on with unmitigated malice, the envoy indicated that he would allow the condemned man another chance to draw.

Will, with great difficulty and much fumbling, at last fitted the arrow to the string and held it there with his left hand while attempting to hook his swollen, mangled fingers into some semblance of an archer's grip. Sweating and shaking with the effort, he did not so much draw back the string as simply hold it and press the bow forward. The arrow flew from the string with little conviction and described a lacklustre curve to plant its point in the turf a good many yards short of the straw target.

The injured criminal passed the bow to the priest and bent down, arms on his knees, gasping, trying to remain conscious as the pain coursed up through his arm like a fire-spitting snake. Meanwhile, his black-robed rival took up the bow and with far more aplomb nocked the arrow to the string. Marshal Guy gave de Glanville a knowing nudge with his elbow and smiled as the visiting dignitary pulled back and loosed his first arrow. Somehow, what seemed an easy draw suddenly went wildly wrong: the missile flew not out as it should have but almost straight up, spinning sideways in a loopy spiral to land behind the onlookers on the green.

Some of the townspeople gathered around laughed. The priest, still smiling, shrugged and held out his hand for another arrow. Marshal Guy gave him another arrow with the admonition to take his time and aim. Nodding, the priest made a gesture of dismissal and handed the bow and arrow back to his opponent.

Will, his face white and beaded with sweat, took up the bow once more and strained with every nerve, the target swimming before his eyes as he strove to pinch the string between thumb and forefinger. When he could hold the string no longer, he released it and sent the arrow forward in a low arc to skid along the grass, almost reaching the foot of the target.

Full of confidence and beaming with bravado, the priest took the bow and received an arrow from Guy, who repeated his counsel to take time, draw, and aim properly. The priest made a reply, which the translator passed along, saying, 'His Eminence is aware of the problem and will adjust his stance accordingly.'

Taking the arrow, he placed it on the string and, gazing hard at the target, narrowed his eyes and drew the string to his cheek, holding the bow straight and strong in front of him. He released after the briefest pause, and the crowd's eyes followed the path of the arrow as it seemed to streak towards the target. But, wonder of wonders, the arrow did not arrive. A second glance confirmed that it had not, in fact, left the string at all, but there remained dangling, caught somehow, one of its feathered flights ripped off and sent halfway across the green. The arrow fell at the embarrassed priest's feet, its iron point in the ground.

More people laughed now.

'The idiot!' grumbled the sheriff. 'This is no contest. Neither one of them can draw worth a fart.'

'I will draw for the priest,' suggested Marshal Guy. 'I can do no worse than he has done.'

The sheriff stared at him. 'Don't be stupid. The contest has begun,' he grumbled. 'We cannot change now; it would not be seemly.'

'Why not?' demanded the marshal. 'You broke that wretch's fingers – that was not seemly. How did you ever agree to such a thing anyway?'

'He said he could draw!' replied the sheriff. He forced a sour smile and nodded at the envoy.

'He is hopeless,' insisted Guy once more. 'Let me take his place.'

'Too late,' answered the sheriff. 'Everyone is watching now. We cannot be seen to force the outcome.' Scanning the pavilion, he caught sight of Count Falkes and Abbot Hugo frowning furiously at the disaster slowly unfolding before them. 'One more arrow,' he said. 'Make certain the envoy understands what is at stake here.'

Taking the last arrow, Guy of Gysburne handed it to Brother Alfonso, saying, 'This is his last chance to win the contest. Make him understand.'

Brother Alfonso made a bow and turned to confer with the papal emissary, who frowned and snatched the offered arrow with a gesture of haughty impatience. As before, the papal cleric stepped close and passed the bow and arrow to Will Scarlet, who drew a long breath as he took the weapon.

'One more, Will,' whispered the priest. 'It is almost over. I will not let you fail.'

It was all Scarlet could do to catch himself shouting, 'Bran?' For the first time he looked into the face of the man he had been drawing against and recognized his lord and friend.

'Shh!' said the priest with a wink.

'Bloody de Glanville broke my fingers!' whispered Will, his voice tight and quivering with pain.

'Do your best, Will,' Bran whispered. 'Try a left-handed pull.'

The condemned man took the bow and, with a groan and gritting of teeth, wrapped his discoloured fingers around the belly of the bow this time and took the strain against the cradle of his palm and thumb. Then, even as the pain sent flags of ragged black misery fluttering before his eyes, he drew with his left hand, steadied the trembling weapon, and loosed. The arrow slanted up, flashing into the air higher and higher; it seemed to hang momentarily before falling, spent, to the ground at the straw man's feet.

This brought a murmur from the crowd, most of whom had by now worked out what was unfolding before their eyes.

The priest, still gracious, took the bow and waited for the final arrow to be passed to him along with the marshal's stern caution to take care and aim properly this time. Nodding, he nocked an arrow to the string and, even as he bent the bow, Guy stepped in behind him and placed his hands over the priest's, steadying his aim as the priest let fly.

The envoy, shocked at this bold intrusion, gave out a yelp and jerked back. But the arrow was already on its way. This time it flew true, but the distance was woefully misjudged, for the missile sang over the straw man's head and flew on, swiftly disappearing into the long grass far beyond the greensward. The condemned man saw it, knew that he had won the contest, and sank to his knees, tears of relief and agony rolling down his bewhiskered cheeks.

Before anyone could intervene, the black-robed envoy summoned his aide, Brother Alfonso, to take the injured criminal under his care. 'Stupid!' roared the sheriff at Guy. 'What did you do?'

'I was only trying to help,' said the marshal. 'It would have worked, too, if he hadn't pulled so hard.'

The black priest accepted his failure with good grace. Beaming with pleasure, he offered his hand to the condemned man, raising him to his feet. Placing his arm around the criminal's shoulders, the slender

329

priest proclaimed in a loud voice so all could hear, 'I declare the contest was fair and the results are conclusive. This man is the winner!' He paused so that Brother Alfonso could relay his words to the gathering. 'I do not know what he has done to merit his punishment, but let his example teach us the humility of forgiveness and redemption. For all men stand in need of salvation. Therefore, as our Lord's vicar on earth, I stand ready to absolve him of guilt and lead him into the paths of righteousness. I accept full responsibility for his life and will do all in my power to redeem him from his reprobate ways.'

As the startled Ffreinc looked on aghast at what had just taken place, he whispered, 'Never fear, Will, I have you now and will not let you go.'

Will Scarlet, dabbing at his eyes with the back of his hand, clung to the black-robed envoy as to a kinsman long lost. 'God bless you, my lord,' he murmured. 'God bless you right well.'

CHAPTER 39

Hamtun Docks

Mérian gently tied the ends of the rag binding Will Scarlet's wounded hand and tucked the ends under. 'If Angharad was here,' she apologized, 'she would know better what to do for you.' She had carefully straightened his swollen and discoloured fingers and bound each one to a bit of hazel twig Iwan had cut and shaped to serve for splints. She surveyed her work with a hopeful smile. 'Does it hurt much?'

'Not much,' Will replied, grimacing even as he said it. 'I am that glad to be feeling anything at all just now. It reminds me I am alive.'

'And back with those who love you,' she said, brushing his finger-tips with her lips as she released him.

'I do thank you, my lady,' he said, his voice thick with sudden emotion. He raised his hand and regarded his bandaged fingers, amazed that something so small could hurt so much. Despite the throbbing insistence of the pain, however, he remained overawed at his rescue, and his friends' continued deception. They had risked all for him, and his gratitude could not be contained. 'My heart has no words to say thanks enough.'

'I only wish we could have come sooner,' said Siarles, who had been hovering at Mérian's shoulder.

'And thanks to you, Siarles,' replied Will, acknowledging the forester's presence. 'It does a body good to see you again. God's truth, I did not recognise any of you. ''Course, I had other things on my mind just then.'

'When Bran said what we were to do,' replied Siarles, 'I told him it would never work — we could never dupe the sharp-eyed sheriff.' He chuckled. 'But Bran would not be moved. He was determined to steal you away and right from under their long Ffreinc noses. We collected Brother Jago from Saint Dyfrig's, and we all dressed up like priests and such and' — he smiled again — 'here we are.'

Iwan, who had been standing watch on the little bower, hurried to rejoin them. 'They're coming back,' he announced. 'Be on your best guard. We are not safe home yet.'

Following the archery contest, Father Dominic had thanked the count and abbot for their inestimable hospitality and announced his desire to resume his journey. In taking their leave of the count the next morning, the papal envoy was surprised to learn that the count had decided to send an escort of knights and men-at-arms to see them safely to their ship at Hamtun Docks. Despite the envoy's protestations that this was in no way necessary, the count — his own resolve bolstered by the insistence of an increasingly suspicious sheriff — would not allow his guests to depart on their own. 'It is the least I can do for our Mother Church,' he insisted. 'If anything should happen to you on the road — may heaven forbid it! — I would never be forgiven, especially since it is so easily prevented.'

'Bloody meddler,' muttered Iwan, when he learned of the plan. 'There is no ship waiting for us. We've never been anywhere near Hamtun Docks.'

'They don't know that,' Bran replied. 'We will go on as we've begun and look for the first opportunity to send them on their way.'

'And if we don't find such an opportunity?' demanded Iwan. 'What then?'

'We can always disappear into the wood,' Bran told him. 'Leave it to me. You keep your eyes on the soldiers and remain alert. If anything goes wrong, I want you ready to break some heads.'

'Oh, aye,' agreed Iwan grimly, 'if it comes to that. I'll be ready right enough.'

They had set off with Count de Braose, Sheriff de Glanville, and ten Norman soldiers – four knights and six men-at-arms – to provide protection from King Raven and his outlaw minions, who haunted the greenwood and preyed on unwary travellers. The papal envoy and his small entourage – the Lady Ghisella and her maidservant, Brother Alfonso the interpreter, and the two lay brothers surrounded by heavily armed Ffreinc men, kept to themselves for the most part. Outwardly, they behaved much as before – cheerful, if quiet, and appreciative of the largess lavished on them by their ever-watchful hosts.

'I do not trust that priest,' the sheriff had said as the travelling party prepared to set off. 'He is no more an ambassador of Pope Clement than my horse. Mark me, there is some deception playing out here, and we are fools if we let them get away with it.'

'You may be right,' conceded Count de Braose. 'But we dare not risk a confrontation until we are more than certain. This way, at least, we can keep a close watch on them.'

'Be sure of it,' growled the sheriff. 'The first time any one of them looks sideways, I'll have him.'

'You are not to antagonise them,' Falkes warned. 'If word of any mistreatment were to reach my uncle – not to mention Pope Clement – we'd be peeled and boiled in our own blood.'

'Never fear, my lord,' replied the sheriff. 'I will be nothing but courtesy itself to our esteemed guests. But I will watch them — by the rood, I will.'

Thus, a forced and wary pleasantness settled over the travellers. Because of the small coach in which Lady Ghisella and her maid rode, and which carried the tents used by the envoy and his company, they could not travel as quickly as the Normans might have wished. At night they made camp separately, each side watching the other, wary and suspicious, across the distance. The only time the foreigners were able to confer openly with one another was when the Ffreinc were occupied with picketing the horses and establishing the guard for the night.

It was during one of these times that Bran moved among the members of his disguised flock, speaking words of encouragement and hope. He also apologized to Will and begged the forester's forgiveness. 'I am sorry, Will. It was my fault you were taken, and I grieve that you suffered because of it.'

'I suffered a little, true,' Will granted. 'But Gwion Bach would have suffered more, I reckon. Still, I forgive you free and fair. I won't say I didn't think ill of that night, all the same.' He smiled. 'But you've more than made up for it by saving my scrawny neck from that hide noose. And for that I truly thank you, my lord.'

'We're not out of danger yet,' Bran said. 'So you might want to wait until we say farewell to our nosey friends before thanking me.'

'Whatever happens,' replied Will, 'we're square, my lord, and no hard feelings.'

The party endured four more days of anxious watching, until at last coming in sight of the bluffs overlooking the river estuary at Hamtun.

'What if there is no ship?' Iwan wondered. 'What will we do then?'

'You should pray there is no ship,' Siarles observed. 'Then we can at least say they have gone to get supplies, or some such thing. The Ffreinc are not about to wait around many days to see us away.'

'But what if there is a ship?' demanded Iwan, plainly worried.

'We will take it,' concluded Bran. 'Either way, it could not be simpler.'

Simple as the choices may have been, the doing was only slightly more difficult. When, the next day, as they followed the road over the bluff and started down into the river valley, they caught sight of the docks on the waterfront below the town, the travellers could see there was, indeed, a ship waiting there — a sturdy, broad-beamed vessel built for hauling men and horses across the sea. To all appearances, it was just the sort of vessel that the patriarch of Rome might provide for his personal ambassador.

'Well, there is your boat,' muttered Iwan. 'Now what?'

Bran glanced around. The sun was low, and the wind freshening out of the west. The count and sheriff had picked up the pace and were drawing closer, expressions of keen anticipation lighting their watchful eyes. 'Ride to the ship and secure it. Take Siarles and Jago with you. Go now before the Ffreinc prevent you.'

'And what do you suggest I tell them when I take their ship?'

'Tell them the pope's ambassador needs it,' replied Bran. 'Tell them we will buy our passage. Tell them anything, but just secure it and keep the sailors out of sight when we get there.'

Scowling with determination, Iwan signalled to Siarles and Jago, and all three galloped away. Bran, turning to Will, Mérian, and Cinnia, quickly explained that they were to continue on in the wagon and, upon reaching the ship, they were to go aboard as if that was what had been intended from the start. 'Whatever happens,' he said hurriedly, 'the two of you get down below deck and stay there. Mérian,' he said, dismounting and helping her down from the wagon, 'you come with me.'

Will, from his seat in the wagon, cast a last backward glance at the sheriff, then turned and set his face towards the river and the freedom waiting there.

Seeing the monks gallop off, Count Falkes and the sheriff rode directly to Father Dominic for an explanation. 'Where are they going?' demanded de Glanville suspiciously.

'Qué?' replied the envoy with a smile of incomprehension. He gestured towards the ship, waving and nodding as if to indicate that they had arrived at last and all was well. Lady Ghisella, who possessed a smattering of French, tried to explain. 'They go to make ready the sailing,' she said.

'You mean to leave tonight?' asked the count.

'But of course,' replied the lady pleasantly. 'It is the wish of His Eminence to leave at once.'

The sheriff, unable to think of any reason why this should not be perfectly reasonable, looked to the count to mount an objection. 'Are you certain?' Falkes said lamely. 'It will be getting dark soon.'

'It is the wish of His Eminence,' the lady repeated, as if this was all the explanation required.

'Well,' said the sheriff, 'we will attend you to see that nothing is amiss.' He lifted the reins and started down the road once more.

'Please, Lord Count,' said Lady Ghisella, 'you must not trouble yourself.'

'But it is no trouble at all, my lady,' replied the count. 'If anything should happen to you while you remained in our care . . .' He allowed the thought to go unfinished. 'Never fear,' he said with a stiff, somewhat condescending laugh, 'we will see you safely aboard and properly under sail. We could do no less for the pope's personal confidant.'

'That is a relief, to be sure,' replied Ghisella crisply. 'I will tell His Eminence.'

Although it made her uncomfortable to speak to the Ffreinc, her reticent, regal manner went a long way towards easing the count's suspicions. His attraction to her despite her undeniable plainness made him more willing to overlook his doubts. She relayed the count's sentiments to Father Dominic, who gave a nod of approval. 'What are we to do now?' she asked, keeping her voice low to avoid being overheard.

'We see it through,' Bran told her, 'and hope for the best. Thank them, and walk on.'

She smiled, revealing her unfortunate, off-colour teeth. 'His Eminence is delighted with your diligence and care. He will speak of it to His Holiness.'

'The delight is ours alone, my lady,' replied the count.

'They are getting away, and we sit here trading pleasantries,' muttered the sheriff. 'I don't like this.'

'I cannot forbid their departure; they have done nothing wrong.'

'This whole affair is wrong!' grumbled the sheriff.

'Then find a way to stop them if you can,' said Count Falkes. 'But unless you discover something very soon, they will be away on the tide.'

The travellers moved on, descending the narrow road into the valley, passing quickly through the town and its low-built, dark houses and single muddy street to the large timber wharf on the river where the ship was moored. All seemed quiet aboard the vessel – no screams or shouting, no evidence of a struggle or fight – although there was no sign of Iwan or any of the others. Bran, his stomach tightening with every step, prayed that they might yet make good their escape. As they drew near the dock, there appeared on deck a man in a red cap and brown tunic which reached past his knees. He was barefoot and carried a knotted rope in his hand. He scanned the wharf quickly and then hurried to greet the new arrivals. *'Mes seigneurs! Ma dame! J'offre vous accueille. Etre bienvenu ici. S'il vous plaît, venir à bord et être à l'aise. Tout est prêt!'*

At this, the French speakers fell silent, dumbstruck. Lady Ghisella gave a little gasp of pleasure.

'Saints and angels!' whispered Bran tensely. 'What did he say?'

'We are welcome to come aboard,' Mérian told him. 'He says everything is ready for us.'

'Peter and Paul on a donkey!' exclaimed Bran. 'How did they accomplish that?' Before she could answer, he said, 'Hurry now. Get on board. Send Jago back to help me get rid of our friends here, and tell Iwan and Siarles to make ready to cast off.' When Mérian hesitated, he said, 'Quickly! Before something goes wrong.'

Bran, alone now, turned to his obliging, if suspicious, hosts and, summoning up his little store of Latin, attempted to sever the last ties and bid them farewell. *Vicis pro sententia Deus volo est hic, vae. Gratias ago vos vobis hospitium quod ignarus. Caveo, ut tunc nos opportunus.*

This might have lacked the polish of a senior churchman, but it was more than either Sheriff de Glanville or Count Falkes possessed, at any rate. The two Frenchmen stared at him, unable to comprehend what had just passed.

'His Eminence says the time has come to bid you farewell,' explained the one known as Brother Alfonso, hastening to join Father Dominic on the dock just then. 'His Grace thanks you for your hospitality – a debt he can never repay – and wishes you a most wonderfully pleasant and uneventful journey home. Be assured that, owing to your kind and attentive service, your praises will ring in the pope's ears.'

The man in the red hat, who, it turned out, was master of the ship, hurried to greet the papal emissary. He knelt to receive a blessing, which was deftly delivered, then rose, saying, 'My apologies, Your Grace, but if we are to take the tide, we must hurry. The horses must be secured and the ship made ready to cast off.'

'Now see here,' protested the sheriff, still unwilling to see the suspicious foreigners slip away so easily.

'Was there something?' inquired the ship's master.

'No,' said the count. 'Be about your business.' To the sheriff, he said, 'Come, de Glanville, there is no more to be done here.'

When this was translated for His Eminence, Father Dominic gave his Norman hosts a blessing and, with a last promise to mention their care and attention to the pope, released them from their duty of guarding him and his entourage. He walked onto the ship and went below deck. A moment later, the two lay brothers appeared and helped the ship's master lead the horses on deck and secure them for the voyage. When this was done, they helped the master cast off and, using stout poles, pushed the craft away from the dock and out into the river, where it drifted for a little while before finding the current. Then, as they entered the stream, Father Dominic, Lady Ghisella, and Will Scarlet came back onto the deck and waved farewell to the Normans, who, although they could not be sure, thought they heard the sound of laughter carried on the wind as the ship entered the centre of the channel and was carried along by the slowly building tide-flow, and away.

CHAPTER 40

Rouen

King William Rufus, wet and miserable in the driving rain, rode at the head of a company of his best and most loyal knights. The royal ranks were followed by sixty men-at-arms grimly slogging through the sticky mud. Water streamed down from a low sky of seamless grey from horizon to horizon, falling in steady rivulets from helmet, shield, and lance blade, puddling deep in the wheel-rutted road. The farms and villages flung out around the low, squat city of Rouen appeared just as cheerless and desolate as the king and his dreary entourage.

Curse his fool of a stiff-necked brother, he thought. It should be Duke Robert – not himself, the king of England – who was saddle sore and catching his death in the rain. Blast the imbecile and his infernal scheming! Why could Robert not accept his divinely appointed lot and be happy ruling the family's ancestral lands? William told himself that if that had been his own particular fate, he would have embraced it and worked to make something of his portion and not be forever wasting his substance fomenting rebellion and inflaming the rapacious ambitions of France's endless supply of muttering malcontents.

These thoughts put the already irritated king in a simmering rage. And when he contemplated the time and money wasted on keeping his idiot brother appeased and under control, his thin blue blood began to boil.

Thus, William arrived in the yard of the archbishop's palace at Rouen already angry and spoiling for a fight. The palace, a solid square of cut stone three floors high and studded with wood-shuttered windows, occupied the top of a prominent hill a mile or so beyond the city wherein stood the cathedral. William's cool and indifferent welcome by the current incumbent of the palace did little to mollify the king, or sweeten his disposition.

'Ah, William,' intoned Archbishop Bonne-Âme, 'good of you to come.' Heavily robed and leaning on his bishop's staff, the old man puffed, out of breath from his short walk across the vestibule. An honour guard of six knights and two earls entered with the king, the water from their cloaks dripping on the polished stone floor, which sent a bevy of clerical servants scampering for rags to mop up the mess.

'My pleasure,' grumbled William, shedding his sopping cloak and tossing it to a waiting servant. 'Where is he? What's it to be this time? Come, let's get to it.'

The archbishop's pale hand fluttered up like an agitated bird. 'Oh, my lord king, this is to be a most serious conclave. I hope you understand the gravity of the moment.'

'I understand that my brother is as worthless,' quipped William, 'as is anyone who sides with him. Beyond that, there is only the money it will take to buy him off.'

The archbishop stiffened and lowered his head in a bow. 'This way, Your Majesty.'

The archbishop turned and started away with King William a step or two behind; the king's men threw off their wet cloaks and

341

assembled in a double rank behind him. And as servants rushed to pick up the sodden garments, the ageing archbishop led them down a lofty corridor to a large audience room where the king found assembled a few minor lords standing around the blazing hearth at one end of the room. They looked around guiltily as the king of England and his men entered. Duke Robert was not among them, nor anyone William recognised.

'Where is he?' demanded the king. 'I have ridden hard for three days in the rain. I am not playing at games.'

'This is what I wanted to tell you, Majesty,' explained the archbishop. 'Duke Robert is not here. Indeed, few of those summoned to attend have arrived. It's the weather, you see . . . but we expect them at any moment.'

'Do we!' snapped the angry king. 'Do we indeed, sir!'

'We do, Majesty,' the old cleric assured him. 'I have ordered chambers to be prepared for you. If you would like to rest a little before the proceedings, I will have refreshment sent to you.'

William gave a last scowl around the near-empty room and allowed himself to be persuaded. 'Very well,' he said. 'Have wine brought to me in my chambers.' To one of his men, he said, 'Leicester, fetch me dry clothes. I'll change out of these blasted wet things.'

'Of course, Sire. At once,' replied the Earl of Leicester. With a nod and flick of his hand, he sent one of his men to carry out the errand. 'Will there be anything else?'

'No,' said the king, feeling a great weariness settling upon him. He started after the archbishop, saying, 'You and Warwick will attend me. The others are to see to the horses, then take food and rest for themselves.'

'At once, Sire.' The earl gave quick instructions to the rest of the king's guard and sent them away. He and the Earl of Warwick accompanied the king to the apartment that had been prepared for him – a large room with a bed and a square oak table with four chairs. Archbishop Bonne-Âme pushed open the heavy door and stepped into the room, glancing around to assure himself that all was in order for his tetchy guest.

A fire burned in the small hearth, and on the table sat a jug of wine with four cups and, beside these, a platter with loaves of bread and soft cheese wrapped in grape leaves.

William walked to the table and poured wine into three of the cups. 'Thank you, Archbishop,' he said, offering a cup to the nearest earl, 'we are well satisfied with our arrangements. You may go.'

Bonne-Âme bowed his old white head and retreated, closing the door. 'I leave you to your rest.'

'My brother is planning mischief,' observed the king, his nose in his cup as he gulped down a healthy draught. 'I can feel it in my bones.'

'Do you know le Bellay?' asked the Earl of Leicester.

'I know my brother,' replied William.

'If there is to be bloodshed . . . ,' began young Lord Warwick.

The king cut him off with an impatient wave of his hand. 'It won't come to that, I think,' William said, handing him a cup. 'At least not yet.' He drank again and said, 'I wish I knew what he and his sycophants were up to, though.'

'Those men down there,' said Leicester. 'Who were they?'

'God knows,' answered the king. 'Never seen the rascals before. You?'

'I might have met one or another. Difficult to say.' He replaced his cup on the board and said, 'I think I might just go and see if I can find out.'

'Never mind,' said the king. Drawing out a chair, he dropped heavily into it, then shoved a second chair towards the earl. 'Here. Sit. You must be as tired as I am. Sit. We'll drink and rest.'

'With respect, Sire, I would rest easier if I knew who those men are and what they're doing here.'

The king shrugged. 'Go then, but hurry back. And tell the chamberlain we need some meat to go with this bread and cheese.'

'Of course, my lord,' said the Earl of Leicester, moving quickly towards the door. He hoped to catch the archbishop for a private word before the old man disappeared into the cavern of his palace.

'And more wine!' called the king after him.

William leaned back in the chair and closed his eyes. 'Sire?' said the Earl of Warwick, setting aside his cup. He came to stand before the king. 'If you would allow me,' he offered, indicating the monarch's feet, 'I think we might dry those boots a little.'

William nodded, and with a sigh raised his foot so that the young man might pull off the sodden shoe. He guzzled down another draught as the young nobleman attended to the other boot.

'There, now,' said Warwick, when he had finished. 'Better, no?'

'Mmmm,' murmured William into the cup. 'Much.'

The earl carried the wet boots to the hearth and put them on the warm stones to dry, then returned to the table and sat down. He and the king sipped their wine in silence for a time, feeling the tensions of the road begin to ease beneath application of the sweet, dark liquid.

'This is all my father's fault,' mused William after a time. 'If he had not promised my ninny of a brother the throne of England, all would be well. He roused Robert's hopes and, fool that he is, the duke has set the value too high – thinks it worth more than it is.' He drained the cup and then filled it again. 'Truth is,' he continued, 'the blasted island costs more than you can ever get out of it.'

'It was ever thus,' Warwick suggested. 'King Harold never had two pennies to rub together one day to the next, as my father used to say.

344

And Aelfred was in debt from the day he took the crown till the day they took it off him in the grave.'

'This is supposed to cheer me, Warwick?' grumbled the king.

'I merely suggest that your condition is neither more nor less than that which all English rulers have endured. God knows, it is difficult enough even for an earl, much less a duke or a king.'

'Duke Robert does right well,' William pointed out. He took up a loaf of bread, broke it, and stuffed half into his mouth. He chewed heavily for a moment. 'To be sure, most of what he has he got from me.'

'Cut him off, Sire,' suggested Warwick. 'Or make him sign a settlement treaty in exchange for his promise never to raise rebellion again. Get him to put his name to it.'

'Robert would have nothing if it wasn't for me propping him up,' growled William, the bread half-eaten in his mouth. 'No more! No more, hear? This is the end.'

'With your permission, Sire, I'll have a treaty drawn up at once,' the earl suggested, raising his cup. 'We'll get Robert to sign it and be done with him once and for all.'

'If he thinks I'll buy him off again, he's woefully mistaken,' said William. 'If he demands another penny from me, I'll march on him, curse the devil, I will! I swear it.'

'Well,' replied Warwick judiciously, trying to calm the agitated monarch, 'perhaps he will listen to reason this time. Would you like me to arrange for a treaty?'

Lord Leicester returned with another jug of wine and, behind him, a servant bearing a platter of cold roast duck and chicken. 'His Grace the archbishop says that he is retiring for the night. He wishes you a good night's rest and sleep. He will conduct a Mass in the morning and break fast after.'

'And my brother? When is he expected?'

'The archbishop could not say, Sire. Tomorrow, I expect.'

'Well, then,' decided William, 'we could do worse than make a night of it. Here, bring that platter! I'm famished.'

They ate and drank, talking long into the night. Both Lord Leicester and his brother, Warwick, remained with the king, sleeping in chairs beside the hearth while William snored in his feather bed. As dawn cracked the damp grey sky in the east, the chapel bell sounded, calling the faithful to Mass. William and his noblemen stirred at the sound, then went back to sleep, awaking again when they heard a clatter in the courtyard below. Warwick got up and walked to the narrow window, pushed open the wooden shutter and looked out. He could see seven men on horseback, or perhaps five men and two women. On closer inspection, at least two of them appeared to be priests. Although the day was still new, their mounts appeared fresh and fairly unsoiled by the mud on the rain-soaked roads. They had not travelled far, the earl surmised. He watched for a moment, scanning the group, but failed to recognise anyone – in any event, they were certainly not Duke Robert and his entourage. Turning from the window, he went to the king's bed and gave a polite cough. When this failed to rouse His Majesty, he took hold of the royal shoulder and gave it a shake.

'Sire,' he said, 'I think the vultures are gathering. We should be ready for them.'

William opened his eyes and tried to raise his head. The effort was too much and he lay back with a groan. 'Who has come? Is my brother finally here?'

'I do not know, my lord. I did not see him,' replied Warwick. 'A priest or two have arrived, but unless the duke travels in the company of priests now, he is not yet here.'

'Oh,' sighed William, struggling upright. 'Why did you let me drink so much?'

'It is a fault of mine, Majesty,' the Earl of Warwick assured him. 'I must try to do better. Then again, the archbishop's wine is very good.'

'It is,' agreed William, swinging his short, stout legs off the bed. 'Is there any left, do you think?'

Henry walked to the table and began examining the jugs and cups. 'Where is Leicester?' asked the king, stretching his back and yawning.

'He has gone to Mass,' Warwick reported. 'I expect him to return soon. Shall I have someone fetch him for you?'

'No, no,' decided the king. 'Let him be.' Heaving his bulk up onto unsteady legs, he tottered to the table and the cup which Lord Warwick now held out to him. The king took a sip, tasted it, then drained the cup. 'Ah, that's better.'

The young earl disappeared momentarily to summon a servant lurking in the corridor to prepare a basin of water for the king, and commanded another to bring the king's chest to the room. Presently, the servant appeared with a basin of hot water, and while William washed, Warwick supervised the cleaning of the king's boots. 'Get all that muck off there and brush them well,' he ordered, so that His Majesty would not look like a common farmhand before the other noblemen. The chamberlain meanwhile appeared with the king's chest and a message that some people had come and were seeking audience on a most urgent matter.

'What do they want?' asked William, raising the hem of his tunic and drawing it over his head. Warwick opened the chest and withdrew a clean, white tunic.

'They did not say, Your Majesty,' replied the chamberlain. 'I was told only that it was of utmost importance that they speak to you at once, and before you speak to anyone else today.'

'Impertinent lot,' observed William, pulling the tunic over his head. The garment, though handsomely wrought, was made for a slightly smaller frame; the fine fabric stretched over his expansive gut. 'Warwick,' he said, 'go see who it is and find out what they want. I have not broken fast yet, and I'm not in a humour to brook any silliness.'

'To be sure, Sire,' replied the young earl.

William nodded, picked up a scrap of bread from the remains of last night's supper, sniffed it, and took a bite. Seeing the servant still stood staring at him, he threw the rind of dried bread crust at him. 'Bring me my food!' The servant ducked the missile and darted for the door. 'And be quick about it,' William called after him. 'Important people have come. We must not keep them waiting.'

CHAPTER 41

S'truth, I'd never make a sailor. Even the smallest stretch o' water seen from the deck of a ship brings me out in a sweat. If a wave should rock the boat, it's me there hanging onto the rail and spilling my supper into the briny deep. Oh, and I had cause enough. Even the master of the ship said it was the worst storm in many a year o' sailing. And he should know – he's crossed that narrow sea more times than a rooster with a henhouse across the road. Our own small voyage might not have been so bad, and indeed I had allowed myself to imagine that the worst was over when we entered the wide estuary of the Thames and sallied slowly upriver to the White Tower of Lundein to pay our ruddy King William a visit.

Alas, the king was not in residence.

Gone to Rouen, they told us – gone to parley with his brother, not to return till Saint Matthew's Day, maybe not till Christmas.

Never mind, said Bran, we've come this far, what's a little further? 'Master Ruprecht!' he called, and I can still hear those fateful words: 'Cast off and make sail for France!'

As it had turned out, our man Ruprecht, the ship's owner and master, was Flanders born and raised, and could speak both French and English into the bargain. His ship was a stout ploughhorse of a vessel, and he was kept right busy fetching and carrying Ffreinc noblemen and their knights back and forth to England from various ports on the coast of Normandie. Thus, he knew the coasts of both lands as well as any and far better than most. Seizing his ship had been easier than rolling off a stump. We lifted nary a finger, nor ruffled a hair — we simply bought his services.

This easy conquest was not without its moment of uncertainty, however. For as we came in sight of the docks at Hamtun that day and Bran gave Iwan, Siarles, and Jago the command to secure the ship, those three hastened down to the wharf. Cinnia and I arrived close behind and scrambled onto the dock hard on their heels. 'Let me talk to them first,' offered Brother Jago, as they dismounted. 'Do nothing until we see how things stand.'

'Hurry then,' Iwan said. 'We do not have much time before the others get here.'

'What will you tell them?' asked Siarles, swinging down from the saddle. 'Maybe it would be better to take them by surprise.'

'Force is the first resort of the coward,' suggested Jago lightly. 'Peace, Brother. We have enjoyed great success with our disguises until now. We can trust them a little further, I think.'

'Go then,' Iwan told him. 'See if they will talk to you.'

'Whatever you do, make it quick,' said I, urging them on.

'All the same, we will be ready to stifle any objections with our fists,' Siarles called after him.

I myself could not have stifled so much as a sneeze with my fists, weak and miserable as I was just then. My months of captivity had left me exhausted, and the last few days of travel had all but killed me. It took my last strength to clamber down from the wagon and, on Cinnia's tender arm, hobble onto the dock and make my slow, aching way aboard the waiting vessel where, if it had not happened, I would not have believed it: the ship's master himself welcomed us with open arms.

'Greetings, friends!' he called, leaping lightly to the rail to help me aboard. 'My ship and myself are at your service. I am Master Ruprecht, and this is the *Dame Havik*.' His English was flat and toneless, but clear, and the ruddy face beneath his floppy red hat was friendly as it was wind-burned. 'The good brother has told me of your urgent mission. Never fear, I will see you safely to your destination.' He paused to wave at the approaching Ffreinc, and to Father Dominic.

What Jago had told him, in the first part, was that Father Dominic was a papal legate, which was no more than de Braose and his lot already believed. Jago merely added that we were all on a secret embassy to England bearing a message of utmost importance for the king. As it happens, this last part was true enough. Bran did indeed bear an important message for the king – the one I had sent him through Odo from my prison cell concerning the letter we had stolen in the Christmas raid. Now, as a result of his sojourn with Count Falkes and Abbot Hugo, our King Raven knew better what that letter meant. The importance of reaching King William might have been overstated somewhat. But in light of the mounting suspicions of Falkes and the sheriff, it was simple good sense to make the captain think our errand urgent. Even so, that excuse was closer to the truth than any of us could have guessed, and it was to be the saving of us.

The *Dame Havik*'s master had only one small impediment towards our leaving straightaway – he had no crew. He had come to England shorthanded, and with a cargo of fine cloth, which he had sold days before; he had put in at Hamtun to pick up more sailors and a load of hides and wool. 'We will have to wait until I can find some more hands to help with the sails and such. I hope you understand. It should not take long,' he hastened to add, 'no more than three or four days maybe.'

'Even that is too long,' Jago, as Brother Alfonso, informed him. 'Perhaps you would allow my fellow monks and me to serve as your crew at least as far as Lundein. If you tell us what to do, we will do it. And,' he added, 'the king will reward you well when we tell him how you have helped us.'

Ruprecht of Flanders pulled on his chin and cast a weather eye at the sky, then to the river. 'The tide is beginning to run, and the wind is in a favourable quarter.' He made up his mind with a snap of his fingers. 'Well, why not? As soon as His Eminence is aboard, we will cast off. Here! I will show you what to do. Step to the music, friends!'

And just like that, Iwan and Siarles were no longer lay brothers, but sailors. Under Ruprecht's direction, they hauled on the ropes and picked up the poles and, in as much time as it takes to tell it, we were away, leaving the Ffreinc standing on the shore, mouths agape, eyes a-boggle at the swiftness of our departure. The ship, light of its load, spun out into the deeper channel; the tide lifted her and carried her off. We saw the dock and Hamtun town growing small behind us and laughed out loud. We were so relieved to have done with those treacherous Ffreinc, we laughed until the tears streamed down our cheeks.

We made for Lundein, sailing along the coast and up the wide Thames until we came in sight of the White Tower – a splendid thing it is, too, all gleaming pale and tall like an enormous horn rising from the bank of the muddy river. But we had no sooner made anchor and summoned a tender alongside to carry us to shore than we learned that the king was not in England. 'Gone to France,' said the tenderman. He counted the days on his fingers. 'A week or more ago, give or take.'

'Are you certain?' asked Jago.

'Show him this,' said Bran, handing Jago a silver penny. 'Give it to him if he answers well.'

Jago questioned the man closely, and at the end declared himself satisfied that the man was telling the truth; he tossed the boatman the coin. 'What is your wish, my lord?'

'We have no choice,' Bran replied. I saw the keen glint in his eye and knew he'd already decided.

Mérian saw it, too. 'You mean . . . ? We can't!'

'Why not?' said Bran. 'I've been thinking, and the sooner we get this out in the open, the sooner we can reclaim Elfael.'

'What are you talking about?' said Iwan.

Bran turned and called: 'Master Ruprecht! Cast off and make sail for France.'

'France!' scoffed the big warrior. 'I wouldn't set foot beyond the high tide mark on the word of an Englishman.'

'Careful, friend,' I warned, smiling as I said it. 'Some of us Englishmen are that touchy when our honour is called into question.'

Iwan pawed the air at me with his hand. 'You know what I mean.'

'He has a point,' Siarles put in. 'France is a fair size, so I'm told.'

'And full of Ffreincmen,' I added.

'We might want to know where we're going if we aim to meet up with Red William.'

Bran agreed and, with Brother Jago for company, ordered Ruprecht to hire the men to crew the ship and get whatever provisions might be necessary for a voyage to France, and then climbed down into the waiting tender boat. Rhi Bran and Jago went ashore to learn what they could of the king's whereabouts, and we were soon occupied with securing provisions and fodder for the horses, and hauling water aboard. Seeing as how his passengers were ambassadors of the pope, the ship's master also bought a cask of wine and two of ale, and a barrel of smoked herrings, two bags of apples, four live chickens, two ducks, and a basket of eggs. These he bought from the merchant boats plying the wide river, bartering for a price and then hauling the various casks, crates, and cages up over the rail. He then went in search of sailors to make the voyage with us. While he was gone, we stowed all of the cargo away in the little rooms below deck and then waited for Bran and Jago to return.

We waited long, watching the river sink lower and lower as the tide ebbed out. The bare mud of the upper bank was showing and the sun had disappeared below the horizon and Iwan was almost ready to swim ashore to storm the tower, he was that sure Bran and Jago had been taken captive, when Mérian called out, 'Here they are! They're coming now.'

Indeed, they were already in a boat and making their way out to where *Dame Havik* rode at anchor. Moments later, we were pulling them aboard. We all gathered around to hear what they had learned ashore.

'The king has gone to attend a council at Rouen,' Bran said. 'He left with sixty men ten days ago. I know not where Rouen may be, but I mean to go there and lay before him all that we know and suspect.'

'I know Rouen,' volunteered Ruprecht when he returned a short while later leading four Flemish sailors to crew the ship. 'Ten days, you say?' He tapped his chin thoughtfully. 'If they were travelling overland on horseback, we may still be able to catch them before they arrive.'

'Truly?' wondered Iwan. 'How is that possible?'

'My ship draws lightly,' he said. 'We can easily go upriver as far as the bridge. It is but a short ride from there to the town.'

The tide was on the rise, so we had to wait until it had begun to ebb again. We settled down to a good meal which the ship's master and

Jago prepared for us, then slept a little, rising again when the tide began to flow. As a dim half-moon soared overhead, we upped anchor and set out once more.

Dawn found us skirting the high white cliffs of the southern coast, and as the sun rose, the clouds gathered and the wind began to blow. At first it wasn't so bad that a fella couldn't stand up to it, but by midday, the waves were dashing against the hull and splashing over the rail. Ruprecht allowed that we were in for some rough water, but assured us that we would come to no harm. 'A summer storm, nothing more,' he called cheerfully. 'Do not fret yourselves, Brothers. See to the horses – there are ropes to lash them down so they cannot hurt themselves.'

Throughout the day, the storm grew. Wind howled around the bare mast – they'd long since taken down the sails – and the waves tossed the ship like thistledown: now up, now down, now tail over top. It was all I could do to hold on for dear life and keep my poor bandaged fingers from smashing against the hull as I tried to keep from getting battered bloody.

As evening fell on that wild day, our ship's master was the only one still cheerful. Ruprecht alone maintained his usual good humour in the teeth of the storm. Moreover, he was the only one still standing. The rest of us – his sailors included – were hunkered down below the deck, clinging to the stout ribs of the ship as she bucked and heaved in the rowdy waves.

More than once, my innards tried to leave the wretched confines of their piteous prison – and I without strength or will to stop them. My stomach heaved with every wave that rolled and tried to sink our vessel. Along with my miserable companions, I shut my eyes against the dizzying pitch and twist, and stopped my ears against the shriek of the wind and the angry sea's bellowing roar.

This seagoing calamity continued for an eternity, so it seemed. When at last we dared lift our heads and unclasp our limbs and venture onto the deck, we saw the clouds torn and flying away to the east and rays of sunlight streaming through, all bright gold and glowing like the firmament of heaven. 'Have we died then?' asked Siarles, grey-faced with the sickness we all shared. The front of his robe was damp from his throwing up, and his hair was slick and matted with sweat.

'No such luck,' groaned Iwan; his appearance likewise had not improved with the ordeal. 'I can still feel the beast bucking under me. In heaven there will be no storms.'

'And no ships, either,' muttered Mérian. Pale and shaky, she tottered off to find water to wash her face and hands. Bran was least affected by the storm, but even he strode unsteadily to where Ruprecht stood smiling and humming at the tiller; summoning Jago to him, Bran said, 'Ask him how many days we have lost.'

'Only one, Your Grace,' came the reply. 'The storm blew itself out overnight. The sea has been running high, but it is calming now. Och! That was a bad one — as bad as any I've seen in a month of years.'

'Are we still on course?' asked Bran.

'More or less,' affirmed the master. 'More or less. But we will be able to raise the sails soon. Until then, have your men see to the horses. Unbind them and give the poor beasts a little food and water.'

While Iwan and Siarles saw to that chore, two of the sailors began preparing a meal for us. Bran and I watched this activity as we leaned heavily on the rail, neither of us feeling very bold or hearty just then. 'What a night,' Bran sighed. 'How is the hand?'

'Not so bad,' I lied. 'Hardly feel it at all.' Looking out at the still-rumpled sea, I asked, 'What will happen when we get to Rouen, if we should be so fortunate?'

'I mean to get an audience with Red William.'

'As Lord Bran,' I wondered, 'or Father Dominic?'

He showed me his lopsided smile. 'Whichever one the king will agree to see. It is the message that is important here, not the messenger.'

'Leaving that aside,' I said, 'I'm beginning to think we're mad for risking our necks aboard this mad ship and storm-stirred sea to save a king we neither love nor honour.'

He regarded me curiously. 'Is that you talking, Will? It was you who put us onto it, after all.'

'Yes, but, I didn't think—'

'If you're right, then it is well worth the risk of a kingdom,' Bran said.

'Whose kingdom, my lord?' I wondered. 'William's . . . or yours?'

We talked until Cinnia called us to our food which, following a little good-natured teasing by the sailors, we were able to get down. After we had eaten, Ruprecht gave orders to his crew for the sail to be run up. Once this was done, the ship began to run more smoothly. We had no more trouble with the ever-contrary weather and reached the French mainland that evening. We dropped anchor until morning, then proceeded up the coast until reaching the estuary of a wide inland river at a place called Honfleur. Although some of our provisions had been damaged by seawater in the storm, we did not stop to take on more provisions because Ruprecht assured us that Rouen was only a day or so upriver and we could get all we needed there at half the cost of the harbour merchants.

So, we sailed on. The storm we had endured at sea had gone before us and was now settled over the land. Through a haze of rain we watched the low hills of Normandie slowly slide by the rail. Although we could not escape the rain, the river remained calm, and it was good to see land within easy reach on either side of the ship. I confess, it did feel strange to go into the enemy's land. And I did marvel that no one tried to apprehend us or attack us in any way. But no one did, and we spent the night anchored in the middle of the stream, resuming our slow way at sunrise the next day. As promised, we reached the city of Rouen while it was still morning and made fast at the wharf that served the city. Iwan and Siarles readied the horses, and Bran meanwhile arranged with Ruprecht to provision the boat and wait for our return.

Then, pausing only to ask directions of one of the harbour hands, we set off once more beneath clearing skies on blesséd dry land. Oh! It was that good to be on solid ground again, and it was but a short ride to the palace of the archbishop where, it was said, the English king had arrived the previous day.

'Here is the way it will be,' Bran said as we entered the palace yard. 'To anyone who asks, we are still ambassadors of the pope with an urgent message for the king.'

'Aye,' agreed Iwan dryly, 'but which pope?'

'Pray we do not have to explain beyond that,' Bran told him. 'At all events, do not any of you speak to anyone. Let Jago, here, do the talking for us.' He put his hand on the priest's shoulder. 'Brother Alfonso knows what to say.'

'What if someone asks us something?' wondered Siarles, looking none too certain about this part of the enterprise.

'Just pretend you don't speak French,' I told him.

The others laughed at this, but Siarles, bless him, was worried and did not catch my meaning. 'But I don't speak a word of French,' he insisted.

'Then pretending should be easy,' Mérian chirped lightly. She patted her hair, working in the ashes that greyed it; then took out the small wooden teeth that were part of her disguise and slipped them into her mouth; they were an off colour and made her jaw jut slightly, giving her face an older, far less comely appearance.

Bran and the others straightened their monkish robes and prepared to look pious. I had no disguise, but since no one in France had ever seen me before it was not thought to matter very much. Then, standing in the rain-washed yard of the archbishop of Rouen's palace, Brother Jago led us in a prayer that the plan we set in motion would succeed, that bloodshed could be avoided, and that our actions would bring about the restoration of Elfael to its rightful rule.

When he finished, Bran looked at each of us in turn, head to toe, then, satisfied, said, 'The downfall of Baron de Braose is begun, my friends. It is not something we have done, but something he has done to himself.' He smiled. 'Come, let us do all we can to hasten his demise.'

CHAPTER 42

We were given a beggar's greeting by the archbishop's porter, who at first thought us English and then, despite his misgivings, was forced to take Bran at his word. For standing on his threshold was a legate of the pope and his attending servants and advisors. What else could he do but let us in?

Thus, we were admitted straightaway and shown to a small reception room and made to wait there until someone could be found who might more readily deal with us. There were no chairs in the room, and no fire in the hearth; the board against one wall was bare. Clearly, it was not a room used to receive expected, or welcome, visitors.

'Pax vobiscum,' said a short, keen-eyed cleric in a white robe. 'Bona in sanctus nomen.'

'Pax vobiscum,' replied Bran. He nodded to Brother Jago, who stepped forward and, with a little bow of respect, began to translate for Father Dominic and his companions.

The man, it turned out, was a fella named Canon Laurent, and he was the principal aid to Archbishop Bonne-Âme. 'His Grace has asked me to express his regrets, as he is unable to welcome you personally.

Your arrival has caught us at a very busy and eventful time. Please accept our apologies if we cannot offer you the hospitality you are certainly due, and which it would be our pleasure to provide under more ordinary circumstances.'

The priest was as slippery and smooth as an eel in oil, but beneath the mannered courtesy, I sensed a staunch and upright spirit. 'How may I be of service to you?' he said, folding his hands and tucking them into the sleeves of his robe.

'We have come bearing an important message for King William from His Holiness, the pope.'

'Indeed,' the canon replied, raising his eyebrows. 'Perhaps if I knew more about this message it would aid your purpose.'

'Our message is for the king alone,' explained Bran, through Jago. 'Yet I have no doubt that His Majesty will explain all to you in the time and manner of his choosing. If you would inform him that we are waiting, we will be in your debt.'

That was plain enough. The canon, unable to wheedle more from our Bran, conceded and promised to take our request to the king. 'If you wish, I can arrange for you to wait somewhere more comfortable,' he offered.

Jago thanked him and said, 'That will not be necessary. But if you could have some food brought here, that would be a mercy.'

'It will be done,' replied the canon as he withdrew.

'That went well,' Bran observed cheerfully.

'Job's bones, Bran,' muttered Iwan. 'You are a bold one. How can you think of food at a time like this?'

'I'm hungry,' Bran said.

'I'm with Iwan,' said Siarles. 'Give me a fair fight any day. This skulking around the enemy camp fair gives me the pip.'

'Steady on, boys,' said Mérian, her voice altered by her wooden teeth. 'All you need do is keep your eyes open and your mouths shut. Let Bran do the rest.' Our lord smiled at her quick defence of him. 'And you,' she said to him, 'see you get us out of here in the same condition we came in, and I might consider marrying you after all.'

'Oh, if I thought that was possible, my love,' he answered, taking her hand and kissing it, 'then you would be amazed to see what I can do.'

How this little dance might have continued we would never learn, for at that moment the door opened and three servants bearing platters of bread and sausage, and jars of watered wine entered the room, and hard on their heels none other than King William of England in the very solid flesh. We knew straightaway that it was Rufus: the fiery red hair; the high, ruddy complexion; the squat, slightly bowed legs; the spreading belly and beefy arms – all of which had been reported by anyone who'd met him. Well, who else could it be?

Attending the king were two noblemen, and our man Canon Laurent, who seemed unable to hold himself out of the proceedings.

The king of England was a younger man than I had imagined, but the life he led – the fighting and drinking and what all – was exacting a price. Still, he was formidable and with long, thick arms, heavy shoulders, and a deep chest, would have made a fearsome enemy on a battlefield. His short legs were slightly bent from a life in the saddle, as his father's were well reputed to have been, and like his father, his hair was red, but grizzled now and thinning. He looked like one of those fighting dogs I'd seen in market squares where their owners set them on bears or bulls for the wagering of a feast-day crowd.

Oh, he'd seen a few fights, had Bloody Red William, and won his share to be sure. As he stumped into the room, the glance from his beady, bloodshot eyes sweeping quickly left and right, he seemed as if he expected to meet an enemy army. Like that marketplace bulldog, he appeared only too ready to take a bite out of whomever or whatever got in his way.

'*Quel est cette intrusion impolie?*' the king demanded, puffing himself up. He spoke quickly, and I had trouble understanding his somewhat pinched voice.

'*Pax vobiscum, meus senior rex regis,*' said Brother Alfonso, bowing nicely.

'Latin?' said the king, which even I could understand. 'Latin? Mary and Joseph, someone tell him to speak French.'

'*Paix, mon roi de seigneur,*' offered Brother Alfonso smoothly, and went on to introduce the king to his visitor.

'When you learn why we have come,' said Bran, taking his place before the king as Jago translated his words for the French-speaking monarch, 'you will forgive the intrusion.'

'Will I, by the rood?' growled the king. 'Try me, then. But I warn you, I rarely forgive much, and fools who waste my time — never!'

'If it be foolish to try to save your throne,' Bran replied, his voice taking an edge the king did not mistake, 'then fool I am. I have been called worse.'

'Who are you?' demanded the king. 'Leicester? Warwick? Do you know this man?'

'No, my lord,' answered the younger of the two knights. 'I have never seen him before.'

'Nor I,' answered the elder. 'Any of them.'

'Save my throne, eh?' said the king. I could see that, despite his bluster, he was intrigued. 'My throne is not in danger.'

'Is it not?' countered Bran. 'I have good reason to believe otherwise. Your brother Duke Robert is raising rebellion against you.'

'Tell me something I do not know,' snorted the king. 'If this is your message, you are the very fool I thought.'

'This time, Lord King,' replied Bran quickly, 'he has the aid and support of Pope Clement and your brother Henry Beauclerc, and many others. It is my belief that they mean to force your abdication in favour of Duke Robert, or face excommunication.'

This stole the swagger from the English monarch's tail, I can tell you. 'I knew it!' he growled. To his knights, he said, 'I told you they were scheming against me.' Then, just as quick, he turned to Bran and demanded, 'You have proof of this?'

'I do, Lord King,' said Bran. 'A document has come into my possession which has been signed by those making conspiracy against you.'

'You have this document, do you?' said the king.

'I do, Sire,' replied Bran.

William thrust out a broad, calloused hand. 'Give it to me.'

Bran put his hand inside his robe and brought out the folded parchment which had been so painstakingly copied by the monks at Saint Dyfrig's abbey. It was wrapped in its cloth, and Bran clutched it firmly in both hands. 'Before I deliver it to you,' he said, 'I ask a boon.'

'Ha!' sneered the king. 'I might have guessed that was coming. You priests are always looking to your own interests. Well, what is it you want? Reward — is that what you want? Money?'

'No, Sire,' said Bran, still holding out the document. 'I want—'

'Yes?' said the king, impatience making him sharp. 'What! Speak, man!'

'Justice,' said Bran quietly. 'I want justice.'

Jago gave our lord's reply, to which William shouted, 'You shall have it!' as he snatched the document away. Unwrapping the thick, folded square, he opened it out and stared at it long and hard. Glancing at Canon Laurent hovering nearby, he lifted a hand to the cleric and said, 'This should be spoken in the presence of witnesses.'

Some have said he never learned to read — at least, he could not read French. 'As it lays, pray you,' he said, thrusting the letter into the cleric's hands. 'Spare us nothing.'

The canon took a moment to study the document, collected himself, cleared his throat, and began to read it out in a clear, strong voice. *'Moi Guillaume par le pardon de Dieu, de Bramber et Seigneur et Brienze, qux trés estimer et reverend Guibert et Ravenna. Salutations dans Dieu mai les tranquillité de Christ, Notré Éternelle Sauveur, rester á vous toujours.'*

It was the letter Jago had read to us that day in Saint Dyfrig's following the Christmas raid. That Laurent read it with far more authority could not be denied; still, though I could understand but little of what he read, I remembered that day we had gathered in Bran's greenwood hut to see what we had got from the Ffreinc. The memory sent a pang of longing through me for those who waited there still. Would I ever hold Nóin in my arms again?

Canon Laurent continued, and his voice filled the room. It seemed that I heard with new ears as I listened to him read the letter again. Adding what I'd learned from Odo to my own small store, the dual purposes behind the words became plain. Yet the thing still held the mystery I had first felt when kneeling in Bran's greenwood hut and staring in quiet wonder at that great gold ring, and the fine gloves, and that wrapped square of expensive parchment. If I failed to see the sense, I had only to look at King William's face hardening into a ferocious scowl to know that whatever he heard in the high-flown words, he liked it not at all.

By the time Laurent reached the letter's conclusion and began reading out the names at the end, William was fair grinding his teeth to nubbins.

'Blood and thunder!' he shouted as the cleric finished. 'Do they think to cast me aside like a gnawed bone?' Turning, he glared at the two knights with him. 'This is treason, mark me! I will not abide it. By the Virgin, I will not!'

365

Bran, who had been closely watching Red William's reaction to the letter, glanced at Mérian, who gave him a secret smile. Straight and tall in the black robe of a priest, hands folded before him as he awaited the king's judgement, he appeared just then more lordly than the ruddy-faced English monarch by a long walk. The king continued to fume and foam awhile, and then, as is natural to a fella like him, he swiftly fell to despatching his enemies. 'How came you by this letter?' he said, retrieving the parchment from the cleric's hands. 'Where did you get it?'

Bran, calm and unruffled as a dove in a cote, simply replied, 'I stole it, Sire.'

'Stole it!' cried William, when Bran's words were translated for him. 'Ha! I like that! Stole it, by the rood!'

'Who did you steal it from?' asked one of the knights, stepping forward.

'It was found among items sent by Baron de Braose to his nephew, Count Falkes in Elfael. The letter, along with a pair of gloves and a papal ring, was taken in a raid on the wagons carrying provisions.'

'You attacked the wagons and stole the provisions?' asked the knight, speaking through Jago.

'I did, yes. The other items were returned to de Braose, along with a careful copy of the letter just read. You have before you the original, and they are none the wiser.'

The knight stared at Bran, mystified. 'Thievery and you a priest. Yet, you stand here and admit it?'

'I am not as you see me,' replied the dark Welshman. 'I am Bran ap Brychan, rightful ruler of Elfael. I was cheated out of my lands by the deceit of Baron de Braose. On the day my father rode out to swear fealty to Your Majesty, the baron killed my father and slaughtered his entire warband. He established his nephew, Count Falkes de Braose, on our lands and continually supplies him with soldiers, money, and provisions in order to further his rule. Together they have made slaves of my people, and forced them to help build fortresses from which to further oppress them. They have driven me and my followers into the forest to live as outlaws in the land our people have owned since time beyond reckoning. All this has been possible through the collusion of Cardinal Ranulf of Bayeux, who acts with the blessing and authority of the crown, and in the king's own name.' Bran paused to let this dagger strike home, then concluded, 'I have come before you this day to trade that which bears the names of the traitors' – he pointed to the letter still clutched in the king's tight grasp – 'for the return of my throne and the liberation of my people.'

Into the silence that followed this bold assertion, Bran added, 'A throne for a throne – English for Welsh. A fair trade, I think. And justice is served.'

Oh, that was well done! Pride swelled in me like a rising sun, and I basked in its warmth and glory. It was that sweet to me just then.

'You shameless and impudent rogue!' snarled the elder of the two knights. 'You stand in the presence of your king and insinuate—'

'Leicester!' shouted King William. 'Leave off! This man has done me a service, and though the circumstances may well be questionable' – he turned again to Bran – 'I will honour it in the same spirit in which it has been rendered.'

At this, Mérian, who had been able to follow most of what was said, clasped her hands and gave out a little gasp of joy. 'God be praised!' she sighed.

'See here, my lord,' protested the one called Leicester. 'You cannot intend—'

'Hold your peace,' cautioned William. 'I do not yet know what I intend. First, I must know what my roguish friend Bran ap Brychan presumes.' To Bran, he said, 'You have presumed so much already, what do you propose for these traitors?'

All eyes were on Bran as Jago conveyed the king's words and Bran answered, his voice steady, 'I leave their punishment in your hands, Sire. For myself I ask only the return of my lands and the recognition of my right to rule my people in peace.'

'You ask a very great deal, thief,' observed the second nobleman.

'And yet it is no more than my due,' Bran countered.

'How do we know this letter is even genuine?' demanded the young knight.

'Do not be an ass,' the king growled. 'The thing is genuine. The imbecile de Braose affixed his seal. I know it well enough. We must think now what is to be done, and that quick. We have a day, likely less, before the others arrive in force. We must work quickly if we are to save ourselves from the trap they have laid for us.'

King William folded the parchment and tucked it under his arm, then stepped forward, extending his hand to Bran. 'My thanks and my friendship. You and your men are forthwith pardoned from any wrong-doing in this matter. Come, friend, we will sit and break fast together and decide what is to be done with those who would steal my kingdom.'

CHAPTER 43

Such palaver with the high and mighty was hard on this simple forester, I can tell you. Ol' Will has had his fill of Ffreinc enough to last him all his allotted days thrice over. If every last one of those horse-faced foreigners were to hop ship back to Normandie, this son of Britain would sing like a lark for joy till the crack o' doom. Nevertheless, here we were up to our neck bones in Normans of every kind, and most of them with sharp steel close to hand.

It fair made me wish for the solace of the greenwood, it did.

And I wasn't the only one with my teeth on edge. Poor Siarles was about as rattled as a tadpole in a barrel of eels. The fella could neither sit nor stand, but that he had to be jumping up every other breath to run to the door to see if any Ffreinc were lurking about ready to pounce on us. Still, though we could hear men moving about the palace, both inside and out, as more of the nobles arrived for their council, they left us to ourselves. The morning passed into midday, and the waiting began to wear on us.

For myself, the pain in my throbbing hand and the toils of the past few days rolled over me like a millstone, and I curled up in a corner and closed my eyes.

'We should go find out what is happening,' I heard Mérian say, and Iwan agreed.

'Aye,' replied the big man. 'Bran might need our help.'

The two had just about worked themselves up to go and see what they could discover, Siarles was fussing and fretting, and Cinnia — too frightened to know what to do — had come to sit beside me, when the door opened and Bran and Jago strolled into the room.

You'd be forgiven for thinkin' they'd been twice around the moon and back the way we ran to greet them. Before either one of them could speak, Iwan swooped in. 'Well?' he demanded.

'What did the king say?' asked Mérian. 'Will he help us?'

'Will he give back our lands?' said Siarles, joining the tight cluster around Bran. 'When can we go?'

I roused myself, and Cinnia helped me to my feet and we joined the others.

'Come, tell us, Bran,' said Iwan. 'What did the king say?'

'He said a great many things,' Bran replied, his voice a sigh of resignation. 'Not all of them seemly, or even sensible.'

To my weary eye, our Bran and Brother Jago seemed a little frazzled and frayed from their encounter with the English monarch. 'King William keeps a close counsel,' Jago added. 'He gives away little and demands much. Yet I believe he has a mind to help us insofar as it helps him to do so. Beyond that, who can say?'

Who could say, indeed!

We had risked all to bring word of high treason to the king — and now that he had it, we were to be swept aside like the crumbs of yesterday's supper.

'He didn't give us back our lands?' whined Siarles.

'No, he did not,' Bran confirmed. 'At least, not yet. We are to wait here for his answer.'

Siarles blew air through his nostrils. 'To think that after all this we are beholden to that fat toad of a king!' he grumbled. 'We should have supported Duke Robert instead!'

'No, we made the right choice.' Bran was firm on that point. 'Listen to me, all of you, and do not forget: we made the right choice. William is king, and only William has the power to give us back our lands. The king is justice for the people who must live beneath his rule. Our only hope is Red William.'

'Duke Robert would have been king and returned our lands to us,' Siarles insisted. 'If we had supported him, he would have supported us in turn, and we'd have what is ours by rights.'

Mérian gave Siarles a glance that could have cut timber. The rough forester glared back at her, but mumbled, 'If I have spoken above myself, I am sorry, my lord, and I do beg your pardon. It just seems that for all our trouble we are no better off than before.'

Bran clapped his hand to the back of Siarles' neck, drew him close, and said, 'Siarles, my friend, if you truly think supporting Robert would avail us anything, you might as well join those traitors who are even now gathering to work their wiles.' Bran spoke softly, but there was no mistaking his resolve. 'But while you are thinking on it, remember that Baron de Braose is one of the chief rebels. It is his hand squeezing our throats and his arm supporting Robert. If Duke Robert were to become king of England, bloody de Braose would become more powerful still, and he would never surrender his grip on our lands.'

'Bran is right,' Iwan declared. 'The only way to get rid of de Braose is to expose him to the king.'

'We have warned Red William in good time, and now he can move to disarm the traitors,' Bran explained, releasing Siarles. 'I have put our case before the king, and we must hope he succeeds in punishing those who have conspired against him.'

'Well,' said Siarles, rubbing his neck. He was still not completely convinced. 'It seems we have no other hope.'

'It has been this way from the start,' Bran said. 'We have done all we can. It is in God's hands.'

See now, Bran was right. Never doubt it. We had no other hope for redress in this world, save William and William alone. But Siarles, bless his thick head, was not wrong to raise the question. Truth to tell, it was something I wondered at first myself – and it was not until Odo told me about the two popes that I began to see my way through that tangled wood. Why would Baron de Braose write a letter like that? Who was it for? Then I remembered who had signed that letter, and although I could not recall all the names, I remembered Duke Robert right enough, and wondered why the king's brother and one of Red William's dearest barons should be makin' up a letter like that.

Oh, it was a right riddle to be sure. But the answer was there starin' us in the face all along. We just didn't see it.

Yet sitting there in that rank pit of a gaol, a fella begins to see lots of things in a different way, if you know what I mean. Ol' Will had time to think and little else.

Even so, when my monkish scribe let out there were two popes, God knows I didn't believe him. Odo was so convinced, his conviction carried me along in the end. I considered it a mite curious that Baron de Braose should take up with Clement when the whole of England, so far as I knew, answered to a pope named Urban. What could it mean?

Two popes. One throne. What else could it mean but that the men who signed the letter had bartered their support for Pope Clement in order to gain the throne of England for their favourite, Duke Robert? Outright rebellion had been tried and had failed; Robert could not be trusted to enter the fray even in his own interest, as many an upright Englishman discovered to his hurt – my old master Aelred included, God rest him. So this time, they meant to use the church somehow. Although I could not rightly say how they meant to force the abdication, the more I thought about it, the more certain I became that the men who had put their names to that letter had formed a conspiracy with the aim of plucking the crown from William's round grizzled head and placing it on luckless brother Robert's. This is why de Braose was so murderously desperate to get that letter back. More valuable by far than the big gold ring or fine leather gloves – mere fancies, after all – that sealed square of parchment exposed the traitors and, if I guessed aright, was well worth a throne.

'God's hands or no,' Mérian was saying, 'I could wish we knew what was happening now. To have come this far only to be shut out sits ill, so it does.'

'Never fear,' Brother Jago replied. 'God's ways may be mystery past finding out, but he hears all who call upon his name. Therefore, be of good cheer! God alone is our rock and our fortress, our friend and very present help in times of trouble.'

'That was a sermon entire, Brother,' observed Iwan. He turned to Bran and asked, 'How much longer are we to loiter here?'

Some little time, I reckoned. As the day wore on, though we heard men moving in the corridors and rooms 'round about the palace, no one darkened our doorway. One by one, we settled back to wait. I sat propped against the wall in one corner, and after a time, Bran joined me. 'How are the fingers, Will?' he asked, sliding down into his place beside me.

'Not so bad,' I told him. 'The pain comes and goes, but not so much as before.' I did not like dwelling on that, so I asked, 'What do you think Red William will do?'

Bran was quick to reply. 'I expect he'll give back our lands,' he said, an edge to his voice. 'Brother Jago was eloquent on our behalf, and I think we made him understand in the end. He promised justice, and we will hold him to it.'

That, of course, was deeply to be hoped. 'We owe you a debt, Will Scarlet,' he said. 'Your quick thinking gave us the chance we needed to save Elfael.'

'Well, it took me long enough,' I allowed, 'but we got here in time. That is all that matters.'

'There's still one thing I wonder,' Bran said. 'How did you work out the nature of the conspiracy?'

'Well, now,' I said, running back over the events of the last days in my mind. 'It was all those days talking to Odo and getting an idea how those Normans think – that's what started it. Then, when I learned about the two popes, it seemed to me that the letter was intended as a treaty of sorts – why else write it all down?'

'A treaty,' mused Bran. 'I never thought of that. You mean Duke Robert and Baron de Braose agreed to support Clement's claim to the throne of Peter, if the pope would support Robert's claim to the throne of England.'

'Our William is not well loved,' I added. 'And, as I know from my old master Aelred, his barons almost succeeded in unseating the king last time they rebelled. I reckoned things have only got worse for them since then. I know William is no lover of the church.'

'He uses it as his own treasure store,' Bran said. 'Helps himself whenever he can.'

'Aye, he does – and that's the nub. Our William milks it like a cow, keeping all the cream for himself. But if that was to stop, his throne would begin to totter, if you see what I mean.'

'With both the barons and the church against him, the king could not stand,' observed Bran. 'I got that much from your message.'

'A bit o' blind luck, that,' I told him, shaking my head at the remarkable string of events that small patch of parchment had set off. 'I wasn't sure what you'd make of it, or what you'd be able to do about it. I didn't even dare hope that scrap would reach you. I had only Odo to depend on, mind. He's a Norman, but he gave good service in the end. I'd like to do something for him one day.' I paused and looked around the bare room and at our unlikely company. 'God's own truth, my lord, I never dreamed it would come to this — squattin' in the palace of the archbishop of Rouen and waitin' for the king of England to decide our fate.'

'My lord!' said Siarles, speaking up from his place across the room. 'Are we to be expected to sit here all day like moss on a log?'

As if to answer his question, there was a bustle in the corridor and the door to our chamber opened. Canon Laurent strode into the room with two clerics dressed in robes similar to his own; with them were three knights from King William's force. All wore solemn expressions. The knights carried swords at their belts, and two gripped lances. The canon held a scrap of parchment and carried it flat between his hands as if the ink was still wet on the surface of the page. 'Peace and grace,' said the canon, which I understood. 'I have come directly from private council with King William, who expresses his highest regards, and sends this message to you.'

Mérian stepped beside Bran and slid her hand into his. They stood side by side, an unlikely pair in their disguises. The rest of us drew near, too, taking our places beside our lord and his lady to receive the judgement of the king. Whatever the king's decision might be, whether for good or ill, we would take it standing together as one.

'Hear the king's words,' said Laurent, raising the parchment. 'Be it known that in gratitude for his good service to our crown and throne, William, by the grace of God, king of England, does hereby bestow the sum of thirty pounds in silver to be used to aid and assist Lord Bran ap Brychan and his company to return home by the way he has come . . .'

'What?' complained Iwan, when this much had been translated for us. 'He's sending us home? What about the return of our lands?'

'Peace, Iwan.' Bran held up his hand for silence. He nodded to Jago.

'Pray, continue,' Jago said to the canon.

'Further,' resumed Laurent, 'His Majesty, King William, serves notice that you are commanded to attend him at the royal residence at Winchester on the third day after the Feast of the Archangels, known as Michaelmas. At that appointed place and time you will receive the king's judgement in the matters laid before him this day.'

Here Laurent broke off. Looking up from the proclamation, he said, 'Do you understand what I have read to you?'

When Jago had finished translating these words, Bran said, 'With all respect to the king, we will stay here and await his judgement. It may be that we can help bear witness against the rebels.'

'No,' answered the cleric, 'after today it will be too dangerous for you to remain here, and the king cannot ensure your safety. The king has commanded that you are to be escorted to your ship at once and you are to make your way home by the swiftest means possible. His Majesty the king wishes you a pleasant journey and may God speed you in all safety to your destination.'

Steal breath from a baby, we were stunned.

We had come all this way prepared to bargain, plead, fight tooth and nail for the return of our lands only to be tossed lightly onto the midden heap like so much dung. It beggared belief, I can tell you. Though Bran tried to get the canon to see the thing as we did, and though the cleric sympathised in his way, Laurent could do nothing. The king had allowed him no room to wiggle; there was nothing for it but to take the money and go.

Red William is every inch as much a rogue as any of his bloody barons, no mistake. The king's knights escorted us to our horses and accompanied us back down the hill and through the town to the river wharf and our waiting ship. We rode in silence all the way, and my own heart was heavy until we came in sight of the *Dame Havik* at her mooring – and then I remembered Nóin. Suddenly, I cared no longer about the doings of the high and mighty. My sole aim and desire was to see my love and hold her in my arms – and each moment I was prevented from doing that was a moment that chafed and chapped me raw. From the instant I set foot on the deck of that ship to the day I stepped off it and onto solid English earth once more, I was a man with an itch I could not scratch.

When on that fine, sunny day we bade our friend Ruprecht farewell and took our leave a little lighter in the pocket, to be sure – for we paid that Flemish sailor well for his excellent and praiseworthy care – it was all I could do to keep from lashing my poor mount all the way back to Elfael. I counted the quarters of the days until I at last saw the greenwood rising in the distance on the slopes of the ridge beyond the Vale of Wye, and then I counted the steps as I watched that great shaggy pelt bristling beneath a sky of shining blue and my heart beat faster for the sight. S'truth, only the man who has journeyed to far distant lands and returned to his native earth after braving dangers, toil, and hardships aplenty can know how I felt just then. I was seized by joy and flown to dizzy heights of elation only to be dashed to the rocks again with the very next thought. For as glad as I was to be going home, I was that afraid something might yet prevent me reaching the one I loved. All saints bear witness, our little company could not move fast enough for me. I fair wore out the goodwill of my companions long before we reached the blasted oak at the entrance to Cél Craidd.

When I came in sight of that black stump, I threw myself from the saddle and was halfway to the lightning-riven oak as through heaven's own gate before I noticed someone standing there.

'Nóin?' I could scarce believe my eyes. She was there waiting for me!

'Is that you, Will Scarlet?' Her voice held a quiver. Surprise? Uncertainty? But she made no move toward me.

I stepped nearer, my heart beating high up in my throat, and put out a hand to her. 'It is . . . ,' I replied, unable to speak above a whisper just then. 'It is Will come home.'

She regarded me with an almost stern expression, her eyes dry. 'Have you, Will? Have you come home at last?'

'That I have, my love.' I stepped nearer. 'Now that I see you, I know I am home at last.'

As many times as I saw this glad reunion in my mind, I did not see it this way. She nodded. I saw her swallow then, and guessed something of what this confrontation – for such it was – cost her. But she did not back down. She held me with her uncompromising gaze. 'I have to know, Will,' she said, 'if you've come back to stay. I cannot wait for you any longer. I have to know.'

'Nóin, my love, with God as my witness, I will nevermore part from you.'

'Don't!' she cried. 'Don't you say that. You don't know.'

'What do you want me to say?' I asked. 'If it is a pledge you seek, tell me what pledge you will accept and I will give it gladly.' As she considered this, I added, 'I love you, Nóin. I loved you every blesséd day I lay in that dark hole, and if I could have come to you even a heartbeat sooner, I would have been back at your side long ere you knew I'd gone.'

She bent her head then, and her long hair fell down around her face. I could see her lips trembling.

'Nóin,' I said, moving closer. 'If you no longer want me, you have only to say the word and I will leave you be. Is that what you want?'

She shook her head, but did not look at me.

I raised my arms and held them out to her. 'Then come to me, my love. Let us return to the happiness we once knew. Or, if that be not possible anymore, let us begin a new and better joy.'

When she raised her head this time, I saw the tears streaking her fair cheeks. 'Oh, Will . . . ,' she sobbed. 'I've missed you so much . . . so much . . . I did not dare to hope . . .'

She came into my arms, and I crushed her to my chest with all the strength I did possess. I held her and felt the hardness in her melt away as she clung to me, her tears soaking into my shirt.

'Will dear, sweet Will, I'm so sorry,' she said. 'I had to be sure. I couldn't live thinking . . . forgive me.'

'There is nothing to forgive. I am here now, and I love you more than ever I did the day I left.'

'And will you yet wed me?' she asked, looking tearfully into my face.

The sight of those tears glistening on her cheeks melted any shreds of dignity I might have had left. I sank to my knees before her and clasped her around the waist. 'Marry me, Nóin. I want you so bad it hurts my heart.'

The words were still fresh on my lips when I felt her arms encircle my neck; she raised me to my feet, and her warm lips bathed my scruffy face in kisses. 'Nóin . . . ,' I gasped when I could breathe again. 'Oh, Nóin, I will never leave you. I swear . . .'

'Shh,' she hushed. 'Don't speak, Will. Just hold me.'

I was happy to do that, no mistake. We stood there in the heart of the greenwood clutching one another so tight we could hardly draw a breath between us. And we were clinging still when the others reached the riven oak where we stood. They dismounted, and Bran let out a wild, withering screech. Instantly, the Grellon began pouring up out of the bowl of Cél Craidd to greet the return of their king and kinsmen.

The next thing I knew, I was half pulled, half pushed through the oak and tumbled down the hillside into the bowl of our hidden settlement. At first glance, everything appeared just as I remembered it – only it was early summer now, and I had left in the dead of winter. Still, all was as it should be, I reckoned, until I began to tell the little differences. The forest folk were right glad to see us, but there was a hollow sound to their laughter, and their smiles, though genuine and heartfelt, held more pain than pleasure. The faces gathered 'round us were greyer than I remembered, the bodies thinner. Winter had been hard for them, yes, and spring no better, I reckoned. Many were gaunt, with skin pinched around their deep-set eyes; their clothes were that much more tattered and frayed; the dirt on their hands and faces was there for good and always.

My heart went out to them. I had endured captivity in the sheriff's odious hellhole, but they were no less captive here. The wildwood of Coed Cadw had become as much a prison as any that the vile de Glanville held key to. It was clear to me then, if never before: this sorry state could not be endured much longer. God willing, our bold King William would soon give us redress, and Bran and all us forest folk could move out into the light once more.

In amongst the young 'uns I saw little Nia's face poking out. I turned and scooped her up. She did not cry out, but twisted in my arms to see who held her. 'Weo!' she squealed, grabbing my beard with both hands. 'Wee-o!'

Bless her, she was trying to say my name. 'It's me, dear heart. Ol' Will is here.'

From among the flock gathering to greet our return, I glimpsed Angharad, hobbling forward on her long staff, her wrinkled face alight with pleasure. 'I bid thee glad homecoming, William Scatlocke,' she crowed, her old voice quavering slightly. 'The Lord of Hosts is smiling on this day.'

'Greetings, Wise Banfáith,' I said, offering her a bow and touching the back of my hand to my forehead. 'It is that good to see you again.'

'And you, Will.' She drew close and stood for a moment, smiling up at me. Then, closing her eyes, she raised her hand and touched two fingers lightly to my forehead. 'All Wise and Loving Father, we thank you for redeeming the life of our friend, delivering him from his enemies, and bringing him back to us in answer to our prayers. Bless him and prosper him for your name's sake, and bless all who think well of him this day and all days henceforth.'

As she prayed, I felt Nóin's hand squeeze my arm. I thanked our bard and then turned to the others who were crowding in to make good my welcome. 'Here now! Here now!' came a shout, and I was enwrapped and lifted off my feet in a rib-cracking embrace.

'Tuck!' I said. 'Are you here, too?'

'Where else should I be, but among my own dear flock on the day of your miraculous return? We've been waiting for this day with a greedy impatience, my friend,' he said, his round face beaming. God bless him, there were tears in his eyes.

'Brother,' I said, pulling Nóin close, 'if you are not too busy, this lady and I are that keen to be married. If you have no objection, I want you to perform the ceremony today.'

'Today!' replied Tuck. 'Today, says he! Well!' To Nóin, he said, 'Is this also your desire?'

'It is my deepest desire,' she replied, her arm around my waist.

'Well, then,' concluded Tuck, 'I do not see any reason to delay.' He glanced around. 'What have you done with Bran and the others?'

Casting a glance behind me, I saw my travelling companions standing on the top of the low natural rampart that surrounded Cél Craidd. I called to them. 'Why were you standing there?' I asked when they had joined us.

'We wanted you to have a proper greeting all to yourself,' Iwan explained.

'And would you leave me standing here alone on my wedding day?' I said.

'Oh, Will! Nóin!' cried Mérian. She pressed Nóin's hands in hers, then kissed me lightly on the cheek. 'This is such good news.'

We then endured the good wishes of Bran, Iwan, and the others in turn, and I was pummelled good-naturedly by one and all. When the festive drubbing was finished, I turned to Tuck and said, 'Friar, I'd be much obliged if you could perform the rites without delay.' I glanced at Nóin and saw the desire in her dark eyes. 'As soon as may be.'

Tuck nodded and adopted a solemn air. 'Is it your wish to be married to this man?' he asked.

'It is, Friar,' she replied. 'I would have done it long since, and there is no better day that I know than this, and I would mark it always in my heart as the day my man was given back to me.'

'Then so be it!'

Turning to the Grellon crowding around, the little friar called, 'Hear now! Will and Nóin have declared their desire to be married. Let us give them a wedding they will never forget!'

If I had any notion of simply saying a few words before the priest and carrying off my bride to a little greenwood bower in the manner of my English father, that idea was dashed to pieces quicker than it takes a fella to spit and say 'I do!' The forest folk fell to with a will. I suppose the safe and successful return of the rescue party was the best excuse any of them had had to celebrate anything in many a month, and the people were that eager to make a fair run at it. Nóin and I were immediately caught up in the preparations for this sudden celebration.

The cooking fire was built up; partridges and quail were pulled from the snares, then plucked and spitted along with half a young wild pig, and six coneys and a score of barley loaves set to bake. The children were sent into the thickets to gather raspberries and red currants, which were mixed with honey and made into a deep red compote; asparagus and wild mushrooms were likewise picked, chopped, and boiled into a stew with borage and herbs; the last of the walnuts which had been dried over the winter were shelled into a broth of milk and honey; and many another dish to make the heart glad. Whatever stores had been set aside against even leaner days were brought out for our wedding feast, and it did rightly make a humble man of me, I can tell you.

While the men constructed a bower of birch branches for us to enjoy our first night together, some of the women gathered flowers to strew our path and for Nóin to carry, and one or two of the younger ones helped dress the bride and make her even more lovely in my eyes.

As for myself, with little else to do, I set about trying to drag a razor through the tough tangle of my beard. I succeeded in cutting myself in such extravagant fashion that our good friar took the blade from my hand, sat me down and, expert barber that he was, shaved me clean as a newborn. He also combed and cut my hair so that I appeared almost a nobleman when my clothes were brushed and my shoes washed. He found a new belt for me and a clean cloak of handsome green. 'There now!' he declared, like God regarding Adam with a critical eye. 'I have made me a man.'

I thanked him kindly for his attentions, and observed that my only regret was that I had no ring to give my bride. 'A ring is a fine thing, is it not?' he agreed. 'But it is by no means necessary. A coin will do; and some, I have heard, have a smith bend the coin to make a ring. You might easily do this.'

This cheered me no end. 'You are a wonder, no mistake,' I told him. 'I can get a coin.' And, leaving the friar to his own preparations, I set off to do just that.

The first person I went to was Bran. 'My lord,' I said, 'I do not think I have asked a boon of you since swearing the oath of fealty.'

Lord Bran allowed that, as he could not think of any occasions, either.

'Then, if it please you, my lord,' I continued, 'I will make bold to request the small favour of a coin to give my bride.' I quickly went on to explain that I had no ring, but that Tuck had said a coin would serve as a suitable token.

'Indeed?' wondered Bran. 'Then leave it to me.'

Well, we were soon caught up in countless small activities and the mood was high. Before I knew it, the sun had already begun its descent when our good friar declared that all was finally ready and we gathered beneath the Council Oak to speak our vows before our friends. Tuck, scrubbed until he gleamed, and beaming like a cherub fresh from the Radiant Presence, took his place before us and called all to solemn purpose. 'This is a holy time,' he said, 'and a joyous celebration. Our Heavenly Father delights in love in all its wondrous forms. Especially dear to him is the love between a husband and wife. May such love increase!'

This brought a rousing chorus of agreement from the onlookers, and Tuck waited for silence before continuing. 'Therefore,' he said, 'let us ask the Author and Sustainer of our love and life to bless the union of these two dear people who have pledged life and love to one another.'

With that he began to pray and prayed so long I feared we would not finish the ceremony until the sun had gone down, or possibly the next morning. Eventually, he ran out of words to say to bless and beseech, and moved on to the vows, which we spoke out as Tuck instructed. There in the greenwood, beneath that venerable oak, we pledged life to life, come what may, and I took Nóin to be my wife. When the time came to give my bride a token of honour, I turned to Bran and, taking my one good hand in both of his, he pressed a coin into my palm. 'With greatest esteem and pleasure,' he said.

I looked down and saw that he had given me a solid gold byzant, gleaming dull and heavy in my hand. I gazed at that rare coin as at a fortune entire. Truly, I had never had anything worth so much in all my life. That he should think so much of me made the tears come to my eyes. The long months of my captivity were somehow redeemed in that moment as I placed that matchless coin in the hand of my beloved, pledging to honour and keep her through all things forever more.

Then it was another prayer – this one for children aplenty to bless us and keep us in our old age – and we knelt together as Tuck placed a hand on each of our heads and proclaimed, 'I present to you Master William Scatlocke and his wife, Nóinina. All praise to our Lord and Kind Creator for his wise provision!'

Of the feast, I remember little. I am told it was very good, and I must have tasted some of it. But my appetite was elsewhere by then, and I could not wait until Nóin and I could be together. We sat on the bench at the head of the board and received the good wishes of our friends. Mérian, with Lord Bran in tow, came by twice to say how much she had longed for this day on our behalf. Iwan and Siarles came to give us an old poem that they knew, full of words with double meanings which soon had everyone screaming with laughter. The celebration was so light and full of joy that I clean forgot about my mangled fingers, and I cannot recall giving them a solitary thought all that fine and happy day.

When the moon rose and the fire was banked high, Angharad brought out her harp and began to sing. She sang a song unknown to me, as to most of us, I suppose, about a beautiful maiden who conceived a love for a man she had seen passing by her window one day. The young woman decided to follow the stranger, braving great hardship crossing mountain and moor in her quest to find him once more and declare her love for him. She persevered through many terrors and misfortunes and at last came into the valley where her love lived. He saw her approaching – her beautiful gown begrimed and bedraggled, her fine leather shoes worn through and wrapped in rags, her beautiful hair dull with dust from the road, her once-fair cheeks sunken with hunger, her slender fingers worn, her full lips chapped and bleeding – and ran to meet her. As she came near, however, she chanced to see her own reflection in a puddle in the road, and horrified at what she saw, she turned and ran away. The man pursued her and caught her, and knowing what she had endured to find him, his heart swelled with love for her. And in that moment, he saw her as she was, and the power of his love transformed her broken form into one even more beautiful than that which had been.

I confess, there might have been more, but I was only listening with half an ear, for I was gazing at my own lovely bride and wishing we could steal away to the birch bower in the wood. Bran must have guessed what was in my mind, for as the song concluded and the people called for another, he came up behind me and said, 'Go now, both of you. Mérian and I will take your places.'

We did not need urging. That quick I was up and out of my seat and taking Nóin by the hand. We flitted off into the wood, leaving Bran and Mérian at the board. By the light of a summer moon, we made our way along the path to the bower, where candles were already lit and the mead in a jar warming by a small fire. Fleeces had been spread on a bed of fresh rushes. There was food beneath a cloth for us to break our fast in the morning. 'Oh, Will!' said Nóin, when she saw it, 'It is lovely – just as I always hoped it would be.'

'And so, my lady, are you,' I told her, and, pulling her close, kissed her with the first of countless kisses we would share that night.

As for the rest, I need not say more. If you have ever loved anyone, then you will know full well. If not, then nothing I can say will enlighten you.

CHAPTER 44

Caer Rhodl

Even though he had known this day was coming, the news caught Baron Neufmarché off his guard. He had just returned from a short trip to Lundein and afterward gone to his chapel to observe Mass and to offer a prayer of thanks for his safe return and a season of gainful commerce. Father Gervais was officiating, and the old priest who usually mumbled through the service in a low, unintelligible drone, perked up when the lord of Hereford appeared in the doorway of the small, stone church tucked inside the castle wall.

Priest and worshipper acknowledged one another with a glance and a nod, as the baron slipped into the enclosed wooden stall which served his family during their observances in the chapel. The priest moved through the various sequences of the daily office, lifting his voice and lingering over the scripture passages so that the baron, whose Latin he knew to be limited, could follow more easily. He chanted with his eyes closed, saying, *'Deus, qui omnipoténtiam tuam parcéndo maxime et miserando maniféstas,'* his old voice straining after the notes that once came so easily.

At those long familiar strains, Bernard felt himself relax; the toil of his recent journey overtook him, and he slumped back on the bench and rested his head against the high back of the stall. He was soon asleep, and remained happily so until some inner prompting woke him at the beginning of the dismissal. Upon hearing the words '*Dominus vobiscum,*' he roused himself and sat up.

Father Gervais was making the sign of the cross above the altar of the near-empty sanctuary. '*Benedicat vos omnipotens Deus Pater, et Filius, et Spiritus Sanctus,*' he intoned, his deep voice loud in the small, stone chapel; and Neufmarché joined him in saying, 'Amen.'

The service concluded, the elderly priest stepped down from the low platform to greet the baron. 'Dear Bernard,' he said, extending his hands in welcome, 'you have returned safely. I trust your journey was profitable?'

'It was, Father,' answered the baron. He stifled a yawn with the back of his hand. 'Very profitable.' The old man took his arm and the two walked out into the brilliant light of a glorious late-summer day. 'And how are things with you, Father?' he said as they stepped into the shaded path between the castle rampart and the rising wall of the tower keep.

'About the same, my son. Oh, yes, well . . .' He paused a moment to collect his thoughts. 'Ah, now then. But perhaps you haven't heard yet. I fear I may be the bearer of bad news, Bernard.'

'Bad news, Father?' The baron had not heard anything on the road, nor in the town when he passed through. None of the household servants had hinted that anything was amiss; he had not seen Lady Agnes since his return, otherwise he would certainly have been informed. His wife delighted in ill tidings — the worse the better. He glanced at the old man beside him, but Father Gervais did not appear distraught in the least. 'I have heard nothing.'

'A rider arrived this morning from your foreign estates — what do you call them? Eye-ass?'

'Eiwas,' the baron corrected gently. 'It is a commot in Wales, Father, ruled by my client, Lord Cadwgan — a local nobleman enfeoffed to me.'

'Ah, your liegeman, yes.' The doddering priest nodded.

'The messenger, Father,' prompted Neufmarché gently, 'what did he say?'

'He said that the king has died,' said the priest. 'Would that be the same one, King Kad . . . Kadeuka . . . no, that can't be right.'

'Cadwgan,' corrected Neufmarché. 'King Cadwgan is dead, you say?'

'I am sorry, Bernard, but yes. There is to be a funeral, and they are wanting to know if you would attend. I asked the fellow to wait for you, but we didn't know when you would return, so he went on his way.'

'When is the funeral to be held?'

'Well.' The priest smiled and patted his temple. 'This old head may not work as swiftly as once it did, but I do not forget.' He made a calculation, tapping his chin with his fingertips. 'Two days from tomorrow, I believe. Yes, something like that.'

'In three days!' exclaimed the baron.

'I think that's what he said, yes,' agreed the priest affably. 'Is it far, this Eye-as place?'

'Far enough,' sighed the baron. He could reach Caer Rhodl in time for the funeral, but he would have to leave at once, with at least one night on the road. Having just spent six days travelling, the last thing he wanted was to sit another three days in the saddle.

A brief search led the baron to the one place he might have guessed his wife would be found. She was sitting in the warmest room of Castle Hereford — a small, square chamber above the great hall. It had no feature other than a wide, south-facing window which, during the long summer, admitted the sunlight the whole day through. Lady Agnes, dressed in a gauzy fluff of pale yellow linen, had set up her tapestry frame beside the wide-open window and was plying her needle with a fierce, almost vengeful concentration. She glanced up as he came in, needle poised to attack, saw who it was, and as if stabbing an enemy, plunged the long needle into the cloth before her. 'You have returned, my lord,' she observed, pulling the thread tight. 'Pleasant journey?'

'Pleasant enough,' said Neufmarché. 'You have fared well in my absence, I trust.'

'I make no complaint.'

Her tone suggested that his absence was the cause of no end of tribulations, too tiresome to mention now that he was back. *Why did she always do that?* he wondered, and decided to ignore the comment and move straight to the meat of the matter at hand. 'Cadwgan has died at last,' he said. 'I must go to the funeral.'

'Of course,' she agreed. 'How long will you be away this time?'

'Six days at least,' he answered. 'Eight, more like. I'd hoped I'd seen the last of the saddle for a while.'

'Then take a carriage,' suggested Agnes, striking with the needle once more.

'A carriage.' He stared at her as if he'd never heard the word before. 'I will not be seen riding in a carriage like an invalid,' he sniffed.

'You are a baron of the March,' his wife pointed out. 'You can do what you like. There is no shame in travelling in comfort with an entourage as befits a man of your rank and nobility. You could also travel at night, if need be.'

The baron spied a table in the corner of the room and, on it, a silver platter with a jar and three goblets. He strode to the table and took up the jar to find that it contained sweet wine. He poured himself a cup, then poured one for his lady wife. 'If I got a carriage, you could come to the funeral with me,' he said, extending the goblet to her.

'Me?' What little colour she had drained from the baroness's thin face; the needle halted in midflight. 'Go to Wales? Perish the thought. *C'est impossible!* No.'

'It is not impossible,' answered her husband, urging the cup on her. 'I go there all the time, as you know.'

She shook her head, pursing her thin lips into a frown. 'I will not consort with barbarians.'

'They are not barbarians,' the baron told her, still holding out the cup of wine. 'They are crude and uneducated, true, and given to strange customs, God knows. But they are intelligent in their own way, and capable of many of the higher virtues.'

Lady Agnes folded her spindly arms across her narrow bosom. 'That is as may be,' she allowed coolly. 'But they are a contentious and bloody race who love nothing more than carving Norman heads from Norman shoulders.' She shivered violently and reached for the shawl that was perpetually close to hand. 'You have said as much yourself.'

'In the main, that may be true,' the baron granted, warming to the idea of his wife's company as he contemplated the more subtle nuances of the situation. To arrive at the funeral on horseback leading a company of mounted knights and men-at-arms would certainly reinforce his position as lord and master of the cantref – but arriving with the baroness beside him in a carriage, accompanied by a domestic entourage, would firmly place his visit on a more social and personal footing. This, he was increasingly certain, was just the right note to strike with Cadwgan's family, kinsmen, countrymen, and heir. In short, he was convinced it was an opportunity not to be missed.

Placing the goblet firmly in her hand, he drank from his cup and declared, 'Ordinarily, I would agree with you. However, my Welsh fief-dom is an exception. We have been on productive and peaceful terms for many years, and your appearance at this time will commence a new entente between our two noble houses.'

Lady Agnes frowned and glared into her cup as if it contained poison. She did not like the way this conversation was going, but saw no way to disarm the baron in his full-gallop charge. 'May it please you, my lord,' she said, shoving back her chair and rising to her feet, 'I will send with you a letter of condolence for the women of the house and my sincere regret at not being able to offer such comforts in person.'

She stepped around the tapestry frame to where the baron was standing, rose up on her toes, and kissed his forehead, then bade him good afternoon. Bernard watched his wife – head high, back stiff – as she walked to the door. Oh, she could be stubborn as a barnyard ass. In that, she was her father's daughter to the last drop of her Angevin blood.

She might balk, but she would do as she was told. He hurried to his chambers below and called for his seneschal. 'Remey,' he said when his chief servant appeared carrying a tray laden with cold meat, cheese, bread, and ale. 'I need a carriage. Lady Agnes and I will attend the funeral of my Welsh client, Cadwgan. My lady's maidservants will attend her, and tell my sergeant to choose no fewer than eight knights and as many men-at-arms. Tell them to make ready to march before nightfall.'

'It will be done, Sire,' replied the seneschal, touching the rolled brim of his soft cap.

'Thank you,' said Neufmarché with a gesture of dismissal. As the ageing servant reached the door, the baron called out, 'And Remey! See to it that the carriage is good and stout. The roads are rock-lined ruts beyond the March. I want something that will get us there and back without breaking wheels and axles at every bump.'

393

'To be sure, my lord,' replied Remey. 'Will you require anything else?'

'Spare no effort. I want it ready at once,' the baron said. 'We must leave before the day is out if we are to reach Caer Rhodl in time.'

The seneschal withdrew, and the baron sat down to his meal in solitude, his thoughts already firmly enmeshed in grand schemes for his Welsh commot and his long-cherished desire for expansion in the territory. Prince Garran would take his father's place on the throne of Eiwas, and under the baron's tutelage would become the perfect tool in the baron's hand. Together they would carve a wide swathe through the fertile lowlands and grass-covered slopes of the Welsh hill country. The Britons possessed a special knack with cattle, it had to be admitted; when matched with the insatiable Norman appetite for beef, the fortune to be made might well exceed even the baron's more grandiose fancies.

The carriage Remey chose for the journey was surprisingly comfortable, muffling the judders and jolts of the deeply rutted roads and rocky trackways, making the journey almost agreeable. Accompanied by a force of sixteen knights and men-at-arms on horseback, and a train of seven pack mules with servants to attend them, they could not have been more secure. The baron noted that even Lady Agnes, once resigned to the fact that there was no escaping her fate, had perked up. After the second day, a little colour showed in her pale cheeks, and by the time the wooden fortress that was Caer Rhodl came into view, she had remarked no fewer than three times how good it was to get out of the perpetual chill of the castle. '*Merveilleux!*' she exclaimed as a view of the distant mountains hove into view. 'Simply glorious.'

'I am so glad you approve, my dear,' remarked the baron dryly.

'I had no idea it could be like this,' she confessed. 'So wild so beautiful. And yet . . .'

'Yes?'

'And yet so, so very, very empty. It makes me sad somehow – the *mélancolie*, no? Do not tell me you do not feel it, my love.'

'Oh, but I do,' answered the baron, taking unexpected delight in his headstrong wife's rare reversal of opinion. 'I do feel it. No matter how often I visit the lands beyond the March, I always sense a sorrow I cannot explain – as if the hills and valleys hold secrets it would break the heart to hear.'

'Yes, perhaps,' granted Agnes. 'Quaint, yes, and perhaps a little mysterious. But not frightening. I thought it would be more frightening somehow.'

'Well, as you see it today, with the sun pouring bright gold upon the fields, it does appear a more cheerful place. God knows, that is not always the way.'

In due course, the travelling company was greeted on the road by riders sent out from the caer to welcome them and provide a proper escort into Cadwgan's stronghold. Upon entering the circular yard behind the timber palisade, they were met by Prince Garran and his three principal advisors – one of his own and two who had served his father for many years.

'Baron Neufmarché!' called Garran, striding forth with his arms outspread in welcome as his guests stepped down from the carriage. '*Pax vobiscum*, my lord. God be good to you.'

'And to you,' replied the baron. 'I could wish this a happier time, but I think we all knew this day would come. Now that it is here, my sympathies are with you and your mother. You have suffered much, I think, the past two years.'

'We struggle on,' replied the prince.

'You do,' agreed the baron, 'and it does you credit.' He turned to his wife and presented her to the young prince.

'Baroness Neufmarché,' said Garran, accepting her hand. 'Rest assured that we will do all in our power to make your stay as pleasant as possible.'

'Lady Agnes, if you please,' she replied, delighted at the prince's dark good looks and polite manner — not to mention his facility in her own language. The baroness thanked her handsome young host and was in turn presented to Cadwgan's widow, Queen Anora. 'My lady, may God be gracious to you in your season of mourning,' Agnes said, speaking in simple French though she suspected the queen did not fully comprehend. Prince Garran smoothly translated for his mother, who smiled sadly and received the baroness's condolences with austere grace.

'Please, come inside,' said Garran, directing his guests towards the hall. 'We have prepared a repast to refresh you from your journey. Tonight we will begin the feast of remembrance.'

'And the funeral ceremony?' inquired the baron.

'That will take place later today at twilight. The feast follows the burial.'

They were led to the hall, where a number of mourners were gathered. Lady Agnes, who had imagined the Welsh to be dressed in rough pelts, their faces tattooed in weird designs, and feathers in their hair and necklaces made from the bones of birds and small animals, was pleasantly impressed with not only the general appearance of the barbarians — most of whom were dressed neither better nor worse than the typical English or French serf of her limited acquaintance — but with their solemn, almost stoic dignity as well. The room was festooned with banners of various tribes and illumined by the light of countless beeswax candles, the warm scent of which mingled with that of the clean rushes bestrewing the floor. On trestles set up in the centre of the room, on a board covered with fresh juniper branches, lay

King Cadwgan himself, covered in his customary cloak, on which was placed a large white-painted wooden cross.

Lady Agnes blanched to see him, but no one else seemed to consider it odd that the deceased should reside in the hall surrounded, as in life, by his subjects and kinsmen. Indeed, every now and then, one of the mourners would come forward to stroke the head of the dead king, whose hair had been washed and brushed to form a wispy nimbus around his head. One by one, the new arrivals were introduced to the other notables in the room, and they were given shallow bowls of mead to drink. Kitchen servants and young girls circulated with trays of small parcels of spiced meat, nuts, and herbs wrapped in pastry, which they served to the funeral guests.

The baroness, although unable to understand anything that was said around her – or perhaps because of it – began watching these courtesies intently. What she saw was a people, whether highborn or low, who seemed to enjoy one another's company and, crude as they undeniably were, revelled in the occasion. A time of sadness, of course, yet the funereal room rang with almost continual laughter. In spite of any previous notions, she found herself drawn to the unabashed sincerity of these folk and was moved by their honest displays of kindness and fellowship.

Thus, the mourners occupied themselves until the sun began to set, at which time a body of priests and monks arrived. As if on signal the mourners began to sing, and though the words were strange and there were no musical instruments, Agnes thought she had never heard music so sweetly sad. After a lengthy stint of singing, a grey-robed priest who seemed to be in charge of the proceedings stepped to the bier and, bowing three times, stretched his hands over the corpse and began to pray. He prayed in Latin, which the baroness had not expected. The prayer, while curious in its expression, was more or less like any she might have heard in Angevin.

When the prayer was finished, the priest was given a crosier – by which Agnes was given to know that he was actually a bishop. Striking the crosier on the floor three times, he gestured to the board. Six men of the tribe stepped forward and, taking their places around the dead king, lifted the board from the trestles and carried it from the hall. The mourners all fell into place behind them, and in this way they were led out into the yard and down from the fortress mound into the valley, eventually arriving in the yard of a small wooden church, where a grave had been dug within the precinct of the low, stone-walled yard. The grave was lined with large flat flagstones, some of which had been roughly shaped for the purpose.

The mourners paused to remove their shoes before entering the churchyard, which Lady Agnes considered very odd; but entering the holy precinct barefoot stirred her soul more profoundly than anything which had happened thus far. When the body on its board was carefully lowered into the hole prepared to receive it by six barefoot men, her ever-watchful eyes grew a little moist at the corners. There were prayers over the grave, and still more when the earth was replaced in the hole, covering the dead king. Then, this part of the service concluded, the people began drifting away in small clumps of two or three.

It was simple, but genuine and heartfelt, and the sincerity of the people winsome. Agnes, more intensely affected by the experience than she could possibly have imagined, became very thoughtful and silent on the way back to the caer. And when, as they mounted the hill and saw the first stars beginning to shine, the mourners began singing, Lady Agnes, for whom life presented nothing more than a series of challenges and hardships to be overcome, felt something tight loosen in her heart, and the tears began to flow. She heard in the melody such indomitable spirit and courage that she was ashamed of her former disparagement of these fine and dignified people. She walked along, slippers in hand, listening to the voices as they mingled in the sweet summer air, tears of joy and sadness glistening on her cheeks.

The baron, walking with Prince Garran and his mother, did not see his wife, or he might well have been alarmed. Later, as they sat down to the first of several feasts in honour of the dead king, he did note that Lady Agnes seemed subdued, but pleasantly so, her smile unforced, her manner more calm and peaceable than he could recently remember. *No doubt*, he thought, *she is tired from the journey*. But as she smiled at him when she saw him regarding her from his place near the prince, he returned her smile and thought to himself that he had been right to insist she come.

The next days were given to preparations for the coronation of Prince Garran who, as the baron had long ago determined, should follow his father to the throne. This decision was roundly ratified by the people of Eiwas, so there was no awkwardness or difficulty regarding the succession, and the coronation took place in good order, with little ceremony but great celebration by those who, having laid to rest the old king, had stayed to welcome the new.

When Baron Neufmarché and his wife took their leave of King Garran two days later, they urged the new monarch to come to visit them in Hereford. 'Come for Michaelmas,' the baron said, his tone gently insistent. 'We will hold a feast in your honour, and talk about our future together.' As if in afterthought, he added, 'You know, I think my daughter would like to know you better – you have not met Sybil, I think?' The young king shook his head. 'No? Then it is arranged.'

'You must come,' added the baroness, pressing his hand as she stepped to the carriage, 'and bring your mother, too. Do promise to bring her. I will send a carriage so she will travel more comfortably.'

'My lady,' replied the new-made king, unable to gainsay his lord's wife, 'it will be my pleasure to attend you at Michaelmas.'

Later, as the carriage climbed the first of many hills that would take the caer from view, Lady Agnes said, 'King Garran and our Sybil, so? You have not mentioned this to me.'

'Ah, um—' The baron hesitated, uncertain how to proceed now that his impromptu plan had been revealed. 'I meant to tell you about that, but ah, well, the notion just came to me a day or so ago, and there wasn't time to—'

'I like it,' she told him, cutting short his stuttering.

He stared at her as if he could not think he had heard her right. 'You would approve of such a union?' wondered Bernard, greatly amazed at this change in his wife's ordinarily dour humour.

'It would be a good match,' she affirmed. 'Good for both of them, I should think. Yes, I do approve. I will speak to Sybil upon our return. See to it that you secure Garran's promise.'

'It will be done,' said the baron, still staring at his wife in slight disbelief. 'Are you feeling well, my love?'

'Never better,' she declared. She was silent a moment, musing to herself, then announced, 'I think a Christmas wedding would be a splendid thing. It will give me time to make the necessary plans.'

Baron Neufmarché, unable to think of anything to say in the presence of this extraordinary transformation of the woman he had known all these years, simply gazed at her with admiration.

CHAPTER 45

Nóin and I spent the rest of the summer luxuriating in one another's love, and talking, talking, talking. Like two blackbirds sitting on a fence we filled the air morning to night with our chatter. She told me all the greenwood gossip – all the doings large and small that filled the days we were apart. I told her of my captivity and passing the time with Odo scribbling down my ramblings. 'I should like to read that,' Nóin said, then smiled. 'That alone would make it worth learning to read.'

'Odo tells me that reading is not so difficult,' I explained, 'but the only things written are either for lawyers or priests, and not at all of interest to plain folk like you and me.'

'I should like it all the same,' Nóin insisted.

As the days passed, I considered making good on my promise to build my wife and daughter a new house. I found a nice spot on a bit of higher ground at one end of Cél Craidd, and marked out the dimensions on the ground with sticks. I then went to our Lord Bran to beg his permission to clear the ground and cut a few limbs of stout oak for the roof beam, lintel, and corner posts.

'Why build a house?' he asked, holding his head to one side as if he couldn't understand. Before I could point out that I had promised it to my bride, and that her own small hut was a bit too snug for three or more he added, 'We will be gone from here come Michaelmas.'

'I know, but I promised Noín—' I began.

'Come hunting with us instead,' Bran said. 'We've missed you on the trails.'

My broken fingers were slowly healing, but as my usefulness with a bow was still limited, I served mainly to beat the bushes for game. 'Don't worry,' Siarles told me after that first time we went out. 'You'll be drawing like a champion again in no time. Rest those fingers while you can.'

In this, he was a prophet, no mistake. I did not know it then, but would have cause to remember his words in times to come.

Thus, the summer slowly dwindled down and golden autumn arrived. I began counting the days to Michaelmas and the time of leaving we called the Day of Judgement. Bran and Angharad held close counsel and determined that we would go with as many of the Grellon as could be spared, leaving behind only those who could not make the journey and a few men to protect them. We would go to Caer Wintan – known to the English as Winchester – and receive the king's decision on the return of our lands. 'The king must see the people who depend on his judgement for their lives,' Angharad said. 'We must travel together and stand before him together.'

'What if he will not see us all in a herd?' wondered Iwan when he learned this.

'He will speak to all, or none,' Bran replied, 'for then he will judge what is right and for the good of all, and not for me only.'

The next day, Bran sent Siarles with an extra horse to Saint Dyfrig's Abbey to fetch Brother Jago, and twelve days before the

Feast of Saint Michael, we set off. It is no easy thing to keep so many people moving, I can tell you. We were thirty folk in all, counting young ones. We went on foot, for the most part; the horses were used to carry provisions and supplies. None of us rode save Angharad, for whom the walk would have been far too demanding. Her old bones would not have lasted the journey, I believe, for it is a fair distance to Caer Wintan from Elfael.

The weather stayed good — warm days, nights cool and dry. We camped wherever we would; with that many people and enough of them bearing longbows, we had no great fear of being harassed by Englishmen or Normans either one. The only real danger was that we would not reach Caer Wintan in time, for as the days of travel drew on, the miles began to tell and the people grew weary and had to rest more often. We moved more slowly than Bran had reckoned. 'Do not worry,' counselled Friar Tuck. 'You can always take a few with you and ride ahead, can you not? You will get there in time, never fear.'

Bran rejected this notion outright. We would arrive together each and every last one, he said, or we would not arrive at all. It was for the people we were doing this, he said, so the king must look into the eyes of those for whom his judgement is life or death. There was nothing for it but that we would simply have to travel more quickly.

That night he gathered us all and told us again why we were going to see the king and what it meant. He explained how it was of vital importance that we should arrive in good time, saying, 'King William must have no grievance against us, nor any cause to change his mind. We must endure the hardships of the road, my friends, for what we do we do not for ourselves alone, but for the sake of all those in Elfael who cannot join us. We do it for the farmers who have been driven from their fields, and families from their homes; for the widows who have lost their men, and those who stood in the shadow of the gallows.

We do it for all who have been made to labour on the baron's hateful strongholds and town, for those who have fled into bleak and friendless exile. We do it for those who will come after us to help shoulder the burden of reclaiming that which we have lost to the enemy. Yes, and for all who have gone before us we do this, theirs the sacrifice, ours the gain.' He gazed at all of those clustered around him, holding their eyes with his. 'We do not do this for ourselves alone, but for all who have suffered under the oppression of the Ffreinc.'

Thus he braced our flagging spirits, speaking words of encouragement and hope. The next day, he became tireless in urging each and every one of us to hasten our steps; and when anyone was seen to be dragging behind, he hurried to help that one. Sometimes he seemed to be everywhere at once – now at the front of the long line of travellers, now at the rear among the stragglers. He did all this with endless good humour, telling one and all to think what it would be like to be free in our own lands and secure in our own homes once more.

The next day he did the same, and the next. He coaxed and cajoled until he grew hoarse, and then Friar Tuck took over, leading our footsore flock in songs. When we ran out of those, he started in on hymns, and little by little, all the urging and singing finally took hold. We walked easier and with lighter hearts. The miles fell behind us at a quicker pace until at last we reached the low, lumpy hills of the southlands.

Caer Wintan was a thriving market town, helped, no doubt, by the presence of the royal residence nearby. Not wishing to risk trouble, we skirted the town and did not draw attention to ourselves beyond sending Tuck and a few men to buy fresh provisions.

We arrived with a day to spare and camped within sight of the king's stronghold – an old English hunting lodge that had once belonged to an earl or duke, I suppose. It was the place where Red William spent those few days he was not racing here or there to shore up his sagging kingdom in one place or another. It reminded me of Aelred's manor, my old earl's house, but with two long wings enclosing a bare dirt yard in front of the black-and-white half-timbered hall. The only defence for the place was a wooden palisade with a porter's hut beside the timber gate.

With a day to spare, we spent it washing our clothes and bathing, ridding ourselves of the road and making ourselves ready to attend the king. At sunrise on the third day after Saint Michael's Day, we rose and broke fast; then, laundered and brushed, washed and combed, we walked to the king's house with Bran in the lead, followed by Angharad leaning on her staff and, beside her, Iwan, holding his bow and a sheaf of arrows at his belt. Siarles and Mérian came next, and then the rest of us in a long double rank. I carried Nia and walked with Nóin; as we passed through the gate, I felt her slip her hand into mine and give it a squeeze. 'I am glad to be here today,' she murmured. 'I will remember it always.'

'Me, too,' I whispered. 'It is a great day, this, and right worthy to be remembered.'

We assembled in the king's yard, and Bran had just asked Brother Jago to inform the king's porter that we had come in answer to the king's summons as commanded and were awaiting his pleasure, when who should appear but Count Falkes de Braose and Abbot Hugo, accompanied by Marshal Guy de Gysburne and no fewer than fifteen knights. They swept in through the gates, heedless of our folk, who had to scatter to let them through.

One look at our straggled lot, and the Ffreinc drew their swords. Our own men set arrows on their strings and took a mark. We all stared at one another, eyes hard, faces grim, until Count Falkes broke the silence. 'Bran ap Brychan,' intoned the count in his high nasal voice, 'Et tous vos compatriotes foule. Qu'une surprise désagréable!'

Brother Jago, taking his place at Bran's shoulder, whispered the count's greeting in our lord's ear. I needed no translation to know that he had insulted Bran by calling us all 'filthy countrymen' and a 'disagreeable surprise.'

'Count Falkes, your arrival is as untimely as it is unwelcome,' replied Bran lightly. 'What are you doing here?'

'One could ask the same of you,' countered Falkes. 'I thought you were dead.'

'I am as you see me,' returned Bran. 'But it would seem you still irk the earth with your presence. I asked why you have come.'

Marshal Gysburne muttered an oath at this reply when Jago had delivered it, and several other knights spat at us. I saw a flicker of anger flit across the count's face, but his reply was restrained. 'We are obeying the king's summons. I cannot think you are here by accident.'

'We likewise have been summoned,' returned Bran. 'Therefore, let us resolve to hold the peace between us for at least as long as we must stand before the king.'

With some reluctance, it seemed to me, Count Falkes agreed, although he really had no better choice. Starting a battle in the king's yard would have gained him little and cost him much. 'Very well,' he said at last. 'We will keep the peace insofar as you keep your rabble subdued.'

I could not tell how much the count knew about our Bran and his busy doings – very little, I guessed, for his remark about Bran having been killed seemed to signify that Falkes did not recognise Bran as Father Dominic, or as King Raven, either. I thought the whole contest would be over once he recognised me, though, but after bandying words with Bran, he feigned disinterest in us and turned his face away, as if we were beneath his regard. I suppose I appeared just a married man with a child in his arms and a wife by his side.

So now, an uneasy truce was established – but it was that thin, I can tell you, a single lance point or arrow tip could have pierced it anywhere along the line. We waited there in the yard, wary and watching one another. Nóin, bless her, stood with her head high and shoulders straight, returning the glare of the marshal and his hard-eyed knights, and little Nia found a pile of pebbles to keep her busy, moving them from one place to another and singing to them all the while.

When it seemed that we must all snap under the strain, the great oak-and-iron door of the king's royal residence opened and out stepped the king's man, accompanied by two other household servants. 'His Majesty the king has been informed of your arrival,' he announced in good English. 'He begs the boon of your patience and will give audience as soon as may be.' Taking in the horde of Welshmen standing with Bran in the yard, he added, 'It will not be possible for all of you to enter. The hall is not large enough. You must choose representatives to attend you; the rest will wait here.'

When Jago had relayed these words to our lord, Bran replied, 'With respect, as the king's judgement will serve all my people, we will hear it together. Perhaps the king will not mind delivering his decision to us here as we wait so patiently.'

The fella made no answer, but simply bent his head, turned on his heel, and scuttled back inside. 'All stand together,' sneered Count Falkes. 'How very Welsh.' The word was a slur in his mouth.

'All hang together, too,' observed Abbot Hugo. His eye fell on me just then, and recognition came to him. His ruddy face froze. 'You there!' he shouted. 'Hold up your hands.'

'Don't do it, Will,' warned Bran, glancing quickly over his shoulder. 'He may suspect, but we need not feed his suspicion.'

I stood my ground, silently returning his gaze, but I kept my hands well out of the Black Abbot's sight. It was then I saw Odo, sitting most uncomfortably on the back of a brown mare. He saw me, too, knew me, and – bless him – held his tongue. He would not betray me to his masters.

'I say!' cried the abbot, growing angry. 'Order your man to show me his hands.'

'As he is my man,' said Bran, 'he is mine to command. I will make no such demand.'

'By the Virgin, it *is* him,' insisted the abbot.

'What are you talking about?' wondered Count Falkes.

'The prisoner!' cried Hugo, jabbing his finger at me. 'Scatlocke – the one they called Scarlet. That is him, I tell you!'

Count Falkes turned his gaze my way and studied me for a moment. 'No,' he decided. 'That is not the man.' No doubt my haircut and shave, and change of clothes and fleshing out a little on my wife's good cooking, had changed me enough to make them just that little uncertain.

'It is him,' put in Gysburne. He looked at Bran and concluded, 'And the last time we saw that one, he gave his name as Father Dominic. I would swear to it.' He gazed at the rest of us, his eyes passing back and forth along the ranks. 'By the rood, they're *all* here!' He pointed at Iwan. 'I know I've seen that one before. I know it.'

'You are imagining things,' remarked the count. 'They all look alike anyway, these Welsh.'

'Say nothing,' advised Angharad, speaking mostly to Bran, but to the rest of us as well. 'Let them think what they will – it no longer matters what they say. Let them rail. We will not stoop to satisfy their accusations.'

So Bran ignored the Ffreinc taunts and finger-pointing which continued to be cast at him and some of the rest of us; instead, he and Angharad turned their faces to the ironbound door and waited. The sun rose slowly higher, and still we waited, growing warm beneath the bright autumn rays. Some of the Ffreinc grew tired of waiting in the saddle and, sheathing their weapons, climbed down from their horses. Others led their mounts away to water them. Most, however, remained to glare and frown and mutter curses at us. But that is the worst of what they did, and we braved it in silence without giving them cause for greater anger.

Then, as the sun climbed toward midday, the door to the royal residence opened once more and the king's man appeared with the two servants. 'Hear! Hear!' he called. 'His Majesty William, King of England!'

Out from the house came the Red King and five attendants: one of them a priest of some exalted kind, robed in red satin with a gold chain and cross around his neck, and another the young Lord Leicester we had met in Rouen; the rest were knights carrying lances. The king himself, surrounded by his bodyguard, seemed smaller than I remembered him; his stocky form was wrapped in a blue tunic that stretched tight across his bulging stomach; his short legs were stuffed into dark brown trousers and tall riding boots. His flame-coloured hair glowed with bright fire in the sunlight, but he seemed tired to me, almost haggard, and there were chapped patches on his cheeks. In his hand, he carried a rolled parchment.

'Which one is the king? Is it the one in red?' whispered Nóin, and I realised that, like most people, she'd never set eyes to the king of England before and had no idea how William or any other king might appear when not tricked out in their regal frippery.

'No, the fat one with orange hair,' I told her. 'That's our William Rufus.'

This information was repeated down the ranks, along with other pungent observations. De Braose and his lot, seeking an advantage somehow, called out greetings to the king, who ran his eye quickly over them but did not respond to their bald attempt at flattery. After this had gone on for a time, the king gestured to his man, who cut short the speeches and called for silence.

With a somewhat distracted air, the king held the parchment roll out to the priest. 'Cardinal Ranulf of Bayeux will read out the royal judgement proclamation at this time,' he declared. Brother Jago relayed these words to the Welsh speakers.

The cardinal known as Flambard stepped forward and, with a short bow, received the scroll from William's hand. He took his time untying it and unrolling it. Holding it high, he stepped forward and began to read it out. It was Latin, of course, and I could make nothing of it. Fortunately, I was standing near enough to Brother Jago to catch most of what he said as he translated the words for Bran and Angharad. Tuck was close by to offer his understanding as well.

'I, William, by the grace of God, king of England, greets his subjects with all respect and honour according to their rank and station. Be it known that this day, the third day after the Feast of Saint Michael, this judgement was made public by the reading hereof in the presence of the same king and those persons summoned by the crown to attend him. Owing to the perfidious nature of certain noblemen known to the king, and because of dissensions and discords which have arisen between the king and the lord king's brother, Duke Robert of Normandie, and a company of rebellious barons of the kingdom concerning William's lawful right to occupy the throne and to rule unimpeded by the slanders and allegations of traitorous dissenters, this recognition has been made before the Chief Justiciar of England, and Henry, Earl of Warwick, and other great men of the kingdom, and has been signed and sealed in their presence.'

Here the cardinal paused to allow the crowd to unravel the meaning of this address. We were by no means the only ones struggling to keep up; the Ffreinc in Count de Braose's camp were having their own difficulties with all that high-flown Latin and were being aided by Abbot Hugo, who was interpreting for the count and others.

When Cardinal Flambard decided that all had caught up with him, he continued, 'Accordingly, I, William, under authority of Heaven, do hereby set forth my disposition in the matters arising from the recent attempt by those rebellious subjects aforementioned to remove His Majesty from his throne and the rightful rule of his realm and subjects. Be it known that William de Braose, Baron of Bramber, for his part in the rebellion has forfeited his lands and title to the crown and is henceforth prohibited from returning to England under ban of condemnation for treason and the penalty thereof. Regarding his son, the Earl Philip de Braose, and his nephew the Count Falkes de Braose, being found to have no part in the wicked rebellion against their lawful king, but owing to their familial proximity to the traitors, it is deemed prudent to extend the ban to them and their households; therefore, they are to follow the baron into exile to whatever lands will receive them.'

The Ffreinc moaned and gnashed their teeth at this, while at the same time it was all we could do to keep from cheering. Oh, it was all we'd hoped for – Baron de Braose was banished, and his noxious nephew exiled with him. The throne of Elfael was freed from the Normans, and victory was sweet in our mouths.

But, as the Good Lord giveth with his right hand, and taketh with his left – so with kings.

'Further,' continued the cardinal, 'it pleases His Majesty to assume those lands now vacated to be placed under Forest Law as a Protectorate of Royal Privilege, to be administered for the crown by a regent chosen to serve the interests of the crown, namely Abbot Hugo de Rainault.

As our regent and an officer of the crown, he will exercise all authority necessary to hold, maintain, and prosper those lands and estates, and with the aid of our sheriff, Richard de Glanville, to more firmly establish the realm in the fealty due its rightful monarch.'

Here the cardinal broke off to allow the translators to catch up. While we were struggling to work out what had just happened, Cardinal Flambard concluded, saying, 'All others professing grievance in this matter, having been rewarded according to their service, are herewith disposed. No further action in regard to this judgement shall be countenanced. Under the sign and seal of William, King of England.'

Owing to the slight murkiness of courtly Latin, it took us a while to get to grips with the outrage that had just been revealed in our hearing. Tuck and Jago held close council with Bran and Angharad. Count Falkes de Braose, astonished beyond words, stared at the king as if at the devil's own manservant; Abbot Hugo and Marshal Guy put their heads together, already preparing to seed more mischief. In both camps, Ffreinc and British, there were dire mutterings and grumblings. Along with many another, I pressed forward to hear what the clerics among us were saying, and caught part of the discussion. 'So, it comes to this,' Tuck said, 'Baron de Braose and all his kith and kin have been banished, never to return to English soil on pain of death – well and good . . .'

'But, see here,' pointed out Jago, 'Abbot Hugo is made regent and remains in possession of the lands granted to de Braose by the king.'

'But the bloody abbot keeps Elfael!' growled Tuck dangerously.

A dull, damp sickness descended over me. Some of those around me swore and called down curses on the head of the English king. 'What does it mean?' said Nóin, pressing close beside me.

'It means we have been used and cast aside,' I spat. 'It means that red-haired rogue has gutted us like rabbits and thrown us to the dogs.'

'That cannot be,' said Bran, already starting forth. 'Heaven will not allow it!' He stepped forward three long paces and halted, calling upon the king to hear him. 'My lord king,' he said, with Jago's help, 'am I to understand that you have allowed Abbot Hugo to keep our lands in Elfael?'

'The king has decreed that the abbot will serve as his regent,' replied Cardinal Ranulf. His eyes narrowed as he gazed at Bran. 'I remember you right well,' he said, 'and I warn you against trying any such foolishness as you attempted last time we met.'

'Then pray remind the king that I was promised the return of our lands and the rule of our people,' Bran countered, speaking through Jago. 'This I was promised by the king himself in recognition of our part in exposing the traitors.'

The king heard this, of course, but glanced away, a pained expression on his face.

'I cannot answer for any promises which might or might not have been made in the past,' responded the cardinal, making it sound as if this had all taken place untold years ago and could have no part in the judgement now. 'After a suitable season of reflection, the king has determined that it does not serve the interests of the crown to return Elfael to Welsh rule at this time.'

'What is to become of us?' cried Bran, growing visibly angry. 'That is our land – our home! We were promised justice.'

'Justice,' replied the silk-robed cardinal coolly, 'you have received. Your king has decreed; his word is law.'

Bran, holding tight to the reins of his rage, argued his case. 'I would remind His Majesty that it was from within the abbot's own stronghold that we learned of the conspiracy against him! Your regent is as guilty of treason as those you have already condemned and punished.'

413

'So you say,' countered the cardinal smoothly. 'There has been no proof of this, and therefore the right practice of justice decrees no guilt shall be laid at the abbot's feet.'

'Call it what you will, my lord, but do not call it justice,' said Bran, his voice shaking with fury. Sweet Jesus, I had never seen him so angry. His face was white, his eyes flashing quick fire. 'This is an offence against heaven. The people of Elfael will not rest until we have gained the justice promised to us.'

'You and your people will conform yourself to the regent's rule,' Flambard declared. 'As regent, Abbot Hugo is charged with your care and protection. Henceforth, he will provide you with the comfort and solace of the king's law.'

'With all respect, Cardinal,' Bran called, fighting to keep his rage from devouring his reason, 'we cannot accept this judgement.'

'The king has spoken,' concluded Cardinal Bayeux. 'The continued prosecution of this dispute has no merit. The matter is herewith concluded.'

King William, impervious to our lord's anger, nodded once and turned away. He and his soldiers and confidants walked back to the house and went inside. The cardinal rolled up the parchment and turned to follow his monarch.

With that, our Day of Judgement was over.

As the door closed on the backs of the royal party, a wide double door opened at the far end of the yard, and soldiers who had been awaiting this moment streamed out to encircle us. Weapons ready, they formed a wall, shoulder-to-shoulder around the perimeter of the yard.

'We must leave here at once,' said Angharad. 'Bran!'

He was no longer listening. 'We will not be denied!' he shouted, starting forth. 'This is not the end. Do you hear?'

She pulled Bran's sleeve, restraining him. Shaking off her grasp, he started after the swiftly retreating cardinal. 'Iwan! Siarles!' she snapped, 'See to your lord!'

The two leapt forward and took hold of Bran, one on either side. 'Come away, my lord,' said Iwan. 'Don't make things worse. They only want half a reason to attack us.'

'You do well to drag him away,' called Marshal Guy, laughing. 'Drag the beaten dog away!'

Gysburne was the only one to find amusement in this disaster, mind – he and a few of the less astute-looking soldiers with him. The rest appeared suitably grim, realising that this was no good news for them, either. Count Falkes looked like a man who has had his bones removed, and it was all he could do to remain in the saddle. His pale countenance was more ghastly still, and his lips trembled, no doubt in contemplation of his ruin.

Iwan and Siarles were able to haul Bran back. Mérian rushed to his side to help calm him. Meanwhile, Tuck and Angharad, fearful of what the Ffreinc might do next, moved quickly to turn everyone and march them from the yard before bloodshed could turn the disaster into a catastrophe.

Obeying cooler heads, we turned and started slowly away under the narrowed eyes and naked weapons of the king's soldiers. As we passed Count de Braose's company, I looked up and saw Odo, his round, owlish face stricken. On impulse, I raised my hand and beckoned him to join us. 'Come, monk,' I told him. 'If you would quit the devil and stand on the side of the angels, you are welcome here.'

To my surprise, he lifted the reins and moved out from the Ffreinc ranks. Some of those around him tried to prevent him, but he pulled away from their grasp; the abbot, sneering down his long nose, told them to let the craven Judas go. 'Let him leave if he will,' said Marshal

Gysburne, snatching the bridle strap and halting Odo's mount, 'but he goes without the horse.'

So my dear dull scribe took his life in his hands, plucked up his small courage, and slid down from the saddle to take his place among the Grellon.

As we marched from the yard, the soldiers tightened the circle and drew in behind us to make certain we would depart without causing any trouble. Abbot Hugo called out one last threat. 'Do not think to return to Elfael,' he said, his voice ringing loud in the yard. 'We have marked you, and we will kill you on sight should you or any of your rabble ever set foot in Elfael again.'

When Jago translated the abbot's challenge for us, I saw Bran stiffen. Turning to address the abbot, he said in Latin, 'Enjoy this day, vile priest – it is the last peace you will know. From this day hence, it is war.'

Abbot Hugo shouted something in reply, and the Ffreinc soldiers made as if they might mount an attack. They drew swords and lowered their shields, preparing to charge. But Bran snatched up a bow, and quick as a blink, planted an arrow between the abbot's legs, pinning the hem of his robe to the hard ground. 'The next arrow finds your black heart, Abbot,' Bran called. 'Tell the soldiers to put up their weapons.' Hugo heeded the warning and wisely called for the king's men to hold and let us depart. Slowly, Bran lowered the bow, turned, and led his people from the king's stronghold.

Heads held high, we strode out through the gate and into our blood-tinged fate.

EPILOGUE

'Are you sure he's the one?' asked Marshal Guy of Gysburne.

'Absolutely certain,' muttered Abbot Hugo. 'There is no doubt. Bran ap Brychan was heir to the throne of Elfael. That idiot de Braose killed his father, and he himself was thought to be dead – but of course that was bungled along with everything else the baron and his milksop nephew touched.'

'To think we had him in our grasp and didn't recognise him,' Gysburne observed. 'Curious.'

Hugo took a deep breath and fixed his marshal with a steely gaze. 'King Raven, the so-called Phantom, and Bran are one and the same. I'd stake my life on it.'

'We should have taken him when we had the chance,' remarked Gysburne, still puzzling over the deception played upon them.

'A mistake,' spat Hugo, 'we will not repeat.'

Count Falkes de Braose had been escorted from the yard by knights of the king, to be taken to Lundein and there put on a ship to Normandie. Abbot Hugo and his marshal were left to consider the unexpected rise in their fortunes, and the threats to their rule. Their first thoughts turned to Bran and his followers. They quickly decided that so long as Bran and his men remained at large, they would never enjoy complete control over the people and lands that King William had entrusted to their stewardship.

'I can take him now,' said Guy.

'Not here,' said Hugo. 'Not in sight of the king and his court. That will not do. No, let the upstart and his rabble get down the road a pace, and follow them. They won't get far on foot. Wait until they make camp for the night, and then kill them all.'

'There are women and children, and at least one priest,' Guy pointed out. 'What shall we do with them?'

'Spare no one,' the abbot replied.

'But, my lord,' objected Guy. He was a knight of the realm, and did not fancy himself a murderer. 'We cannot slaughter them like cattle.'

'Bran ap Brychan said it himself,' countered the abbot. 'It is war. His words, not mine, Gysburne. If it is war he wants, this is where it begins.'

Before Marshal Guy could argue further, the abbot called his knights and men-at-arms — and as many of the count's men who wished to join his army — to gather in a corner of the yard. 'On your knees, men,' he said. 'Bow your heads.' With a clatter of armour, the knights under Guy Gysburne's command drew their swords and knelt in a circle around the abbot. Folding their hands over the hilts of their unsheathed swords, they bowed their heads. Raising his right hand, Hugo made the sign of the cross over the kneeling soldiers.

'Lord of Hosts,' he prayed, 'I send these men out to do battle in your name. Shield them with your hand, and protect them from the arrows of the enemy. Let their toil be accounted righteousness for your name's sake. Amen.'

The soldiers raised their heads as the abbot said, 'For any and all acts committed in carrying out the charge laid upon you this day, you are hereby absolved in heaven and on earth. Obey the will of your commander, who serves me even as I serve God Almighty. For the sake of God's anointed, King William, the holy church, and the Lord Jesus

Christ himself, show no mercy to those who rebel against their rule, and do so with the full knowledge that all of your deeds will be accounted to your favour on the earth and in heaven, and that you bear no stain of guilt or sin for the shedding of blood this day.'

With that, Guy and his men mounted their horses and silently rode from the yard in pursuit of King Raven and his flock.

Here ends the second book in the King Raven
trilogy. The story concludes in

TUCK

THE TURBULENT TIMES
OF WILLIAM SCATLOCKE

In our own time of shifting borders and changing allegiances, forced migration and displacement, religious suspicion and conflict – it is not too hard to imagine the plight of William Scatlocke who, owing to the political upheaval of the eleventh century, suddenly found himself a homeless refugee. One day a valued member of a close-knit society, ancient as the hills and rooted as the oak groves around him . . . and the next a wandering vagabond looking for a community and the protection of a strong leader. Then, as now, a traditional way of life could be shattered in a matter of days, broken so thoroughly that repair was not possible – only something utterly different.

For Will and his countrymen, the Norman devastation and destruction did not end when England's hapless King Harold was cut down on the battlefield at Hastings in the autumn of 1066. That was only the beginning of what would become a generations-long cataclysm of change. Under William the Conqueror and his flame-haired son, William II (William the Red or 'Rufus' as he was often called) the centuries' old structures that supported life for the largely Saxon population of England were subjected to merciless assault. The intricate system binding lord and vassal in a tightly intertwined chain of mutual loyalty, support, and protection perfected by the Saxons was broken, throwing the well-ordered nation into turmoil. New rulers of the realm meant strange new laws in the land. One of the most hated was known as Forest Law — a set of highly questionable legal codes designed solely for the benefit of the crown-wearer and his cronies, and not at all confined to 'forests' as we understand the word (areas of dense woodland), but could encompass large tracts of grassland, marsh, and moorland. Entire villages were razed and burned to the ground, sometimes because the settlement occupied land that the king, or members of his court, had identified as prime real estate for hunting. Other times destruction was inflicted as punishment for an infraction — such as rebellion or treason — by the local lord. In either case the newly seized land would be confiscated and declared a royal possession and special preserve belonging to the king, who delivered these often-vast estates to the management and protection of a 'shire reeve,' or *sheriff*, his personal representative on the scene. Such a claim on what had previously been common land and livelihood for many — available for hunting, gathering, grazing, timber, and sundry uses — represented a seismic shift in the established social order.

All of a sudden, it was a serious crime to trespass on royal land, and the hapless victim caught within the royal forest precinct faced losing a hand or an eye at best, or if worse came to worst, death by hanging.

So, here come the Normans, falling upon the land like wolves on a peaceful sheepfold. Through no fault of his own, Will — and countless others like him — are driven from their homes by the over-bearing overlords who displaced their masters and seized their mas-ters' lands, leaving the common folk — the farmers, the craftsmen, the peasants — to their own slender devices. And if nowadays it is not uncommon to learn that the man driving your taxi was actually a heart surgeon in his own country, or that the woman who cleans the office building was a university lecturer before she was driven out of the land of her birth . . . then neither was it uncommon in Will Scarlet's day to meet drifters, beggars, thieves, and outlaws who had previously been the bedrock of traditional communities now laid waste by the invaders. And in spite of the rigours of Forest Law, many sought a greenwood refuge in the desperate hope of finding food and shelter in the wilderness.

And if there wasn't trouble enough on the secular front, the spiritual realm was suffering its own clash of cultures. Although church affairs were the purview of an educated elite and the aristocracy, trouble at the top of the social ladder affected those clinging to the lower rungs, and did so severely. We who live in 'Christian' countries that have become largely post-Christian may have some difficulty appreciating the depth of passion aroused by the changes introduced to the English church by the Normans. We have only to look at the present turmoil resulting from conflict between religious powers in certain parts of the world to appreciate just how violent these struggles can become. The devastation and bloodshed is clearly visible to one and all, and hardly needs mentioning to anyone within range of CNN or Al Jazeera. Yet, it is worth pointing out that in the medieval world, when disease and death were constant, grim companions and the grave an all-too-likely prognosis for everything from toothache to plague, the church with its promise of eternal salvation was the solitary hope and ultimate sanctuary for those who lived beneath its sheltering wings: virtually every man, woman, and child alive in the land.

Thus, when even relatively minor changes – such as replacing the user-friendly English-speaking Saxon cleric with his more imperious Norman counterpart – could wreak spiritual and temporal havoc for the locals, what of the great challenges of the day such as which of two competing popes to support? This particular predicament did occur during William II's reign, and the waves of that disturbance spread far and wide throughout Europe. Pope Clement in Rome and

Pope Urban in France were battling for supremacy of the One Holy Catholic and Apostolic Church, and excommunicating opposing parties right and left. Kings and princes, dukes and barons, cardinals and archbishops all chose sides and lined up beneath the banner their favourite candidate. The result of decisions taken by the high and mighty in the rarified air of courtly affairs proved disastrous to those on the ground as the contest descended into physical violence: houses were looted, shops set ablaze, streets erupted in riots between rival camps, and lives were lost.

But all was not black and stormy; here and there small, stray rays of light broke through. For although the church was dominated by the rich and powerful, men with aristocratic connections whose commitment to the core tenets of Christian belief and practice was not always in ready evidence, it too had its countercultural element to be found in people like Friar Tuck, humble servants of the faith who eschewed riches, lived on small donations, and helped pave the way for the later, wildly popular and much needed Franciscan movement.

Will Scatlocke was, then, a man of his time. Denied his traditional way of life, with little or nothing to lose, he threw in his lot with Bran and his tribe of outlaws, who championed the cause of right and justice for those powerless to protect themselves from the abuses of the rapacious invaders. In the final book of the King Raven Trilogy, Friar Tuck – the simple mendicant monk – will take centre stage as the increasingly heated conflict between Welsh and Norman interests reaches its white-hot conclusion.

It has been gratifying to hear from readers who are eager for the next book and who want to know when the next instalment will appear. Generally speaking, it does take far longer to write a book than to read one – always a problem – and at this point I must beg your further indulgence as the writing and publication of *Tuck*, the third volume in the trilogy, will be delayed on account of a serious illness. Thanks to restored health and strength, I am working away at the conclusion of the series, and thank you for your patience and understanding.

— Stephen Lawhead
Oxford

PRONUNCIATION GUIDE

Many of the old Celtic words and names are strange to modern eyes, but they are not as difficult to pronounce as they might seem at first glance. A little effort — and the following rough guide — will help you enjoy the sound of these ancient words.

Consonants — As in English, but with the following exceptions:

c:	hard — as in *cat* (never soft, as in *cent*)
ch:	hard — as in Ba*ch* (never soft, as in *church*)
dd:	a hard *th* sound, as in *th*en
f:	a hard *v* sound, as in o*f*
ff:	a soft *f* sound, as in o*ff*
g:	hard — as in *girl* (never soft, as in *George*)
ll:	a Gaelic distinctive, sounded as *tl* or *hl* on the sides of the tongue
r:	rolled or slightly trilled, especially at the beginning of a word
rh:	breathed out as if *h-r* and heavy on the *h* sound
s:	soft — as in *s*in (never hard, as in *his*); when followed by a vowel it takes on the *sh* sound
th:	soft — as in *th*istle (never hard, as in *th*en)

Vowels — As in English, but generally with the lightness of short vowel sounds:

a:	short, as in c*a*n
á:	slightly softer than above, as in *a*we
e:	usually short, as in m*e*t

é:	long *a* sound, as in h*ey*
i:	usually short, as in p*i*n
í:	long *e* sound, as in s*ee*
o:	usually short, as in h*o*t
ó:	long *o* sound, as in w*oe*
ô:	long *o* sound, as in g*o*
u:	usually sounded as a short *i*, as in p*i*n
ú:	long *u* sound, as in s*ue*
ù:	short *u* sound, as in m*u*ck
w:	sounded as a long *u*, as in h*ue*; before vowels often becomes a soft consonant as in the name Gwen
y:	usually short, as in p*i*n; sometimes *u* as in p*u*n; when long, sounded *e* as in s*ee*; rarely, *y* as in wh*y*

The careful reader will have noted that there is very little difference between *i*, *u*, and *y* – they are almost identical to non-Celts and modern readers.

Most Celtic words are stressed on the next to the last syllable. For example, the personal name Gofannon is stressed go-FAN-non, and the place name Penderwydd is pronounced pen-DER-width, and so on.

Stephen R. Lawhead is the author of many acclaimed historical fantasy novels, including the Pendragon Cycle and the Celtic Crusades. He lives in Oxford, England. Visit his website at www.stephenlawhead.com

Find out more about Stephen and other Atom authors at
www.atombooks.co.uk

THE WARLOCK LORD

by

Terry Brooks

Living in the remote hamlet of Shady Vale, the young half-elf Shea Ohmsford knows little of the outside world. And yet, in the desolate, ruined lands of the far north, a dark-hearted sorcerer is plotting his death.

The ancient warlock has dispatched a band of deadly Skull Bearers to track Shea down and murder him. For Shea is the last descendant of an ancient Elvin king, and the only person living who can wield the fabled Sword of Shannara – a weapon with the power to thwart the Warlock Lord's terrifying plans.

Only the druid Allanon knows where the sword is hidden and even now he rides to Shady Vale to offer his aid. But the Skull Bearers are swift and ruthless, and Shea Ohmsford's destiny may be over before it has begun!

And so begins the incredible legend of The Sword of Shannara – a classic story of magic, adventure and epic conflict, from one of the world's greatest living storytellers.

THE MAGICIANS' GUILD

by

Trudi Canavan

Each year the magicians of Imardin gather to purge the city streets of beggars, urchins and miscreants. Masters of the disciplines of magic, they know that no one can oppose them. But their protective shield is not as impenetrable as they believe.

As the mob is herded from the city, Sonea, a young street girl, furious at the authorities' treatment of her family and friends, hurls a stone at the shield, putting all of her rage behind it. To the amazement of all who watch, there is a flash of blue light and the stone passes straight through the barrier and cracks a magician on the temple, rendering him unconscious.

After five hundred years of order, the guild's worst fear has been realised – an untrained magician is loose on the streets. She must be found, and quickly, before her uncontrolled powers unleash forces that will destroy both her, and the city that is her home.

www.atombooks.co.uk

THE HUNDRED-TOWERED CITY

by

Garry Kilworth

What awaits Jack, Annie and Davey when they are transported back in time to the gothic city of Prague, to search for their missing parents? Trying to avoid capture by the secret police, they find themselves running through dark and dangerous cobbled streets and meet some very shady characters.

Where are their parents and who has stolen the key to the time machine?

Alchemists, mythical creatures and a man with a hook for a hand hold the answers they're looking for.

Will our young heroes be in time to save their parents from eerie Karlstein Castle? And even if they do, how will they return to the present day without the key?

www.atombooks.co.uk

WINTER ROSE

by

Patricia A. McKillip

They said later that he rode into the village on a horse the colour of buttermilk. But I saw him first — as a fall of light. And then as something shaping out of the light. So it seemed. There was a blur of gold: his hair. And then I blinked and saw his face more clearly . . .

From that moment, Rois is obsessed with Corbett Lynn. His pale green eyes fill her thoughts and her dreams are consumed by tales of his family's dark past. Of son's murdering fathers, of homes fallen to ruin, and of a curse that, as winter draws in, is crawling from the frozen forest to engulf them all.

www.atombooks.co.uk

WINTER ROSE

by

Patricia A. McKillip

THE EXTRAORDINARY AND UNUSUAL ADVENTURES OF HORATIO LYLE

by

Catherine Webb

In Victorian London at the height of the industrial revolution, Horatio Lyle is a former Special Constable with a passion for science and invention. He's also an occasional, but reluctant, sleuth. The truth is that he'd rather be in his lab tinkering with dangerous chemicals and odd machinery than running around the cobbled streets of London trying to track down stolen goods. But when Her Majesty's Government calls, Horatio swaps his microscope for a magnifying glass, fills his pockets with things that explode and sallies forth to unravel a mystery of a singularly extraordinary nature.

Thrown together with a reformed (i.e. 'caught') pickpocket called Tess, and a rebellious (within reason) young gentleman called Thomas, Lyle and his faithful hound, Tate, find themselves pursuing an ancient Chinese plate, a conspiracy that reaches to the highest levels of polite society and a dangerous enemy who may not even be human. Solving the crime will be hard enough – surviving would be a bonus . . .

www.atombooks.co.uk